Charlotte Betts began her working life as a fashion designer in London. A career followed in interior design, property management and lettings.

The Apothecary's Daughter is her debut novel and won the YouWriteOn Book of the Year in 2010, the Romantic Novelists' Association Joan Hessayon Award for New Writers in 2011 and the RoNA's Historical Category award for 2013. The sequel, *The Painter's Apprentice* was published in 2012 and shortlisted for the Festival of Romance's Best Historical Read Award in 2012. *The Spice Merchant's Wife* was published in 2013 and won the Festival of Romance's Best Historical Read Award in 2013. *The Palace of Lost Dreams* was shortlisted for the Romantic Novelists' Association's Historical Romantic Novel RoNA award in 2019 and *The Fading of the Light* in 2022.

Visit Charlotte's website at www.charlottebetts.com.

By Charlotte Betts

The Lost Daughter of Venice

Charlotte Betts

PIATKUS

PIATKUS

First published in Great Britain in 2023 by Piatkus
This edition published in 2023 by Piatkus.

1 3 5 7 9 10 8 6 4 2

Copyright © 2023 Charlotte Betts

The moral right of the author has been asserted.

*All characters and events in this publication, other than those
clearly in the public domain, are fictitious and any resemblance
to real persons, living or dead, is purely coincidental.*

A CIP catalogue record for this book
is available from the British Library.

ISBN 978-0-349-43271-7

Typeset in Caslon by M Rules

Printed and bound in Great Britain by
Clays Ltd, Elcograf S.p.A.

Papers used by Piatkus are from well-managed forests
and other responsible sources.

Piatkus
An imprint of
Little, Brown Book Group
Carmelite House
50 Victoria Embankment
London EC4Y 0DZ

An Hachette UK Company
www.hachette.co.uk

www.littlebrown.co.uk

To my daughter Polly.

I love you for the little girl you once were, for the amazing woman you have become and for the precious daughter you will always be.

Chapter 1

Venice

October 1919

The train rattled onto the long causeway that connected the Italian mainland to the city of Venice. Fat drops of rain splattered against the carriage window as I looked out at the grey and choppy waters of the Lagoon. The sky was equally grey and fog melded water and sky together at the horizon. Silhouettes of low-lying islands, no more than dark humps, appeared like semi-submerged sea creatures. Every now and then a glowing cinder from the engine flew past the window like a shooting star.

It had been seventeen years since I'd left Venice. I'd neither wanted nor ever expected to return but the telegram I'd received from Aunt Lavinia had been difficult to ignore.

Come to Venice. Please, Phoebe, do not fail me.

1

Despite what had happened and the acrimonious words that led to our long estrangement, I had many reasons to be grateful to Aunt Lavinia. And perhaps it was time for me to tell her I was sorry. The railway carriage rocked and swayed as it carried me onwards into the swirling fog.

Dusk was falling by the time I disembarked from the train at Santa Lucia station but the rain had ceased. Since I had no intention of staying in Venice any longer than I had to, I carried only a small valise. I rarely travelled without my photographic equipment but it was too cumbersome on such a short visit.

I waved away the porters and small boys who attempted to carry my luggage down the station steps, to where the waters of the Grand Canal lapped the quay. I bought a ticket and joined a group of women and a priest waiting for the water bus. There was a pervasive odour of decaying fish but the sight of the great green dome of the church of San Simeone Piccolo on the opposite side of the canal drove it from my thoughts. Now I was truly back in Venice.

A uniformed soldier stood on the steps, his scarred face and blind eyes turned up to the sky, singing an aria from *La Bohème*. I dropped a handful of lire into his hat. It was so cruel that, only a year after the war had ended, some of those who'd fought for their country were forced to beg for their living.

The vaporetto steamed up to the quay and the small crowd of passengers surged forward to board. It was strange to hear Italian voices again and I eavesdropped on the conversations around me.

Briny gusts of the penetrating October wind fluttered my scarf; the brackish smell of the waterway was immediately familiar to me. Gondolas, barges and sailing boats passed by. The grand palazzi of the city's once pre-eminent trading empire lined the Grand Canal, their warm daytime colours leached away by the increasing gloom.

Shivering by the time the vaporetto had travelled the two miles of the Grand Canal, I was pleased to step off the boat and onto the narrow walkway beside the water. I hadn't assumed I'd be invited to stay with my aunt and, in any case, wouldn't have felt comfortable there, given the terms on which we'd parted.

I asked a passer-by for directions to the Hotel Danieli and, before long, saw the welcoming glow of lamps lighting the entrance. By now thoroughly chilled, I was relieved to settle into my room and change before dinner.

After breakfast the following morning, the doorman found a gondola to take me to the Palazzo degli Angeli. As I sat on the cracked leather cushions inside the small cabin, the pale sunshine gleaming on the Grand Canal tempered my apprehension about the imminent meeting with my aunt.

The canal was much busier at this time of day. Barges laden with fruit and vegetables, vaporetti and a myriad of smaller craft bustled about their business. The gondola approached the low iron bridge of Ponte dell'Accademia and, a few minutes later, turned into Rio della Toletta, a narrower canal.

As we drew closer to the palazzo, I realised the neighbouring property was now an hotel. There were smart scarlet awnings over the water steps and gondolas were tied up to the scarlet and black-striped mooring posts. Bay trees in terracotta pots flanked the entrance, over which was a sign painted in red and gold with the black silhouette of a bird of prey. Hotel Falcone.

The gondola swayed past the hotel and then, there was the Palazzo degli Angeli. Built during the Renaissance, it was three storeys high with a balustraded balcony running the full width of the first floor. The pale Istrian stone of the lower façade and the bases of the fluted columns were stained green and black by the high tides but the upper floors gleamed ochre yellow. Since I'd last seen the palazzo, some of the stucco had fallen away, exposing the brickwork beneath.

The boat slid up to the landing stage next to the Conte's old *sandolo*. The gondolier offered his hand to me when I stepped out of the boat and I was glad of it when my shoe slipped on green slime. The wrought-iron water gate was ajar so I didn't ring the bell. It wasn't as if I didn't know the way. I paused for a moment to glance up at the winged angel carved into the keystone above the high arch of the opening. 'Hello, old friend,' I murmured.

Pushing open the gate, I entered the *portego*. The undulating marble floor was cracked and walls that once had been adorned with frescoes of angels and cherubim were flaking with damp. I walked through an archway into the courtyard and climbed the exterior staircase. Opening the heavy door at the top, I entered the hall.

Murano chandeliers cast a dim light over walls covered in claret-coloured damask and I realised electricity had been installed since I left.

I was staring up at the high ceiling where painted angels peeped over rose-pink clouds when one of the hall doors opened, revealing an angular figure. My sister Eveline. I tensed, waiting for her to speak.

'What on earth are you doing here?' she said. 'You should have waited for the housekeeper to bring you upstairs. How did you know?'

'Know what?'

Eveline frowned. 'That Aunt Lavinia is dead, of course.'

'Dead!' My hand flew to my throat. 'But I received a telegram from her telling me to come and see her only a few days ago. What happened? Was she ill?'

'You'd better come into the drawing room.' My sister led the way.

I felt sick. Aunt Lavinia – gone! I'd always imagined that, one day, we'd be reconciled and now I'd lost the opportunity. Full of self-loathing, I knew I should have overcome my stupid pride and visited her years ago.

Eveline poked her head around the door. 'Aren't you coming?'

The windows overlooking the canal were tightly shuttered, out of respect for the dead. The cluttered room was lit only by two lamps, leaving most of it in shadow.

'How did Aunt Lavinia die, Eveline?' Shivering, I held my shaking hands towards the fire that burned in the marble fireplace. 'Was she ill?'

'Would you have cared?'

'Of course I would!'

Eveline shrugged. 'She slipped on the landing stage and drowned in the canal.'

I pressed my fingers to my mouth. It had been only moments since I'd slipped there myself.

'Signor Benedetti, Aunt Lavinia's man of business, had come to visit her. She lost her footing and knocked her head. Fell into the water and drowned. Benedetti jumped in, but it was too late.'

'How brave of him!'

'An heroic but futile act,' said Eveline. 'It's the funeral tomorrow. You'll need to find yourself something suitable to wear.' She frowned at my marine blue coat with the velvet collar and matching hat.

'I hoped I'd never have to wear black again, now the war is over.'

'I'm still wearing mourning for my husband,' said Eveline, plucking at her black skirt.

I noticed how drawn and pale her face was. 'I'm very sorry to hear that. So we're both widows. John fell at the Somme.'

'I daresay he left you well provided for, though, unlike my

husband. Matteo didn't die a hero's death. He caught influenza – just as the war ended – so there's no widow's pension for me either.'

If past history was anything to go by, anything I said in reply would only make her more resentful. 'What time is the funeral?' I enquired.

'You must be here by half-past ten tomorrow.' She stood up.

Clearly dismissed, I left.

𝄢

The following morning, I studied my reflection in the hotel mirror. The new hat didn't suit me and the dress and coat I'd bought in a hurry from a small shop were too short since I was taller than the average Italian woman. There hadn't been time for me to see a dressmaker and have something altered or made.

At half-past ten, I presented myself at the palazzo. This time, the water gate was locked and I rang the bell.

A plump middle-aged woman wearing a housekeeper's sober clothes came to unlock the gate.

'Valentina!' I said. 'Is it really you?'

She smiled and her face lit up, eyes almost disappearing behind the apples of her cheeks. 'Signora Wyndham. So many years!'

'I never imagined you'd still be here.'

'My husband Jacopo – you remember Jacopo?'

'So you married him!'

'Poor man.' Valentina assumed a pious expression but her eyes twinkled. 'It wasn't fair to make him wait any longer. We have a fine son, too. Franco is working with his uncle in Mestre.' Her expression sobered. 'The other servants left or died during the war until only Jacopo and I remained. And now, both the Conte and the Contessa have gone, too.' She dabbed at her eyes. 'Signora Rizzio is waiting for you.'

Eveline stood by the fireplace. She didn't come forward to greet me.

I refused to be intimidated. My footsteps clipped across the parquet floor as I navigated through the gloom, sidling between scagliola-topped tables and gilded chairs.

Eveline wore a black coat with threadbare cuffs, which was at odds with her elegant velvet hat with a wide brim and black ostrich feathers.

I came to a halt at the sight of two children sitting on the sofa.

'This is my son Carlo, who is ten, and my daughter Rosetta,' said Eveline, moving to rest a hand on the girl's shoulder. 'She's eight.'

My heart lurched. My sister's children. Children of my own blood. 'What a wonderful surprise!' I said. 'I'd no idea you had children, Eveline.'

'Why would you, since we never communicate?'

Choosing to ignore her antagonistic tone, I smiled at my niece and nephew. 'I'm your aunt Phoebe. I'm delighted to meet you both.' I held out my hand to Carlo.

He stood up, his expression sullen.

'How tall you are!' I said.

Rosetta stared at her feet. I saw that her dark plaits were tied with black ribbons.

'And you look so like your mamma when she was young,' I commented.

Neither child seemed inclined to speak.

'Do you have children?' asked Eveline.

I shook my head and tried not to notice the gleam of satisfaction in my sister's eyes.

'The water hearse will arrive shortly,' she said.

It was then that I saw a figure sitting on the carved armchair that had once been Uncle Emiliano's favourite seat by the window. I froze, remembering how he'd often gravitated there to read his

7

newspaper in the afternoons. It had distressed me when, before the war, Aunt Lavinia sent me a terse note informing me he'd died. Would I have gone to his funeral if I'd been invited? I'm not sure. In any case, the note came too late for that.

The man stood up and walked towards me, smiling. I blinked. The Conte had been clean-shaven whereas this man had a moustache.

'This is Signor Benedetti,' said Eveline. 'My sister – Signora Wyndham.'

He was about my age, handsome in the Italian manner. 'I remember a Signor Benedetti,' I said, 'but ...'

'You remember an older man?' He shook my hand. 'My father managed the Conte and Contessa's affairs for a long while. He retired two years ago.'

Signor Benedetti the Younger had black hair. His father's had receded and I'd never seen him in a suit as beautifully tailored as the one his son wore today.

'May I express my deepest condolences for your loss, Signora Wyndham?' he said.

I realised he still held my hand and Eveline was staring at us. Hastily, I disengaged my fingers from his grip. 'It is shocking,' I said, 'even though my aunt and I were no longer close.'

'She spoke of you many times.'

'Oh, dear!' I said. 'I doubt she had anything good to say.'

'Not at all!'

I couldn't help noticing that he had the remnants of a black eye. That intrigued me; he didn't look like a man who would involve himself in a fight.

'After the funeral, Signor Benedetti will disclose the contents of Aunt Lavinia's will to us,' said Eveline.

'My presence won't be required for that,' I said. I neither hoped for nor expected any bequest. Long ago, Aunt Lavinia had made *that* perfectly clear in a searing denouncement of my character and morals. 'I plan to return to London early tomorrow morning.'

'It won't take long,' said Signor Benedetti.

Valentina came in to murmur something to Eveline before leaving the room.

My sister stood up. 'The pallbearers are waiting and the mourners are gathering on the canal.' She pulled down the black veil attached to her hat and motioned to the children to come to her side.

Signor Benedetti buttoned his overcoat and we all went silently downstairs. The doors to one of the store rooms in the *portego* stood open. There, in the flickering candlelight, six pallbearers stood waiting around a coffin.

I jerked in alarm. The lid was open.

'I was sure you'd want to pay your respects properly to Aunt Lavinia,' said Eveline.

I knew what was expected of me. My sister's steely gaze was like an icy finger running down my back as I approached the flower-filled coffin.

Aunt Lavinia's hair was white now, her expression remote and her once sparkling eyes forever shuttered. Dutifully, I bent to press my lips to her waxen forehead and tried not to recoil at the chill of her skin. Behind me, Eveline sighed as if she were disappointed.

We waited while the pallbearers closed the coffin and draped it with a gold-embroidered cloth. When they carried it aloft through the water gate, we all followed.

The other mourners waited in respectful silence in their gondolas, the men removing their hats when the coffin came into view.

The water hearse was handsomely coated in shiny black varnish. Wider than a normal gondola, the prow was adorned with a golden angel, wings unfurled, and carved gilt embellishments.

I watched while the coffin was placed on the bier under a

black-curtained canopy with gilded finials and a great deal of gold rope and tasselled decoration. Irreverently, I couldn't help thinking the bier looked like a rather grand four-poster bed. But Aunt Lavinia would have enjoyed the pomp and circumstance of this, her final journey.

A hired gondolier, dressed in black with a gold sash, helped us into his craft. It was a raw, damp day and there was no cabin, perhaps so that the chief mourners remained on view for others to assess the depth of our grief.

I stared straight ahead, struggling with the sense of unreality that had overtaken me since the moment I'd heard my aunt had died.

A moment later the funeral party set off, a flotilla of a dozen gondolas and other small vessels following the bobbing progress of the water hearse to the island of San Michele, where the City of Water buried its dead.

Chapter 2

Once Aunt Lavinia had been interred next to her husband in the di Sebastiano family vault, the funeral party broke up. One by one the mourners' gondolas slipped away from the procession. It wasn't Venetian custom to hold a reception after a funeral and I was relieved not to have to make stilted conversation with people I didn't know.

Only one gondola followed us all the way back to the palazzo and it moored up to one of the red and black posts outside the Hotel Falcone. A man of upright bearing alighted and stood watching us as we disembarked.

When he raised his hand in acknowledgement, I couldn't help noticing his aquiline nose and high Slavic cheekbones. He walked into the hotel. 'Who was that?' I asked Eveline.

'Signor Falcone, the owner.'

'Falcone is a troublemaker,' said Signor Benedetti.

'In what way?' I asked.

He gave a dismissive shrug. 'Shall we go inside, out of the cold?' Eveline hurried through the water gate.

Valentina came to greet us in the hall, her expression sober.

'Jacopo has attended to the fire and the drawing room is warm for you. Signor Falcone has sent us food from the hotel kitchens.'

'Thank you, Valentina,' said Eveline.

The housekeeper dropped her gaze. '*Prego*, Signora Rizzio. Lunch will be ready in ten minutes.' She tiptoed away.

I couldn't remember Valentina ever moving so quietly before. As a girl, she'd clattered about everywhere, singing to herself with her dimples flashing and a cheerful word for everyone, whether they wanted it or not.

'Why did Signor Falcone send food?' I enquired.

'It's usual to receive such gifts after a death,' said Signor Benedetti, once we were warming ourselves by the fire. 'The household of a grieving family isn't expected to cook.'

'Mr Falcone is very kind then,' I said, 'for a troublemaker.'

Signor Benedetti grimaced but ventured no further comment.

Feeling curious, I covertly studied my sister's children. With eyes downcast, they were unnaturally quiet.

Conversation was stilted. It was a relief when Valentina returned and announced lunch was served.

We trooped into the shuttered dining room, where a cobweb-draped chandelier cast shadows over the sixteen-seater table. The walls, still hung with ruby and gold paper, were crowded with gilt-framed paintings of the Conte's ancestors, mostly now also adorned with cobwebs. I remembered how Uncle Emiliano had liked to tell anecdotes about them, guffawing all the while at their outrageous exploits. His family had originated from Rome but his grandfather had made his fortune investing in the railways and bought the Palazzo degli Angeli after falling in love with Venice.

Valentina served us an excellent seafood risotto, followed by a rich beef stew and polenta. The children ate with gusto and lost some of their reserve so I asked them about their schooling.

'Carlo and Rosetta are both *excellent* students,' said Eveline, almost as if she expected me to dispute the fact.

'I'm sure they're a credit to you,' I said.

After Valentina had cleared the dishes and brought us coffee, Eveline told the children to go and read in the library. Obediently, they slipped away.

Signor Benedetti sipped his coffee. 'It is time for me to tell you about the Contessa's will,' he said.

Eveline sat up very straight, hands folded on the table in front of her. There was a tinge of pink in her cheeks and an expectant gleam in her eyes.

Signor Benedetti took a folded document from his jacket pocket and read it aloud.

The will was written in complicated Italian legal phrases that went over my head. I leaned back and wondered how soon I could leave. Uncle Emiliano had been the last in a long line of an obscure noble family and Aunt Lavinia had already told me I would never inherit anything from her. Although since the lawyer had requested my presence here today, possibly she'd changed her mind and left me some trifling gift.

I suppressed a yawn. My visit to Venice, combined with the painful emotions it had evoked, had been draining. It was dispiriting to know I had to face the reverse journey in the morning when I returned to my lonely life in St John's Wood.

'NO!' Eveline reared up so abruptly that I jumped. Her chair fell backwards and crashed onto the parquet. 'She *promised*! All these years of running her errands and putting up with her interference ...' Pressing her knuckles to her mouth, she said, 'How could she?' She turned to Signor Benedetti. 'You *knew*, didn't you? I didn't understand at the time but that's why you—'

'Calm yourself, Signora Rizzio!' He shrugged. 'I merely carried out the Contessa's bidding.'

Eveline turned to me, her expression furious. 'How long have you known?'

'Known what?'

'Oh, that's right! Pretend innocence as usual.' She pushed her face close to mine, voice shaking with anger. 'But I know how far from innocent you are. You were always the pretty and attentive sister, weaselling your way into our uncle and aunt's good books. You've *always* managed to have things your own way, haven't you?'

'I don't know what you mean,' I stammered. 'I haven't seen either you or Aunt Lavinia for years.'

'I saw Lorenzo first and still you took him ...'

'Eveline, I told you all those years ago, he *never* thought of you in that way.'

'You encouraged him to fall in love with you, didn't you? And then there was John Wyndham. *I* was the elder sister and should have been married first. He could have given me a comfortable position in the world. But what happened? *You* snatched him from right under my nose.'

'It wasn't like that!' I refrained from telling her that John had remarked she was unsuitably bold for him. Choosing my words carefully, I said, 'Uncle Emiliano insisted I leave the palazzo. I was seventeen with nowhere to go, so when Aunt Lavinia wanted me to marry John Wyndham, I had little choice.'

'You've *always* taken what should have been mine and I hate you for it!' hissed Eveline. 'And you too, Cosimo Benedetti. May you both burn in hell!' She rushed from the room, shouting for her children to follow her. Two minutes later, the front door slammed.

In the sudden silence, the dining room seemed to ring with the echoes of her outburst.

I swallowed. 'I don't understand why she suddenly reopened old wounds.'

Signor Benedetti pursed his lips. 'I believe she had expectations that the Contessa would leave her the Palazzo degli Angeli. It came as a shock to her to discover that it is now yours.'

'*Mine?*' Confused, I said, 'That isn't right. Aunt Lavinia would never leave it to me.'

'The Contessa made her wishes perfectly clear,' he said.

Panic gripped me. 'But I don't want the palazzo!' Venice held such painful memories for me, all I wanted was to leave. 'It must be a mistake.'

'You're shaking!' His brown eyes were sympathetic. 'Do not distress yourself, Signora Wyndham.'

'Why would Aunt Lavinia do this?'

Signor Benedetti steepled the tips of his fingers. 'Your sister lived here at the palazzo during the war. After Signora Rizzio was widowed, she and the Contessa had a disagreement and your sister moved out into her own apartment.'

I wondered why they'd argued. 'I'll make the palazzo over to Eveline,' I said. 'She has children to care for.'

'The Contessa made it abundantly clear to me that your sister must not have the palazzo.'

'But why?'

'She wouldn't say.' He placed his hand lightly on my wrist and spoke soothingly. 'If you don't want the palazzo, there's no difficulty. I'll help you to find a suitable buyer.'

'How soon?'

'I might know someone I can approach.' He patted my hand. 'I must go now but I'll call upon you in the next few days to discuss the matter further.' He stood up. 'In the meantime, try and enjoy a little holiday at the Palazzo degli Angeli.'

'But I can't stay here!'

'You must. The palazzo will be yours to sell once the necessary paperwork has been approved but it's your responsibility to clear your aunt's effects. In view of the circumstances, I doubt your sister will wish to assist you.'

I was sure Eveline would go out of her way to make things even more difficult for me.

'I'll send the housekeeper to you,' he said. 'A glass of brandy perhaps, to soothe your nerves?'

'Thank you, Signor Benedetti.'

He made a formal little bow and left the room.

The following morning, I awoke to the sound of church bells. I sat bolt upright in bed, disorientated until I realised I was in the bedroom of my girlhood. The familiar mahogany wardrobe and dressing table, even the blue damask curtains were the same, although now the sun had faded them to tatters. Nothing had changed, except that there was no longer a washstand and towel.

After a moment, I got up and went to the bathroom. The previous night I'd discovered a splendid marble-clad temple to cleanliness with hot and cold water that spouted from gold taps shaped like dolphins. As I bathed, I wondered what had become of the sturdy girls who used to deliver fresh water in brass buckets to the earthenware storage urns in the kitchen.

Downstairs, I peeped into the ballroom. The parquet floor was dusty and the tasselled silk curtains closed. Gold-painted chairs lined the walls and the chandeliers were tied up in bags of muslin. There was a general air of neglect and I supposed there had been no dances or parties at the Palazzo degli Angeli since before the war.

I walked through the palazzo, ghosts from the past echoing in my mind. The rooms were stuffed to the rafters with antique furniture in want of a good polish: heavily carved stools, marquetry-inlaid bureaux, ebony torchères in the shape of blackamoors, corner cupboards painted in the Venetian style and myriad objets d'art. It shocked me to see how run-down everything looked. When I was a girl, everything had shone and there were always fresh flowers. Of course, there had been many servants then.

I waited for my breakfast in gloomy splendour at one end of the long dining table, mulling over how to begin to clear the palazzo for sale. I felt weighed down by the thought of it.

Valentina brought in a tray and placed a basket of bread, apricot jam, butter and a pot of coffee on the table. 'Rolls fresh from the oven, Signora Wyndham.'

'Thank you, Valentina.'

'After your breakfast, shall I come to your study for my orders?'

'Orders?'

'For your lunch and dinner.'

'Oh, I see. Just bring me something simple for lunch. A sandwich maybe.'

Valentina's eyes widened. 'But there are many gifts of food for you in the kitchen.'

'Whatever you think best then.'

'Signora ...' She twisted her apron in her hands.

'What is it, Valentina?'

'Signor Benedetti said you are not coming to live here?'

'I must stay for a while but my life is in London. The palazzo must be sold.'

Valentina's brown eyes glistened with tears. 'But *my* life is at the Palazzo degli Angeli. And Jacopo's too. I have worked here for over twenty-five years. What shall we do if you send us away?'

'You'll have some time before the sale to find new situations,' I said, uncomfortable in the face of her distress. 'And I'll give you both good references.'

Valentina sniffed noisily.

17

'I'm sorry,' I said, 'but I cannot live here. Perhaps the new owner will take you on?'

She dabbed at a tear with the corner of her apron. 'It will not be the same as if you lived here.'

I didn't know what to say to comfort her. 'I'll be here long enough to sort through the Contessa's personal belongings. Will you advise me what to do with them? A worthy cause, perhaps.'

Valentina blew her nose noisily. 'The churches distribute clothing to the poor. There are so many widows and men too damaged to work since the war.'

'I was only expecting to be in Venice for a day or two and I travelled very light,' I said. 'I must write to my housekeeper and ask her to send some of my things.'

'Perhaps there is something of the Contessa's you might wear until they arrive? She was tall and slender like you.'

'I'll take a look.'

Valentina returned to the kitchen, her expression so tragic it filled me with guilt.

A little while later, fortified by strong coffee, I went into Aunt Lavinia's study. The desk drawers were full of papers and, in the bookcase, ledgers of household accounts stretched back several years.

Opening the dusty shutters, I looked down at the canal. Mist drifted across the water before a shaft of pale sunshine broke through, reminding me of a beautifully ethereal photograph I'd taken of the Embankment at home. That image was the frontispiece of my recently published book, *Landscapes of London*.

I took a sheet of the creamy, deckle-edged writing paper that Aunt Lavinia had always used and wrote to my housekeeper in England. I asked her to forward my camera and tripod together with some clothes and gave her careful instructions on packing things safely. Since I might have to be here for a few weeks, I decided I would use the opportunity to photograph Venice, even if I couldn't develop the plates until I returned to my darkroom in St John's Wood. Despite everything that had happened, it made me smile to think that I'd taken my very first photographs on the Brownie camera Uncle Emiliano gave me. That timely gift had set me on my journey to becoming a professional photographer.

I placed the letter on the hall table for Jacopo to post then set off up the curving staircase. I knew I must face up to sorting through Aunt Lavinia's possessions.

In her bedroom I stood in the shadows, listening to the silence. There was a faint hint of gardenia perfume in the air, the one Aunt Lavinia always used to wear because the Conte loved it so. As children, Eveline and I had often watched Carmela, our aunt's maid, dressing her mistress's thick blonde hair – hair that was exactly like my own. Eveline's was darker. Sometimes Aunt Lavinia had asked our advice on which brooch or necklace to wear and we'd been allowed to select an item from the glittering treasures in her jewel box.

I threw back the shutters to let in the light and dispel the ghosts. From this vantage point I looked down on the garden. A man with a drooping moustache, Jacopo I guessed, was raking up leaves. The dark pillars of two cypresses framed a marble statue of Venus ranged against the garden wall. The fig trees were bare but a climbing rose on the pergola still bore a few withered blooms. In the summer heat, this garden had always been a cool, green oasis. Since space in the city was so scarce and most properties were tall rather than wide, the garden would be a useful talking point when it came to selling the palazzo.

A long time ago, on velvety summer nights, I'd met my lover under that pergola to exchange illicit kisses. For a moment or two, I remembered the feel of his hands in my hair and the urgency of his lips against mine as he promised to love me forever and ever.

Melting inside and quivering with the pleasure of his touch, I'd known then with absolute certainty that I'd never love anyone else. That part of our whispered promises had certainly been true.

I rested my forehead against the glass and surrendered my thoughts to the past.

Chapter 3

Venice

February 1901

It was a bright Sunday morning and the bells of Chiesa di San Trovaso pealed a tumultuous and urgent reminder to all good Catholics to hurry to Mass. The ringing of myriad competing summonses to worship ebbed and flowed on the breeze from all quarters of the city.

On the narrow walkway beside the buildings that lined the San Trovaso canal, Eveline and I trotted along behind Aunt Lavinia and our uncle, the Conte di Sebastiano.

As we reached the arched bridge, Aunt Lavinia came to an abrupt halt, pressing a hand to her side.

The Conte strode on ahead.

'Emiliano!' she called. 'Wait for us!'

He stopped and turned back. 'I'm sorry, my dears. Was I going too fast for you?'

'You always forget you have much longer legs than us, Uncle Emiliano,' I said.

'And much sturdier shoes,' added Aunt Lavinia, slightly out of breath.

The Conte offered her his arm. 'I shall be more mindful of that in future. Shall we proceed, ladies?'

Since I was sixteen and still at school, I grinned at my sister, secretly pleased to be called a lady. Eveline, a year older and leaving school at the end of the year, assumed what I guessed she imagined was a haughty, ladylike expression and imitated Aunt Lavinia's gliding steps. I copied her.

Eveline scowled at me. 'Don't!'

I was tired of being considered a child and looked forward to that magical day when I was grown up and no one could tell me what to do any more. I imagined being a married lady and inviting my friends to gossipy tea parties like Aunt Lavinia did.

The clamour of the bells intensified as the campanile and then the church came into view. The doors to the canal-side entrance were open and the Conte led us in and settled us into our usual pew. The church smelled of incense and mould.

Shivering despite my thick black stockings and woollen coat, I kneeled down beside my sister to pray. The congregation rustled and murmured. A baby cried and someone coughed, hollow echoes bouncing back from the ceiling far above.

Eveline nudged me with her elbow. 'Phoebe,' she whispered, 'there's Giulia two pews in front. In the dark blue coat.'

'Who?'

My sister rolled her eyes. 'I *told* you. The new girl who sits next to me in class.'

Aunt Lavinia leaned forward to frown at us and press a finger to her lips.

I peered around the excessively large hat of the woman in the pew in front until I could see Giulia. She sat between a lady dressed in black, a widow perhaps, and a young man with broad shoulders.

22

The service began and I stood, kneeled and made my responses automatically as the flow of Latin words washed over me. Eveline and I went to the altar rail with our aunt and uncle but bowed our heads to be blessed instead of receiving the Eucharist.

Orphaned six years before, we'd come from our boarding school in London to live in Venice with our mother's sister. Her husband, the Conte, had wanted us to receive instruction into the Roman Catholic faith but Aunt Lavinia had put her foot down.

'It's too much!' she'd said. 'The poor little mites have already had their lives turned upside-down. As it is, they'll have to learn the language before they can begin to make friends here. Besides, as an Anglican minister, my brother-in-law would turn in his grave at the very idea.'

'But you converted when you came to Italy and married me,' argued the Conte.

'That was my choice,' said Aunt Lavinia. 'And the girls are free to follow that path when they're old enough to make up their own minds.'

The Conte had shaken his head. 'Well, I hope your decision doesn't damage their marriage prospects.'

The service ended and we left through the other set of doors, stepping out into the sunshine. Every Sunday morning the congregation gathered in the large square at the front of the church to greet friends and neighbours.

'Aunt Lavinia, may Phoebe and I go and speak to Giulia Albani, my new schoolfriend?' asked Eveline. 'She moved to Venice recently and doesn't know many people yet.'

'By all means, so long as you stay within my sight. Where is she?'

'Over there by the well with her mother and brother.'

'Since the family is new to Venice, why don't we all say hello?' said the Conte. Leading the way across the square with his loping stride, he waved to friends and shook hands with acquaintances as we passed. He introduced himself and then the rest of us to Giulia's mother.

Signora Albani, her face as beautiful and distant as the statue of the Madonna inside the church, presented Giulia and her brother, Lorenzo.

I liked Giulia at once. She didn't have her mother's beauty but her smile was warm and her expression open and friendly.

Lorenzo shook my hand. Two or three years older than I, his hazel eyes were thickly fringed with dark lashes. Struck dumb by sudden shyness, the breath hitched in my throat. He was quite the most handsome young man I'd ever met. After he released my hand, his touch still tingled against my palm. When he turned away to greet Eveline, I felt as if the sun had disappeared behind a cloud.

'I understand you've recently arrived in Venice, Signora Albani?' said the Conte.

She inclined her head. 'My husband and I both came from Venice but his business was in Rome. He'd inherited his family house here in Calle dei Frati and so, after he went to his eternal rest, I chose to return to the city of my birth.'

'You have family and friends here?' asked Aunt Lavinia.

'Only my children now.' Signora Albani glanced at Giulia and Lorenzo.

'They must be a comfort to you,' said my aunt. 'Calle dei Frati is only a step or two away from us at the Palazzo degli Angeli on the Rio della Toletta. I'd be delighted if you'd call on me during one of my Thursday afternoon At Homes. You'll see the angel carved in stone over the water gate.'

Too diffident to push myself forward, I watched Lorenzo from beneath my lowered lids. Eveline had no such qualms and laughed and chatted easily with him and his sister.

She waved to a group of young people standing by the old

24

gondola workshop then tucked her arm under the crook of Giulia's elbow. 'Come and meet my other friends,' she said. 'You too, Lorenzo.'

Smiling, he turned to me. 'Are you coming?' he said.

It seemed to me that the sun had appeared from behind the clouds again.

After that, I eagerly anticipated Sunday mornings and the opportunity to exchange a few words with Lorenzo. Our conversation wasn't particularly memorable; it was the way he looked deep into my eyes as if he really *saw* me that made me fizz with suppressed excitement.

Eveline had been struck by Lorenzo, too, and chattered to me about his well-shaped eyebrows and the dimple in his chin. She paid great attention to her appearance on church mornings, fussing with her clothes and pinching her cheeks to make them rosy. Aunt Lavinia always said my blonde hair was my best feature and, I confess, on these days I brushed it until it shone, hoping Lorenzo would notice.

One Sunday, the young people had gathered as usual beside the gondola workshop in the square outside the church, while our parents chatted.

Eveline had made sure she was close by Lorenzo's side. 'Did Giulia tell you she was top of the class in our last test, Lorenzo?'

'She did,' he said. 'I'm very proud of my little sister.'

Giulia turned to Eveline. 'Lorenzo has been helping me with my studies before he goes to the university in Padua this autumn.'

My stomach clenched. Padua was so far away!

'I'll be home for the holidays,' he said, looking straight at me, as if he'd known what I was thinking.

'How clever you are, Lorenzo!' said Eveline, fluttering her

eyelashes. 'How I wish I had a brother to help me with my homework.'

I scowled, irritated by her flirtatious manner.

'I'd be happy to help you, too,' he said.

'How terribly kind!' she gushed.

'Perhaps Giulia and I could accompany you both back to Palazzo degli Angeli after school one day each week?' he said. 'We could spend an hour or two studying and then I'd take her home afterwards?'

Eveline squealed in delight and hurried off to seek Aunt Lavinia's permission for the scheme.

I glanced at Lorenzo.

His mouth twitched. 'I do hope I'll be able to help you with your homework, too, Phoebe.' He gave me the suspicion of a wink.

It was the highlight of my week when, on Wednesday afternoons, we sat around the vast table in the dining room at the Palazzo degli Angeli and Lorenzo tutored us. It annoyed me when Eveline pretended she didn't understand and asked him repeatedly for help. He would stand behind her to peer over her shoulder at the exercise book.

Frequently, Lorenzo caught my eye when the other girls' heads were bent over their work. He looked back at me with a steady gaze and a half-smile until I blushed and turned away. I hugged the memory of his secret glances deep in my heart and relived them later.

When the studying was finished, Lorenzo initiated interesting discussions about poetry and literature, theology and science.

At four o'clock precisely, Signor Giordano the butler served tea in the English style. Aunt Lavinia had imported this tradition from her home country and the Conte had adopted it with enthusiasm. We demolished the dainty sandwiches, scones and cakes while we continued our discussions.

The dining-room door was always left open and Aunt Lavinia made frequent appearances to ensure we were behaving appropriately. Sometimes, the Conte came to join in a discussion, bringing a book of poetry or posing a philosophical question.

One afternoon, once we'd closed our books for tea, Giulia, her eyes sparkling, said, 'I have an announcement to make.'

Lorenzo gripped his hands together on the table and a muscle flickered in his jaw.

Always attuned to his mood, I wondered what had perturbed him.

'I wanted to share my joy with you,' his sister said. 'It's taken me a long time to be sure but now I know what I want to do with the rest of my life.'

Eveline clapped her hands. 'You're getting married!'

Giulia laughed. 'In a way. I'm going to be a Bride of Christ.'

'A nun?' I stammered.

Eveline's mouth had fallen open and she was uncharacteristically lost for words.

'Mamma has always wanted me to take my vows but I've waited until I was quite sure it was right for me.'

'You want to leave the world and live cloistered with only women?' Eveline shook her head. 'But why?'

Giulia leaned forward eagerly. 'Because I want to be free. I shan't be confined by the restrictions imposed upon a wife and mother. I've chosen not to enter a silent order because I wish to work for the greater good. Teaching or nursing perhaps.'

'You don't need to be a nun for that,' said Eveline. She turned to appeal to Lorenzo. 'Can't you make her change her mind? Giulia has always been so . . . ' She waved her hand while she thought of the appropriate word. 'So full of life. And now she'll wither away in her convent if you don't stop her.'

'Stop her?' Lorenzo looked at Giulia with a half-smile. 'You don't know my sister. She's chosen her path to Heaven. Who am I to come between her and her faith?' He looked down at his clasped hands. 'To have that absolute certainty must be a wonderful thing.'

'Lorenzo is going to Padua and now you're going to be a nun.' Eveline sounded close to tears. 'I thought we'd all be friends forever.'

'I shan't enter the convent until September,' said Giulia. 'We still have this summer and I intend to make the most of every single minute of it.'

Eveline sighed. 'We'll have to store up as many happy memories as we can to keep you going for the rest of your life.' She looked at Lorenzo and smiled. 'But you'll come back to Venice in the holidays and when you've finished university, won't you?'

Spring arrived, bringing warmer weather, and I went into the garden one afternoon to sit under the pergola and daydream about how I might be alone with Lorenzo. If only Eveline wouldn't keep pushing between us! The warmth in his eyes when he spoke to me convinced me he felt the same.

My secret longings were disturbed when Valentina came pattering up the garden path with a basket of laundry on her hip.

'All on your own today?' she said, and began to peg out the sheets on the line strung between the pergola and the ancient fig tree.

Valentina had been a thirteen-year-old scullery maid when I, aged ten and grieving for my parents, had first arrived at the palazzo. She'd brought me little treats of cake or a freshly baked biscuit filched from the kitchen, and she'd hugged me and dried my tears. Now, Eveline said Valentina's behaviour with me was over-familiar but I hadn't forgotten how kind she'd been.

'Have you seen Jacopo?' asked Valentina, looking about the garden.

I shook my head. He was the young man employed to help the gardener, see to the fires and clean all the shoes at the palazzo.

'He bought me a bracelet,' she said. Her dimples deepened. 'He doesn't speak much but he says he loves me.'

'Do you love him?' I asked.

'Oh, yes, but I'm not telling him that.'

'Why not?'

Valentina rolled her brown eyes heavenward. 'Don't you know *anything* about boys? Once they're sure of you, they stop bringing you presents and telling you how pretty you are.' She pegged up a pillowslip. 'Surely there's a boy you love? What about that Lorenzo? He's very handsome, isn't he?'

Warmth suffused my cheeks.

'Go on then, tell me about him. Apart from family, there's nothing more important than love, is there?'

'There's nothing to tell. We're never alone,' I said, 'but I like him very much. And I think he likes me more than Eveline.'

'Boys need a bit of encouragement sometimes. Why don't you ask the Contessa if I can be your chaperone while the four of you go for a stroll? The alleys and canal paths are narrow. Surely you could find a way to walk beside Lorenzo while Eveline and Giulia go in front?'

I pursed my lips. 'I'm not sure if Aunt Lavinia would consider you a suitable chaperone.'

Offended, Valentina put her hands on her hips. 'Why not?'

'She'd probably prefer us to be accompanied by somebody much older,' I said, diplomatically, 'but I'll ask her anyway.'

I found an ally in my sister when I said how good it would be for her to be able to walk and chat with Giulia, making the most of the time left to them before her friend entered the convent. Eveline persuaded Aunt Lavinia to allow Valentina to chaperone us once a week, provided Signora Albani found the idea acceptable. Since Giulia would be accompanied by her brother, she made no protest.

The following Saturday afternoon, the four of us strolled along the walkways beside the canals, chaperoned by Valentina walking behind. Once Giulia and Eveline were deep in conversation, Valentina overtook Lorenzo and me, stationing herself behind the older girls and giving me an impudent glance over her shoulder.

I pretended to be extremely interested in a passing gondola until my blushes had faded.

'It's good to talk without the others listening, isn't it?' said Lorenzo. 'Your sister always interrupts when I speak to you.'

'Mmm,' I said, not daring to tell him it was because she wanted him for herself.

'If you like,' he said carefully, 'perhaps we could arrange to meet sometimes without the others. I'd love to take you out in my boat.'

'My aunt would never allow me to meet you alone.'

'I suppose not.' He ran a hand through his hair. 'It's impossible to say all the things I'm thinking when we're watched all the time.'

We stepped aside to let another couple pass and his hand brushed against mine.

A frisson of pleasure shivered up my arm. I couldn't stop myself from asking, 'What are you thinking?'

A slow smile spread across his face. 'I'm thinking how modest you are for such a beautiful girl and how I'd like to stroke your glorious blonde hair. And how I think about you all the time we're apart and wish we could spend more time together.'

'I'd like that, too,' I murmured.

'And I keep thinking how very much I want to kiss you.'

I caught my breath. It shocked me that he'd spoken to me in such a way, but it thrilled me that he was as attracted to me as I was to him. Hesitating only a moment, I decided to be bold. 'No one is watching us now.'

Lorenzo glanced at Valentina's back several yards in front of us on the path and then at Giulia and Eveline, who were considerably further ahead. He came to a standstill and tilted my chin with his finger and thumb.

My heartbeat pounded in my ears. Transfixed, I felt my head swim as his face came closer to mine. What if someone saw us? I closed my eyes and his mouth pressed against mine. It was only a heartbeat before he stepped back again but, in that moment of my very first kiss, I felt newborn, like a butterfly emerging from a chrysalis.

Chapter 4

Aunt Lavinia was in a frenzy of activity preparing for the annual palazzo ball: hiring musicians, florists and a French chef. She took Eveline and me to her own dressmaker because, for the first time, we were invited to attend.

On the evening of the ball, Aunt Lavinia's lady's maid, Carmela, assisted us to dress. I was overjoyed with my gown of draped ivory chiffon with an underskirt of lilac. Eveline wore white with a blue underskirt. Carmela put our hair up and clasped necklaces of seed pearls, a gift from Uncle Emiliano to mark the occasion, around our newly exposed necks,

I stared at my reflection, barely recognising myself. I looked like a younger version of Aunt Lavinia. I felt beautiful and was sad that Lorenzo, who hadn't been invited to the ball, wouldn't see me in my finery.

'What beautiful young ladies you are!' said Uncle Emiliano, kissing our fingertips. 'And you, too, as always, my dear.' He kissed Aunt Lavinia's cheek and led her downstairs.

'Who knows?' murmured Eveline. 'Perhaps tonight is when I'll meet my future husband.'

The palazzo was lit with a thousand candles and perfumed with roses as Eveline and I followed our aunt and uncle downstairs to the hall to receive the guests.

Afterwards, we went into the ballroom, where musicians were playing and our guests laughing and gossiping with their friends.

'*He's* rather handsome, don't you think?' Eveline whispered.

I glanced at the young man with black hair who was studying the frescoes on the ceiling. 'He's been here before. Isn't he Signor Benedetti's son?

'Uncle Emiliano's lawyer?' Eveline watched him for a moment. 'Aunt Lavinia would consider him eligible, wouldn't she?'

Our aunt brought a Mr Wyndham to meet us. At least he wasn't as old as Uncle Emiliano and I readily agreed to add Mr Wyndham's name to my dance card.

Later, as I progressed around the ballroom with him, he told me he was an architect. He admired the palazzo and waxed lyrical about the harmonious proportions and symmetry of Renaissance design. I took little notice since I was watching Eveline as she danced with the younger Signor Benedetti. Besides, I had no thought for any man except Lorenzo.

The evening passed in a whirl of music and dancing, sips of sparkling wine and fulsome compliments from Uncle Emiliano's friends on how I'd blossomed into a beautiful rose. By the time I'd enjoyed the buffet supper and danced twice with most of the guests, I was happy to retire to bed.

A few days later, Uncle Emiliano called me into his library to show me a new book of photographs of the Swiss Alps. I was awed by their depiction of beauty and majesty far greater, in my opinion, than anything I could see in a painting in a church. He was delighted by my interest and gave me a Brownie camera for my birthday the following week.

I brought it on our walks with Lorenzo and Giulia and discovered a growing talent for composing interesting photographs. It was bitter-sweet to capture precious memories of Lorenzo before he went to university and of Giulia's last summer before she entered the nunnery.

One afternoon we were feeding the pigeons in Campo Santa Margherita and I was laughing as I photographed the birds landing on Eveline's wrist.

'You both look so happy,' said Lorenzo. 'Tell me, did it take you long to recover from the shock of losing your parents?'

'I don't really remember them now,' I said. 'I was only seven when Mama brought Eveline and me from Bombay to our boarding school in London. She told us we had to go there because children could die if they caught a fever in India.' I scattered more crumbs for the pigeons. 'But she didn't tell me that parents could die that way, too.'

'The school was horrible,' said Eveline. 'We hated the cold and the teachers weren't kind like our ayah had been in India. We cried piteously when Mama left.'

I shuddered at the memory. 'We'd have cried even more if we'd known we'd never see her again. I think I'd have died from misery if Eveline hadn't been there.' I reached out for her hand.

'We needed each other,' said my sister. 'Then, three years later, we were called to the headmistress's study. I thought we must have broken the rules again because her lips were all pinched together. An elegantly dressed lady was with her and the headmistress told us this was our aunt, the Contessa di Sebastiano.'

'We'd never met her but she gathered us into her arms,' I said, remembering the flowery perfume of her hair and how

34

soft her fur coat had felt against my cheek. 'And then she broke the terrible news that our parents had perished from cholera out in Bombay.'

'I was bereft when my father died,' said Lorenzo, 'but to lose both your parents at once must have felt like the end of the world to you.'

His expression was so full of compassion that I had to restrain myself from hugging him. 'It was dreadful, but then Aunt Lavinia told us she hadn't been blessed with children and she was going to take us to Venice to live with her.'

'It's like a fairy tale,' said Giulia. 'Imagine if you'd been sent to an orphanage!'

'We were very lucky,' I said. 'Aunt Lavinia is everything a mother should be.'

On our way back to the palazzo, Eveline pushed me aside to flirt with Lorenzo until Giulia said, 'Walk with me, Eveline. I want to remember these times together.'

Once they'd gone on ahead, closely followed by Valentina, I smiled at Lorenzo.

He lifted my hand, kissed my palm and curled my fingers over it. 'That's for you to keep until later,' he murmured. 'How I wish we could be alone.'

'Me too.'

He cast a furtive glance at his sister. 'If you'll unlock the back gate of the palazzo, we could meet in the garden tonight.'

My eyes widened at his audacity. 'What if someone sees us?'

'Slip out when the household is asleep. If you haven't unlocked the gate by midnight, I'll go home.'

I didn't answer straight away. Aunt Lavinia had solemnly warned Eveline and me that we must never risk our good reputations by being alone with a man but, whatever danger it was she perceived, surely it wasn't applicable to Lorenzo? And how could it upset my aunt if she didn't know about it? 'Just for a few minutes then,' I said, and was rewarded by Lorenzo's smile.

That evening, after dinner, I watched the hands of the clock on the drawing-room mantelpiece moving painfully slowly as they marked the passage of time. I was so fidgety that the Conte looked up from his book and balloon of brandy to frown at me.

At last, Eveline said good night and we went upstairs together. Leaving my door ajar, I sat on the bed until Aunt Lavinia's footsteps came up the stairs. Soon, my uncle's followed.

An hour later, the butler's measured tread rang through the palazzo as he locked up and turned down the lamps.

When all was silent, I crept downstairs and paused in the hall, listening, before easing back the bolts on the front door. And then I was outside in the darkness, running lightly down the exterior staircase, into the courtyard and through the moonlit garden to the back gate.

The bolt was stiff but then the gate swung open.

Lorenzo, waiting in the alley behind, slipped into the garden and took me in his arms. He kissed me fiercely, setting my senses alight.

My lips parted and there was a sweet ache deep inside me.

'Oh, Phoebe!' Lifting my fingers to his warm mouth, he said, 'I've waited so long to hold you like this. I dream about you every night, imagining you in my arms.'

He kissed me again and his hands felt hot against my back. When one palm cradled my breast, I jerked away. 'Lorenzo! No!' Overwhelmed by feelings I'd never experienced before, I found myself gasping for breath. 'You must go now.' I freed myself and opened the gate.

'Phoebe, let me stay a little longer,' he pleaded.

'No. You're frightening me.' I bundled him back through the gate and bolted it behind him. My heart was racing as I hurried away up the garden path.

Too agitated to sleep, I alternated between dreaming up ways

I might be able to meet him alone again and then telling myself that must never happen.

I could barely look at Lorenzo after church that Sunday. He didn't attempt to speak to me. Slighted, I was gnawed by anger and jealousy when Eveline made him laugh at a funny story. It was a relief to walk sedately back to the palazzo beside my aunt. And yet, I was wretched that he'd ignored me.

The next time we met was when the four of us and Valentina went down to Zattere, the long quayside looking towards the island of Giudecca.

I remained silent, staring steadfastly ahead at Valentina's back. I couldn't find the words to explain my turbulent emotions; the intensity of my yearning and my terror that I was on the brink of an unseen abyss.

'I'm sorry,' murmured Lorenzo. 'I shouldn't have ...'

I jumped when his hand brushed against mine.

'This week, when I thought you might never speak to me again, has made me realise how much I care for you,' he said. 'Forgive me?'

I made him wait for a full two minutes while I made up my mind. 'You're forgiven,' I said. 'And if we can find a way, I'd like to see you alone again.' My voice was so quiet I wasn't sure he could hear it. 'But you'll have to behave.'

His whole face lit up when he grinned at me.

We had two more midnight meetings in the garden, sitting under the pergola, holding hands and whispering to each other. The first time, Lorenzo kissed my cheek chastely before he departed, leaving me deeply disappointed.

The second time, when he brushed my cheek with his lips, I whispered, 'Kiss me properly!'

I drowned in that kiss, my arms around his neck, and this time, when he tentatively stroked my breast, I didn't push him away.

The following morning, I yawned throughout breakfast.

Uncle Emiliano announced he had a business meeting on Monday in Verona. He planned to take Aunt Lavinia and us with him and stay overnight. 'It will be a little holiday,' he said, 'and I daresay you girls will be interested in the Roman ruins.'

Eveline glanced at me and grimaced.

'And there are excellent shops, too,' said Aunt Lavinia with a knowing smile.

Eveline squealed in delight.

Then I had a clever idea. If I pretended to be ill, the others might go without me and I could meet Lorenzo unobserved.

'The ruins must be fascinating!' I said, startled by how easily I uttered such deceitful words. All I had to do now was to let Lorenzo know the good news on Sunday.

On the morning we were due to catch the train to Verona, I declared I had a sick headache. I persuaded Aunt Lavinia that, rather than cancel the trip and spoil it for the rest of them, I would stay at home with the housekeeper, Signora Lucioni. Reluctantly, Aunt Lavinia agreed.

Once the others had left for the station, I asked the housekeeper not to disturb me for the rest of the day while I slept off the headache. As soon as I could, I slipped out of the palazzo and let myself out by the water gate.

A little further along the canal, Lorenzo was waiting for me in his *sandolo*. He rowed me along the smaller canals, where we were unlikely to be noticed, and then out into the Lagoon.

I photographed him with his sleeves rolled up and a smile in his eyes as he stood in the prow, working the oar. I knew I'd have to keep that photograph hidden from my family when the film came back from the developers!

We moored up in one of the creeks amongst the marshes of sea lavender, with only the sound of water lapping at the side of the boat and the call of the curlews to disturb us. I thought I was in Heaven.

We sat side by side on the wooden plank that served as the little boat's seat and shared the picnic Lorenzo had brought: bread, ham and grapes washed down with lemonade.

All the while we ate, I was remembering the delicious sensations I'd felt when he'd touched my naked skin the last time we'd met in the garden. 'I wish today could go on forever,' I said.

He kissed me until I was liquid with desire. When he eased me off the seat and laid me down on a blanket on the ribbed floor of the boat, I barely noticed how uncomfortable it was. And then my skirt was around my waist and, drunk on his kisses, I clung to him while his hand slid up my leg. His lips were hot on my throat and breasts and I gasped as his fingers caressed between my thighs.

'I love you, Phoebe,' he whispered, as he moved to lie on top of me, 'and I want us to be together always.'

'I want that too.'

What followed seemed to me to be the natural consequence of our love.

After our passion was spent, we clung together until our breathing steadied and I knew with clear and absolute certainty that nothing would ever be the same again. I breathed in the musky, male scent of his skin in the sunshine and was overcome with love and tenderness for him.

Lorenzo nuzzled my neck. 'I meant what I said, Phoebe. I want us to be together for always, especially now.'

'We belong together, don't we?' I said.

'Forever.'

I eased my back against the uncomfortable floor of the boat. 'I must go home before I'm missed,' I said.

We barely spoke while Lorenzo rowed back, each absorbed in our own thoughts. He moored the *sandalo* near the palazzo.

'Meet me tomorrow?' he said.

I shook my head. 'I daren't risk the servants discovering I'm missing. Besides, I don't know what time my family will return.'

'Come to the garden the night after.'

'If I can.'

He tried to kiss me when he handed me out of the boat but I hurried away, fearful someone I knew would see us.

I crept through the water gate, tiptoed up the outside staircase and let myself into the hall. The butler and the housekeeper were talking in the kitchen passage. Holding my breath, I inched my way upstairs and into the safety of my bedroom.

After such a momentous happening, I imagined I must look different. Standing before the mirror, I saw I'd caught the sun on my cheekbones and my mouth was bee-stung by Lorenzo's kisses. Incredibly, there was no other outward sign of our passion.

I changed into my nightdress and climbed into bed. I was just in time. There was a soft knock on the door and the housekeeper entered with a tisane to enquire if my headache was improved.

It was late the following day when the family returned and Eveline was full of tales of the pleasures I'd missed.

I barely listened, counting the hours until I'd see Lorenzo again.

At last, the time arrived and I crept out of the sleeping house and ran through the garden to unlock the gate.

'I thought you weren't coming,' he whispered.

'I had to wait until Eveline blew out her candle.'

He kissed me and laid me down on the grass and I surrendered myself to his love-making.

Later, we sat entwined on the bench beneath the velvet-dark sky with the sweet perfume of honeysuckle filling the air.

'Phoebe,' said Lorenzo. 'I have something important to ask you.'

'Yes?'

'Will you marry me?'

My heart skipped a beat. Did he mean it? His expression was serious and I was filled with elation. 'Oh, yes!' I breathed.

He smothered me in kisses until I was breathless with laughter. 'But I must warn you,' he said, 'my mother won't be happy about this.'

I didn't think anything made his mother happy. She never smiled and hadn't accepted any of Aunt Lavinia's invitations to her Thursday afternoon teas. 'She'll think we're too young?'

He hesitated. 'She's a devout Roman Catholic. Already she's expressed concern that Giulia and I are spending too much time with you because you and Eveline are not of the true faith.'

'I could convert – like Aunt Lavinia.'

'Would you do that for me?'

I tried not to think of what my father might have said. Lorenzo was here and my father was not. 'Of course!' I said. I would do anything to be his wife.

'That may not be enough to persuade her.' He rubbed at his jaw. 'I don't want any unpleasantness to spoil our happiness,' he said. 'Why don't we elope, Phoebe? And then, what can any of our family do, except be happy for us?'

'But where would we live?' I asked.

'I won't go to university, after all,' he said. 'My uncle in Treviso is a wine merchant and I'm sure he'll give me work. It'll be tough at the beginning, but I promise to do everything possible to

41

provide for you. For a start, I'll go to the bank and withdraw the money I inherited from my father. It may take a day or so.'

'But then we'll be together for always,' I said, hugging him.

'Pack only what you can carry,' he said, 'and meet me in the alley behind the palazzo at four o'clock on Saturday morning. We'll catch the first train to Treviso and find a priest to marry us. And then,' he kissed my nose, 'we'll make beautiful babies together.'

Intoxicated by love, I returned his impassioned kisses.

After we'd said a reluctant good night, I crept back indoors, my body still vibrating from his touch.

Eveline appeared out of the shadows in the hall. 'Where have you been?' she said.

I gave a guilty start. 'You frightened me! I was too hot to sleep and went to sit in the garden.'

Her face expressionless, my sister stared at me.

With my heart hammering, I went upstairs to bed.

The next day, Valentina came to dust my room and found me surrounded by clothes spread all over the bed. 'My, what a mess! Have you lost something, Signorina Phoebe?'

'Oh! I'm looking through my summer wardrobe,' I said. 'Some of my things are too small.'

'That's because you're a young woman now.' She gave me an appraising look.

'Will you come back later, please?' I said. 'I'll let you know when I've finished.'

After she'd gone, I folded another dress and placed it in the portmanteau I'd kicked under the bed when she came in. That was it; there wasn't room for another thing. I hid the bag in the bottom of the wardrobe. Now I had nothing to do except wait impatiently until Saturday morning.

Downstairs, Aunt Lavinia and the Conte were sharing a pot of coffee in the drawing room. I experienced a stab of guilt imagining their distress when they discovered I'd gone, but I wouldn't be able to bear it if they made me wait for years to marry Lorenzo.

'Have you seen Eveline?' I asked.

'She went to visit Giulia,' said Aunt Lavinia. 'Carmela accompanied her.'

'Why didn't she ask me to go, too?'

'Don't look so cross! Giulia is her special friend and Eveline is sad they won't see each other after this summer.'

I thought Saturday would never arrive. I packed and repacked my travelling bag. I was full of misgivings that I was behaving in such an underhand way but certain that Lorenzo and I were meant to be together. Before the mirror, I practised introducing myself as Signora Albani and then grimaced to think I'd share the name with Lorenzo's mother.

Eveline was irritable after her visit to Giulia and I stayed out of her way, instead spending as much time as possible with my aunt and uncle. I sat with the Conte in the drawing room and we worked together on his crossword puzzle. He patted my hand and called me a sweet child.

I sought out Aunt Lavinia to give her a hug and tell her how grateful I was that she and Uncle Emiliano had given me such a happy home, just in case it was a while before they forgave me for eloping.

At last, it was time. The alarm clock under my pillow woke me from a fitful doze. My clothes were on the chair and my fingers shook as I fumbled to do up the buttons. I placed the note I'd written on the dressing table and picked up my portmanteau.

The palazzo was silent as I crept into the garden. I unlocked the gate and slipped into the alley.

Something moved nearby and joy blossomed in my breast. 'Lorenzo!' I whispered.

A cat stalked out of the shadows and I sighed with disappointment.

Lorenzo was late.

I waited for what felt like hours, shifting from one foot to the other, impatient to start our journey. Pacing back and forth along the alley, I grew increasingly agitated and annoyed. Had he overslept? The one thing I was sure of was that he wouldn't let me down.

The first glimmer of light appeared on the horizon and, heavy-hearted, I watched it spread across the inky sky. Finally, I was forced to accept something had happened to delay Lorenzo. The servants would be up at any moment and I had no choice but to return to the palazzo. My shoulders drooping, I slunk back to my bedroom.

Chapter 5

As I sipped my breakfast coffee, I half-listened to Aunt Lavinia chatting to Eveline about her visit to the dressmaker that afternoon. The Conte read his newspaper. It was an ordinary day for my family. They had no idea I was so agitated. The worst thing was that I couldn't ask for any comfort. Pushing away my coffee cup, I mumbled an excuse and returned to my room, where I fretted about what could have prevented Lorenzo from meeting me.

Later that morning, Valentina tapped on the door. 'A manservant brought you a note.' She lingered a moment, her eyes alight with curiosity.

My spirits lifted. It had to be from Lorenzo. 'Thank you, Valentina,' I said. As soon as she'd gone, I ripped open the envelope.

Phoebe,

After searching my heart, I have realised I do not truly love you but have been blinded by lust. We are too young for marriage. My decision is final and I will already have left Venice by the time you read this.

May God forgive us our sins.

Lorenzo Albani

Utterly undone, I wept for my shattered dreams. I'd never imagined it was possible for Lorenzo to be devious; he'd been so loving and excited about our elopement the last time we'd been together. What had changed his mind? I read the note again. It was definitely his handwriting but surely he would never want to cause me such pain? I screwed up the note and flung it to the floor. Of course he wouldn't! His mother must have discovered our plans and made him write the letter.

I waited until Aunt Lavinia went to visit her dressmaker and then hurried out of the palazzo. It wasn't far to Calle dei Frati and I'd be back before she returned.

I arrived at the house and asked to speak to Signora Albani. After being kept waiting for a nerve-wracking fifteen minutes, I was admitted to the drawing room.

Lorenzo's mother clasped the heavy gold crucifix she wore on a chain around her neck. In glacial tones, she said, 'Lorenzo has told me you persuaded him to make you promises he couldn't keep.'

'I didn't need to persuade Lorenzo to ask me to marry him.' I quailed before the contempt in her expression.

'Surely you must know you're an entirely unsuitable bride for my son? In any case, he left Venice two days ago.'

I was filled with bitter hatred for her. 'Where did you send him?'

'Somewhere you won't be able to follow him. Furthermore, Giulia has entered her convent a few weeks early. There will be no further contact between our families. You will leave my house now.' She rang for the servant to show me out.

Distraught, I stumbled back to the palazzo. Had Lorenzo betrayed me after all? Aunt Lavinia had cautioned me time and again never to be alone with a young man and I'd blindly ignored her warnings.

Eveline was sitting in the garden with her book when I came through the gate. 'What's wrong?' she asked.

'Lorenzo has left Venice,' I said, in tragic tones. 'We were going to elope.' Eveline gasped. 'He didn't come to meet me and Signora Albani told me he changed his mind.'

'It serves you right,' snapped my sister. 'You knew he liked me and still you pushed your way between us. He would have been the perfect husband for me and you stole him from under my nose!'

'But he never thought of you in that way,' I protested.

'He did!'

'Giulia has been sent to her convent, too.'

'No!' wailed Eveline. 'I haven't said goodbye to either of them. Because of your wickedness, I've lost my best friend as well. You've spoiled everything!'

Over the following weeks, I never stopped hoping Lorenzo would write to say it had all been a mistake, but no letter arrived.

Eveline was so filled with anger that she barely spoke to me.

Then I became unwell with a recurring stomach upset.

Aunt Lavinia called the doctor and, after he'd examined me, he had a whispered conversation with her outside the bedroom door. She let out a cry of horror.

I'll never forget either my own shock or my aunt and uncle's anger and distress when we were told I was expecting a baby.

They sent me to my bedroom. Several hours later, Eveline came to see me.

'You've ruined your life,' she said, her lips twisted with disgust. 'Thankfully, Aunt Lavinia says she won't let your immorality ruin my reputation. You'll be sent away so no one will know what you've done. We'll tell everyone you've gone to a finishing school in Switzerland.'

'But when I come home with my baby ...'

Eveline laughed scornfully. 'Your ill-gotten child will be sent to an orphanage and you don't imagine they'll want you back here, do you?'

I was removed from school and confined to the palazzo. Two weeks later, Aunt Lavinia instructed me to pack a bag and took me downstairs, where a middle-aged woman waited for us in the hall.

'This is Signora Peralta,' said Aunt Lavinia. 'You are to go with her and do exactly as she says.'

'But . . .'

Aunt Lavinia's chin quivered. 'Oh, Phoebe,' she whispered. 'What have you done to us all?' Then she turned and hurried away.

Signora Peralta was squat and solid with a dour expression. She escorted me in silence to the vaporetto stop on the Grand Canal. We boarded the steamer to the station and caught a train to the mainland.

Desolate, I stared out of the carriage window as the train carried me far away from those I loved. Had Lorenzo ever loved me? I didn't know any more.

Hours later, we arrived at a country station and continued the journey in a carriage to a remote rural cottage in the Po valley.

I soon learned Signora Peralta was little more than my jailer. Forbidden to leave the cottage, I was locked in my attic room each time the Signora went to buy food in the village. I lay on the bed, wishing I was dead.

My warden provided thin soup and dry crusts for me to eat, insisting that I must do penance for my sins or I would go to Hell. I was made to wash the dishes and scrub the floors. My only reading matter was the Bible.

I became stick-thin apart from my expanding abdomen. And then, one day, I felt a tiny movement inside me. I laid a hand on my stomach and kept very still until it happened again.

Signora Peralta gave me a sharp look. 'The child has quickened?'

For the first time, I thought of the baby inside me as a separate entity; a tiny person created out of the love I thought I'd shared with Lorenzo.

During that long, lonely winter, I stroked my belly and crooned to the baby that I would name Sofia if it was a girl and Aldo if it was a boy. It was unthinkable to allow this precious child to grow up in an orphanage. I wrote a long and impassioned letter to Aunt Lavinia begging her to help me keep my baby. I never received a reply.

One bitterly cold February night, my waters broke and the pains began. Some hours later I was in agony. Terrified, I begged Signora Peralta to send for a doctor.

She shook her head. 'Don't fuss. I'm a midwife. There's no need for a doctor.'

The pain felt as if it was splitting me apart by the time she jabbed a syringe into my thigh. I fell into a twilight sleep full of vivid and frightening dreams of pain and the urgent cries of a new-born.

It was morning when I awoke. My body ached and my head felt full of stones. Then I remembered. I struggled to sit up. 'My baby?'

Signora Peralta shook her head. 'She was stillborn.'

'No!' I whispered.

'It's a blessing in disguise.' The midwife busied herself changing my blood-stained sheets.

'I don't believe it,' I said. My breath came in panicky gasps as my gaze raked the room. 'I felt her moving just before you sedated me and then I heard her cry!'

'You imagined it. Rest now or you'll bleed.'

'Please, I beg you, let me see her!'

'The doctor took the body away.'

All the pain and distress of the past months boiled up inside me and I let out a shriek. Once I began, I couldn't stop. I slid my

49

feet over the side of the bed so I could search for my baby daughter but found I was bleeding. My knees buckled.

The midwife manhandled me back to bed, held me down and jammed the syringe into my thigh again.

Two weeks later, Signora Peralta deemed I'd recovered sufficiently to travel.

I didn't care if I stayed at the cottage or returned home. My thoughts were trapped in a nightmare world where I hadn't even had the chance to hold my dead daughter or kiss her forehead and whisper that I'd love her forever.

Signora Peralta escorted me to the palazzo and handed me back to Aunt Lavinia, as if I were an unwanted parcel.

I stood the hall, leaking milk through the bindings around my breasts; milk that should have been nourishing my baby. I was a mother but I would never be my little girl's mama.

Aunt Lavinia was pale and unsmiling. She stared at me. 'You're dreadfully thin.'

'I was kept hungry,' I said. I wanted her to know how I'd suffered after she abandoned me. 'That woman only gave me thin soup and stale bread. She told me I must do penance for my sins or I'd go to Hell.'

Her eyes widened. 'Signora Peralta told me you were shockingly insolent and refused to eat. Come with me. I need to speak plainly to you.'

I followed her into the drawing room where I slumped on a sofa.

'You've let us all down,' said Aunt Lavinia, 'and your uncle will not allow you to stay here for longer than a few weeks.'

That shocked me bolt upright. 'But where will I go?'

'You'll have to take employment as a companion or a governess, somewhere far from Venice. Or else find a husband.'

'But I don't know anyone to marry,' I protested. The full reality of my situation came home to me then and I was frightened.

'I might be able to help you there. Do you remember John Wyndham, an acquaintance of your uncle's?'

I shook my head.

'You danced with him at our ball. He and his business partner Mr Dunne have an architectural practice in New York and make regular visits to Venice seeking design inspiration. Mr Wyndham is wealthy and unmarried and mentioned he thought it was time he found a wife. I'll invite him to dinner when he returns to Venice in six weeks' time and suggest to him you might be a suitable bride. If you make an effort to recover your looks and manners, you might secure him.'

Now my life was in ruins, I imagined marriage to a wealthy man must be preferable to a precarious existence as a governess. 'Thank you, Aunt Lavinia,' I said, meekly. And perhaps, although no child could ever replace my Sofia, another baby might alleviate my grief.

Over the following weeks I took care of my appearance, never spoke unless spoken to and kept my gaze modestly lowered. Meanwhile, Eveline avoided me as if my disgrace was contagious.

It distressed me that Uncle Emiliano barely acknowledged my existence, so one day I cornered him in his library.

'I've come to apologise,' I said. 'I didn't understand what could happen if I was alone with a man.'

He cleared his throat and his eyes glistened with unshed tears. 'I loved you as if you were my daughter,' he said, 'but now I realise I never knew you at all.'

That, far more than any recriminations he could have made,

brought home to me how much I'd disappointed and hurt him after all his previous kindness to me.

John Wyndham returned to Venice and accepted Aunt Lavinia's invitation to dinner.

Carmela buttoned me into a new rose-pink gown and I looked in the mirror and saw a pretty girl. I felt ugly inside.

Eveline was already in the drawing room. She wore the yellow dress that made her complexion look sallow. 'Aunt Lavinia promised to find me a husband,' she said bitterly. 'You should be in disgrace and yet she's bought you a new dress for the meeting with Mr Wyndham.'

'She wants to be rid of me.'

'But I'm older than you and should be married first!'

When Mr Wyndham arrived, he seemed pleasant enough and almost handsome. I knew this was the best opportunity I'd have to avoid a servant's life, so I made every effort to be charming and to respond intelligently to his conversational gambits.

Eveline became extremely animated and attempted, without noticeable success, to draw his attention away from me.

After dinner, Aunt Lavinia led us into the drawing room while Uncle Emiliano and our guest drank their port.

'You made a spectacle of yourself, Phoebe, flirting with Mr Wyndham like that,' said my sister.

'On the contrary,' said Aunt Lavinia. 'Phoebe behaved well, which is more than I can say of you, Eveline.'

My sister burst into tears and ran from the room.

I was relieved when the evening ended.

Two days later Mr Wyndham called on Uncle Emiliano. Then Aunt Lavinia sent me, alone, into the drawing room, where Mr Wyndham waited for me. He came straight to the point.

'We barely know each other,' he said, 'but I return to America in three weeks. I own houses in both London and New York. I'm looking for a wife who will be a charming and well-dressed hostess to entertain my business connections. I believe you are suitable. In return, I'd give you a comfortable life.'

I stared at my hands folded neatly together on my lap. He hadn't mentioned love, for which I was grateful. I'd never again allow myself to be deceived by promises of love.

'Thank you, Mr Wyndham,' I said.

He held up his hand. 'Before you accept my offer, I must speak bluntly. Our marriage would be subject to certain conditions. You will not pry into or comment upon my private life and we will not share a marital bed. Provided you are discreet, however, I'll turn a blind eye if you choose to have liaisons.'

Shaken by his forthright words, I could not meet his eyes. 'I do not anticipate any such event,' I said.

'To be quite clear: there is no place in my life for children and I will divorce you and put you out on the street if you have a child.'

I drew in breath sharply. If I married this man, I would never have another child. I recalled stroking the contours of my unborn baby and hope died within me then. But there would be compensations; a comfortable life without any of the distressing complications of love.

'I understand,' I murmured. 'The marriage is to be a business arrangement.'

John Wyndham gave a sad smile. 'But I hope that we will be friends, as far as is possible.'

After he'd left, Uncle Emiliano announced my engagement and then retired to the library.

Aunt Lavinia pressed a hand to her breast. 'Thank God!'

'You don't deserve it,' said Eveline. 'Lorenzo liked *me* until you seduced him. And now you've stolen what should have been *my* opportunity for a good marriage.'

'Since I'm being cast out of this family,' I said, 'I have no choice.'

'You could have worked as a companion!' yelled Eveline. 'You should be made to suffer for your immorality, not rewarded with a good marriage.'

Aunt Lavinia put her hands over her ears. 'Stop it! Go to your rooms, both of you, and reflect upon your behaviour! Phoebe, you will stay there until you're safely married and Mr Wyndham takes you away to New York.'

The pain of knowing my sister and my aunt no longer loved me made my temper flare. 'Willingly. I don't *ever* want to see either of you again!'

Aunt Lavinia's voice shook with anger. 'You ungrateful wretch! After everything your uncle and I have done for you—'

'You sent me away with that cruel witch to a godforsaken hovel and it's *your* fault my baby died,' I shouted.

'Don't be ridiculous!'

'*You're* the one who should reflect upon your actions. It was *you* who instructed Signora Peralta to punish me by starving me so that Sofia was too weak to survive. How can you live with yourself after murdering my child?'

Aunt Lavinia pressed a hand to her chest. 'But—'

'I *hate* you and I hate Eveline and I never want to see either of you ever again!' Sobbing, I ran upstairs and locked the bedroom door behind me.

Chapter 6

October 1919

I moved away from Aunt Lavinia's bedroom window, my head throbbing under the deluge of painful memories I'd done my best to forget for the past seventeen years. But I had never forgotten my baby daughter.

Turning my back abruptly on the echoes of the past, I pulled open the wardrobe doors. That dreadful time had passed and the sooner I made a start on turning out Aunt Lavinia's things, the sooner I'd be able to return to London.

Later, I went down to the dining room for luncheon, pondering on the progress I'd made sorting out my aunt's clothes. There wasn't a great deal to throw away since most of the garments were of good quality. I'd set aside several items to wear myself until my trunks arrived from London. There was nothing that would fit Valentina, who had grown from a plump girl into a solid matron. Some things would surely be useful to my sister, including a coat with a fur collar. There were also several pairs of exquisite shoes that were almost new. I decided to store them for now and offer them to Eveline when she'd had time to simmer down.

Valentina came into the dining room. 'Signor Falcone from the hotel is here,' she said. 'Shall I tell him to wait?'

'No, I've finished here.' I dabbed my mouth with a napkin and went to the drawing room.

Signor Falcone stood with his back to the fireplace. 'I hope I'm not intruding during your period of mourning?'

'Not at all. Please . . .' I indicated an armchair by the fire and sat down in another. I noticed he was olive-skinned but his eyes were an unusual light green, like the peridot necklace in Aunt Lavinia's jewel box. 'I intended to call and thank you for the kind gifts you sent from your hotel kitchens. The pumpkin ravioli was delicious.'

He smiled. 'It's one of my favourite dishes.' There was an awkward pause. 'I knew your aunt well and feel that we became friends. It was a shock when she died.'

'For me, too,' I said. 'She sent a telegram only a few days before, asking me to visit her. I didn't know she'd died until after I arrived here.'

Signor Falcone watched the dancing flames in the fireplace. 'The Contessa often talked about you.'

I tensed. Surely Aunt Lavinia wouldn't have disclosed the reason for my banishment from Venice? 'I'm surprised. We rarely communicated unless it was with news of a death.'

'And her telegram foreshadowed her own demise.' Signor Falcone clasped his hands together in his lap. 'Perhaps you should know she regretted a disagreement you'd had and that her unkind words had made it impossible for you to feel able to be reconciled with her.'

Slowly, I let out my breath, remembering my own bitter taunts. With the hindsight of maturity, I understood now why Aunt

56

Lavinia had sent me away. It would have been unthinkable for me to have kept Sofia, if she'd lived, in the strict, close-knit society of pre-war Venice. We would have been pariahs.

'It was a long time ago,' I said, 'and now I regret not coming here before to reconcile myself with my aunt.' I sighed. 'Of course, I was in New York for years so it would have been difficult. My husband sold his architectural practice there and we moved to London in 1915 so that he could enlist.'

'The Contessa worried about you after she received your telegram informing her your husband had died.'

'John fell at the Somme.'

'You must have been proud of him, giving up everything he'd worked for to return to his homeland and do his patriotic duty?'

'We all did what we could, in various ways, to protect our homelands, didn't we?' I didn't say John had only enlisted to remain close to his lover and hadn't wanted to live after Cyril was killed by a shell.

'Absolutely. Well, I mustn't keep you.' Signor Falcone rose from his chair and, hesitating as if he was considering his words carefully, said, 'I understand the Contessa left the palazzo to you. Will you remain in Venice?'

I glanced away from his penetrating glance. 'For a while. I must deal with my aunt's effects.'

'If you require assistance in any way, do call on me. Or if you and your sister would like to have dinner at Hotel Falcone one evening, I'd be honoured if you came as my guests.'

'That's very kind,' I said, smiling wryly at the idea of having a pleasant dinner with Eveline.

He followed me into the hall, shook my hand, and I closed the door behind him.

It was time to tackle Aunt Lavinia's paperwork.

The study was cold and I put a match to the fire laid in the hearth. Opening the top drawer of my aunt's satinwood desk, I lifted out the first handful of papers.

Two hours later, I'd extracted a pile of unpaid bills and filled the wastepaper basket with cryptic notes on scraps of paper, discarded sweet wrappers, pencil stubs and several empty bottles of ink. I decided to ask Signor Benedetti to see if funds were available to settle my aunt's outstanding accounts or if I'd have to write to my bank manager in London. Now I was over the immediate shock of Aunt Lavinia's death and my unexpected inheritance, I needed to discover the extent of any financial obligations.

Tapping the desk with my pen while I thought, I wondered why Aunt Lavinia had cut Eveline out of her will. If she'd forgiven me, surely she could have made us joint beneficiaries? It was unfair my sister had been excluded from the will, but the angry scene she'd made, and those unfounded and jealous accusations, didn't incline me to hand over my inheritance to her.

Picturing my niece and nephew's sullen expressions, I concluded that Eveline had poisoned them against me. And that was hurtful. Now that I'd taken the painful step of visiting Venice, I'd have liked to get to know Rosetta and Carlo. I'd lost my own child but perhaps I could be a good aunt, just as Aunt Lavinia had been to me. Regret and self-reproach nagged at me again.

I went to look at the bookcase. When Aunt Lavinia married the Conte, she'd brought with her the works of Charles Dickens, volumes of romantic poetry and novels by Henry James and Thomas Hardy. There was a photograph album, together with maps, a train timetable and old catalogues from previous Biennale exhibitions.

I opened the album and there was Aunt Lavinia and Uncle Emiliano's wedding portrait. I'd forgotten how beautiful she was. Then I smiled at a studio portrait of the woman in a large hat that I knew was my mother. She held me, a chubby baby, on her knee and a toddler, presumably Eveline, sat beside her. There were studio portraits of Eveline and me in our school uniform and some family snapshots I'd taken with my Brownie.

On the top shelf of the bookcase were household account ledgers and I remembered Aunt Lavinia balancing her accounts at the end of every month. Running a finger along the spines of the dated ledgers, I paused at 1901. Pulling it down from the shelf, I carried it back to the desk.

This was the year I fell in love; the year when everything changed. If only I'd listened to Aunt Lavinia's warnings! I'd been so beguiled by Lorenzo that I'd given him myself, body and soul. In the end my love hadn't been enough for him and he'd allowed his mother to end our relationship. After that, I'd vowed never again to make myself vulnerable by allowing myself to fall in love. And I hadn't, though in the inner recesses of my heart I'd never quite stopped loving Lorenzo, or rather the memory of him, despite his cruel and cowardly desertion of me.

Sighing, I blew the dust off the ledger and turned over the pages. In the May of that year were entries for the hire of musicians, florist's and dressmaker's bills for the summer ball. Oh, the excitement of that ball! That was the night I first met John, though I promptly forgot him after our dance because, by then, I was already in love with Lorenzo.

Dusk was falling and I switched on the desk lamp. I came to the month of September, shuddering when I remembered what a painfully tumultuous time it had been. Skimming down the entries, the name Signora Peralta jumped out at me. I pictured the woman who still sometimes haunted my nightmares. Payments had been made monthly to her. They included a generous allowance for the food supplies she ate herself, leaving me with only dry bread and meagre bowls of soup. Perhaps Aunt Lavinia hadn't known about that, after all.

I fetched the ledger for 1902 and the same regular payments continued to her through to January. At the end of February, that hateful, fateful February I could never forget, was a double payment to Signora Peralta before they ceased altogether.

On February the eleventh of that year, there was a payment to a Dottor Sabbino, presumably for his late attendance at the birth and the removal of my stillborn baby. Every single year since that terrible time, I'd mourned the anniversary of Sofia's death on February the eleventh.

And then, a day later, was a huge payment to a Signor Luigi Vianello. I stared at it, thinking. The coincidence of such a large payment on that particular day was too great to ignore. Who was he? And why had Aunt Lavinia given him that enormous sum of money? A log crumbled to ashes in the hearth, sending a shower of orange sparks up the chimney. I stared at the entry in the ledger, lost in thought.

It was completely dark when Valentina came to tell me dinner was ready. While I ate I continued to ruminate on what I'd discovered.

Early the following morning, I returned to the study and trawled through several more ledgers, searching for any references to Luigi Vianello that might explain matters. Engrossed in my search, I found significant payments to him on my baby's birthday every year, up to and including 1912, when they ceased. Might this unknown man somehow have discovered my disgrace and blackmailed my uncle and aunt?

I returned to the 1902 ledger and searched February and March for a payment to an undertaker. Nothing. I wept at the thought of my unbaptised infant being buried in an unmarked grave in an overgrown corner of a cemetery. Surely though, since she was born at full-term, there must have been a proper burial and who else would have paid for that but Aunt Lavinia?

And then I had a truly shocking idea. If Sofia hadn't had a funeral, perhaps she hadn't died after all. What if Aunt Lavinia had arranged to send her to an orphanage? She might even have thought it would be kinder if I believed the baby had died so that I was free to start a new life.

My heart raced and my palms were damp. I paced across the study. Sometimes, from the depths of my dreams, I woke in a panic, convinced I'd heard my baby crying after Signora Peralta sedated me.

I closed the ledgers and put them away with trembling hands. Then I had another preposterous idea. What if Aunt Lavinia had paid Signor Vianello to adopt Sofia? If that were true and not simply wishful thinking, Sofia must still be alive. I knew I was putting two and two together to arrive at the answer I wanted but, oh, what a wonderful thought it was.

I was daydreaming about what my daughter might look like now if she'd lived, when Valentina brought me a pot of coffee.

'Valentina,' I said, 'do you know Signor Luigi Vianello?'

'Luigi Vianello? Why do you ask about him?'

'*Do* you know of him?' I held my breath.

'Don't you remember when he came here?'

'No, or I wouldn't have asked you!'

'You remember Carmela, don't you?'

'My aunt's personal maid.'

Valentina nodded. 'Clever fingers, that one. She made such neat stitches ... once she mended a great tear in my skirt and, afterwards, you'd never know it was ever there.'

'Valentina,' I said, attempting to keep my temper, 'what has Carmela to do with Signor Vianello?'

'She was excited about him coming to visit. It was before

61

Christmas one year. A long time ago, it was.' She frowned and then her expression cleared. 'Ah, that's why you don't remember! It was the Christmas you were at school in Switzerland. Yes, Carmela was excited because her sister Angelina was coming to visit with her husband – Luigi Vianello.'

I let out my breath. 'The Christmas of 1901,' I murmured.

'The Conte and the Contessa were very gracious,' said Valentina. 'They received Angelina and Luigi in the drawing room and spoke to them for a long time. I took them coffee and panettone.' She grinned. 'I remember that because there was a piece left over. I ate it before I returned to the kitchen.'

'Where do Angelina and Luigi live now?'

The housekeeper shrugged.

'Please, see if you can remember!'

'Carmela will know.'

'And where is she?'

'She left the palazzo during the war. It was hard here.' Valentina sucked air through her teeth at the memory. 'The City of Water has no cellars where civilians could shelter from the bombs. It was terrifying.'

'Where did Carmela go?'

'She wanted to be near her sister. Benaco, was it? I'll see if I can find her address for you.'

I waited impatiently until she returned and handed me a scrap of paper. 'As I thought,' she said, 'it's in Benaco.'

Once the door closed behind her, I glanced at the address. *Lombardi Carmela, via Garibaldi 5, Benaco.* I scanned the bookcase before pulling out a map of the Veneto and unfolding it on the desk. It seemed Benaco was a village on the outskirts of Rovigo, south of Padua.

I rifled through the various leaflets in the bookcase and crowed with triumph when I pulled out the train timetable. I'd first have to travel to Padua and then change for Rovigo. Glancing at my watch, I saw that if I made haste, I could travel there and back in the day.

I hurried down to the kitchen, finding Valentina and Jacopo drinking coffee together. Jacopo nodded at me and sloped off through the back door.

'Valentina, would you make me a packet of bread and cheese? I'm going on a train journey and won't be here for lunch.'

I hurried upstairs to put on my coat and adjust my travel hat before the age-spotted mirror. I studied my reflection for a moment then took off the hat. Just supposing Sofia was there with the Vianello family . . . Of course, it was too much to hope for, but just *suppose* she was there, I must look my best.

In Aunt Lavinia's room, I pulled hat boxes down from the top of the wardrobe and found a black velvet hat. It was so much smarter than the black felt I'd made do with for the funeral.

I rushed out of the palazzo by the garden gate and made my way down the alleys until I reached the Grand Canal. Turning left there, it was only a few hundred yards to the water bus stop. A small group of people had gathered, indicating there wouldn't be too long to wait. Nevertheless, I shifted impatiently from foot to foot, anxious to get on with my journey.

I was soon seated on the train to Padua. Excitement and hope thrummed through my veins, alternating with the sick realisation that my faint hope of finding my daughter would probably soon be dashed. I felt far too queasy to eat my bread and cheese.

Chapter 7

I changed trains at Padua and arrived at Rovigo with little trouble. Outside the station was a large square and I was relieved to find some horse-drawn taxis there and a driver willing to take me to my destination and wait until I'd finished my business. We set off at a brisk pace. Once we'd left the outskirts of town, the road became narrow and rutted.

I clung to the hanging strap as we jolted through farmland and wondered if I'd completely lost my senses, undertaking such a journey solely on a hunch. How could I *possibly* have deluded myself that my baby had lived, purely on the strength of a payment made to a servant's relative? Surely no doctor would risk his professional reputation by lying about a baby's death?

I'd fretted myself into an agitated state by the time we entered the village of Benaco and drew up outside a neat little house in Via Garibaldi. I sent the driver to ask for directions.

He returned and we set off again.

A few minutes later, the carriage drew up outside the Ristorante Angelina. It appeared respectable enough with lace curtains and fresh green paintwork.

I descended from the carriage and peered through the windows, wondering if Sofia might be inside. But what would I do then? I berated myself for procrastinating and went inside.

Several people lingered over a late lunch but I was despondent to see there was no sign of any young girl.

A balding, middle-aged waiter came forward to greet me with a welcoming smile.

'May I speak to Signor Vianello?' I asked.

The waiter pressed his hand to his chest. 'I am Signor Vianello. As you can see, I'm busy now but soon the restaurant will close. Do you wish to take lunch, Signora?'

I glanced at a young waiter carrying a cheeseboard to one of the tables and, all at once, was ravenously hungry. I nodded.

He showed me to a table and brought me bread and a carafe of water. 'A moment,' he said, 'and I will bring you something delicious.'

I watched him walk away, stopping here and there to clear empty plates or exchange some cheerful words with his customers. All the while I wondered if he could be Sofia's adoptive father. But how on earth was I going to summon the courage to ask him?

Uproarious laughter came from the adjacent table where four young men were sharing a bottle of wine. One of them sat in a wheelchair. He had a barrel chest but his arms and legs were curiously truncated so that he was no taller than a six-year-old child. His back was bowed and, when he felt my gaze and looked back at me, his whole body turned as if his neck didn't move easily. He raised his glass to me politely, his dark eyes bright with laughter.

I smiled back and looked away.

A moment later, Signor Vianello returned with a half carafe of white wine in one hand and a plate of mixed fried fish in the other. He placed them before me with a flourish.

The fish was dipped in a light batter and deliciously crisp and lemon-scented. I ate every last morsel.

Except for the four young men, the other customers had left by the time I'd finished.

Signor Vianello returned with two glasses of grappa and sat down opposite me. 'You wish to speak to me?'

I hesitated, my stomach churning with nerves. 'I have something of a delicate nature to ask you.'

He eyed me warily.

I sipped the grappa to buy myself a few more seconds. 'Seventeen years ago, the Contessa di Sebastiano made a large payment to you after you and your wife visited her in Venice. Will you tell me what that payment was for?'

'Why do you ask?'

His tone was sharp and I quailed. He could have blackmailed Aunt Lavinia, whether Sofia had lived or died. 'The Contessa was my aunt,' I said.

'Was?'

'She died last week.'

'I'm sorry to hear that.' His voice had softened.

'Please,' I said, 'will you tell me the purpose of that payment?'

He drank his grappa. 'Seventeen years is a long time ago. How do you expect me to remember financial transactions after so long?'

'It's hard to forget such a large sum.' I realised I'd twisted my napkin into a knot. 'This is very important to me.' I heard the quaver in my voice.

He scrutinised my face and then stood up abruptly. 'Excuse me.' He walked through the door to the kitchen.

Did he mean I should leave? But how could I walk away from this chance to discover what had happened? I remained seated.

A few minutes later, he returned from the kitchen bringing with him a woman still wearing an apron. Her brown eyes were wide with apprehension when he introduced her as Angelina, his wife. She sat down beside me, plump hands folded as if she were praying.

'Please,' I said to her, 'will you tell me why my aunt made such a large payment to your husband?'

She looked down but said nothing.

Signor Vianello sat beside her and let out a sigh. 'Are you the baby's birth mother?' he asked.

My stomach lurched. Forgetting any attempt at pretence, I said, 'Was my baby stillborn?'

Signor Vianello made a small sound and laid his hand on my wrist. 'No. She was a beautiful healthy baby and she grew up strong.'

My breath caught in my throat and my head swam. I was barely able to comprehend that what I'd hoped for was true. 'Please,' I said, 'may I see her?'

'She's not here,' said Angelina Vianello. Her gaze slid away from me. 'She left us when she was ten years old.'

I groaned. 'No! Don't tell me she's dead?'

Signor Vianello shook his head.

The party at the adjacent table laughed uproariously at something the young man in the wheelchair said. Signor Vianello shook his head and frowned at him.

'Then where is my daughter?' I asked. 'What happened?'

Angelina glanced at her husband, who gave a brief nod. 'I will explain.'

I leaned forward. 'Tell me everything, from the beginning,'

'It was like this,' said Angelina. 'The Contessa was very distressed after you left the palazzo but Carmela had guessed you were expecting. She offered the Contessa a possible solution. Your aunt agreed and Carmela wrote to us with her proposal.'

'That you should adopt my daughter?'

Angelina shook her head. 'Only foster her.' She shrugged. 'Perhaps the Contessa thought, once you were married, she would tell you that Sofia lived. If your husband would accept the child, you might have claimed her later.'

'She never suggested that to me,' I said. But then, I'd refused almost all contact with Aunt Lavinia after I'd married, returning her letters unopened. 'Did you have no children of your own?'

'We had our son Tommaso,' said Angelina. 'And that was why we agreed to foster Sofia.' She looked directly at me. 'It was one of the Contessa's conditions that we should call the child Sofia, the name her mother had chosen for her.'

'Tommaso was five years old,' said Signor Vianello. 'When he was born, he screamed and screamed. The doctor found he had broken ribs. We thought the midwife must have dropped him, though she denied it. And then, when he began to crawl, he fell down a step and broke his leg. The doctor realised he had a condition that causes brittle bones. It could not be cured, only managed. The continuing treatment was very expensive and we were in despair. Also, we were advised not to have more children.'

'Then the letter came from Carmela,' said Angelina. 'The Contessa would pay us a large sum of money to foster the baby and we would be able to pay for Tommaso's medical care for the next few years.'

'It was a gift from Heaven,' said Signor Vianello.

'Carmela brought Sofia to us when she was a day old,' said Angelina, a half-smile on her face. 'She had a mouth like a rose-bud and a fuzz of dark hair.'

'I never even saw her before she was stolen from me,' I whispered.

'I loved her for herself,' said Angelina, 'not just for what the money could do for Tommaso.'

'And look at our son now,' said Signor Vianello. He pointed to the young man in the wheelchair at the other table.

I glanced at him, laughing and enjoying his friends' company, and could only be happy for him that my uncle and aunt's money had eased his pain. 'What happened when Sofia was ten?'

Angelina's face clouded over. 'She was helping me in the restaurant when a lady came in. Expensively dressed, wearing a gold cross ... but her face was so cold it might have been carved from marble. I called Luigi because I didn't like the way she pinched our little girl's chin and turned her head so as to study her face.'

Signor Vianello narrowed his eyes as he recalled that day. 'Her name was Signora Mancini and she told us the Contessa had decided Sofia must go to a convent to receive a good education. She showed us a letter from the Contessa's lawyer confirming that Signora Mancini was to take charge of Sofia.'

'I told her the girl was happy at her school in the village,' said Angelina, 'but she said, "If you care for the child, you will want better than this for her." If you'd seen her curl her lip in disgust as she looked around our restaurant ...'

'So we had to let her take Sofia away,' said Signor Vianello.

'But where is she now?'

Angelina's chin quivered and she glanced at her husband.

'I wrote to the Contessa,' he said, 'asking if she would return Sofia to us. And then, a few days later, your aunt visited us, very upset. She hadn't sent us that letter from her lawyer and she didn't know where Sofia was.'

My hand flew to my mouth. 'Signora Mancini stole her from you?' I drew a ragged breath. 'You let her take my child!' My voice rose in anger. 'Why didn't you ask the Contessa to confirm her instructions first?'

'We have asked ourselves that a thousand times since,' said

Signor Vianello, unhappily. 'We are simple people and Signora Mancini had a legal letter—'

'Have you seen my daughter since then?'

'No,' murmured Angelina. 'The Contessa said she would make enquiries but she never found her. Luigi visited all the local convents but Sofia wasn't there. We have missed her every day.'

She sounded so sad that, despite my anger, I couldn't help but pity her. 'Now I know Sofia survived,' I said, 'I shall search for her. And I won't give up until I find her.'

Chapter 8

I arrived back at the palazzo, reeling from the shock of what I'd discovered, and remained awake half the night thinking about it.

The following day, I still couldn't think straight. One moment I was overjoyed to know I had a living daughter, the next overcome by wretchedness because she was missing. I needed to find her and hear that she was safe and happy.

I went over and over Angelina and Luigi's account in my mind a hundred times and my thoughts kept returning to Signora Mancini. Angelina had mentioned she'd been elegantly dressed. Something tugged at my memory but my mind was too woolly from lack of sleep to remember what it was.

It was impossible to go back to my normal life in London until I'd discovered what had happened to Sofia. I returned to Aunt Lavinia's study in the hope of finding further information.

There was a large cupboard I hadn't opened yet. I lifted out a stack of old newspapers and several notebooks filled with lists and miscellaneous notes. There was a scrapbook, too, and I was about to open it when Valentina peeped into the room.

'Signor Benedetti has come to see you,' she said, frowning at the discarded heaps of newspapers and the overflowing waste bin. 'He's in the drawing room.'

Headachy and irritable, I didn't want company. 'I'm busy,' I said. 'You'd better bring him in here.'

Valentina gathered up the waste bin and left the room.

I flicked through the scrapbook until something caught my attention. A cutting from the *New York Times* of 1913 showed a photograph of John and I looking at an exhibition of my landscape photography. My husband had allowed me to train with New York photographer Solly Goldman on Fifth Avenue. Now and again, Solly had given display space for my work in his gallery. I'd sent the newspaper cutting to Aunt Lavinia, secretly hoping she'd be proud of me, and was touched she'd kept it in her scrapbook.

Valentina returned with the visitor.

'Do sit down, Signor Benedetti,' I said, hoping my face wasn't as smudged with dust as my fingers. His black eye had faded, I noted.

'Some good news for you, Mrs Wyndham.' His slightly crooked teeth were white against his warm complexion when he smiled. 'I have a buyer for the palazzo. The offer is perhaps a little on the low side,' he shrugged, 'but the building is not in good condition.'

'I haven't noticed anything wrong with it. The bathroom has been updated and electricity installed so it meets modern requirements.'

'Any property like this needs continual, and often expensive, attention. Venice is built on a swamp and rising tides rot these ancient properties from the foundations up.'

'I lived here for long enough to know that. Who is this potential buyer?' I asked. 'And when does he wish to view the palazzo?'

'That isn't necessary. He was a frequent guest of the Conte and Contessa and knows it well. He prefers to remain anonymous until the deal is done.'

'It's not as if I'd know him anyway.' I glanced at the scrapbook and straightened it so that it aligned perfectly with the edge of the desk. 'I may not, however, be quite ready to sell yet,' I said, 'especially if the price is low.'

Benedetti's smile disappeared. 'But you said you don't want to live in Venice?'

'There's some business I must conclude before I leave,' I said. 'Afterwards, I'll see what my plans are.'

'Business? What *business* could you wish to do here, a lady like you?'

His sceptical tone, indicating that he assumed me incapable of such a thing, riled me. But I couldn't confess to searching for my illegitimate daughter, a child I'd believed had died at birth but who had been unexpectedly resurrected. He'd think I was a lunatic as well as immoral.

'Signor Benedetti,' I said, my voice as smooth as honey, 'you underestimate me. Perhaps you're not aware I'm a professional photographer? My work has been exhibited in New York several times.' I opened the scrapbook and showed him the cutting. 'This was taken at the opening of an exhibition of my work.'

He stared at it in astonishment.

'Subsequently,' I continued, 'I've had two books of landscape photography published. During the war, after I was widowed, I travelled to France to do voluntary work. Perhaps you've heard of Alice Bellanti, the war correspondent?'

He nodded.

'Some of her newspaper reports were illustrated by my photographs. And my book *Behind the Lines on the Western Front* was published last year and is on its third reprint. My latest book, *Landscapes of London*, has just been delivered to my publisher and I was looking for a new idea to work on. I have now found that idea.'

'But—'

'Yes,' I said with a brilliant smile, to give me time to improvise. 'My next photographic book will be called ...'

Signor Benedetti waited while I paused for effect.

'... *The Glory of Venice*.'

He pinched the bridge of his nose. 'And how long will this masterpiece take to produce? The buyer may not be prepared to wait.'

'Oh, I expect another will come along,' I said. 'Send me a formal offer in writing and I'll consider if it's worth my while to sell the palazzo and move into an hotel for the duration.'

'I'm sure it would be.'

'I'll decide that for myself once I have the written offer.'

Signor Benedetti sighed heavily. 'Your aunt possessed the same...' he paused then continued '... *independent* frame of mind.'

I smiled. 'Are you trying to say "stubborn"?'

'The Contessa always knew her own mind,' he said. 'Except in financial matters when she was happy to take my advice.'

'Really? I've been looking through her ledgers and she kept very clear accounts.'

He gave me a sharp look. 'Her ledgers? Why would you wish to do that?'

'Now the palazzo is mine, I need to understand what the expenses and obligations may be. There are several unpaid bills and then there are the servants' wages. I wanted to ask you how much there is in my aunt's bank account?'

'There are certain papers to be filed before that passes into your hands. If you give me the bills, they can be settled out of the estate.'

I opened the desk drawer and pushed the unpaid bills across the desk to him.

'There is one other thing,' said Signor Benedetti. 'The prospective purchaser has offered to take the furniture. I assume that would be helpful, to save you the trouble of sending it to an auction house?'

I considered this. Although generally in need of polish and

repair, some of the antique furniture was beautiful and quite possibly valuable. 'I'll wait to see what the offer is before I make any decision on that.' I stood up. 'Is there anything else we need to discuss? I'm really very busy.'

He gave me a curt little bow. 'I'll return when I have more information or documents for you to sign. Meanwhile you must open a bank account here in Venice, ready for when the funds from your aunt's estate are released.'

Once he'd gone, I leaned back in the desk chair with my hands clasped behind my head. Staring out of the window, I looked at the canal glittering in the afternoon sunshine. A steamer passed by and the water churning in its wake caused a mesmerising undulation of reflections on the study ceiling.

I'd been very crotchety with Signor Benedetti when he'd only done what I'd asked and found a buyer for the palazzo. I supposed I'd have to apologise if I wanted him to continue to help me. I looked at my watch. Half-past three. Dusk would fall in about an hour but there was still time for me to take a walk in the fresh air and clear my head.

I fetched my hat and coat and went to the kitchen to tell Valentina I was going to Piazza di San Marco.

'You'll need rubber boots,' she said. 'There's an *acqua alta*. Last night was a full moon and the high tide often occurs then, especially when the wind is blowing across the Lagoon from the Adriatic.'

'How annoying. Aunt Lavinia's boots will be too small for me, I fear.'

'There are boots in many sizes. The Contessa liked to keep them for her guests. Come, I will show you.'

I followed her through the *portego* into a store room where a row of gum boots was arranged on a low shelf. I soon found a pair that fitted me.

I left by the garden gate and set off towards the Ponte dell'Accademia. It had been a long time since I'd needed to navigate the streets and alleys of Venice but I found the bridge with no trouble. Halfway over its shallow arc, I stopped and leaned my elbows on the handrail while I looked down the Grand Canal. The water was blue in the sunshine and busy with gondolas, steamers, fishing boats and barges. The wind channelling up from the Lagoon buffeted the brim of my hat but I caught it before it was snatched away.

Descending to the other side of the bridge, I headed off in the general direction of Piazza di San Marco, only to be confounded by a dead end. Retracing my steps, I turned in a different direction until I came to a minor canal. There was a narrow walkway alongside it and I was glad of the borrowed boots since the water had overflowed.

The walkway opened out into Campo Santo Stefano. The sizeable brick and tile church at one end gave the square its name. Seawater bubbled up through the drains, forming wide pools that I skirted. A passage led out of the square and I found my way by trial and error through an infuriating network of backstreets, frequently coming up against a brick wall or a canal with no bridge over it.

I asked an elderly lady for directions and received a barrage of quick-fire instructions in the Veneziano dialect, made even more incomprehensible by her lack of teeth. Nevertheless, I caught the essence of it and passed La Fenice opera house, crossed another canal bridge and walked along yet more cobbled streets until I arrived at Piazza di San Marco.

The Lagoon, a glorious turquoise today, bordered the large open space of the piazza, most of which was now ankle-deep in seawater. Seagulls screamed overhead and men shouted instructions at each other as they set up raised walkways before the colonnaded buildings with practised efficiency.

The two columns of San Marco and San Teodoro, their bases underwater, marked the original entry point to the city from the Lagoon. The campanile, soaring up towards the azure sky, was perfectly placed to act as a watchtower for sighting approaching ships, as well as a landmark to guide ships safely into harbour.

I had a fleeting memory of the very first time I came here. It had been a blisteringly hot day. I remembered the feel of my hand, slightly sticky with ice cream, clasped in Uncle Emiliano's palm as he told me about Venice's great trading history. His stories were so vivid I could almost smell the spices and see the silk merchants.

Now, I watched with delighted awe as the sunset gradually washed the Byzantine domes of the Basilica di San Marco with apricot and gold. Excited anticipation thrummed in my veins at the prospect of the magnificent photographs I hoped to take. I would hand-tint some of the finished prints to convey the splendour of the sunsets. There was no doubt that the City of Water was a paradise for photographers. Next time I came to the piazza, perhaps I'd climb the campanile an hour before sunset and capture the views from all around the bell tower.

The golden evening sunshine soothed away the remnants of my headache. Sofia must be somewhere. No matter what it took, I would continue to search until I found her.

The sun sank behind the buildings and, reluctantly, I splashed across Piazza di San Marco to find my way back to the palazzo before darkness engulfed the city.

That night, I awoke crying out from a dream where I was running after Lorenzo while he raced along a narrow alley between towering brick walls. He looked back over his shoulder, urging me onwards to find our daughter. Every time I almost caught up with him, he turned down another alley.

Moonlight cast a silvery gleam across the bed. I fumbled under my pillow for a handkerchief to dry my tears. Even after all this time it was hard to comprehend that he had abandoned me. I suspected his mother had forced him to leave Venice but, if he'd really cared for me, surely he'd have found some way to communicate with me?

Suddenly, I sat up in bed. Lorenzo's mother! That was the thought that had been tugging at my memory earlier. I recalled Angelina's description of the woman who'd taken Sofia away. *Expensively dressed, wearing a gold cross . . . but her face was so cold it might have been carved from marble.* That was it! On that awful day all those years ago, when I'd received Lorenzo's note, I'd braved a visit to Signora Albani. She'd clasped a gold cross to her breast while she crushed my last hope of a lifetime of happiness with her pitiless gaze and cold-hearted words.

I could only assume Lorenzo's mother must have been masquerading as the mysterious Signora Mancini who took Sofia away from the Vianello family.

Chapter 9

In the morning, I buttoned my coat and put on Aunt Lavinia's black velvet hat. I left the palazzo to catch the vaporetto, secure in the knowledge that I looked more composed than the distraught seventeen-year-old girl who had once sobbed in Signora Albani's drawing room.

Later, standing on the doorstep of her house, I hesitated for only a heartbeat before knocking on the door. A liveried manservant admitted me into the shadowy hall and took my calling card away on a silver tray.

Waiting on a hard wooden chair, I studied an oil painting of a patiently suffering St Sebastian punctured by arrows. I tried, and failed, to imagine a youthful Lorenzo, so full of life, ever living in such a mausoleum.

After twenty minutes, the servant returned and I was led upstairs.

Signora Albani sat in a chair with a high back and carved arms, like a throne. Time had not been kind to her. Her back was bent and she rested a hand twisted with age on an ivory-topped walking stick. But there was nothing feeble about the hard stare she gave me from hooded eyes.

Since she didn't speak, I said, 'I am Phoebe Wyndham. Some years ago I was a close friend of your son's.'

'I know who you are.' Her lip curled. 'He made a gross error of judgement by involving himself with a slut such as you.'

I gasped at the insult and the heat of anger seared my cheeks. 'On the contrary,' I snapped, 'I was the one who made an error of judgement in believing him when he promised to marry me.'

'You cannot seriously have imagined my son would wish to be permanently saddled with a promiscuous female who is not of the True Faith? He was young and you made a failed attempt to seduce him.'

'No,' I said firmly, 'I did not. And he loved me. You forced him to leave Venice and he was weak enough to obey.'

'When someone told me they'd witnessed you, in a garden, making improper advances to my son, I did what was necessary to save him from a lifetime of misery with a girl of low morals.'

'It wasn't like that!'

'It was exactly like that,' said Signora Albani, her fingers reaching for the gold cross on her breast. 'And the truth of it was proved when the Contessa came to tell me your sin had led you to fall from grace. She had the audacity to demand my son should marry you.'

The breath caught in my throat. Aunt Lavinia had never told me she'd interceded on my behalf.

Signora Albani fixed me with a gimlet stare. 'I told her a girl of your moral depravity would have many lovers.'

'That's a lie!' Rage made me shake.

'There was no proof Lorenzo was at fault and the Albani family accept no responsibility for the result of your promiscuity.'

'There was only *ever* Lorenzo and we truly loved each other. But you ...' I clenched my fists '... you ruined our lives.'

Signora Albani gave a scornful laugh. 'I assure you, Lorenzo is perfectly happy without you.'

'Where is our child, *Signora Mancini*? You stole her from the Vianello family on the strength of a forged letter from my aunt.'

The old woman's gnarled knuckles grew white as she gripped her stick. 'Lorenzo has no child.'

'He is Sofia's father. Where did you take our daughter?'

'Enough!' Signora Albani reached out to a side table and rang a handbell. 'I will not allow you to sully my son's reputation with your malicious allegations. Leave this house immediately! If you ever return, there will be legal consequences.'

'Tell me where you took Sofia!'

Signora Albani raised her stick, her mouth twisted with anger. 'Leave my house!'

'Where is she?' I shouted.

The door opened and the manservant entered. Lorenzo's mother hunched down in her chair, clutching her cross. In a quavering voice, she said, 'She's frightening me. Take her away!'

If I hadn't seen Signora Albani transform herself in a heartbeat into a fragile old lady, I'd never have believed it possible. Shaking with anger, I knew there was nothing to be gained by remaining. A few moments later, after the manservant had escorted me downstairs and shut the front door firmly behind me, I could barely restrain myself from kicking it.

Later, arriving at the palazzo, I was still seething. Signora Albani would never tell me where she'd taken Sofia but perhaps Lorenzo might know. If I could contact him. His abominable mother had said, "Lorenzo is perfectly happy without you." Surely that must mean he'd survived the war?

Valentina was rearranging the dust on the mantelpiece in the drawing room when I returned. I bit back a sharp comment about it being a good idea to shake the duster out of the window every now and again. To be fair to her, there had been a full complement of servants to run the palazzo before the war when now there was only herself, Jacopo and a visiting washerwoman.

'Valentina,' I said, 'I want to talk to you.'

'Signora Wyndham?' Her expression was apprehensive. 'You have sold the palazzo?'

'No, I promised I'd let you know if that happens. Do you remember Lorenzo Albani, the brother of one of my school friends?'

'But of course.' She smiled until her dimples appeared. 'Such a handsome boy!' She kissed her fingers. 'But I remember he broke your heart when he left Venice so suddenly. That was before you went to Switzerland, wasn't it?'

'It was. Do you know if he ever returned to Venice?'

'I never saw him again.' Her eyes widened. 'You're looking for him? Do you still love him?'

'Of course not!' But was that entirely true? 'It was a long time ago,' I said. 'He'll be married with a brood of children by now.'

'Probably,' agreed Valentina. She gave me a sly, sideways look. 'But now you're a widow, it wouldn't do any harm to find out, would it? Perhaps Signora Rizzio knows where he went?'

'I have no romantic feelings for Lorenzo Albani,' I said firmly. 'And perhaps you'd better get on with the dusting?'

The gleam in Valentina's eyes was extinguished. 'Yes, Signora Wyndham.'

I retreated to the study and sat at the desk with my chin cupped in my hands, brooding over Signora Albani's antagonistic attitude.

I believed now that Lorenzo hadn't chosen to desert me but that his overprotective mother had coerced him into doing so. But if that were true, why hadn't he contacted me later? It was painful to think of it but perhaps he'd made a new life for himself and relegated me to nothing more than a pleasant memory. Meanwhile, I'd continued to yearn for a different, happier, life where nothing had come between us.

I reached for a sheet of writing paper and wrote to Angelina Vianello, asking her to speak to Carmela in case she knew of Lorenzo's whereabouts.

The doorbell rang downstairs and a moment later Valentina tapped on the study door. 'Signor Benedetti has come to see you, Signora,' she murmured.

I'd been very sharp with him the last time we'd met. 'Thank you, Valentina. Show him into the drawing room.'

He stood up as I entered and held out a magnificent bouquet of orchids. 'Signora Wyndham, I hope you will accept these, together with my sincere apologies for the way I spoke to you at our last meeting?'

'How beautiful they are! You arrived at a difficult time and I'm afraid I was curt with you.'

'I was fully at fault.' He smiled ruefully. 'I should have learned from the Contessa that Englishwomen are refreshingly free-spirited and unconventional in comparison to Italian ladies.'

'Even in London,' I said, 'it's difficult for a woman to gain acceptance for her achievements.' I smiled. 'As you may have noticed, that irritates me.'

'But your husband approved of your success? I saw the newspaper cutting of you both at your exhibition.'

'As an architect, he was interested in the arts in all their forms.' In fact, John had encouraged my passion for photography since it kept me busy and out of his way. He'd preferred to spend his free time with Cyril.

'Do you like opera?' asked Signor Benedetti. 'La Fenice is reopening with Verdi's *Otello* next week and I wondered if you'd do me the honour of accompanying me? We might make up a party with my sister and her husband and dine afterwards at a very good little restaurant I know.'

I opened my mouth to make a polite refusal but then thought better of it. I knew no one in Venice and the opera visit would be a distraction from my present concerns. 'Thank you,' I said. 'I'd like that.'

A broad smile spread across Signor Benedetti's handsome face. 'I shall anticipate the evening with great pleasure.'

Chapter 10

Following my unpleasant encounter with Signora Albani, I knew I must endure another difficult meeting, this time with my sister. Thinking back, I'd remembered the night when Eveline caught me creeping in from the garden after secretly meeting Lorenzo. I burned with shame at the possibility she'd witnessed the intimacy between us. The following day, I recalled, she'd visited Giulia. Now I could only conclude that my sister had betrayed Lorenzo and me to Signora Albani.

A long time ago, my sister and I been close and it was a sad state of affairs that currently I didn't even know where she lived. After breakfast, I rummaged through the desk in the study and found Aunt Lavinia's address book. Eveline's address wasn't written inside it.

I asked Valentina if she knew where my sister lived.

'She had a big fight with the Contessa.' The maid rolled her eyes. 'You could hear her shouting from the other side of the Grand Canal! After that, she moved into an apartment in Santa Croce. It isn't at all what she was used to. Her husband was a dentist and, after she was widowed, Signora Rizzio didn't get enough money out of his business partner to rent somewhere better.'

'That must have been hard for her.' I felt a flicker of pity for Eveline but suspected her quick temper had been her downfall. 'Can you tell me how to find the apartment?'

'If you like, I could take you there tomorrow morning?' said Valentina. 'She lives near the fish market by the Rialto Bridge. It's Friday so I'll go there to buy your dinner. But we must go early. All the best fish will be gone by eleven.'

It was barely light when we boarded the vaporetto to the Ca' d'Oro water bus stop on the north side of the Grand Canal. It was only a brief walk from there to a wooden jetty in Campo Santa Sofia, where we waited for the *traghetto*, our collars turned up against the wind. It had been years since I'd been ferried across the canal in a *traghetto*, a larger and more workmanlike gondola, in which up to ten passengers remained standing for the short journey.

I was relieved to maintain my balance and step out on the other side without mishap, despite the vigorous rocking of the boat when a vaporetto steamed past.

'Oh!' I said, when I saw the fish market's hall, colonnaded with Neo-Gothic arches. 'It looks different.'

Valentina laughed. 'They rebuilt it after you left. It's very fine, don't you think?'

The two market halls were indeed impressive, with paved floors, lofty timber ceilings and stone columns carved with designs of fish. A salt-laden breeze gusted in through the arches that opened onto the canal and stirred up a pungent, fishy smell. The market was noisy and bustling, crowded with gossiping housewives and porters pushing trolleys laden with shellfish and sardines as silvery as new-minted coins. Beady-eyed seagulls perched on the canopies of the stalls, waiting for an opportunity to swoop down and steal a fish.

I stared in wonderment at row upon row of trays laid out with glistening arrays of squid, spider crabs, sole, swordfish and oysters on beds of crushed ice and knew I must return another time to take photographs. 'What a feast for the eyes!' I said.

'And a feast for the stomach later,' said Valentina, kissing her fingers.

The fishmongers kept up a flow of lively chatter with their customers, flipping the produce onto paper squares and deftly wrapping it into neat packages before presenting it as if it were a priceless treasure.

Valentina visited various stalls, peering into a basket of writhing eels and prodding the merchandise before making her purchases. Full of quick-witted repartee, she bantered with the stallholder. He laughed and threw an extra couple of scallops onto the pile of seafood she'd selected.

'There will be an excellent fish stew tonight,' Valentina said, tucking the parcel into her basket. 'Come with me now and I will take you to Signora Rizzio's apartment.'

I noted landmarks as we walked through narrow streets and crossed canal bridges before arriving in a little square bordered by dilapidated houses and a church with a bell tower. A plane tree in the centre would provide welcome shade in the summer but now it was leafless. Washing hung from the balconies and a feral cat stalked a pigeon pecking in the dust. The smell of fried onions hung in the air.

'There,' said Valentina. She pointed to a building, once painted salmon pink, but now scabbed and peeling. 'When the Contessa found out your sister was living here, she tried to persuade her to return to the palazzo, but she wouldn't. The Contessa was very unhappy about that.'

Eveline always had been stubborn. I remembered Aunt Lavinia saying, "Your sister would cut off her nose to spite her face rather than admit she'd made a mistake."

'I must hurry to buy the vegetables,' said Valentina. 'Can you find your way home after you've seen Signora Rizzio?'

'Someone will direct me to the fish market,' I said. 'I can find my way from there.'

Valentina nodded and set off the way we'd come.

I crossed the square to my sister's building. There was a list of names on a wall plaque, including Rizzio E., so I knew I was in the right place.

Inside the hall, a bicycle and perambulator were parked under the stairs and there were apartment doors to either side. Neither bore Eveline's name so I climbed the staircase. Damp stained the walls and the terrazzo steps were chipped. On the landing, illuminated by a small skylight, a tap dripped into a sink.

A door opened and there stood Eveline.

'I saw you loitering in the square,' she said. 'So, you've come from your palazzo to gloat at my humble abode, have you?'

I gritted my teeth. This was going to be as tiresome as I'd expected. If I were to extract any information from her about Lorenzo's whereabouts, it would take a great deal of self-control not to accuse her of betraying me to Signora Albani. 'May I come in?'

Eveline blocked the doorway for a moment before abruptly turning inside, the soles of her shoes noisy against the bare floorboards.

I followed, making an effort to keep my expression neutral. In truth, I was shocked. The living room was chilly and black mould marked the walls. A window shutter hung crookedly, anchored by a piece of string. A primus stove resting on a battered wooden cupboard appeared to be the only kitchen facility, apart from the tap on the landing.

I glanced at the fireplace, where a few sticks of firewood and some crumpled newspaper remained unlit.

Eveline wrapped her shawl more tightly around her shoulders. 'I light the fire when the children return from school.' Her tone was defensive. 'Not everyone is as affluent as you.'

'If you hadn't argued with Aunt Lavinia and left the palazzo in such a sulk, you'd have inherited it instead of me.' Curious, I asked, 'What did you quarrel about?'

'None of your business!'

Another door allowed a glimpse into a bedroom with a narrow single bed and two camp beds beside it. 'I didn't know you were living in such straitened circumstances,' I said. 'You and the children should come back to the palazzo.' I hated the idea because she was so difficult but she was still my sister, whatever she'd done.

'I don't want your pity!'

'I'm thinking of the children but I can't force you to stop being a martyr, if that's what you prefer. If you change your mind . . .'

'I won't.'

I perched on one of the shabby armchairs. 'I've been looking through Aunt Lavinia's effects. There are some items of clothing and some shoes you might like. And a wool coat with a fur collar that would suit you.' I studied her expression as desperation warred with pride.

'I don't want charity,' she said.

'I'm not offering charity. Do you have to take offence at everything I say? If you accept them, it will mean I don't need to decide what to do with them,' I said, giving her a chance to save face.

'I suppose I could take them off your hands.' Evelyn's tone was grudging.

'Then I'll ask Jacopo to deliver them.' I glanced at a rickety table with three mismatched chairs around it. 'There's a great deal of furniture, too, if you'd like to come and choose some items.'

'And where would you like me to put them?' asked Eveline. 'In the ballroom or the library, perhaps?'

I flushed at her sarcastic tone. 'Look,' I said, 'I'm only trying to help.'

'What would have helped me most of all would have been to have had what Aunt Lavinia promised me. But, as usual, you've pushed in and snatched away everything that was important to me.'

I was instantly so filled with rage that I thrust myself out of the armchair and pointed a finger at her. 'You can say that to me, after what *you* did? All these years I thought Lorenzo had deserted me but now I know the truth. His mother sent him away but *you* were the one who, in a fit of jealousy, betrayed us to her.'

'I didn't.' Eveline gripped the arms of her chair and looked away.

'Liar! You spied on Lorenzo and me making love and you betrayed us to Signora Albani. It makes me sick to think of it. You ought to be ashamed of yourself!'

'You're the one who should be ashamed!'

I folded my arms to prevent myself from slapping the smug smile off her face. 'The huge grudge you nurse against me for my imaginary misdemeanours is *nothing* compared to the terrible harm you did me that day. Lorenzo and I loved each other. And when your malicious and interfering tale-telling ripped us apart, the consequence was that that my child had to grow up without knowing the love of either her mother or her father. How would *you* feel if, purely out of spite, my actions had snatched your children away from you?'

Eveline shrank from my fury. 'But your baby died.'

'No, she didn't. I've discovered that the child I've mourned, *every single day* for the last seventeen years, didn't die after all. Aunt Lavinia instructed the midwife to drug me during the birth and then to tell me Sofia had died.'

'Sofia?'

'My daughter's name.' My face crumpled. 'And that's the only thing I know about her because I never had the chance to hold her or even see her face, thanks to what *you* did.' I hid my face in my hands then and wept, my harsh sobs noisy in the silence.

'Phoebe?' Eveline was ashen-faced. 'When I told Signora Albani, I didn't know then that you were expecting. Seeing you with Lorenzo that night was so upsetting to me that I confided in Giulia. She made me tell her mother.'

I drew a shuddering breath. 'Can you imagine what it was like for me to believe Lorenzo had stopped loving me, and then to discover I was to bear his child, alone and in disgrace?' I shook my head. 'I was such an innocent. I hadn't realised that the love we shared was how a baby was made.'

'The two of you were too young to marry—'

'That wasn't for you to decide! I still believe our love would have given us the strength to make a successful marriage, but your jealousy and malice destroyed that chance.'

'Where is Sofia now?'

'I don't know!' I twisted my fingers together. 'I met her foster parents, who told me a woman took her away from them seven years ago. I'm sure it was Lorenzo's mother, even though she denies it. I need you to tell me if you know where he is now.'

Eveline's laughter sounded incredulous. 'You don't imagine he's still in love with you, after all this time? If he'd wanted you back, he'd have come to find you.'

'I'm not stupid,' I said. 'I need to ask him if he'll find out from his mother where she took Sofia.'

'I never saw Lorenzo or Giulia again.'

There was a sick, hollow feeling inside me. The trail had gone cold and I had no idea where to turn next. But what if Eveline, however unwillingly, could still be persuaded to help me? 'Finding my daughter is all I care about and I shan't rest until I know she's safe and well. Would you cease searching if it were Rosetta who was missing?'

Eveline looked away, giving a barely discernible shake of her head. 'Giulia mentioned something about an uncle who was a wine merchant in ...' She tapped her fingers on the wooden arm of the chair while she thought.

'Where, Eveline!'

She shrugged. 'I only remember because she once mentioned that Lorenzo might eventually take over his business. I liked the idea of being a vintner's wife.'

'You know people in Venice,' I said. 'If you bring me information that leads me to Sofia, I'll settle a sum of money on Carlo, sufficient to give him a university education, and an additional amount for Rosetta. And perhaps I'll share the palazzo with you.'

Eveline's eyes widened but then her excited expression fell. 'But I have no idea where to look!'

I shrugged. 'If Carlo and Rosetta are as precious to you as Sofia is to me, I'm sure you'll find a way.'

I left the apartment. When I crossed the square, I glanced back over my shoulder to see the pale blur of Eveline's face staring out at me from behind a broken shutter.

Signor Benedetti arrived at the palazzo in the evening to escort me to the opera. His hair was Brilliantined to a shine rivalling that of his patent leather shoes and a white silk scarf was draped over the collar of his coat.

I too had made an effort with my appearance. My clothes hadn't yet arrived from London and so I'd been obliged to rifle through Aunt Lavinia's wardrobe. Since I was still in mourning, I'd selected a beaded dress of black silk georgette, a long rope of jet beads and a black velvet opera coat lined with purple silk.

'You look magnificent!' said Signor Benedetti, kissing my hand. He presented me with a white orchid corsage and insisted on pinning it to my shoulder.

I recognised the lemony aroma of his cologne as Acqua di Parma since my husband had worn it on his final home leave before he'd died. Uncomfortable at Signor Benedetti's close proximity, I turned my face away as he fixed the orchid in place.

Downstairs, Jacopo had lit the torchères by the water gate and they cast a wavering yellow light on the black water of the canal slapping at the wooden jetty. A gondola was tied up to one of the mooring posts and a lamp hung from its curved prow.

Signor Benedetti handed me into the boat, where two other passengers awaited us.

'Signora Wyndham,' said Signor Benedetti, 'may I present my sister Livia and my brother-in-law Francesco Rinaldi.'

I shook their hands and we made small talk about how lucky we were that the weather was clement and how much we were looking forward to the opera.

'Though, in my opinion, *Rigoletto* is a superior work to *Otello*,' said Signor Rinaldi.

'What nonsense!' said his wife. '*La Traviata* is far more accomplished. Don't you agree, Signora Wyndham?' She had an imposing Roman nose and an imperious manner.

The gondolier cast off and the boat undulated its way along the Grand Canal. Other watercraft slipped by in the darkness, only detectable by brief glimpses of lamplight and the creaking of their oars. After a while, we turned into a narrower canal and soon found ourselves in a queue of gondolas waiting until there was space for passengers to disembark at the brightly lit water steps of

La Fenice. There was a buzz of chatter and laughter as operagoers anticipated the evening ahead.

The opera house was very grand and we settled into one of the carved and gilded boxes, luxuriously draped with ice-blue curtains fringed with gold.

I would have been content simply to watch the crowd and marvel at the glittering chandeliers and extravagant decorations but Livia Rinaldi was determined to involve me in lively conversation. It was a relief when the curtain rose and the auditorium hushed for the performance.

Music swelled to fill the soaring space and I endeavoured to concentrate on the dramatic story unfolding before us while my thoughts kept returning to the confrontation with Eveline. Despite my anger, it had distressed me to see the conditions in which she and her children lived. It was no wonder she was furious with me for "stealing" the palazzo from her, especially since John had left me well provided for. Aunt Lavinia must have known Eveline was in need of assistance so I didn't understand why she hadn't left the palazzo to my sister. Of course, Eveline's abrasive manner might well have been at the root of it.

However bitter I felt towards my sister for the harm she'd caused, I knew I must improve things for her and her children. It angered me that she was too pig-headed to stay with me, even though the idea of living in such close proximity to her made me shudder.

Signor Benedetti leaned closer.

'Are you unwell?' he murmured, his expression concerned.

'Not at all,' I whispered. 'The performance is very moving, isn't it?'

He smiled and patted my hand.

I fixed my gaze on the stage, wondering how I might find Sofia. And it was then that I remembered. Eveline told me Giulia had mentioned an uncle who was a wine merchant. Heat suddenly radiated through my body. I gripped the armrests and forced myself to sit still. When Lorenzo planned our elopement, he'd said we'd stay with his uncle who was a wine merchant. Of course, he might have had more than one uncle, but it wasn't likely that more than one would be a wine merchant. I remembered now that the uncle had lived in Treviso. If only I could find him, he might lead me to Lorenzo.

I blinked as the auditorium lights went on, signifying the interval.

Signor Benedetti gave a soft laugh. 'I could see you were passionately absorbed in the story of Otello's self-destructive jealousy, Signora Wyndham.'

'Jealousy is such a powerful emotion,' I said.

'Shall we stretch our legs and find some refreshments?' asked Livia Rinaldi.

The rest of the evening passed pleasantly. After the opera, Signor Benedetti guided us to a nearby restaurant, where he was received as a regular and respected guest.

The dinner was delicious and I enjoyed being in company again. When the war had siphoned all the pleasure out of everyone's lives for four years, I'd wondered if I'd ever feel carefree again.

Signor Rinaldi, while appearing more reserved than most Italian men, proved to have a dry wit. He watched his wife with a half-smile and a raised eyebrow while she grilled me about my family, my husband, my life in London and New York, and whether it was possible, or even advisable, for a woman to be a good photographer.

I deflected her probing questions with the experience gained from acting as my husband's hostess.

'Records of our ancestors show that the Benedetti family were spice traders, merchants and explorers documented back to the fourteenth century,' said Livia. 'Oral history tells us that our fore-bears first came to Venice to escape Attila the Hun.'

'How fascinating! Do tell me more,' I said, to divert the inquisition from myself.

'Sadly, the Benedetti fortunes declined two generations ago.' She gave her brother a pitying glance. 'Cosimo would have inherited it all but only a few properties remained.'

'Enough, Livia!' said Signor Benedetti. 'All this talk of the past. Signora Wyndham will think you're boasting.'

'I boast no more than you do, Cosimo.'

The waiter came to pour more wine and the conversation moved to the restoration, a year after the war had ended, of the bombed Scalzi church.

After dinner, our party strolled back to the canal and embarked on a gondola to take us home.

Mist drifted across the surface of the water and I shivered in the damp chill. Despite my protests, Signor Benedetti placed his coat around my shoulders, the satin lining warm from his body.

I smiled and thanked him.

Livia Rinaldi watched the exchange closely.

It came into my mind that perhaps she had questioned me in such detail because she wondered if her brother had a romantic interest in me. Since I hardly knew him, I brushed the thought away as absurd.

Later, when the gondola moored outside the Palazzo degli Angeli, I said good night to the Rinaldis and Signor Benedetti helped me safely onto land.

At the adjacent jetty, another party was disembarking from their gondola and chattering loudly on the water steps to the Hotel Falcone.

I saw Signor Falcone standing in the lamplight, talking to another man. Almost as if he'd felt me looking at him, he lifted his hand in acknowledgement. Before I could respond, Signor Benedetti took my arm firmly and guided me to the water gate.

'Thank you for a lovely evening,' I said, slipping his coat from around my shoulders and returning it to him.

'The pleasure was mine.' He kissed my hand. 'Perhaps you will allow me to invite you to dine on another occasion?' Leaning closer, he murmured, 'Next time without my inquisitive sister.'

'I should enjoy that,' I said. Livia was still watching us. I waved and went through the water gate into the palazzo.

Chapter 11

The following morning, I arrived in Treviso. It was only five or ten minutes' walk from the station to the town centre, where I arrived in a charming square. Piazza dei Signori was bordered by brick-built arcaded shops and the fourteenth-century Palazzo dei Trecento.

I went into a cake shop under one of the arches and asked the assistant where I could find a wine merchant.

She laughed. 'Did you not see there is one two doors down?'

A moment later, I pushed open the door to the wine merchant's premises.

A man with bushy eyebrows came forward to greet me. 'How may I help you, Signora?'

'I haven't come to buy wine,' I said.

He smiled. 'Since you are a lady, I didn't imagine that you had.'

I bit back an acerbic retort to the effect that I was perfectly capable of ordering a case of wine without a husband to advise me. 'Have you worked in these premises for long, Signore?' I asked him.

'Forty years.'

'I'm looking for Signor Lorenzo Albani,' I said. 'I've lost touch with him since the war but he told me that his uncle was a wine merchant in Treviso.'

The man shook his head. 'I regret to inform you that my sister's children are all girls.'

I wasn't sure if I was meant to commiserate with him for his sister's failure to produce a son. 'I see,' I said, feeling disappointed. 'Then, I wonder if you know of any other vintners in Treviso?'

'There are two that I know of. One is behind the Duomo and the other is to be found in Via Carlo Alberto.'

'Would you be so kind as to give me directions?'

I found the premises behind the Duomo but the merchant had never heard of Lorenzo Albani.

I set off for the final wine shop, confident that this time I'd be successful.

I was dismayed when a young assistant told me the business was under new ownership.

'Is the owner here today?' I asked.

The assistant nodded. 'Shall I fetch him?'

A few minutes later, a middle-aged man appeared from the back office.

'I'm searching for Signor Lorenzo Albani,' I said. 'I believe he may be the nephew of the previous owner of this business.'

'That is perfectly possible,' said the merchant, 'since the owner's name was Alfredo Albani.'

I let out a sigh of relief. 'Then will you give me his address so I may write to him with my query?'

He shrugged. 'It won't do you any good.'

'I'd like to try, Signore.'

'The man you seek was a childless widower. He now lies next to his wife in the cemetery outside the town.'

'Oh, no! I was so hopeful I'd find him.' I thought for a moment. 'Who sold the premises to you?'

'A land agent in Verona. I'll write down his name and address, if you like?'

I thanked him and left the shop clutching a scrap of paper.

Downhearted at discovering yet another dead end, I set off for the station.

That afternoon I was writing a letter to the land agent in Verona when Valentina tapped on my door to tell me Signor Falcone had come to call. When I went into the drawing room, he was standing by one of the windows looking down at the canal.

'Signora Wyndham, I hope I do not disturb you?' I saw that his clear green eyes were an exact match to the watered silk panels that lined the walls.

'Not at all.'

'I saw you returning to the palazzo last night,' he said. 'I would have come to speak to you then but didn't wish to intrude while you were with friends.'

'Signor Benedetti, my aunt's lawyer . . .' I frowned. 'My lawyer now, I suppose, invited me to the opera.'

'Yes, I know him,' said Signor Falcone. 'I was there when the Contessa slipped into the canal. He jumped in after her but was unable to bring her to safety. I swam out to them and dragged them both onto the jetty. Sadly, it was too late for the Contessa.'

'I had no idea you were involved,' I said. 'My sister told me Signor Benedetti jumped into the canal to save our aunt.'

'He was very near to exhaustion from all that thrashing around.' Falcone's expression was bland. 'His exquisitely tailored suit was entirely ruined, I believe.'

'Then, on behalf of my aunt, I must thank you for your efforts.'

Signor Falcone gave a small bow. 'The Contessa was my friend. I wish I'd been able to save her.'

'I wish that, too,' I said. 'Would you like some coffee?'

He spread his hands and smiled. 'How could I say no? I am Italian and coffee runs in my veins.'

I rang the bell for Valentina, who must have been hovering outside the door, judging by how quickly she appeared.

'I will bring coffee,' she said, 'and almond biscuits.'

'My favourite!' said Signor Falcone.

Valentina simpered. 'I know.' She left the room with a coquettish glance over her shoulder.

I wondered if it was normal in Italy for a housekeeper to flirt with a guest, or if it was only Valentina who behaved in that way. In either case, I would have to reprimand her.

Signor Falcone laughed. 'She is irrepressible, isn't she?'

'So it would seem.'

'I used to visit the Contessa regularly for a game of backgammon,' he said, 'and it amused her that Valentina often baked little treats for me.'

I was curious about his friendship with Aunt Lavinia, who was so much older than himself.

'Your aunt was a most interesting lady and I miss our conversations very much. My mother died twenty years ago and, after I bought the hotel, I discovered the Contessa was as wise a counsellor as Mamma had been.'

'It was deeply upsetting for me when we became estranged,' I said.

'And for her. She mentioned it to me several times and still hoped to be reconciled with you one day.'

'I wish that had happened, too.'

There was an awkward silence.

'How long have you owned the hotel?' I asked him.

'I bought the building over ten years ago. My father comes from a long line of restaurateurs and, as we grew up, my brothers and I learned every part of the business – from washing up in the kitchens to waiting at table, choosing the wines and ordering supplies, hiring staff . . . When my father bought a second restaurant, he trusted me to manage it. It was a success but I wanted more.'

'And now you have your own hotel.'

'I knew the big money was in the tourist trade. I worked hard and saved hard until I managed to buy a share in a run-down pensione. A year later, I sold my share to an investor for a significant profit.'

Valentina pushed open the door and put a tray on the table. She placed a plate of *cantucci* in front of Signor Falcone and left the room, swaying her hips.

His lips twitched with suppressed laughter.

I poured the coffee and handed him a cup. 'So now you have the Hotel Falcone,' I prompted.

'It needed a great deal of work – at times, I despaired of ever having it ready for guests. Finally, in 1909 it opened and I invested the profits into upgrading it, to provide the kind of luxury foreign tourists sought. The war years were difficult but Frederico Fortini, my hotel manager, kept it going while I was away at the battlefront.'

'And do your ambitions end there,' I asked, 'or do you want to buy more hotels?'

He laughed. 'I see you already have a clear picture of my character. In fact, I've recently purchased the building behind the hotel and have plans to join the two by means of a loggia and a courtyard.'

'How enterprising!'

'I'll open more bedrooms in the annexe but also a breakfast room and a billiards room on the ground floor.' He took a contemplative bite of his *cantuccio*. 'I should tell you that, when your aunt died, we'd almost completed negotiations for me to buy the Palazzo degli Angeli.'

'She was going to sell it? But she loved it!'

Signor Falcone nodded. 'She did but after the Conte died she lost her appetite for hosting parties. She was worried about the future – growing old and being alone. The palazzo is very large for one person and she said there were too many ghosts in it. And I wanted more canal frontage and a garden for Hotel Falcone, so I came up with a solution to suit us both.'

'And what was that?'

'I would make her a two-bedroomed apartment with a balcony overlooking the canal. She would have her own permanently reserved table in the dining room and the freedom to use the public areas whenever she wished. And I planned to instal a lift so that, if she became infirm as she grew older, she wouldn't be trapped upstairs.'

'Did she agree to that?'

'She did. My lawyer was drawing up the contract when she died.'

I was perplexed. 'I can see that your plan would suit her but . . .' I picked at a loose thread on my skirt while I thought. 'Did you know she'd changed her will and left everything to me?'

'Often we would chat by the fire in the evenings with a glass of whisky.' He crossed his legs. 'Sometimes we exchanged confidences, so, yes, I did know.'

I glanced at him, my heart lurching. Could she have told him about my baby? Carefully, I said, 'Did she say why she changed her will?'

'We sat up late one night, discussing the final details of her apartment, and she said she had regrets about certain decisions she'd made in the past.' Signor Falcone drained his coffee cup. 'She spoke of you and Eveline and how you were orphaned. "My heart was broken," she said, "when I saw those little girls, grieving and afraid. I made a promise to myself that I'd love them and do my utmost to make them happy. But in the end, I failed them both."'

I swallowed the lump that had swelled in my throat while he spoke. 'Both the Conte and Aunt Lavinia made every effort to make us happy. And we were. But then we came to a difficulty that couldn't be overcome and we quarrelled bitterly.' I poured my guest another cup of coffee to give me time to compose myself.

'The Contessa was saddened by the thought of selling the palazzo but she knew it was a practical way forward.' Signor Falcone smiled. 'And she drove a hard bargain because she knew how much I wanted that canal frontage and the garden. She would have had plenty of money to ensure her comfort for the rest of her life. And, later, plenty to leave to her heirs.'

'I'm sure she originally intended to leave everything to Eveline. I don't understand why she changed her mind.'

'It was only in the last year that your aunt's relationship with your sister grew strained. I don't know what happened but they had a disagreement and your sister and her children moved out.' Thoughtfully, he stared into his coffee cup. 'The Contessa was on her third glass of whisky one night when she said something strange. "Whatever happened in the past, I know that Phoebe won't fail either me or Eveline," she said. "But I must be careful. Dark forces are moving in."'

'Dark forces?' I gave an involuntary shiver. 'Whatever did she mean by that?'

Signor Falcone shrugged. 'I wish I knew.'

'She sent me a telegram that said, "Come to Venice. Please, Phoebe, do not fail me." We so rarely communicated but I knew there was something wrong and felt I had to come straight away.' There was a tightness in my chest. 'Now I regret I didn't attempt to make up our differences straight after the war.'

'It's too late to punish yourself with regrets.' He stood up. 'I must go, I have a banquet to arrange. But there is one thing I'd like to say. The offer I made to the Contessa still stands, should you be interested?'

'My plans are unclear at present. There's something I must do while I'm in Venice. And I've already received an offer, though I'm not sure if I'll accept it.' I didn't say it was for a disappointingly small sum.

He sighed. 'Then I shan't press you but I'll write to you with my offer for your consideration. Either with or without an apartment for your own use.' He bent to pick up another *cantuccio*. 'Do you mind if I take one with me?' His mischievous smile made me laugh.

'Of course not. Valentina will be pleased.' I could quite understand why Aunt Lavinia had been fond of him.

I was restless after Signor Falcone left and went into the library, intending to empty Uncle Emiliano's desk and filing cabinet. I imagined I could still detect the faint aroma of his favourite after-dinner cigars and was overtaken by nostalgia. Perhaps the smoke had permeated the upholstery and curtains, mingling with the scent of mildewed books?

When I was young, Uncle Emiliano could sense if something worried me and listened attentively when I told him about my troubles. The mahogany shelves were filled with his lovingly collected leather-bound volumes. I felt it would be a betrayal of his memory to sell them. They belonged in this library. When I sold the palazzo, I'd include them in the sale.

I sat down at the desk and wondered how long it would be before I had a response to my enquiry to the land agent in Verona. Tracing Lorenzo was my best chance of finding Sofia. I wracked my brains to think of other ways to discover where she was but, unless Eveline came up with new information, I didn't know what else I could do. There was an emptiness in my heart, a desperate, painful yearning to find Sofia, to hold her and to *know* her.

Meanwhile, it didn't do any good to sit about moping. Fresh air and a brisk walk would be a good antidote to gloom. I decided to visit the station to see if my camera had arrived from London.

The sun was setting when I arrived there. I called into the left luggage office and discovered two large parcels had recently arrived for me. They were too bulky to fit comfortably in the vaporetto without giving inconvenience to other passengers but a porter carried them down to the quay and procured a gondola for me.

I installed myself with the parcels propped on the seat opposite and the gondola glided away, the oars making a gentle plash. Vapour curled up from the darkening waters of the canal and I recalled Signor Falcone telling me what Aunt Lavinia had said. "Dark forces are moving in." It was a chilling sentiment, almost as if she'd known her days were numbered. But what could have frightened her?

The air smelled of low tide in the Lagoon, salty and foetid with mud and rotting seaweed, perfectly in tune with my dispirited state of mind. I was still brooding on where else I might search for Sofia when the gondola drew up outside the palazzo.

I called for Jacopo to carry the parcels upstairs to my room. My housekeeper in London appeared to have sent all the personal items I'd asked for and I was relieved to have my own clothes to wear again. The second box revealed my precious Century camera and folding tripod. I ran my fingers over the fine grain of the polished mahogany and cherrywood of the body of the camera, relieved it had arrived undamaged. I found my precious long-focus lens, removing the crumpled newspaper that had been packed around it, and then paused. The boxes of dry plates I'd requested hadn't been included. There was a note at the bottom of the box.

Dear Mrs Wyndham,

I have put in everything you asked for except them boxes of dry plates because they weren't on the shelf in your darkroom as you said.

I have done a good dusting, beaten the carpets outside and cleaned out the larder. If you write to inform me of your return date, I will make sure there are kitchen supplies ready for you.

Yours sincerely
Elsie Deevers (Mrs)

Irritated with myself for not previously replacing the glass plates I'd already used, I knew this put paid, for the time being anyway, to beginning my new photography project.

I sat on the bed and wondered where on earth I might find somewhere that sold photographic supplies in the tortuous alleys of Venice.

Chapter 12

In the morning, I woke after a troubled night spent imagining Eveline and her children shivering in that miserable apartment.

Once dressed, I went into Aunt Lavinia's bedroom and took from the drawer the garments I'd set aside for my sister. I folded the coat with the fur collar and placed it in one of my aunt's suitcases, along with two cashmere cardigans, several silk scarves and some blouses. I added a warm dressing gown, some almost new velvet slippers, embroidered handkerchiefs, a green woollen day dress and a claret evening dress I thought would suit Eveline. In a second case, I packed several pairs of shoes and some handbags.

As an afterthought, I went into Eveline's old bedroom and found the gaily embroidered bedspread that Uncle Emiliano had brought back for her after one of his business trips. I crammed it into the case with the shoes, closed the lid and buckled up the leather strap. Then I went to the kitchen to find Valentina.

'Will you tell Jacopo to deliver the suitcases that are in the Contessa's bedroom to Signora Rizzio?' I said. 'You can give him the address and he can take the Conte's *sandolo*.'

While I was eating breakfast, I decided to call in to the Hotel Falcone later on. Whoever manned the reception desk might be able to tell me where I could buy glass plates for my camera. I smiled at the title for my new work that I'd plucked out of the air when Cosimo Benedetti belittled my photographic ability. *The Glory of Venice*. It had a nice ring to it.

Leaving the palazzo by the water gate, I discovered it was foggy again. In my memories of girlhood, Venice had always been kissed by the sunshine of an eternal summer.

I stepped onto the narrow path, little more than a ledge, that led along the front of the buildings to the Hotel Falcone's entrance. Remembering Aunt Lavinia's accident, I took special care since it was green with algae and made a mental note to ask Jacopo to scrub this away.

A bell boy, smartly dressed in a scarlet uniform with brass buttons, opened the entrance door for me as I approached. He ushered me inside with a polite, 'Good morning.'

The *portego* walls were decorated with trompe l'oeil arches framing painted views of the Grand Canal by the Rialto Bridge. I chose not to take the lift, shaped like an elegant gilded bird-cage, but climbed the staircase to the main floor of the hotel. The reception lobby was a vision of gleaming white marble, islands of plush red carpets, mirrored tables and leather wing chairs. There was a small shop selling Venetian masks, painted fans, velvet slippers and Murano glass ornaments likely to appeal to tourists. Small groups of guests conversed quietly or read their newspapers.

At the reception desk, a man with silver hair greeted me.

'I wonder if you might be able to tell me where to find a photographer's studio or a photographic supplier?' I said.

'Perhaps you would like me to arrange for a photographer to call upon you?'

'I'm not a guest here,' I said. 'I live next door in the Palazzo degli Angeli but have recently arrived in Venice. I thought you might know of somewhere I can buy dry plates for my camera.'

Smiling, he said, 'Of course, I shall be pleased to assist a neighbour.' He launched into a detailed description of how to find the premises. When I looked confused, he sketched a map on a sheet of hotel writing paper.

I was bending over it, trying to work out how to follow the route, when Signor Falcone appeared from the back office.

'Signora Wyndham, how delightful! I thought I recognised your voice. I hope my General Manager has been able to assist you?'

'He's been very helpful. I'm looking for somewhere that sells dry plates for my camera.'

'You look a little doubtful.'

'I'm afraid I don't have a very good sense of direction and it's been so long since I lived here . . . '

'And it would be easier if you had a guide? Please, take a seat for a few moments, then I'll be free to come with you.'

'Oh, I couldn't possibly—'

'It's no trouble. I have some errands to run in that part of the city. Wait a moment and I'll fetch my coat.'

He was as good as his word and was soon leading me towards the Accademia bridge.

'We'll take the vaporetto to Piazza San Marco,' he said. 'It's only a short walk from there.'

The fog was so thick on the canal that it was an eerie experience as we steamed along, forging our way through a vaporous world where other watercraft appeared suddenly and then glided past, to be swallowed up in the murk again moments later. Gondoliers' cries of warning, footsteps and the sound of church bells, drifted through the air like ghostly echoes.

After the short boat ride, we walked across the open space of Piazza di San Marco where, even away from the water, mist still clouded the air.

Signor Falcone reached into his overcoat and brought out a street map. 'This is for you,' he said. 'I'd hate to think of you lost and wandering in circles.' He waved aside my thanks and led me through a maze of narrow streets.

I tried to memorise each intersection and turning – here a corner shrine lit by a flickering candle sheltering a statue of the Blessed Virgin; there a pink-painted wall with a family of feral cats draped along the top and a glimpse of a canal at the end of an alley.

'The Contessa told me you were a photographer,' said Signor Falcone. 'She mentioned how impressed she was when you sent her a newspaper cutting of your exhibition in New York.'

'I discovered that cutting the other day,' I said. 'I was touched she'd kept it.'

Signor Falcone halted outside a photographer's studio. The window displayed several wedding photographs on a plinth draped with dusty white tulle and silk roses. He pushed open the door and a brass bell jangled.

The assistant, a man in his later years, greeted us from behind the counter. 'May I help you, Signore?'

'The Signora wishes to buy some dry plates for her camera.'

I stepped forward. 'Good morning. I require two boxes of Kodak dry plates. The six and a half inches by eight and a half, please.'

He gave me a quizzical look. 'For your husband's camera?'

'I'm a widow.'

'My condolences.' He remained silent in a moment's respect.

'They're for my Century camera,' I said, conscious of keeping Signor Falcone waiting.

'Are you sure? Glass plates of that size are more commonly used by professional photographers.'

'Exactly,' I said. 'I *am* a professional photographer.'

His eyebrows almost disappeared above his hairline but, aware of my tight-lipped annoyance, he turned to the mahogany cabinet behind the counter and opened a drawer.

Signor Falcone caught my eye and made a comical expression, obliging me to suppress a giggle as the assistant turned around.

'I have only one box in stock,' he said, 'but I'll order more if you require them?'

'Perhaps you'd better send for another two. And do you have a box of the five- by seven-inch plates?'

'For another camera?'

I shook my head. 'For exposure tests.'

'You're aware they won't fit the plate holder?'

'Of course. I have an adapter.'

Sighing, he placed the two boxes of glass plates on the counter and then wrote my order in his book, asking for my name.

'Phoebe Wyndham.'

He glanced up at me, his eyebrows rising again. 'Not the same Phoebe Wyndham who wrote and illustrated *Behind the Lines on the Western Front*?'

'The very same.'

'I'm delighted to make your acquaintance, Signora Wyndham.' He gave a small bow. 'I am Signor Tonello. I bought a copy of your book. I can't read English but your exquisite photographs speak for themselves.'

'I'm pleased you found it worthy of your attention, Signore.'

'It certainly didn't disappoint,' he said. 'I anticipate your goods will be here in a week and I shall look forward to seeing you again then.'

I paid for the plates and he wrapped the boxes in brown paper.

Signor Falcone opened the door and we went into the street.

'Allow me to carry your parcel,' he said, taking it from me. 'I'm intrigued. I had no idea your work was famous. I shall order your book this very afternoon.'

'I hope you won't think me too arrogant if I say the photographs are of high quality, but the book's success has been greatly aided by the subject matter.'

Signor Falcone took my arm as we walked, as if it were the most natural thing in the world. 'I'm sure you aren't arrogant,' he said.

'The book is particularly popular with women because, by and large, their husbands and sons rarely discuss the awfulness of their experiences during war. The photographs also show the men relaxing in the YMCA huts so the book brings their wives and mothers some measure of comfort that they weren't suffering all the time.'

'And you went to France especially to take the photographs?'

'After my husband died, I joined the Women's Auxiliary Committee of the YMCA. Since I had no family ties, I volunteered to assist in the rest and relaxation huts behind the lines.'

'A worthy occupation.'

'The huts were a "home from home" where exhausted men could write letters, buy cigarettes or play a game of cards. I soon discovered what so many of them really needed was a little kindness, a cup of tea and a sense of normality.'

Signor Falcone nodded in agreement. 'My regiment was stationed in the Alps. It was bitterly cold and if we'd been able to retreat to a place such as you describe, even for an hour or two, it would have greatly improved our spirits.' He glanced at his watch as we entered Piazza di San Marco again. 'Shall we go to Caffè Florian for hot chocolate?'

'What an appealing idea,' I said.

Pigeons fluttered into the air around us as we walked across the piazza towards Caffè Florian, set under the arcades of the Procuratie Nuove. I remembered Uncle Emiliano buying ices from Florian for Eveline and me in long-ago summers. We would sit at a table on a baking hot pavement and think we were in heaven. Today, though, I was happy to retreat from the cold and sit inside on one of the red velvet banquettes.

'I'd forgotten how impossibly grand Caffè Florian is,' I said, studying the mirrored, panelled and gilded walls.

'What sights and sounds this place must have seen over the last two hundred years,' said Signor Falcone. 'It positively breathes history! Mozart, Byron, Dickens, Keats and Proust have all visited this place.'

The cafe was crowded and waiters weaved between the tables with silver trays of mulled wine and hot chocolate held high above their heads.

'Sitting here in gilded comfort, you'd never know there had been a war,' said Signor Falcone. 'Sometimes guilt weighs me down because I survived to enjoy simple pleasures like this, while comrades who were lost will never have the opportunity.'

His voice was so bleak that I wanted to comfort him. 'You aren't alone in that,' I said. 'Time and again in the YMCA huts, I saw men moved to tears by such thoughts. Your comrades were fighting to give us all a better future, as you were, and we must make the most of what they made possible for us. If we don't, their sacrifices were wasted.'

He nodded. 'Thank you,' he said.

We made small talk and watched the other customers in the eternal reflections of the mirrored walls until a waiter brought our hot chocolate.

I sipped the rich and delicious drink, warming my hands on the cup.

'I'm curious as to why you still use dry plates for your camera?' Signor Falcone observed. 'Isn't modern film easier?'

'Infinitely,' I said. 'Anyone can take a photograph with a simple Brownie camera. I had one myself when I was young. It was fun to take snapshots but the results can be disappointing. You send the camera away to have the film developed by a technician who doesn't care about any nuances the photographer might have wished to capture.'

'It's true that snapshots are often unflattering. Perhaps the camera may not have been held perfectly straight so that a building looks as if it's falling over. Or maybe a lamp post seems to be growing out of your friend's head.'

I chuckled. 'There are many challenges when attempting to capture a good photograph. There's the necessity of spending sufficient time composing the picture, perhaps by turning the camera half an inch or so. Then the light must be exactly right and it's important to calculate exposure time correctly. And there are endless variations and permutations when developing the negatives and making prints.'

'Can you develop your negatives at the palazzo?'

'Unfortunately, I'll have to wait until I return to my darkroom in London.'

Signor Falcone nodded. 'I see now that you're as passionate about photography as I am about running my hotel.'

I sipped my chocolate. 'I hope I haven't bored you?'

'Not at all.' He sounded as if he meant it.

'I was impressed with what I saw of Hotel Falcone today,' I said. 'It's very chic and equals many of the smarter hotels in New York.'

'Thank you. The wealthy American visitors in particular can be very exacting but I'm aiming to attract them back to the hotel now the war is over.'

I drained the dregs of my hot chocolate. 'You have errands to run and I mustn't keep you any longer.'

'I'm going to find a Christmas present for my nephew,' he said. 'I've promised him a wooden train and I'm hoping to find one in the market near the Rialto Bridge. There will be Christmas stalls selling trinkets, sweets and other festive produce. You're welcome to accompany me if you wish.'

'What fun!'

The bustling alleys that linked Piazza di San Marco with the Rialto were lined with small shops and I promised myself I'd be back to window shop here another day.

The market was in full swing. Stalls with striped awnings were laden with pyramids of produce: pumpkins, cabbages, shiny red apples and legs of cured ham, dried sausages and pungent cheeses. Housewives bargained noisily with the market traders, sniffing the salami and pinching the fruit to see if it was ripe.

There was a tantalising aroma of frying sausages and onions drifting from one stall and we watched a girl dextrously flipping crab fritters at another.

Jostled by a woman with a basket of smoked eels, I stumbled over a loose cobblestone but Signor Falcone caught hold of my elbow to steady me.

We meandered amongst stalls displaying Christmas wares, my eyes wide at the beautifully crafted leather goods and exquisite glassware from Murano. I bought a box of *mandorlato*, a sweet popular at Christmastime, for Valentina. Signor Falcone stopped to look at a toy stall, carefully examining some colourful toy trains.

'How old is your nephew?' I asked.

'At five, Bruno is the youngest of my nieces and nephews. This little wooden train will be suitable for him.' He grinned. 'Having no children of my own, I look forward to when he's old enough for a proper metal train set. Will you buy gifts for your niece and nephew?'

'I don't know their tastes,' I said, 'or even if Eveline will allow me to give them presents. She's so angry with me for inheriting the palazzo.'

'It's so sad you aren't close to your sister. I cannot imagine how it would be not to have the love and support of my large family.'

'I've never known what it's like to be part of an extended family. I suppose I might invite her and the children to come and share my Christmas Eve dinner,' I said, 'though I daresay she'd refuse.' And, if she did accept, I wondered if she'd foil my efforts to make it a joyful occasion.

'Perhaps you might give the children some small presents?' said Signor Falcone. 'Nothing extravagant but some trifles they will enjoy. Look, what about these?' He drew my attention to some wooden whistles carved in the shape of birds. 'These warble in the most delightful way.'

I laughed. 'I had one as a child.' I pounced upon a cardboard tube containing brightly painted wooden sticks. 'I wonder if Rosetta would like these Spillikins?'

A short while later, Signor Falcone purchased a scarlet train for Bruno. I waited while the stallholder wrapped up my parcel of bird warblers, together with Spillikins for Rosetta and a model aeroplane kit for Carlo. It was impossible not to feel sad that I'd been deprived of the pleasure of buying Christmas gifts for Sofia for the last seventeen years.

'There's just one more thing before we return,' said Signor Falcone and led me to a glowing brazier where an old man cooked chestnuts on a shovel set upon the coals. He bought two newspaper cones filled with roasted chestnuts.

'A satisfactory shopping expedition, don't you agree?' He blew on his fingers as he peeled a hot chestnut and handed it to me.

'This has been the most enjoyable day I've had since I returned to Venice,' I said.

'Then I suggest we go shopping together more often.' He smiled at me, his green eyes full of mischief.

Chapter 13

Every day, I hoped the postman would deliver a letter from Verona, bringing me news that might lead to Lorenzo and thence to Sofia. Every day, I was disappointed. If the land agent hadn't written to me by early the following week, I had determined to travel to Verona and ask for the information in person.

Meanwhile, I kept Signor Falcone's street map close to hand and made several expeditions with my camera. I rose early and captured the fishermen unloading their catch in the misty dawn at the fish market. From the top of the campanile in Piazza di San Marco, breathless from the climb and the loveliness of the view, I took two shots of the setting sun over the rooftops of the city. There wasn't sufficient light to take more photographs that day but I noted the interesting effect of the contrasting light and shadow under the repeating Gothic arches of the Doge's Palace and promised myself to return.

Jacopo rowed me in the *sandolo* down some of the quieter canals. He stood at the stern and used the single oar with the casual skill born of long usage to propel the long, narrow boat through the water. I asked him to stop, to allow me to photograph the faded beauty of several ancient houses whose wavering twins were reflected in the water. It saddened me that they were sinking inexorably into the mud beneath the city.

I'd set up my camera and tripod beside a narrow canal when a young woman came out of a first-floor room and leaned over her balcony. So perfect was the composition, I called up to her, begging her not to move.

She pulled the pins from her hair and let down it down in a waist-length cascade of silken tresses over the balustrade, just as if she were Rapunzel waiting for her prince. A canary in a cage hanging from a hook by the door began to trill.

Enchanted, Jacopo watched her with a smile on his lips.

The girl remained motionless while I adjusted the camera setting and took the photograph. My heart ached when I realised that she was only a year or two older than Sofia must be. I couldn't help wondering if my daughter had dark hair like Lorenzo or blonde like mine. I took another shot of Rapunzel using my long-focus lens to capture her in close up before calling out my thanks.

She lifted her hand in acknowledgement and then coiled and pinned her hair before returning inside.

Jacopo kissed his fingers in her direction and I had to speak to him twice before he heard my instruction to set off along the canal again.

When we returned to the palazzo, Valentina was waiting for me.

'Signor Benedetti called,' she said. 'There are papers for you to sign. He left his card and asked if you'd visit his office in Campo Santa Margherita.'

'I'll go tomorrow morning.' I hoped the signatures would finalise the legal transfer of Aunt Lavinia's assets. 'Are there any letters for me?'

'On the hall table.'

'Thank you, Valentina.' I snatched them up, noticing the

address was typed on one of the envelopes – a business letter. I hoped it was from the land agent and hurried into the study before I tore open the envelope.

The letter was from the agent but disappointment made me groan aloud. He wrote that the proceeds from the sale of the wine merchant's premises had been sent to the widow of his client's brother, a Signora Albani of Calle dei Frati in Venice. My hopes were dashed. I knew Signora Albani wouldn't give me the information I needed and, yet again, my search had come to nothing.

I opened the other letter, which was brief and to the point.

Phoebe,

It seems I must be grateful to you for sending me Aunt Lavinia's hand-me-downs. You have seen how my children and I live so I cannot deny that I am glad to have them, even though it is humiliating to accept charity from you.

Eveline

Crumpling up my sister's missive, I tossed it in the fire. I hadn't expected Eveline to be grateful but it was uncomfortable to be reminded of the quandary I was in as to whether or not I should share the inheritance with her. If Aunt Lavinia had had a valid reason to disinherit my sister, I didn't want to ignore her wishes. But what could that reason be?

It wasn't until Lorenzo came into our lives that my sister's jealousy had caused difficulties between us. When I told Eveline that Sofia had survived, she'd shown real distress at the far-reaching effects of her spiteful interference. I was sick of this breach between us and had to find a way to heal it.

Before I could change my mind, I penned an invitation to my sister and her children, asking them to come for dinner on

Christmas Eve. I hurried to find Jacopo and asked him to deliver it straight away.

Afterwards, I collected the photographic equipment that I'd left in the hall and carried it upstairs to my room. It was frustrating that, since I had no darkroom, I couldn't develop the plates straight away. The critical thing was to keep them safe from unplanned exposure until I could work on them back in London.

Wrapping the storage boxes in a light-proof bag, I placed them in the bottom drawer of my wardrobe beside the others. The paper drawer lining had become crumpled in one corner and, when I attempted to smooth it, I found a piece of thin card beneath. I experienced a little jolt of shock when I saw it was a faded photograph of a youthful Lorenzo. I remembered now that I'd concealed it beneath the drawer liner, all those years ago, in case Aunt Lavinia or Eveline found it. Lorenzo's shirtsleeves were rolled up as he rowed his *sandolo* and there was a smile in his eyes. My heart skipped a beat. Early-morning sunshine caught the planes of his face and, instantly, I was transported back to that illicit excursion. I remembered the sun hot on my shoulders, the brackish smell of the Lagoon and the euphoria of being young and in love. I wondered how much the passage of time had changed him.

Sighing, I placed the photograph in my jewel case. Then I removed my hat and coat and went downstairs.

The next morning, I set off for Signor Benedetti's place of business. Valentina had described how to find the building and marked the location on my map, a short walk away in the same area of Dorsoduro as the Palazzo degli Angeli. I took my time and explored a part of the city I hadn't walked since I was a girl.

Crossing a delightful small canal, the Rio San Barnaba, I

paused on the humpbacked Ponte dei Pugni. I'd stood in exactly the same place with Lorenzo, all those years ago.

Eveline, Giulia and Valentina had walked on ahead and we'd leaned on the railings, side-by-side, while he told me the history of the bridge. His arm had brushed mine and I'd felt his nearness like a bolt of lightning tingling down my spine. He'd translated the name as the "Bridge of Fists" and explained it had come about in the seventeenth century when two rival gangs, the Castellani and the Nicolotti, had fought there to settle their differences. There had been no railings then and the losers were thrown into the canal.

I rediscovered a quiet area of little squares and narrow streets, all leading to the open space of Campo Santa Margherita. Recalling Valentina's directions, I found the *pasticceria* she'd mentioned with a tempting array of cakes and pastries on the counter inside. Opposite the shop was a building painted saffron yellow.

Crossing the square, I read the brass plaque, inscribed "Benedetti" beside the entrance door. I knocked and was admitted by a young man.

'Signora Wyndham,' I said. 'Signor Benedetti asked me to call upon him.'

He led me through an entrance hall to a waiting room. 'I'll see if Signor Benedetti is available.'

I sat down in a high-backed armchair. Newspapers and periodicals were fanned out on a table beneath a Venetian mirror and a stuffed bird of prey under a glass dome stared down at me with beady eyes from the mantelpiece. I flicked through a periodical to avoid the bird's unsettling gaze.

The young man appeared again. 'If you will come with me, please?'

I followed him to a room across the corridor.

'My dear Signora Wyndham!' Signor Benedetti came to greet

me, hands outstretched. He ushered me to a chair. 'I called to see you yesterday but your housekeeper told me you were not at home.'

'I was exploring the canals,' I said. 'There are so many picturesque views to photograph.'

'For your book, *The Glory of Venice*?'

Smiling, I said, 'I'm surprised you remembered the title.'

'How could I forget, after you so firmly put me in my place?'

'Perhaps you think me over-sensitive but men rarely recognise female achievements, not even those made during the war.'

'Might that be because most men were too busy fighting for the freedom of their families at the time to have witnessed the achievements of a few women?'

He'd begun to annoy me again. 'Women played a valuable role in keeping the factories and hospitals functioning,' I said, 'while also maintaining homes and families for their returning heroes.'

Signor Benedetti turned up his palms. 'Let us not argue.'

'I wouldn't dream of it,' I said, 'but I like to keep the record straight.' And to have the last word, especially when being patronised.

'Shall we move to the business of the day?' he asked. 'The Contessa kept an inventory of her goods and possessions and either you or I must check it. This is required to establish the final value of her estate. I'm afraid there would be an addition to my fees if I undertake this myself.'

'I'll do it.' It would be onerous but preferable to having Signor Benedetti poking around in the palazzo. 'I've disposed of some items already – mostly old papers and nothing of any value. I've set aside some of the Contessa's clothes to give to the poor.' I didn't mention giving a few to my sister.

'We needn't worry about those,' he said. He handed me a sheaf of foolscap papers. 'Once you've signed and returned the inventory to me, I'll add it to the paperwork I've almost completed. These

124

documents will be submitted to the authorities for final approval and then your aunt's assets, less estate duty and my administration fees, will be officially made over to you.'

'Signor Benedetti ...' I hesitated. 'Do you know why my aunt left everything to me? It's very odd. Years ago, she made it clear that I was not to expect any inheritance from her and, truly, my sister is in far greater need than I.'

He steepled his fingers and pursed his lips. 'The Contessa relied on me for advice after her husband died and, I believe, thought of me as a friend.'

I smiled to myself. Aunt Lavinia must have been all of sixty when she died but, apparently, she'd still enjoyed the company of good-looking younger men. Both Signor Falcone and Signor Benedetti had been charmed by her.

'In this matter, however,' he continued, 'she didn't confide in me. As I mentioned previously, the Contessa had been very fond of your sister but then some difficulty arose between them. It upset her greatly and she grew short-tempered, very unlike her old self. She came to me one day and told me she wanted to change her will. I asked her why and she ...'

'What exactly did she say?'

Spots of colour flared in his cheeks. 'She said it was none of my business and to do as I was told.'

'How ill-mannered!'

'She'd *never* spoken to me in that way before and I was shocked.' He smoothed down his already sleek black hair as if the comment still ruffled him. 'I did as she asked and didn't question her again.'

'She was usually sunny-natured,' I said, 'and I rarely heard her say a cross word to anyone.' At least, I thought, not until I made her angry when I risked bringing shame upon the family.

'I can only assume the Contessa had good reason to cut your sister out of her will.'

'But I've seen where Eveline lives. It's an awful place to bring up her children. I feel I should at least share the inheritance with her.'

He held up his hand. 'I strongly advise you not to go against your aunt's wishes.'

I supposed I could always give Eveline a share of the inheritance in due course.

'Once you've completed and returned the inventory to me,' he said, 'I'll bring the legal matters to a close. And then, after you've finished your photographs for *The Glory of Venice* and the palazzo is legally yours, you'll be free to sell it.' He gave me a wintry smile. 'You may then choose to share some of the proceeds with Signora Rizzio.'

He took a manila envelope from his desk drawer. 'Allow me to put the inventory in here for you.'

I took the envelope from him and he ushered me towards the door.

'I wonder,' he said, 'would you care to dine with me one evening next week – Thursday perhaps?'

On the point of finding an excuse to refuse his invitation, I hesitated. I had already spent too many lonely evenings fretting over how I might find Sofia. 'Thank you,' I said.

I walked back to the palazzo in a contemplative mood. How strange that my return to Venice, an event I'd vowed would never happen, had led me to make new friends. Moreover, there was the astonishing and undreamed of gift of discovering that my daughter was alive. That changed everything. At least, it would if I could only find her.

Chapter 14

On Sunday morning I went to Mass at Chiesa di San Trovaso. I didn't recognise any of the congregation until Signora Albani hobbled up the aisle, leaning on her cane. I was sitting near the back and turned away as she passed, my pulse racing.

It was strange to slip back into half-remembered Roman Catholic rituals. At the end of the service, I hung back until Lorenzo's mother had gone. One of the last to leave, I exchanged a few words with the priest, explaining that I was visiting Venice.

'I lived with the Conte and Contessa di Sebastiano when I was a girl,' I said. 'We worshipped here at San Trovaso.'

The priest expressed his sorrow that my aunt and uncle had passed on and I asked if he knew the Albani family.

'Why, you've just missed Signora Albani,' he said. 'She was here a moment ago.'

'I was always a little in awe of her,' I confessed. 'But I was friends with her children, Giulia and Lorenzo. Do you know where they are now?' I held my breath.

'I've only been here for five years,' he said, 'and I've never met them.' He smiled, his face creasing into wrinkles. 'If you hurry, perhaps you can catch Signora Albani and ask her?'

On Thursday morning, I visited Signor Tonello's photographic studio again and, this time, he greeted me enthusiastically. The boxes of glass plates had arrived and I promptly placed an order for more.

'I've used them more quickly than I expected,' I said. 'It's almost impossible to find a view of Venice that isn't beautiful.'

'You will do the city justice, Signora Wyndham,' he said, 'unlike some of the tourists I see snapping away without a thought for framing the view.'

'Shall I collect my order next week?'

Signor Tonello gave me a formal bow. 'I shall anticipate your visit with pleasure, Signora.'

I returned to the palazzo, planning to work on the inventory for the rest of the day. I was sure that, when Signor Benedetti came to escort me to dinner that evening, he was bound to ask how much progress I'd made.

Climbing the stairs from the courtyard, I went into the hall and found two letters waiting for me on the console table. The first was from Eveline, thanking me for the invitation to dinner on Christmas Eve but informing me that she and the children had a prior engagement. Her response wasn't unexpected but I experienced a surprising flash of regret that not only would my own Christmas be lonely, but I had missed an opportunity to bring about a reconciliation between us.

The second letter was from Angelina Vianello. After a polite enquiry as to my health, she wrote:

I spoke to my sister Carmela to enquire if she had any knowledge of where Lorenzo Albani is living now. I am sad to say that she does not but she remembers that he called upon the Contessa. Carmela was mending her mistress's dress in the bedroom when she heard a man's voice shouting downstairs and leaned over the banister to see what was happening. The Conte strode across the hall and went into the drawing room and there was more shouting. Then young Signor Albani ran out of the front door.

Carmela remembers the Contessa was very upset and my sister had to put her to bed in a darkened room. She sat beside her, massaging her temples with lavender oil until her mistress had cried herself to sleep.

I asked Carmela when this was and she said it was a month or two after your wedding. She never saw or heard of Signor Albani again after this.

I folded the letter, my heart racing. It looked as if Lorenzo had come back to find me after all, though it had been too late. Why, oh, why, hadn't he come for me sooner? How different everything would have been then; we could have been a family with Sofia. Instead, I was a mother without her child, deprived forever of even the memory of holding my baby. My desperate longing to find Sofia and to be able to tell her I loved her twisted inside me like a rusty knife. I *had* to find my daughter!

During the afternoon, I worked on checking the inventory but my thoughts constantly returned to the new knowledge that Lorenzo had come back for me. Now I wanted to find him even more, not only in the hope that he'd lead me to Sofia, but because I still carried the hurt of his desertion and it was unfinished business I needed to settle.

At half-past seven, I went to change. I wasn't in the right frame of mind to have dinner with Signor Benedetti but it would be discourteous to decline his invitation so late. I put on a crepe dress I'd bought after John died. The shape suited me, even if black made my complexion look too pale. Loosening my hair, I re-pinned it into a neat chignon. In London, I'd planned to have it cut in the modern fashion – so much easier to keep it tidy without a lady's maid to assist me – but I hadn't noticed any women in Venice with shingled hair.

I dabbed my favourite perfume, Roses de Syrie, onto my wrists and buttoned the ankle straps on my shoes. In New York, I would have applied a dusting of powder and rouged my lips but I suspected that would be frowned upon here.

Signor Benedetti arrived a few minutes late. 'I apologise for my tardiness,' he said. 'I had to meet the elderly tenant of a warehouse I own nearby.' He sighed. 'The war ruined his business and he can no longer pay the rent. I shall have to seek a new tenant.' He kissed my hand. 'You look as elegant as always. The evening is dry and bright. Shall we walk? It isn't far.'

He guided me through the cobbled streets to a delightful restaurant where candlelight cast a warm radiance over the diners and silken drapes framed a view of the Grand Canal.

The head waiter seated us beside one of the arched windows. 'I reserved your favourite table, Signor Benedetti,' he said, pulling out a chair for me. He advised us of the chef's special dishes of the day. I chose the spider crab and grilled fish, caught that day in the Lagoon.

Signor Benedetti commended my choice and ordered the same before selecting a bottle of Soave to complement the dishes.

'It's very romantic, isn't it?' he said, watching me as I studied the view.

Moonlight shimmered on the inky blackness of the canal and

lights glowed in the windows of the palazzi on the opposite bank. A vaporetto steamed past, leaving a wake of shimmering ripples. Outside the restaurant windows, a row of flickering hurricane lamps were suspended from a pergola on the terrace. 'It's beautiful,' I agreed.

'In the summer,' he said, 'diners arrive by gondola and eat on the terrace overlooking the waterfront. Sitting in the balmy evening air and watching the sun set over the Grand Canal is an experience not to be missed. Do you plan to be in Venice when the warmer weather arrives?'

'I'm not sure yet.' Much depended on whether my search for Sofia was successful.

'Your decision depends upon when you complete your photographs for *The Glory of Venice*, I suppose?'

I took a sip of water while considering how to answer. 'Not entirely. I hadn't expected to find anything here in Venice to persuade me to stay but ...'

His gaze searched my face. 'Something, or someone, you've found here has changed your mind?'

I glanced away, hoping he wouldn't notice how my cheeks suddenly burned. How could I possibly explain I hoped to find an illegitimate daughter I'd believed to be dead? 'I'd forgotten how lovely Venice is, even in winter,' I stammered.

The waiter arrived with an ice bucket and made a performance of uncorking the wine and pouring a little into a glass for Signor Benedetti to taste.

'Have you made progress on the inventory, Signora Wyndham?' he asked, after the waiter had moved on.

'Not much, I'm afraid,' I confessed. 'My husband often used to chide me for procrastinating.'

'If it isn't too painful,' he said, 'tell me about him.'

'He was a successful architect with a practice in New York,' I said. 'My uncle met him on one of his visits to Venice and they became friends. John was fascinated by the beauty of the city.'

'You married young, I believe?'

'I was eighteen,' I said. 'John was eight years older. He wanted a bride who was young enough to ...' I'd meant to say "be malleable and turn a blind eye", but stopped myself. 'He knew Aunt Lavinia was an excellent hostess and he hoped I'd learned those skills from her.'

'And had you?'

'I'm a good organiser. I arranged many successful parties for my husband's business acquaintances.' And at every dinner, Cyril, John's bosom friend, had watched me with a supercilious smile on his lips, looking for an opportunity to slide an acid comment about me into the conversation, cloaked by a honeyed turn of phrase.

'You must have been a golden couple,' said Signor Benedetti. 'The gifted architect and his beautiful and creative wife.' He hesitated. 'But you had no children to complete your perfect marriage?'

Abruptly, I pushed away my wine glass. 'My husband had no desire for them in his carefully ordered life.'

'I apologise if my remark was intrusive,' he said. 'You're a young and very beautiful widow, Signora Wyndham. Perhaps you will marry again and this time ...'

'I like my new-found independence,' I said. Besides, at thirty-four years old, any man who had returned unscathed from the war was probably already married or seeking a much younger wife.

The waiter arrived with our first course and I was relieved Signor Benedetti was distracted from questioning me further. Really, he was almost as bad as his inquisitive sister!

By the time coffee was served, I'd forgotten my irritation. He was a handsome, attentive and amusing companion. A fount of knowledge about the history of Venice, he described in fascinating detail how the City of Water had been created and how it evolved into a rich and powerful trading empire. Although I'd learned this at school, he made history come alive with his descriptions of merchant adventurers, pirates, crusades and illustrious Venetian artists.

'How I wish I'd been born a few hundred years ago,' he said wistfully, 'and lived the life of a wealthy Venetian merchant.'

Laughing, I said, 'I can picture you dressed in velvet with a feather in your hat, swirling your fur-trimmed cloak around your shoulders.'

'And you might have been sitting on your balcony with an enigmatic smile on your face, having your portrait painted by an Old Master, while you watched the world pass by.' He sighed. 'Those were the days.'

'Perhaps,' I said, 'though I confess, I'd find it hard to give up the luxury of hot water coming from a tap whenever I wish and electric light available at the flick of a switch.'

'I suppose you're right. Though perhaps you have the best of both worlds. You have a beautiful palazzo, which has hot and cold water on tap and electric lighting. Even if the building does have serious issues with subsidence.'

'Subsidence?'

'Many properties in the Floating City are troubled by subsidence. Venice is sinking and it's an ongoing struggle to keep replacing the timber piles that shore up the buildings.'

'I haven't noticed any problems at the Palazzo degli Angeli.'

'You will,' said Signor Benedetti. 'Or perhaps you'll decide to sell it before one corner of the building collapses into the water of the Rio della Toletta. If that happens, no one will buy it until it's been rebuilt.'

'What an alarming thought!' But surely he was exaggerating?

'You must have seen the repair works going on all over the city? Everywhere you go you see barges laden with building materials and hear the tap-tap of stonemasons' hammers.' He chuckled. 'Sometimes I wish I owned a construction company – I'd make a fortune!' He signalled to the waiter, indicating that he wanted the bill. 'I can send a surveyor to take a look at the Palazzo degli Angeli, if you like?'

'I suppose it would be reassuring to know there aren't any problems,' I said.

We left the restaurant and took our time walking back to the palazzo. Signor Benedetti pointed out one of the grander houses. 'That is Ca' Foscari,' he said. 'Henry III of France lodged there in 1574.'

'You know so much about the history of Venice and its population,' I said. 'I wonder if you know anything about a family called Albani? I used to be at school with Giulia Albani but I lost touch with her. I believe she's a nun now.'

'Albani?' He thought for a moment. 'Ah, yes. Parvenues. Silk traders who arrived from Rome in the eighteenth century. The family home is in Calle dei Frati, near the Palazzo degli Angeli. I believe Widow Albani still resides there, all alone in that great house. Cesare Albani died of a fever some twenty years ago and I understand his widow turned to the Church.'

'Giulia had a brother, too,' I said. 'Lorenzo.' I held my breath, desperately hoping Signor Benedetti might shed some light on Lorenzo's current location.

Signor Benedetti shook his head. 'I don't believe he's living in Venice now.'

My hopes crushed, my responses to his flow of conversation became stilted.

'You're very quiet,' he said as we turned into the alley behind the palazzo. 'I apologise if I've tired you by suggesting we walk.'

I summoned a smile. 'Not at all. And I've enjoyed the history lesson.'

A few minutes later, I opened the garden gate and Signor Benedetti accompanied me along the path and into the courtyard.

We stood beneath the lantern at the foot of the stone staircase. 'It's been a lovely evening,' I said.

Signor Benedetti lifted my hand to his lips. 'I hope you will allow me to take you to dinner again?'

'I should be delighted.'

'And, since your aunt and I were such good friends, perhaps you will call me Cosimo, as she did?'

I didn't see any reason why I shouldn't. 'Good night, Cosimo,' I said, 'and please, call me Phoebe.' I freed my hand and felt his gaze upon me as I climbed the steps to the front door.

Chapter 15

I was struggling to board a gondola by the water gate when Signor Falcone appeared on the jetty.

'May I help you?' he asked.

'Oh, Signor Falcone! Thank you. Would you hold the tripod while I stow the camera safely? I'm worried I might drop it in the canal.'

Once I was seated, I held out my hand for the tripod.

'I'm pleased to have seen you,' he said. 'I was going to call by later today to say I'm holding a small party for family and friends next week, on Christmas Eve. If you're free, I'd be delighted if you'd join us?'

'How very kind!' In Italy, Christmas Eve was an important celebration and I hadn't wanted to be lonely at dinner. 'I should like that very much.'

His lips curved in a smile. 'I'm so pleased. There's just one thing I should tell you . . .'

'Yes?'

'I invited your sister and her children, too, and she has accepted.'

'Oh! She wrote to tell me she had a prior engagement after I invited her to come to the palazzo.'

'I took the liberty of asking her after we went to Caffè Florian,' he said. 'It's so sad that you and your sister aren't close. I hoped that, if you both came to the hotel, you'd meet on neutral territory and perhaps there'd be less opportunity for discord.'

'That's thoughtful of you. I promise there will be none on my part.' I shrugged. 'But I cannot speak for Eveline.'

'You have presents for your niece and nephew and I doubt she'll want to spoil their Christmas,' he said.

A barge laden with timber rowed past and its wake made the gondola rock from side to side.

Signor Falcone took a step back. 'I must let you go on your photographic expedition before the light changes but I look forward to welcoming you on Christmas Eve. Eight o'clock?'

'Thank you,' I said.

The gondolier cast off and the boat slid out into the canal.

I waved to Signor Falcone as he walked towards the hotel. I thought how lucky I was to have such a considerate neighbour. I could quite see why Aunt Lavinia had enjoyed his friendship.

The day before Christmas Eve, Cosimo Benedetti took me to a concert of Vivaldi's music at the church of Santa Maria della Pietà, a stone's throw from Piazza di San Marco. He told me the church had been built in the eighteenth century but the marble facing to the façade had been left unfinished until 1906.

'So it wasn't completed until after I left Venice, then,' I said.

Cosimo nodded. 'The work was carried out to the design drawn up by the original architect,' he said, 'but the most interesting thing is that Antonio Vivaldi once worked here as the choirmaster.

There was an orphanage attached to the church, where the boys learned a trade and the girls studied music.'

'I remember my uncle telling me that.'

'The most talented were offered a place in the choir where they sang in the stalls, protected by grilles from the stares of the general public.' He smiled. 'Despite that, many of the girls attracted notice and went on to make good marriages.'

The interior of the church was crowded. When the concert began, a hush fell over the congregation as Vivaldi's music soared upwards, filling the air and resonating through my bones. My gaze rested upon an oval cartouche on the ceiling, gloriously frescoed by Tiepolo.

I imagined the orphaned and abandoned girls lifted from the gutter and given the opportunity to develop their voices by singing this ethereal and sublime choral music. I wondered how Sofia fared at her convent. Had she, perhaps, been given the chance to find her own talent in some way, like Vivaldi's choir girls? Most importantly, was she happy?

After the concert ended, we walked in silence while the music still filled our thoughts. Arriving at Piazza di San Marco, we stopped at a stall selling spiced wine. We warmed our hands around the glasses while we sipped. Our breath floated away in little drifts of vapour on the frosty air.

Later, Cosimo took my arm and walked me back to the palazzo.

'Thank you,' I said. 'The concert was beautiful.'

He lifted my fingers to his lips. 'It was a pleasure to spend an evening in your company.' I gently withdrew my hand from his. 'I don't like to think of you on your own on Christmas Eve and I wish we might have dined together,' he said, 'but I'm obliged to celebrate with my parents. They're elderly now and . . .'

'Really,' I said, 'there's no need to explain. It's good to know you are a dutiful son. Besides, I shan't be alone.'

'You're meeting friends? Old school friends, perhaps?'

'Signor Falcone has invited me and my sister to a small party at his hotel.'

'You are dining with Signora Rizzio?' He puffed out his breath. 'I hope you don't suffer from indigestion afterwards.'

I couldn't contain my laughter. 'You're too bad! It was generous of Signor Falcone to invite us out on what is usually a night for families to spend together. He has an ulterior motive, you see.'

'I'm sure that he has,' said Cosimo drily. 'You know he pressured your aunt to sell the palazzo to him so he could extend his hotel? He'll do his utmost to persuade you now.'

'He mentioned he'd like to buy it,' I said, the smile slipping from my face, 'but he's put no pressure upon me. The motive I spoke of is merely to bring about good relations between my sister and myself.'

'Well, I hope you're right.' Cosimo shook his head. 'I don't trust him at all.'

'I'm sure you're mistaken.' There was an awkward silence and then I said, 'Thank you again for taking me to the concert.'

'It was my pleasure. Good night, Phoebe.'

'Good night.' I nodded and went inside.

The next morning, Valentina and Jacopo, dressed in their outdoor clothing, came to see me in my study.

'So you're all ready to go to Mestre?' I said.

'Are you sure you'll be all right without us?' asked Valentina with a worried frown.

'Of course I will! I live alone in London, so I'm quite used to it.'

'Don't forget to put coal in the range,' said Jacopo, 'or there won't be any hot water for the bathroom. I've filled the hods and the fires are all laid, ready for you to light.'

'Thank you, Jacopo.'

'And I've left you ravioli to cook in capon broth for tomorrow,' said Valentina. 'It's the traditional lunch on Christmas Day.'

'I remember,' I said.

'There are cold meats and breadsticks. And a stew of eels in garlic and tomato sauce and a nice piece of Montasio cheese.' She shook her head. 'You'll have to warm the stew in a pan—'

'I'm perfectly capable of doing that! In any case, I shall be dining at the Hotel Falcone tonight. Now you both go and have a good time with your son and your brother's family. I'll see you in a few days.'

'Tell Signor Falcone to look after you,' said Valentina.

'I'll be absolutely fine on my own,' I said. 'And I won't forget to give him the *cantucci* you made for him.' Laughing, I made a shooing motion with my hands. 'Now go on with you or you'll miss your train!'

After they'd gone, I dressed warmly and went out. The sky was a clear blue and the sun shone, even though the air was bitingly cold. I caught the vaporetto to Piazza di San Marco and then wandered through the narrow streets towards the Rialto area. It was along that route I'd seen some interesting little shops when I was walking with Signor Falcone.

Meandering along the alleyways, I called into any establishmentthat caught my fancy. I put a handful of notes into a one-legged soldier's hat, saddened that he was reduced to begging after being wounded on active service for his country.

I bought a few Christmas gifts: some perfumed soap from an old-fashioned apothecary for Eveline, and for Signor Falcone a notebook bound in fine-grained tan leather with marbled endpapers.

I stopped in a cafe for an espresso and a brioche and watched a pair of nuns laughing together as they walked past the window.

Although Luigi had told me that he and Aunt Lavinia had written to various convents in their search for Sofia, that had been some years ago. It gave me an idea. Immediately after Christmas, I'd visit the priest at San Trovaso to ask him for names of nearby convent schools and orphanages. Then I'd write to them all. Invigorated by the idea of a new direction for my search, I took the vaporetto back to the Accademia bridge.

The palazzo was quiet without Valentina and Jacopo's presence and I crept into the kitchen, feeling like a trespasser when I heated soup for a late lunch and replenished the coal in the range.

I laid out the newly purchased gifts on the kitchen table: a pretty trinket box decorated with painted kittens for Rosetta, the notebook for Signor Falcone and Eveline's soap. For Carlo there was a splendid jigsaw of a Venetian Trireme with pennants flying and oarsmen straining against the waves.

The final present had been an impulse buy. I ran the soft wool of the aqua green shawl through my fingers and wondered if Eveline would throw it back at me, saying she didn't want my charity. Sighing, I remembered the damp chill of her apartment. It was up to her if she rejected a present given out of a genuine desire to help.

Upstairs, I arranged my evening clothes on the bed. I didn't know how formal the dinner would be but it was a special occasion so I laid out Aunt Lavinia's black beaded dress that I'd worn to the opera. The bedroom was cold so I lit the fire to warm it for when I changed for the party.

Downstairs, I lit the library fire, chose a book, and curled up in my uncle's scuffed leather armchair. Apart from the occasional hiss of steam escaping from the coal and the rustle of turning pages, the palazzo was silent. Outside, church bells rang in the distance and a dog barked. It had never been so quiet when I'd lived there with my aunt and uncle. They had many friends and loved to meet new people, collecting visitors to Venice as if they

141

were trophies, and inviting them to their *salons* of literary and artistic acquaintances. They'd hosted marvellous parties.

I remembered, as a child, sitting with Eveline at the top of the stairs in our nightgowns and peering through the banisters at the dancing below. The palazzo had been lit by a hundred flickering candles and had felt like a fairy palace. Sometimes, Aunt Lavinia had slipped upstairs to bring us a plate of sweetmeats. She'd ruffled our hair and told us not to stay up too late, before running downstairs in a swirl of taffeta and lace to rejoin her guests.

I felt guilty now, imagining how lonely it must have been for her after Uncle Emiliano died. And then came the 'war to end all wars', leaving in its wake so many grieving and lonely widows.

Outside, the light faded. I turned on the lamp and read another chapter of my book. It was cosy by the fire and I almost wished I wasn't going out. Above all, I hoped Eveline wouldn't make a scene.

When it was time to dress for the party, I walked around the echoing rooms, closing the shutters and turning on lights to dispel the ghosts and shadows. Upstairs, I ran a bath and sprinkled in the salts I'd bought in the apothecary shop that morning.

Later, my melancholy mood dispelled by the perfumed bath, I dressed and coiled up my hair. Aunt Lavinia's jet beads looked too sombre for a Christmas party so I draped my rope of pearls around my neck. I slipped on the velvet opera coat and went downstairs to gather up the gifts before walking next door to the Hotel Falcone.

Chapter 16

The *portego* of the hotel was milling with guests greeting each other with kisses and cries of delight. I smiled at the impossibility of an Italian talking without reinforcing the meaning and drama of the conversation with hand gestures.

Upstairs, the reception area was thronged with guests and music drifted through the open doors to another room.

Signor Falcone, debonair in his dinner jacket, was waiting to receive his guests as they arrived. 'Signora Wyndham, welcome!' he said, holding out his hands to me. 'How elegant you are!' He kissed both my cheeks and murmured, 'Your sister and her delightful children have just arrived.'

I glanced over his shoulder but couldn't see Eveline.

'She's in the cloakroom. You may care to leave your coat, too? Afterwards, just follow the noise towards the dining room and, as soon as I've greeted all the guests, I'll introduce you to my family and friends.' A chattering group of people arrived and Signor Falcone went to meet them.

The ladies' cloakroom was crowded when I handed my coat and the presents to the attendant. I'd give the gifts to Eveline and the children when we left. Glancing in the mirror, I tensed when I glimpsed my sister's reflection. Pasting a smile on my face, I turned and said, 'Hello, Eveline.'

She acknowledged me with a dip of her head. Her cheeks were flushed and her eyes bright.

'I see we're both wearing outfits plundered from Aunt Lavinia's wardrobe,' I said.

Eveline ran a hand over the skirt of her garnet silk dress.

'That colour really suits you.'

'I was worried it would look disrespectful to Aunt Lavinia's memory,' said Eveline, 'but I didn't have anything else suitable for tonight.'

'It's hardly a garish colour and no one will be offended, least of all Aunt Lavinia, if she's looking down at us.' I couldn't see Rosetta and Carlo amongst the guests. 'Are your children here?'

'Making friends with some of Signor Falcone's nieces and nephews.'

'Shall we go out together to join the other guests? It's a bit daunting not knowing anyone here.'

Eveline gave me an uncertain glance before following me.

We were drawn to the dining room by the sound of harp music and halted in the doorway.

'How the children will love this!' said Eveline.

The room was decorated with paper lanterns and garlands of greenery tied with scarlet ribbons. Long tables draped with white linen were lit by flickering pillar candles grouped with gold-sprayed fir cones, sprigs of rosemary and silk bows. Glass baubles strung between the Murano chandeliers gleamed in the candlelight.

'It reminds me of the parties Aunt Lavinia and Uncle Emiliano used to host,' I said.

'I miss those days,' murmured Eveline. She coughed and then

couldn't seem to stop so I fetched her a glass of wine from a passing waiter.

'Thank you,' she said, taking a sip. 'I'm getting a cold but didn't want to stay at home when the children were so looking forward to coming. Oh, look – there's Rosetta.' She set off towards a group of children huddled together on the other side of the room and I followed, cheered because we hadn't exchanged even one cross word. Signor Falcone's idea of keeping to neutral territory was a good one.

The children were clustered around a magnificent Nativity scene set up on a low table. Carved from wood in intricate detail and beautifully painted, it was truly a thing of wonder. The inn nestled into a hillside setting and the doors to the stable were open wide. Light glowed from within where the baby Jesus lay serenely in his manger, while his kneeling mother clasped her hands to her breast and watched him in awe. Joseph stood protectively at their side and sheep and cattle clustered round. A shining star was suspended over the stable.

Carlo looked up and recognised me. I smiled but was saddened when he immediately looked away. Perhaps Eveline's embittered comments had prejudiced him against me.

Rosetta, her eyes wide, slipped her hand into her mother's. 'Look, Mamma, isn't it beautiful?'

Eveline stroked her daughter's cheek and bent down beside her to study the details of the Nativity.

Jealousy crept into my heart as I watched their tender exchange. It was immensely painful that I'd never had the chance to share such cherished moments with my daughter.

As if she felt my gaze boring into her back, Eveline turned to glance at me. She flushed and looked away.

'Signora Wyndham.'

I blinked furiously, realising Signor Falcone was beside me.

'The children seem to like the Nativity,' he said.

'It's wonderful.'

'It was made in a local monastery. Some of the figures were given to me when I was a child. And, of course, on the sixth of January, Epiphany, I shall add the Three Wise Men when they arrive with gifts for the Holy Child.'

Eveline stood up. 'What a beautiful Nativity, Signor Falcone.'

'Thank you. Allow me to introduce you both to some of my family.'

He exchanged a few cheerful words with his nieces and nephews and instructed them to look after Carlo and Rosetta, before leading us towards a small gathering nearby.

We smiled and shook hands with several people, including Signor Falcone's father, but there were so many of them that their names became a blur in my mind. I remembered Signor Falcone's older brothers, Alfonso and Salvatore, because they had his high cheekbones and merry smile, though not his light green eyes. Their wives were friendly and welcoming and it transpired that Eveline was acquainted with Alfonso's wife Paola, since her son Alessandro was in the same class as Carlo.

Eveline chatted to Paola and, although her cough troubled her, it was encouraging to see that she still remembered how to smile.

Signor Falcone was called away by a member of his staff and asked Flavia, his other sister-in-law, to look after me.

'It will be my pleasure, Dante.' She hooked her arm through the crook of my elbow and drew me to one of the groups of chairs arranged against the walls of the dining room. 'Dante said you lived in New York,' she said. 'Salvatore can never take leave from the restaurant for long enough for us to travel so I'm dying to hear what New York is like.'

'My husband's business was there,' I said. 'He was an architect

146

and the city was expanding rapidly so he was busy with one project after another.'

'Was it very exciting?' Flavia leaned forward, eager to hear more. 'I go to the picture house and see films made in America but it seems to be a very dangerous place.'

I laughed. 'That depends. We lived in a respectable area and I never saw any trouble, but I was sensible. I never carried too much money or wore jewellery if I was going to take photographs in the poorer areas. And I was careful not to walk alone anywhere after dark.' I smiled at her. 'But that's the same for most cities, isn't it?'

'Is it?' asked Flavia. 'I don't find that in Venice, though I know some visitors have complained of bag snatchers.'

We talked about the theatres and galleries in New York and I liked Flavia for her enthusiasm.

The guests were summoned to the table for dinner and I was pleased Flavia had been seated opposite me. Rosetta was to my left with Eveline beside her and Carlo on her other side. It seemed Signor Falcone had used his diplomatic skills by separating two possibly quarrelsome sisters. Discreetly, I read the name card by the vacant place to my right just as Dante Falcone arrived to sit down beside me.

'I apologise for disappearing so suddenly,' he said, 'there was a small crisis in the kitchen.'

'A crisis?'

'The chef cut his hand so badly the sous-chef had to take over.' He grimaced. 'Chef was determined to make the point that the sous-chef could not do as good a job as he would have done, and so the sous-chef threatened to walk out.'

'Who would have thought such rivalries would take place in a kitchen?' I said.

'If only you knew,' said Signor Falcone, shaking his head sadly, though there was a glint of laughter in his eyes.

A waiter filled our glasses and placed baskets of bread on the table.

'Since you're staying in Venice for the time being and since we're neighbours,' said Signor Falcone, 'I wondered if you would think it very forward of me to ask if you would consider calling me Dante?'

I smiled. 'Not at all, on condition you address me as Phoebe.'

He lifted his glass and touched it to mine. 'How is your sister behaving?' he whispered.

'Surprisingly well, though she was mostly talking to Paola while I had a very pleasant conversation with Flavia. We're going meet for lunch.'

He beamed. 'I'm pleased to hear that. She's a good wife to Salvatore and it will be good for you to have friends here in Venice.'

I remembered Cosimo's sharp comment about him. 'So you aren't trying to persuade me to sell the palazzo and return to London as quickly as possible, then?'

'Of course not!' He pressed a hand to his chest and looked hurt. 'You must do as you wish. In fact, I had an idea that might make you want to remain in Venice. You said it was frustrating you couldn't develop your photographs until you returned to London so I wondered if you might make yourself a darkroom in one of the storage spaces off your *portego*?'

I stared at him. 'That's a marvellous idea! The only problem is that I might then never go and where will that leave your plans for expanding the Hotel Falcone? I can't imagine I'll easily tire of the photographic opportunities here.'

'In that case, I shall be delighted to have such a charming neighbour,' he said. 'Actually, I have another reason for suggesting the darkroom.'

'Oh?'

'I have plenty to do for the moment as far as plans go for expanding the hotel. The building works start on the new extension at the back after Christmas. Once it's finished, I shall need some high-quality photographs for our brochure. I was hoping I might commission you to take them?'

'What an interesting idea,' I said, 'and, assuming I'm still in Venice when your building works are completed, I'd be delighted to take on such a project.'

He lifted his wine glass. 'Let's drink to that!'

The waiter brought an excellent risotto made with Venetian clams and I turned to Rosetta and asked her who was her best friend at school.

Eveline coughed frequently but nevertheless kept a watchful eye on us as the little girl chatted about her friends and school and books she'd read. After a moment, she distracted her daughter's attention so I continued my conversation with Flavia.

Later, after an excellent five-course dinner, the children were each given a little purse of sweets and allowed to get down from the table. Coffee and tiny glasses of Amaro, a bitter-sweet digestif, were served, along with candied fruits.

Eveline was still coughing and her forehead was shining with perspiration. 'Are you all right?' I murmured.

She blotted her brow with a handkerchief. 'I'll be fine,' she said. 'I mustn't spoil Christmas for Rosetta and Carlo.' She glanced at the corner of the room where the group of children had congregated.

'Why don't you go home to bed?' I asked, thinking that might be the only place she could keep warm in that horrible apartment. 'Then you'll probably shake it off by tomorrow. I'm sure the doorman will find you a gondola if you don't want to walk.'

Eveline shuddered convulsively. 'Perhaps you're right. I don't feel at all well and I have the most dreadful headache.'

'I'll come with you and help put the children to bed.'

'Please, don't fuss! I can manage. I've always had to manage on my own,' she said, her tone bitter.

Dante overheard the last part of our conversation. 'Is there some difficulty? May I help?'

'No,' said Eveline.

'Yes!' I said simultaneously. 'Eveline is unwell. Would your doorman find a gondola for her?'

'Of course.'

'I'm quite well enough to walk!' Eveline stood up and her complexion turned chalk-white. She swayed and then her knees folded and she crumpled.

Dante stepped forward and caught her before she hit the floor.

'That settles it,' I said. 'I'll take her and the children home with me.'

He helped me to support my sister back to the palazzo and chatted reassuringly to the children while I hurriedly put fresh sheets on the bed in Eveline's childhood room, lit the fire and laid out one of my nightgowns for her. I returned to the drawing room.

'I'll come at once if you need help,' murmured Dante. 'Shall I sit with the children while you put your sister to bed?'

'Thank you. And I left their presents in your cloakroom.'

'I'll fetch them later and leave them in the hall.' He smiled reassuringly.

I assisted Eveline upstairs.

'Let me help you undress,' I said.

'I'm not a child! I can do it myself,' she said, sounding exactly like a fractious child. 'Turn your back.'

Sighing, I did as I was told.

A minute or two later, the bed creaked. 'I'm ready,' she croaked.

She was sitting with one foot on the bed and the other still on the floor while she struggled to control another fit of coughing. The hem of her nightgown had ridden up and I stared at the scattering of small purple scars on the pale skin of her thighs. Each one was the size of a cigarette tip.

'Eveline!' I said. 'Who did this?'

She saw my horrified gaze and hastily covered herself.

I persisted. 'Was it your husband?'

Lying down, she pulled the covers up to her ears. 'Not all marriages are as good as yours was,' she said. 'Now leave me to sleep.'

'Eveline—'

'Go away!'

I hesitated briefly then left the room, closing the door quietly behind me.

Chapter 17

I woke early on Christmas morning to the sound of myriad church bells ringing in celebration of the birth of Christ. I lay still for a moment, remembering the events of the previous night. The burn marks on Eveline's thighs had shocked me. Had it been her husband Matteo who'd inflicted the wounds? Clearly, she didn't want to talk about it, and while she was ill I wasn't inclined to press her.

The children had been tired and anxious about their mother the previous night and Rosetta had cried while I made up the twin beds in one of the guest rooms. I'd told them a story, even though Carlo said he was too old for fairy tales. I sat beside them, stroking Rosetta's hair, until finally they both fell asleep.

Now, the pealing of the bells grew ever-more insistent as other churches joined in. I slipped on my dressing gown and hurried across the landing to peep into the children's room. Carlo lay on his back, one arm outflung, looking younger and more vulnerable asleep than he did awake. Rosetta was curled up under the eiderdown with her dark hair tumbled over the pillow.

I crept away. It had been a late night for them and I didn't want to wake them. Further along the corridor, I'd left the door of

Eveline's room ajar in case she needed anything during the night. The sound of coughing came from within. Tapping gently on the door, I waited until she told me to enter.

Eveline struggled to raise herself and her breath wheezed in her chest.

I helped her to sit up and arranged the pillows to support her back. Resting a palm on her forehead, I was shocked. 'You're burning hot, Eveline!'

'I've a horrible feeling it's influenza,' she croaked. 'My head hurts so much and everything aches. Influenza killed Matteo last year, just as the war was ending and when we thought we'd all be safe.' She gripped my wrist. 'Don't let the children come near me! They mustn't catch it!'

'That's a sensible precaution.' A shiver ran down my back. Three of my acquaintances had died of Spanish Flu. What if ... but I mustn't let myself think about the worst that could happen. 'I'm going to call a doctor to take a look at you.'

'No!'

'Of course you must see a doctor!'

'I can't ...'

I opened my mouth to speak and then wondered if she was worried about the cost. 'I'll make you some honey and lemon to soothe your throat,' I said. I'd see to the children and then fetch a doctor, whatever Eveline said.

'The bells hurt my head.' She put her hands over her ears.

'I'll leave the shutters closed then.' I made up the fire again and then went towards the door.

'Phoebe?'

'Yes?'

'You must wear a mask when you come near me. If you fall ill, what will the children do?'

'I'll improvise something.' Her suggestion of a mask was

sensible. While the influenza pandemic had raged, I'd always covered my face while I was out and about.

Downstairs in the kitchen, I riddled the range, added more coal and set the kettle to boil. There was a lemon and a jar of honey in the pantry and I foraged through the dresser drawers until I found some old tea towels, the linen worn thin with use.

Once I'd made the honey and lemon, I carried it upstairs, tied the tea towel over my nose and mouth and returned to the sickroom. After Eveline finished the drink, I brushed her hair and brought a flannel and a basin of warm water to bathe her clammy hands and face. I resisted distressing her by asking again about the scars on her thighs.

She sank back against the pillows, utterly exhausted.

'Can I bring you something to eat?' I asked. She shook her head. 'Then rest now. There's a glass of water here beside you. I'm going to dress and make breakfast for the children when they're awake.'

Later, as I came out of the bathroom, I heard their voices and tapped on the door. 'Good morning and a happy Christmas to you both!'

Carlo was already dressed but his hair stood up in spikes. 'How is Mamma?'

Rosetta ran forward. 'Can we see her now? Please?' Tears sparkled on her eyelashes.

'She's having a nap,' I said, making myself sound more cheerful than I felt. 'Why don't we have breakfast and then we'll see if you can say hello? I thought we might make pancakes together.'

'Pancakes?' said Carlo. His lip curled. 'For breakfast?'

'When I lived in New York, we had pancakes for breakfast every day.'

His eyes widened. 'You lived in New York?'

'In a place called Manhattan,' I said. 'It was near Central Park and I used to like to walk there to get away from the traffic some-times. There was a menagerie, too.'

'What kind of animals were there?' asked Rosetta.

'Mostly rather moth-eaten ones, as I remember.'

'Are there motorcars in New York?' asked Carlo. 'And did you see any skyscrapers in Manhattan?'

'Hundreds of them,' I said. Still answering their questions, I led them to the kitchen.

An hour later, the two children pushed away their plates, each having eaten a stack of American-style pancakes. There wasn't any maple syrup but I'd improvised with a sauce made from honey and butter. The kitchen was littered with eggshells, and flour liberally dusted the table and floor.

'Did you enjoy those?' I asked. Carlo leaned back in his chair and kissed his fingers in true Italian style, making me laugh.

'My skirt is sticky,' said Rosetta. She scooped up a drizzle of batter and licked her finger.

'Mamma isn't well enough for you to go home today,' I said, 'so we'd better go to your apartment and fetch some more clothes for you.'

'Can we see her now?' Rosetta's chin quivered.

'She's worried that you'll catch her chill but we'll stand in the doorway and you can speak to her if she's awake. Let's wash the dishes first to give her a little longer to rest before we disturb her.'

Rosetta nodded and began to stack the plates.

When the kitchen was tidy again, we trooped upstairs and, finger to my lips, I carefully opened the door to Eveline's bedroom.

She opened her eyes and smiled weakly when she saw the children. 'Don't come any closer!'

'We made pancakes for breakfast, Mamma!' said Rosetta.

'How lovely,' she murmured.

'Aunt Phoebe is going to take us home to fetch our clothes,' said Carlo. 'I had to sleep in my vest.'

I smiled at the indignation in his voice. 'May I take your door key, Eveline? I can bring your nightgown and slippers and anything else you'd like to have here.'

'But I must go home.' She pushed herself up a few inches and then sank back against the pillows.

'As soon as you're well enough,' I said in my firmest voice. I tied on my improvised mask and stoked up the fire, then brought her handbag to her.

She sighed. 'The key's in the side pocket.'

'Will you be all right if we leave you for a while?'

'I only want to sleep.'

We tiptoed away.

Christmas Day was cold and bright. Strangers smiled and wished us a happy Christmas as we walked towards Accademia Bridge.

'I saw a doctor's brass plaque on the door of a house near the bridge,' I said. 'We'll ask him to come and visit your mamma.'

A maid answered the door and told me the doctor was at a confinement. She said she'd give him the message when he returned but warned me that was unlikely to be until later that afternoon.

We set off for the vaporetto stop and didn't have long to wait before we saw the black plume of smoke heralding the approaching water bus. Since it was Christmas Day there were few barges on the canal, though gondolas were busy ferrying people back and forth. The air reverberated with the pealing of bells and sometimes the cacophony was so loud as we steamed past a church that it was hard to hold a conversation.

We left the vaporetto at the Rialto stop. The fish market was closed and the children shrieked as they chased seagulls, footsteps echoing across the stone floor beneath the Gothic arches.

I listened to their breathless laughter and, just for a moment, imagined these children were mine. But my marriage to John could never have provided the happy family life children need to flower.

Rosetta and Carlo guided me to the apartment. When we arrived, Carlo took the key from me. 'Mamma says I'm the man of the house now so it's my job to unlock the door.'

Inside, although everything had been left neat and tidy, the apartment was as cold as a crypt and the mould made it smell like one too. It tugged at my heartstrings that the mantelpiece was decorated with a single church candle and a row of red and green paper chains.

'We made those,' said Rosetta with a proud smile. 'Mamma said it would make everything look festive, even if she couldn't afford to give us presents this year.'

I'd never seen a room look less festive. They'd managed far better in the YMCA huts behind the front line in France. 'The paper chains are very pretty,' I said. 'Now, we need to pack some things. Can you help me?'

Carlo went into the bedroom and pulled Aunt Lavinia's suitcase from under the bed.

The cover I'd sent for Eveline was placed over the children's two mattresses, side-by-side on the floor, while her own bed was covered by a pitifully thin blanket and a worn dressing gown. 'Will you both pack your clothes and anything else you'd especially like to bring?' I opened the chest of drawers and lifted out my sister's carefully mended lingerie and darned stockings, along with Aunt Lavinia's blouses that I'd sent her.

A short while later the clothing was folded into the suitcase, along with toothbrushes and flannels. It troubled me that the children had so few clothes and I wondered how Eveline managed to wash and dry them in time for the next wearing. Surely Matteo Rizzio, however bad a husband he might have been, must have left *some* means of support for the welfare of his family?

'Do you have everything?' I asked.

Rosetta nodded, a rag doll clutched to her chest.

Carlo carried a box of coloured pencils and a book of adventure stories for boys. 'So I don't have to listen to any more fairy tales,' he said.

'Then let's hurry back to the palazzo before the doctor arrives.'

Carlo locked the door behind us and I pocketed the key.

Chapter 18

Eveline still burned with fever.

I bathed her face and neck and supported her while she sipped some water.

The children watched from the doorway, their eyes round with apprehension.

I led them away. 'Mamma is going to rest now but you shall see her later.' As they went downstairs, Rosetta's hand slid into mine. The little girl's face was tear-streaked and I crouched down beside her. 'What is it, sweetheart?'

'Aunt Phoebe, is Mamma going to die? My papà died in the war.'

Carlo came to an abrupt halt on the step beside them, his anxious gaze fixed on my face.

All at once the chilling memory flooded back of Aunt Lavinia telling me that Eveline and I were orphans. I sat down on the step and drew the children towards me, though Carlo remained rigid in the circle of my arms. 'I know it's worrying but I promise we'll do everything we possibly can to look after her.' I didn't dare promise that their mamma would recover because too many people had been carried off by the influenza pandemic in the past two years. 'Come with me,' I said, 'I have some gifts for you.'

We sat by the fire in the drawing room and I set aside my fears, happy to see the delight on the children's faces when they opened their presents.

Carlo smiled at the sight of the model aeroplane kit and let out his breath in a whistle when he unwrapped the jigsaw. 'I've never had such a large puzzle before.' He spread out the pieces on the floor and lay on his front, searching for the edge pieces.

Rosetta forgot her tears when she unwrapped the wooden trinket box, decorated with painted kittens. 'I've always wanted a cat but Mamma says it wouldn't be fair to keep one in an apartment,' she said.

'Well, now you have *five* kittens!' I said, making her giggle.

The doorbell clanged and I hurried to answer it.

A short, stout man stood on the doorstep. 'Dottor Bucchi. I believe you sent for me?'

'Please, come in.'

He took off his hat and coat and handed them to me. 'And where is the patient?'

'Upstairs. It's my sister, Signora Rizzio. I think she may have influenza.'

He tutted under his breath. 'I have encountered a few cases again recently.'

I placed his hat and coat on the hall stand, led him upstairs and waited while he washed his hands in the bathroom.

Outside Eveline's room, he took a mask from his doctor's bag and carefully tied it over his lower face.

I tied on my own makeshift face covering and we went inside. 'Eveline? The doctor has come to see you.'

Her breath rasped in her chest when she tried to sit up. 'I told you, I don't want a doctor!'

'You may not want one but you need one,' I said briskly, 'and Dottor Bucchi's account will be sent to me.' I stood at a discreet distance while the doctor looked down Eveline's throat, felt her glands, took her temperature and listened to her chest.

He asked a few questions and nodded at the patient's murmured replies. 'Good,' he said, putting away his stethoscope. 'I shall give your sister instructions for your care, Signora Rizzio, and you must do exactly as she says.'

'But I need to go home!' wailed Eveline.

'Absolutely not! Any failure to comply could lead to severe complications. Or worse. Good day.' He shooed me out of the room ahead of him.

The children had crept up the stairs and were waiting for us. 'Is Mamma going to be well soon?' asked Rosetta.

The doctor untied his mask and bent down to speak to her. 'You can help her get better by being as quiet as two little mice. Mamma is infectious so you must keep away. It would make her very worried if you caught influenza too.'

Rosetta nodded solemnly.

He turned to me. 'A light diet: chicken soup, bread and milk and so on. Plenty of water to drink. Aspirin for her headaches and feverishness, and sponge her down if she gets too hot. If her cough worsens or she has difficulty breathing, you may give her a steam infusion. Call me if you're worried.'

'Thank you, Dottor Bucchi.'

After he'd gone, I took the children into the kitchen and heated the traditional festive meal of ravioli *in brodo* that Valentina had prepared. I took a cupful of the broth to Eveline and she drank a few mouthfuls. I made up the fire and tiptoed out of the room when she fell asleep again.

The afternoon passed quietly. I taught Rosetta how to play Spillikins. Distracted from his jigsaw by his sister's laughter, Carlo played a round with her and I took the opportunity to pen a thank you note to Dante for the party.

The doorbell jangled again and I found my neighbour on the doorstep.

'I came to enquire after Signora Rizzio's health,' he said.

'How kind of you! Unfortunately, the doctor says it's influenza.'

'Then it's not surprising she felt so unwell last night.'

'Won't you come in? I've just written a note to thank you for the wonderful dinner yesterday and for your kindness in helping me bring Eveline home.'

Dante followed me inside and I handed him the note.

'And I must thank you, too, for the very handsome notebook,' he said. 'I'll keep it by my side for the interminable lists I need to make to keep the hotel running smoothly.'

'I'm pleased it will be useful.'

'How are the children today? I saw that Rosetta was upset.'

'We're getting to know each other but, naturally, they're anxious. They enjoyed making pancakes for breakfast and so far I've distracted them with their Christmas presents.'

In the drawing room, the children were lying prone on the floor, squabbling over a game of Spillikins.

'Time to find something else for them to do,' I said with a wry smile.

'If they'd like to, why don't they come and spend an hour or two with my nieces and nephews?' said Dante. 'Would you like that, children?'

Carlo looked up. 'Is Alessandro there?'

'He certainly is,' said Dante. 'He hoped you'd come and see him. And Isabella said she would like to play with Rosetta again.'

'May we go, Aunt Phoebe?' asked Rosetta.

'Do you promise to be good?'

They both nodded their heads vigorously.

'The hotel is closed for a few days,' said Dante, 'and Flavia and Paola are staying so they'll watch out for Carlo and Rosetta. I'll bring them home in time to say good night to their mamma.'

'Thank you.'

'Phoebe, will you be all right here alone?'

'Of course,' I said. 'I'm used to being alone.'

He drew breath, as if he were about to say something, but after a moment's pause he held out his hands to the children. 'Come,' he said. 'Let's go and find the others.'

The following few days settled into a routine. I took the children out for a walk in the mornings and bought them another set of clothes. After lunch they went to the hotel to play with Dante's nieces and nephews. Valentina and Jacopo returned from Mestre and were shocked when they heard about Eveline's illness.

Valentina reclaimed her kitchen and set to work making chicken soup and other dainties suitable for an invalid. I was relieved to leave Jacopo to tend to the fires again and Valentina to keep an eye on Eveline while I took the children out for some fresh air.

Eveline remained feverish. When her breath rattled in her chest, Valentina prepared herbal infusions. I made a tent with a towel over Eveline's head so she could breathe in the rosemary-scented steam.

One evening, Valentina answered the door to Cosimo. He'd brought me a box of *mandorlato* sweets but when she told him it was a house of sickness, he backed out of the hall. He sent me a message apologising for not calling before to wish me a merry Christmas due to several family engagements. He promised to return after Eveline's influenza had passed.

The following day, he sent me a huge basket of fruit tied with a yellow satin bow.

On the fifth afternoon Eveline's temperature came down. She still coughed but her headache was gone.

I assisted her from the bed to a chair by the fireside and tucked a blanket around her knees. Later, I fed her bread and milk. When she'd finished, I placed two parcels on her lap. 'I was going to give you these on Christmas Eve,' I said, 'but you weren't well enough.'

Eveline shot me a suspicious glance. 'What are they?'

'Open them and see.'

Slowly, she unwrapped the paper and took out the oval bar of rose-perfumed soap. She held it to her nose and breathed in the perfume. 'It's lovely. I didn't expect you ...'

'Now the other one,' I said.

She untied the ribbon and folded back the paper before lifting up the turquoise shawl with a sharp intake of breath. She stared down at it in silence.

I took it from her and arranged it around her shoulders. 'Don't you like it? I hoped you'd find it cosy for the winter.'

Eveline bowed her head.

'If you prefer another colour ...'

'Don't!' A tear dropped onto the shawl. 'Don't you understand how hard it is for me to accept gifts from you?'

I stepped back, hurt. 'But as you pointed out to me,' I said, 'I can afford them.'

'Why do you have to make it so hard for me to hate you?'

'My intention wasn't to upset you.'

'You've nursed me as if you really care about me—'

'You're my sister! Give me some credit for a little human kindness.'

'But how can you be so kind to me when you know what I did?'

164

She hid her face in her hands. 'I loathed you for always being prettier than me, cleverer than me, more popular than me—'

'Don't say that!'

'But it's true,' she wept. 'I desperately wanted Lorenzo and I was so sure he liked me. When I saw you two together in the garden that night, it was like a dagger in my breast to realise it had always been you he loved. But I promise you, I didn't know you were carrying his child when I sent that note to his mother, and I didn't have any idea that the consequence would be that you'd lose your daughter.' She let out a sob. 'I've hardly been able to sleep since you told me.'

I folded my arms tightly against my chest. 'I wish we could be friends, Eveline. I can't go on making myself miserable thinking about what might have been if you hadn't sent that note. All I want now is to find Sofia and make it up to her. And you must rest and recover, for your children's sake.'

'I can't give you expensive gifts,' she said, 'but I may be able to give you something else you want.'

'You don't need to give me presents.'

'You'll want this.' Eveline's mouth twisted into a bitter smile. 'You see, I've found out where Lorenzo is living now.'

Chapter 19

It had been a tiring journey, involving changing trains several times and then waiting for a horse-drawn cab to take me and two other passengers to the small town of Molina. It was long after dark when I finally arrived at the only hotel and far too late to start knocking on doors asking for Lorenzo.

Eveline had explained how, despite having lost contact with most of her old friends since she'd married Matteo, she'd visited or written to as many of them as she could find, to ask if they knew of Lorenzo's whereabouts.

'I was on the point of abandoning my quest,' she'd said, 'when I remembered Anna Esposito, one of Giulia's friends. I went to ask her for news of Lorenzo and she told me she'd met him, quite by chance, as she came out of a butcher's shop one winter's day the year before. He told her he'd recently been discharged from the army and was visiting his mother before moving to Molina to take up a new position. Anna remembered he'd said he had a house opposite Chiesa San Giovanni.'

I'd been in turmoil ever since Eveline had told me, wondering not only if Lorenzo could lead me to Sofia, but how I would feel when I saw him again. Many years had passed but, for me at least, there was still the unfinished business of the painful ending of our affair to discuss.

I waited a few days, until I was sure Eveline was recovering, and then left Valentina to look after the invalid and her children.

In Molina, after a tolerable dinner in the hotel dining room, I paced the floor of my room, planning what I would say to Lorenzo when – if – I found him. Later, I slept fitfully, my dreams vivid with images of a young man with the light of love in his eyes while a baby cried behind a door I couldn't open.

The following morning, I put on my smart marine blue coat with the velvet collar and matching hat. I studied my reflection, imagining Lorenzo's thoughts on seeing me seventeen years older. My figure was still slender and my hair the same honey-blonde but there were a few lines around my eyes now, as was to be expected at thirty-four. Shrugging, I turned away from the mirror. This meeting was about my search for Sofia, not about rekindling a long-ago love affair with a man who'd probably been happily married for years. And yet . . .

The hotel manager directed me to the church of San Giovanni in Via Vittorio off Molina's main square. It was an old town of undistinguished stucco buildings with terracotta roofs, an arched bridge crossing the river and views of distant hills. A low rumble of thunder made me glance up uneasily at black clouds gathering in a sullen sky and wish that I'd brought an umbrella.

The great oak door of the church was ajar and I stood on the doorstep to study the opposite side of the street. There was only one house there. It was painted cream with brown shutters and crammed between an ironmonger's and a baker's shop. My mouth was dry as I imagined Lorenzo, perhaps reading a newspaper or drinking coffee, unaware of my presence outside. Would he be shocked, happy or angry to see me? The worst thing would be to find him indifferent.

And then I realised I'd been foolish. At this time of day, he'd probably be at his place of work. If I knocked on the door I might have to explain myself to his wife, assuming he had one.

I was dithering, wondering if I should leave a message for him to call on me at the hotel, when a gust of wind caught the brim of my hat. A flash of lightning sliced across the leaden sky, followed immediately by a deafening crack of thunder. I flinched and, even before my heart had ceased thudding, the heavens opened. Hailstones fell with the force of a cartload of gravel being tipped onto the road, clattering as they bounced off the cobbles. In my anxious frame of mind, it seemed like an ominous portent from above. I cupped my hands over my ears and backed into the church.

The interior was shadowy and silent, though I could still hear hailstones rattling on the pavement outside. Shivering, I closed the door behind me and straightened my hat. How ridiculous to have been so superstitious!

Tiptoeing up the aisle, I slipped into one of the pews. Out of habit, I knelt down and folded my hands even though I hadn't been able to pray for years.

A whisper came from the nave ahead and I peered over my clasped hands to see a priest, his back turned to me, rising from his knees before the altar. His cassock swayed as he walked ahead with measured steps to straighten one of the pillar candles.

I closed my eyes and tried to pray but still didn't know what to say to the God who had allowed me to lose both my child and the man I'd once loved so much. For years I'd daydreamed about meeting Lorenzo again. Now I was so close to finding him, I was fearful.

What if he refused to speak to me, poisoned by his mother's insinuations that I'd been unfaithful to him? Or perhaps he might have lost his *joie de vivre* and become narrow and embittered, like Signora Albani. I was afraid my precious memories of our love, that had supported me through the lonely years, might be shattered if I met him again. If I left Italy now and returned to St John's Wood, I could avoid the emotional turmoil of recriminations and regrets that might arise from a disappointing reunion.

But if I wasn't brave enough to face Lorenzo, I'd lose my last hope of finding Sofia. I would never forgive myself for such cowardice.

I walked slowly back down the aisle towards the entrance door. A plaster statue of the Virgin Mary looked down at me impassively from a niche in the wall. Her bare foot protruded from under her blue robes, the paint worn away by the kisses of the faithful. An impulse caused me to touch it. Perhaps I only imagined the sense of calm that descended upon me then but all at once I knew for certain I must call at Lorenzo's house and leave him a message.

The iron ring handle on the church door was stiff and I struggled with both hands to turn it.

'Let me help you.'

A deep voice came from behind me and I turned to see the priest smiling at me. Then the smile faded from his still-handsome face and his hazel eyes widened. 'Phoebe?' he whispered. 'Is it really you?'

I stared at Lorenzo's cassock and any lingering secret dreams of reconciliation, of our becoming a family with Sofia by our side, exploded with the intensity of a flash lamp. Shaking, I gripped my handbag to my chest as if to raise a barrier between us. 'Lorenzo. I didn't know ...'

'That I'm a priest?'

Trapped behind a door I couldn't open, I glanced over his

shoulder for another means of escape. I wasn't ready to face him and wondered if he could hear the frantic pounding of my heartbeat.

'Are you here with your husband?'

'No.' My lips were numb and it was hard to form the words. 'He fell at the Somme.'

'I'm sorry. So sorry.' He closed his eyes momentarily and a tic flickered in his jaw. 'There have been such terrible times . . .' His voice trailed away.

Mustering my resolve, I said, 'Lorenzo, I must speak to you.' I glanced back at the statue of the Virgin, serene in her blue plaster robe. 'This isn't the right place. Is there somewhere we can go?'

He gave a shaky smile. 'God sees and hears all, wherever you are, but my housekeeper will make us some coffee. My house is close by.'

'Thank you.'

He opened the heavy door and I saw that the hailstorm outside had given way to drizzle. We walked in silence across the road and he led me to the house. He showed me into a small, cold sitting room before going to speak to his housekeeper.

It was a simple room, as befitted a man of the cloth, with bookshelves on one whitewashed wall and a crucifix on another. There was a potted fern on a small side table, a rag rug on the polished floorboards and a desk by the window. Shivering and still stunned by the revelation of Lorenzo's path in life, I perched on one of the armchairs.

He returned and I couldn't help noticing that the priest's garb suited his lean figure.

'You're cold,' he said. He lit the kindling laid in the fireplace and waited to ensure it had caught before sitting down on the chair opposite me. 'Where shall we begin?' he asked. His hands were restless in his lap.

'I haven't come to cause you any trouble,' I said.

'I didn't imagine you had.'

'Nevertheless . . . ' I took a calming breath. 'I need to talk about what happened. It changed my entire life.'

'Oh, Phoebe! I never meant—'

I held up my hand to stop him. 'Please, let me have my say.'

He nodded.

'When I received your note on the day we'd planned to elope,' I said, 'I thought your mother must have dictated it. I went to see her but she told me in no uncertain terms you'd changed your mind about me and gone away.' I swallowed the lump that had risen in my throat. 'I'd been so sure you loved me and had no idea what I'd done to displease you.'

'Nothing!' He ran his fingers through his dark hair. There was a sprinkling of grey around his temples now. 'My mother was furious. She said I'd destroy our family's standing if I ran away with you – a non-Catholic. I said we wouldn't need to elope if she'd accept our marriage. I told her of your willingness to convert. And then she said someone had seen us together in the garden at night.' He flushed and looked away.

'You don't have to explain,' I said, equally flustered. 'It was Eveline.'

'Your own sister?'

'She wanted you for herself.'

'But I never gave her any reason to imagine . . . ' He wiped his face with his palm. 'Mother threatened to besmirch your name. Said a girl of low morals would be utterly condemned, while society would remain far more lenient towards a man who'd associated with such a slut.'

'Your mother would have *deliberately* ruined me?' Anger blazed inside me and I longed – oh, how I longed – to make her suffer as she'd made me suffer.

'She saw it as her duty to save me.' He swallowed. 'I couldn't allow her to destroy you and your family. She gave me a choice. I could train to be a priest or learn my uncle's business as a wine merchant. I chose my uncle, intending to write to you and explain we'd have to bide our time until I had some savings. I thought about running away to come and get you, but I had no money. Also, if it went wrong, I knew my mother would make good her threat to ruin you.'

'Why didn't you write?' I asked.

'Uncle Alfredo kept me under close supervision and locked me in my room when I wasn't working. I discovered later that he'd intercepted the letters I wrote to you.'

'So you did write?' My spirits lifted. 'I thought you'd stopped loving me.'

The door opened and an elderly housekeeper brought in a tray of coffee and placed it on the desk.

'I *never* stopped loving you,' said Lorenzo, after she'd gone. 'Mother made me write that note. Each word was as painful to me as if I were carving it into my own skin, but I knew she wouldn't hesitate to make good her threat to dishonour both you and your family if I refused. It nearly destroyed me, thinking you'd imagine I'd deserted you.' He went to pour the coffee while he recovered his composure. 'Then, a few weeks later, she wrote to tell me you'd gone to Switzerland.'

I took a cup from him, my hands trembling so much it rattled on the saucer.

'Early the next year,' he continued, 'she wrote to say you were married. I didn't want to believe it, hoping she'd lied to stop me pining for you, but I had to be sure. I stole money from the cash box, pushed Uncle Alfredo aside when he tried to stop me and went straight to the Palazzo degli Angeli. Your aunt and uncle confirmed you'd made an advantageous marriage and had gone to live in New York.'

'Oh, Lorenzo!'

'I wish you'd waited for me.' His voice was low and despairing. 'After that, Uncle Alfredo wouldn't have me back. Mother had always wanted me to train for the priesthood, a path I'd rejected. But after I learned of your marriage, I didn't care what happened to me any more. It was impossible to marry the woman I loved and I knew I'd never love another, so I went along with her plan. And, eventually, I found solace in my new calling.' He looked up at me with a wavering smile. 'At least I knew you were safe and happy with your husband.'

I let out a laugh that turned into a sob. 'It wasn't like that at all. We never loved each other, the marriage was merely a business arrangement.'

A muscle twitched in his jaw. 'So we were both made unhappy?'

There was such sorrow in his voice I could hardly bear to hear it. 'But that's not the worst of it. I didn't go to Switzerland for my schooling. That was a story my aunt and uncle put about to conceal the truth.'

'What truth?'

I gulped the coffee, black and bracing. 'That they'd hidden me away in the country until I gave birth to your child.'

Lorenzo's mouth fell open. 'My *child*?'

'Our child. The midwife told me our baby was stillborn. Every day for the last seventeen years, I've mourned her death. I called her Sofia.'

He pressed the back of his hand to his mouth, his eyes glistening. 'How you must have suffered – disgraced and alone.'

'The story doesn't end there. Aunt Lavinia died recently and I returned to Venice. While I was going through her effects, I found something that made me think Sofia hadn't been stillborn after all.'

He shook his head. 'I don't understand.'

I explained how I'd followed the trail and how it led me to believe his mother had removed Sofia from the Vianello family and taken her to a convent school.

Lorenzo's gaze never left my face while I was speaking. 'My mother and I have never been close,' he said, 'but how *could* she have been so cruel as to withhold knowledge of our child from us?'

'I assure you, it is the truth.'

He stood up abruptly and paced across the room.

'But where *is* Sofia?' I said. 'And is she safe and happy? I have to *know*, Lorenzo.'

'We both need to know,' he said. 'I never imagined . . .'

'It's a shock for you but I couldn't think where else to search for her. I hoped you would have heard of this.'

'Did you have any other children, Phoebe?'

'No,' I said. 'But even if there had been, it wouldn't make any difference to my need to find Sofia. Lorenzo, I *have* to find her. She had good foster parents for the first ten years of her life but who is there to love her in that convent? Now she's no longer a child, will the nuns press her to take vows? Or might she be sent out into the world to make her own way? I want her to know I didn't abandon her and that she was born out of love.'

'The poor child.' Lorenzo's complexion had paled. 'How alone she must have felt, snatched away from everything she knew.'

'But where did your mother take her?'

He shook his head. 'I'll go and see her, ask her, but she can be . . .' he chewed at his lip ' . . . obstinate and unyielding. Furthermore, she's dying.'

I gasped. '*Dying*? But then you *must* make her tell you where she took Sofia, before it's too late!' I heard the panic and despair in my voice and took a deep breath.

'I believe the bitterness in her soul is what has caused a canker to grow in her stomach,' said Lorenzo. 'I doubt she has long to wait to meet her Maker.'

I couldn't bring myself to be sorry for Signora Albani but I was sorry for Lorenzo. 'I apologise for my outburst. That was selfish of me.'

'I'll do everything in my power to persuade her to tell me the truth.'

'Thank you.'

His expression was troubled. 'I'll have to tell my superiors I have a child born out of wedlock.'

'Must you?'

'I'm a priest, Phoebe. I must make my confession and seek guidance.' There was quiet determination in his words.

'I suppose so.' After a moment, I said, 'I never felt that what we did together was a sin. Our love was innocent and beautiful. We should have had the chance to become a family with Sofia.'

He bowed his head. 'Yes, we should. We were very young, too young, and I don't know how we'd have managed, but I believe that, together, we'd have found the way.'

I yearned for the past, wishing we could go back in time and take a different path. I reached out and brushed his arm. His palm, warm and dry, caught my fingers and, for one blissful moment, he pressed them to his lips.

'You must go now,' he said, releasing my hand, 'before this becomes any more distressing to us both than it is already. I have arrangements to make before I can leave my parish to visit my mother.'

My fingers tingled where he'd kissed them. 'Will you come and see me at the Palazzo degli Angeli, to tell me what she says?'

'For better or worse, I promise to let you know.' He looked at me steadily. 'Phoebe, you do know it's too late for us now, don't you?'

I closed my eyes, my heart breaking all over again. 'Yes,' I murmured, but that didn't make giving up my secret dreams any the less painful.

Chapter 20

On my return journey from Molina the following day, I brooded upon my encounter with Lorenzo. For years I'd nurtured a tiny spark of hope that, one day, we'd meet again and he'd take me in his arms and tell me he still loved me. That youthful daydream had supported me throughout the lonely years of my marriage but now I must look to the future. A future that I hoped with all my heart would include Sofia.

I arrived at Palazzo degli Angeli after dark and entered through the gate in the rear alley. Walking along the garden path, I was comforted by the glow of light behind the windows. I'd have felt even more wretched if I'd returned to the palazzo to find it cold, dark and empty.

The courtyard and outside staircase were lit, presumably in anticipation of my return, and the front door was unlocked. I placed my overnight case at the foot of the stairs to take up later. The door to the drawing room was ajar and I pushed it open, smiling at the sound of children's voices. They lay on their stomachs on the hearthrug, working on Carlo's jigsaw puzzle by the light of the fire. The rest of the room was in darkness.

'I'm back,' I said.

Carlo turned and Rosetta scrambled to her feet and ran to hug me. 'Aunt Phoebe! You've been away for ages!'

My heart melted at the little girl's embrace and I bent to kiss the top of her head.

Carlo was more reserved but he stood up and held out his hand to me, palm up. 'Look!' he said. 'The very last piece of my jigsaw puzzle. I've been saving it for you to complete.'

'What an honour!' I said. 'Now, let's see if I can find where it fits.'

Rosetta laughed. 'There's only one place it can go.'

'Silly me!' I pushed the piece into place. 'There!' My unhappiness dissipated at the children's affectionate welcome. 'Now, tell me how you have been. And how is your mamma?'

'Recovered,' said a voice.

'Oh, I didn't see you there!' I turned on a table lamp.

Eveline, her eyes watchful, sat in a wing chair, swathed in her new shawl. 'Was your meeting successful?' she asked.

I glanced at the children. 'Rosetta, Carlo, would you go and find Valentina and tell her I've returned? Perhaps you might ask if she'll make some coffee and, if there's any left, cut us some slices of panettone?'

Eveline coughed and dabbed at her nose with a handkerchief. 'Did you find Lorenzo?' she asked, once the children had left the room. Her expression was intent.

'I did.' I sat down. 'Unfortunately, he doesn't know where Sofia might be.' Eveline sagged in her chair, probably anxious that the promised funds for the children might not be forthcoming if the information she'd passed on didn't lead me to Sofia. The children deserved a better start in life than their mother could provide for them, though. I wouldn't say anything yet but I'd ask Cosimo to set up a trust fund for Carlo and Rosetta, whether or not I found Sofia.

'Can't he ask his mother?'

'He's going to visit her and see if he can persuade her to tell him.'

'Good. How was he?' she asked.

'Shocked. He didn't know he had a child.'

'I can imagine, especially since he's . . .' Her voice trailed away.

I stared at her. 'Eveline? You *knew*, didn't you? You *knew* he's a priest now.'

My sister stared at her hands. 'Anna might have mentioned it.' She lifted her chin defiantly.

'Why didn't you warn me?'

'You've already said it's too late for you to be together so it's irrelevant.'

Arguing with my sister only ever left me feeling irritable. 'Signora Albani is dying,' I said. 'I hope Lorenzo will persuade her to tell him where she took Sofia, before it's too late.'

The sound of laughter echoed in the hall. The door burst open and the children ran in, followed by Valentina carrying a tray. She poured the coffee, enquired after my journey and gave me an update on Eveline's recovery. Handing the children a plate of panettone, she pinched their cheeks affectionately and closed the door behind her.

'Have you kept yourselves busy while I've been away?' I asked the children.

They were full of chatter about their friends Alessandro and Isabella and how Signor Falcone had visited every day and taken them into the hotel kitchen, where the chef had taught them to bake star-shaped biscuits.

'I hope you tidied up the mess afterwards,' I said, remembering the pancakes we'd made together.

'There wasn't any mess!' said Carlo indignantly. 'Well, not much anyway.'

Eveline, her lips set in an expression of disapproval, was silently watching me.

'Shall we go out tomorrow,' I said, 'and give your mamma some peace? Where would you like to go? We could take a boat ride and visit one of the islands in the Lagoon. Or we might go to Caffè Florian for a hot chocolate and climb up the campanile to look at the view.'

'Hot chocolate!' squealed Rosetta.

'A boat ride!' said Carlo.

'Perhaps we can do both,' I said.

'That won't be possible,' said Eveline. 'We're returning home tomorrow.'

'But Mamma—' chorused the children.

'Home!' I said. 'Eveline, you aren't nearly well enough yet.'

'We can't stay here forever. Not now that we have no right to be here.'

'I'm not going to be drawn into a discussion about that,' I said, giving a meaningful nod at the children, 'but you need time to recover.'

'We've been here too long already,' she said. 'I don't care to be beholden to you and I can't sit here watching you alienating the affections of my children.'

'What!' Shocked, I shook my head. 'How could you even imagine that?'

'I don't have to imagine it. I can see what's going on before my very eyes. The presents, the new clothes, the outings . . .'

'Are you still so jealous of me that you'd deprive your children of a few simple pleasures because you won't allow me the enjoyment of seeing them happy?'

'You've taken everything else away from me,' said Eveline, 'so why would you stop at my children?'

'That's not true!' I said. I gave a bitter laugh. 'Though, if I had, perhaps it would only be what you deserve for depriving me of what should have been *my* family.'

'Don't you dare raise your voice to me!' Eveline rose unsteadily to her feet.

'Mamma?' Rosetta ran to her mother and hugged her. 'Don't fight with Aunt Phoebe!'

'We'll leave in the morning,' said Eveline, 'so you won't be further inconvenienced by our presence. Come, children!'

Hardly able to believe such rancorous words had blown up between us so quickly, I watched silently as she shepherded them from the room.

Carlo hesitated in the doorway and glanced back at me, his face tight with tension, before following his mother.

My hand shook as I lifted a cup to my mouth. The coffee was cold. I leaned my head back against the chair and stared into the fire, trying not to weep.

Breakfast the next morning was an awkward affair.

'Eveline, I wish you'd stay a little longer,' I said.

Her face was pale except for the shadows under her eyes but the set of her jaw was stubborn. 'I want to go home.'

'But I don't want to leave the palazzo,' said Rosetta, her eyes filling with tears. 'Why can't we stay with Aunt Phoebe, Mamma?'

'Because she lives a different kind of life from us and I won't have you being spoiled,' she snapped.

'Aunt Phoebe hasn't spoiled us,' said Carlo, 'and I want to stay, too. Our apartment is freezing cold and I'm tired of soup for every meal—'

'Be quiet!'

He flinched.

'Go and pack your clothes. You too, Rosetta.'

The children gave her anxious glances and left the room in silence.

I wanted to plead with Eveline to stay but knew that I'd only make things worse. 'I'll ask Jacopo to find you a gondola then, so you won't catch a chill.'

'I don't want anything from you, except for you to leave us alone.'

My patience snapped. 'Are you so resentful and selfish you'd risk pneumonia, simply for the sake of your pride?' I thrust myself to my feet. 'Contrary to your accusations, I'm not attempting to steal your children but, if you aren't sensible, they'll end up motherless and will have to come and live with me anyway.' I held up my hand. 'No! Don't argue. You will go home in a gondola. Jacopo will accompany you, bringing a portable stove and a can of paraffin to heat your apartment. Valentina will pack you some food and bring groceries to you every day until you are well.'

'I don't want charity!'

'Not that old refrain! Like it or not, you're my sister and I won't let it be on my conscience that I allowed you to go to your death!' Shaking with anger, I hurried from the room before I said anything else I might regret.

Ten minutes later, I stood on the jetty while Jacopo assisted Eveline and the children into the gondola. My sister steadfastly refused to look at me, even when the gondolier cast off and manoeuvred the boat out into the canal.

Carlo glanced back at me and surreptitiously lifted his hand in farewell.

Later that day, unsettled and irritable, I went to visit the priest at San Trovaso and he obliged me with a long list of convent schools and orphanages. I decided I would write to every one of them and, if there was no response, I'd go and bang on their door until I was sure Sofia wasn't there.

All the following week, torrential rain fell from a louring sky, pockmarking the surface of the canal and turning the garden into a quagmire. I made use of the dreary spell of weather by starting to write to the convents.

New Year arrived and passed without any celebration on my part, only relief that the previous war-filled decade was over. I was unsettled and irritable. I'd heard nothing from Eveline but received a box of candied plums and a note from Cosimo, promising to visit me once the palazzo was free from influenza. I didn't write to tell him Eveline had left.

Valentina returned, drenched, from the market one morning and reported that high water had turned Piazza di San Marco into a lake again. On my instructions, she'd delivered groceries to Eveline's apartment. The children had opened the door to take them inside and simply nodded when questioned about their mother's health. 'I'm sure Signora Rizzio had forbidden them to speak to me,' she said indignantly.

The palazzo was too quiet now the children had gone and I sat in the gloom of the study every day, writing my letters and watching raindrops running down the window panes. I'd heard nothing from Lorenzo and didn't know if he'd managed to visit his mother.

One afternoon I was closing the shutters as darkness fell when Dante called.

'How lovely to see you,' I said, my spirits lifting. 'I'm feeling very cooped up. The rain makes everything so dismal, doesn't it?'

His smile was warm. 'Spring isn't far away. I came to tell you that, subject to the weather next week, the builders will be starting work on the new annexe.'

'How exciting!'

'It really is,' he said. 'The war is still causing difficulties in obtaining building supplies but we can move forward now. The builders will construct the loggia to connect the two buildings first. I hope you won't find the work too noisy and disruptive. Please don't hesitate to come and tell me if it inconveniences you.'

'It's considerate of you to forewarn me,' I said, 'though, at present, I might welcome some noise. It's deathly quiet since Eveline and the children left.'

'Signora Rizzio is well and happy again?'

'Not entirely.' I grimaced. 'We quarrelled, I'm afraid. She has some notion that she's indebted to me.'

'I daresay she has her pride.'

'She certainly has.' It hurt to remember the hard words we'd exchanged. 'Won't you sit down?'

'Thank you but I must hurry back,' said Dante.

I didn't want him to go. I liked his company and it had been a lonely week. 'What a shame,' I said, smiling to mask my disappointment.

'But I hoped you might come to the hotel to have dinner with me tonight?'

'I'd like that *very* much,' I said.

Dante returned at eight o'clock to escort me to the hotel's dining room. The service was discreet, the dinner delicious, and wine and conversation flowed. I liked the way he listened to what I was saying without interrupting. I was interested to hear about the alterations that were to be made to the new annexe, including bedrooms, bathrooms and a lift.

'I wondered,' said Dante, 'if you would take some photographs before the renovations begin? The guests might find it interesting to compare views of the building before and after the works. I could frame the photographs and hang them in the corridors.'

'What a good idea!' I said. 'I'll need to order flash lamps from Signor Tonello since I'll be working indoors. Then I must waste no time in setting up a darkroom.'

'Do you need assistance? I could ask my building contractor to call upon you.'

'That would be helpful.' I was pleased to have a new project to keep me occupied while I was waiting for responses to my letters.

'On another subject,' said Dante, 'Flavia asked me to tell you that she's planning to invite you to lunch for a good gossip.'

I laughed. 'All the gossip will have to be from her side since I know so few people here.'

'She'll invite Paola and some of her other friends, too, so you can get to know them.'

'How kind of her!' I was delighted Flavia wanted to meet me again. 'I envy you your family, Dante.'

'We all have strong opinions and argue much of the time,' he said. 'Families are a mass of contradictory emotions but, in the end, there's nothing more important, is there? Except,' he smiled, 'perhaps, love. Now, shall we have a digestif with our coffee?'

We lingered until all the other guests had left.

'I must go home,' I said, reluctant to leave him. 'Your staff will be waiting to go to their beds.'

Dante called for my coat and umbrella and took my arm to escort me home through the rain.

'It's been a lovely evening,' I said, shaking raindrops off my umbrella. 'I was very gloomy after my quarrel with Eveline and being confined indoors because of the miserable weather but now I'm looking forward to setting up my darkroom.'

'It's always invigorating to have a new project,' said Dante, 'and it's good to see the sparkle back in your eyes.' He took a step closer. 'A diamond,' he said. Lightly, he touched my cheek and showed me the raindrop on his finger. Then he leaned forward and kissed me softly on the mouth.

It was only for a heartbeat but my pulse skipped.

'Good night, Phoebe.'

'Good night, Dante,' I murmured.

He dashed out into the rain and disappeared into the darkness. Smiling, I touched a finger to my lips.

Chapter 21

The next morning, I investigated the store rooms off the *portego* to decide which one would be best to convert into a darkroom. There was electric light in both, albeit very dim, and both were cluttered with dusty boxes and broken furniture. As was so common in Venice, the salt water of the Lagoon beneath had risen up through the building, causing some of the plaster to fall away and reveal the underlying brickwork. Salty crystals blossomed on the lower part of the walls and the floor was littered with flakes of paint.

I chose the store room that had only one small window set high up in the wall. It would be useful for ventilating any chemical vapours but small enough to cover with a wooden shutter to exclude the light. I pushed away my memory of Aunt Lavinia lying here in her coffin and turned my attention to the abandoned furniture. There was a kitchen table, also a wardrobe and some shelves suitable for storing chemicals and photographic equipment.

When the rain ceased, I ventured out to visit Signor Tonello. He greeted me like an old friend and was interested to hear that I intended to set up a darkroom and would remain in Venice for the time being. 'So I have a rival for my business,' he said.

'Not at all. I don't take studio portraits and I hope I might prevail upon you to advise me on the supplies to order, rather than having everything sent from London?'

'There's no need for that!' he said. 'Italy produces the finest photographic supplies you will find anywhere in Europe. Now let me show you these catalogues.'

Half an hour later, I left the shop carrying the flash lamps I'd need for the indoor photographs of Dante's annexe and confident I'd ordered everything necessary for my darkroom. There was a spring in my step as I strode through the streets, avoiding the puddles. I smiled at the memory of Dante's good night kiss. It had been very brief, so I wasn't sure if he'd meant it purely as a friendly gesture or if he had romantic feelings for me. No man besides Lorenzo had ever kissed me on the lips before. Now that I was certain there would never be a future for me with him, I felt strangely free.

I returned to the palazzo and went to change into a plain skirt and blouse and an apron borrowed from Valentina. Hurrying down to the store room, I looked through the boxes it contained, setting aside bric-a-brac and threadbare curtains, together with a broken chair, a fire screen and a worn footstool for Jacopo to burn. Dragging the boxes through the *portego* and into the other store room, I stacked them beside the boot rack. I swept the floor in what would be the darkroom and was crouching down with a dustpan when a shadow fell over me. I glanced up and scrambled to my feet.

'I didn't mean to startle you,' said Lorenzo. He was deathly pale and there were shadows under his eyes.

My heart thudded and my mouth was dry. 'What is it?' I stammered. 'Have you found Sofia?'

'May we go inside for a moment?'

I led him out of the store room and followed him up the

outside staircase. There was thick mud on his shoes and the hem of his cassock.

Valentina appeared as we entered the hall and I asked her to bring coffee for my guest.

She stared curiously at the priest as he slipped off his shoes and placed them neatly by the front door. 'I apologise,' he said. 'The *acqua alta* remains in places. Despite the duckboards, I couldn't avoid the flood water.' He removed his hat but kept on his pellegrina cape.

'Come and dry your feet beside the fire.' I caught sight of myself in the hall mirror and surreptitiously wiped a smudge of dust from my cheek.

Lorenzo followed me into the drawing room.

'Rest your feet on the fender to dry,' I said. He had a hole in his sock and there was something peculiarly intimate about seeing his bare toe. I looked away and sat in the armchair to the other side of the fireplace. 'What news, Lorenzo?'

'I arrived in Venice yesterday afternoon,' he said. 'My mother was very unwell. We talked but then ...'

'Yes?' I said, sitting on the edge of my chair. 'Did you find out where Sofia is?'

'Mamma passed away during the night.'

'Oh, how dreadful! I'm ... I'm so sorry,' I stammered, though truthfully I couldn't mourn Signora Albani. Apprehension made my stomach churn. What if she'd died before she told Lorenzo about our child's whereabouts?

'I hadn't expected it to happen so soon,' he said, 'or for it to be so painful to watch her breathe her last. She was the best mother to us when Giulia and I were young, but after my father died ...' He smoothed his cassock over his knees. 'Well, we had many differences of opinion. But she always wanted what she thought was best for us.'

189

'She was wrong about what was best for you and me. And for our child.'

'We cannot go back in time.'

'No.' I had to ask the question that was burning inside me. 'Did she say where she took Sofia?'

'She denied Sofia's existence at first.' He shaded his eyes with his hand. 'I told her I knew she wasn't telling me the truth. We argued and now I blame myself because she became so distressed, she couldn't get her breath.' He met my gaze. 'She said it wouldn't do me or Sofia any good for us to know each other. And then ... then it was too late.'

Anger flared, white-hot, in my breast. 'How *dare* she make that decision for us! Sofia is *our* daughter.'

'But, Phoebe, she doesn't even know us.'

'Of course she doesn't!' There was a sharp edge to my voice. 'How could she when your mother and my aunt conspired to steal her from us?' Tension made my head ache.

The doorknob rattled and I snatched open the door to admit Valentina. 'Put the coffee on the table,' I ordered her.

My housekeeper backed hastily from the room.

'Have you considered that Sofia might not welcome us intruding on her life?' said Lorenzo.

'Why wouldn't she want to know us?' I poured coffee into a cup and thrust it into his hands.

'We're complete strangers to her.'

'But she should be allowed to make that decision for herself and your mother has denied her, and us, the opportunity to meet! Even if *you* don't want to find our daughter, I do.'

'I didn't say I don't want to find her.'

I shivered and huddled back into my armchair. 'But we have no idea where she is.' My voice cracked. 'I mourned our baby every day for the past seventeen years. *Seventeen years!* That's half my lifetime. And then, like a miracle, I discovered she was alive after all. Don't you see, Lorenzo? I simply *have* to find her.'

'I do understand. I'll search my mother's papers and see if I can discover anything.' He turned his head at the sound of voices in the hall and then the door opened.

Valentina stood in the doorway, her expression anxious. 'Signor Benedetti has come to see you, Signora Wyndham. 'I said you had a visitor but—'

Cosimo appeared beside her, smiling broadly and carrying a basket planted with flowering narcissi. 'I was sure you wouldn't refuse to see me for a moment or two.'

'Thank you, Valentina,' I said. 'That will be all.'

Cosimo stepped into the room but halted when he noticed Lorenzo. 'Oh! Excuse me, Father.'

Lorenzo hastily removed his stockinged feet from the fender and stood up.

'This is Father Albani,' I said.

Cosimo placed the basket of narcissi on the table. 'These are for you, Phoebe.' He turned to Lorenzo. 'Albani? Ah, I remember now. Signora Wyndham was asking me only a few weeks ago if I knew of you. You're old friends, I believe?'

'Yes,' said Lorenzo. 'My parish is in Molina but I returned to Venice to visit my mother.'

'A dutiful son. She must be proud of you.'

'She died last night,' he said, 'and I came to inform Signora Wyndham.'

'My condolences,' said Cosimo.

'I'll take my leave,' said Lorenzo. 'I have arrangements to make.'

'Please take a seat, Cosimo, while I show Father Albani out,' I said. Silently, I accompanied Lorenzo into the hall.

He slipped on his shoes and hat. 'I'm sorry I couldn't bring you the information you so desperately want.'

'I'll *never* stop looking for Sofia,' I said, my chin quivering. 'I've spent hours writing to convent schools and orphanages in case someone knows of her whereabouts.'

'If I discover anything . . .'

'Yes,' I said, opening the entrance door for him.

Lorenzo hesitated. 'I'm sorry for everything that makes you sad. I wish very much that things had been different. But now . . .'

'I know.'

He placed his hand on my head. 'May God go with you.'

I closed the door behind him and rested my forehead against the polished timber. Lorenzo had gone, taking all my dreams with him. I took a few moments to master my emotions, and then I returned to the drawing room.

'Well,' said Cosimo, 'so your old friend is a priest? When you enquired about him, I imagined there had once been some special relationship between you.'

I found I couldn't talk about Lorenzo. 'How kind of you to bring me such lovely flowers,' I said, sniffing the narcissi.

'I hoped they'd brighten your day. It must have been difficult having your sister and her children to stay?'

'Eveline was far too unwell to do anything but keep to her bed and the children are delightful,' I said. 'I'm glad you called, Cosimo. I wonder, is the paperwork now in order to finalise my inheritance from Aunt Lavinia?'

'It's been submitted to the authorities,' he shrugged, 'but in Italy it's impossible to hurry our bureaucracy.'

He gave me a questioning look. 'Are you in financial difficulties?'

'Not at all.'

Cosimo nodded and waited.

'You advised me not to formally set aside any of my aunt's estate to provide for Eveline and, after consideration, I agree with you. She'd be too proud to accept it at the moment so I'll wait and see what I can do for her later. I do, however, wish to set up a trust fund for the benefit of her children.'

'I see.' Cosimo pursed his lips. 'I hope you'll forgive me for asking but, since it may take some months for the Contessa's estate to be passed to you, perhaps you might have funds readily available for the proposed trust from the proceeds of your husband's estate? You see, I'm concerned that essential repairs to the Palazzo degli Angeli may use up a considerable proportion of your inheritance from your aunt. You should be prepared to set aside a significant sum.' He gave a dry smile. 'The drawback to owning an ancient palace.'

I dismissed his comment with a wave of my hand. 'I'm not so sure the palazzo has severe structural problems. Perhaps a little decorative work and some updating is required.' I remembered the flaking walls in the store rooms. 'I wish to ensure Carlo has sufficient for a university education and for an equal amount to be settled on Rosetta.' I knew what it was like to be financially dependent upon a husband and I didn't want that for my niece.

'Are you perfectly sure you wish to do this? Your relations with your sister are far from cordial.'

'It's not *for* Eveline,' I said. 'The trust would be for the sole use of her children. Let me assure you, I know my own mind. What do you think would be an appropriate amount for each child?'

We spent an hour or so discussing the terms of the trust and the necessary sum to cover my intentions. Cosimo and I would both act as trustees, releasing funds when required.

'I'll draw up the paperwork to set up the trust,' he said, once we'd finished our discussion.

'Thank you, Cosimo.' The see-sawing emotions of the previous week had given me a throbbing headache. 'Let me show you out.'

In the hall, he squeezed my hand. 'You look tired.'

'A headache,' I said.

He released my hand. 'Not influenza?'

'No.'

'Phoebe . . .' He hesitated. 'I don't want you to think I'm interfering with your decisions; it's only that you're alone in the world and I don't want anyone to take advantage of you.'

'I can look after myself,' I said, smiling to soften my acerbic tone.

'Nevertheless, please know you may call upon me any time you need help or advice. And when you're quite recovered, perhaps you'd care to accompany me to the opera again?'

'Thank you,' I said, and closed the door behind him.

Valentina was lurking in the passage to the kitchen. 'Was that priest Lorenzo Albani?' she asked. Her eyes gleamed with speculation.

'Yes,' I said. 'It was.' I returned to the drawing room and closed the door. Stirring the embers of the fire, I thought about how Signora Albani had maintained her power over the lives of others, even in death. She would take the secret of where she'd hidden Sofia to the grave with her. The logs on the fire crackled and hissed and, just for a moment, I imagined I heard the Signora's mocking laughter.

Chapter 22

Over the following days, I received several replies to my letters from various convent schools but none brought me the news I longed for. I wrote to four more orphanages and took the letters to the post office.

Dante brought his builder, Enzo, to meet me. In the proposed darkroom, I explained what needed to be done and he agreed to make a light-proof shutter, paint the walls black, bring in a water supply and instal a large sink with drainage.

'Phoebe, come and look at this,' said Dante.

I moved over to where he was standing in the shadows. 'It looks like a door.'

'I've not noticed it before but it must lead into my hotel's furniture store.' He tried the ancient iron handle. 'Locked,' he said. 'I imagine the previous owners of one of our properties once rented out their store room as additional warehouse space to the other. I have a collection of old keys that came with the building when I bought it. Enzo could fix some battens across the door to make it secure for you.'

'That won't be necessary,' I said. 'The door appears to have been locked for years.' I turned to the builder. 'When will you be able to do the work?'

He scratched his grizzled head and frowned while he thought. 'I'll come tomorrow and bring my apprentice with me. Then we'll finish in time to start on Signor Falcone's annexe.'

'Splendid,' I said.

'Tomorrow then,' said Enzo. He nodded and left.

'It was his building firm I used to refurbish the hotel,' said Dante. 'He's a good workman.' He glanced around the store. 'So this is where the magic will happen and you'll make your photographic prints?'

'It doesn't look very magical at the moment, does it?' I sighed as another flake of paint fluttered to the floor. 'The walls are terribly damp so I shan't be able to store the paper in here.'

'In the past, the merchants always built their living quarters on the upper floors. You can't stop the rooms and boathouses at this level from becoming damp.'

'Cosimo Benedetti tells me the Palazzo degli Angeli needs a great many expensive remedial works,' I said.

Dante's eyebrows rose. 'All these old buildings need constant maintenance, especially after flooding, but you don't need to worry that your palazzo is going to suddenly collapse.'

'I sincerely hope not!' I was reassured by his words. 'Since Enzo will be starting on your annexe very soon, I ought to take photographs of the building as it is now, before it's too late. Will you show me the views you'd like?'

'If you have time to look today, I'll fetch the keys and the plans so you can see how it's all going to work.'

Ten minutes later, he led me out of the back of the hotel and into a small courtyard. 'As you can see,' he said, 'there's too little outside space presently for guests to use comfortably.' He opened a gate in the rear wall and we stepped into another yard with a house behind. 'The new annexe and its yard run for the length of your garden, with the alleyway behind both the properties.'

'So the annexe is on a plot of land the same length as my garden?'

'Exactly! The previous owner was an elderly widow and the place had become very run-down. She's living with her son now.'

Dante showed me how a covered walkway would link the two properties. The adjoining courtyards would be landscaped with a fountain pool and benches. Inside the building, several small rooms and a kitchen would be opened up to provide a generous sitting area, a billiard room and a breakfast room. Upstairs, there was room for eight new bedrooms, several bathrooms and a linen store.

'Now it's stopped raining and the light is good,' I said, after we'd finished the tour, 'I'm free to start straight away, if that's convenient?'

I returned to the palazzo to pack my photographic bag and collect my camera and tripod. I turned off the light in the store room and, feeling my way in the darkness, withdrew a box of dry plates from a black velvet sack. I unwrapped one and rubbed it gently to identify the smoother, emulsion side of the glass. Then I loaded the plates, emulsion side up, into the holders and put them in the camera.

Returning to the annexe, I set up the tripod for the first photograph. Completely absorbed in the project, time passed quickly for me until the light began to fade. Finally, satisfied with my progress, I locked the annexe and returned the keys to the hotel reception desk.

Early the following morning, Enzo and his apprentice Marco arrived to start on the new darkroom. Once they were busy sawing and wrestling with pipework, I returned to the hotel with my photographic equipment.

Later, I heard footsteps approaching along the passage. The door creaked open just as I set off the flash lamp and took a photograph. A shocked exclamation came from behind me and I saw Dante, blinking in the doorway.

'Sorry, did the flash startle you?' I asked. He shook his head but the colour had drained from his complexion.

'Just for a moment,' he said, giving an uncertain laugh, 'I thought I was back in the trenches and it was a shell landing. I saw some terrible things, Phoebe.' He stared out of the window and then shook his head as if to free himself from a disturbing vision.

It distressed me to hear that, as for so many men, Dante's wartime experiences were still vivid in his mind. I rested my hand on his arm. 'Shall we go outside?'

He forced a smile. 'I came to ask if you'd like to have lunch with me?'

I glanced at my watch. 'Heavens! Is that the time?'

'Leave your camera and equipment here,' he said. 'It will all be quite safe if we lock the building.'

A short while later we were sitting at a table in the dining room overlooking the canal. Dante ordered spaghetti with clams for us and glasses of white wine and we discussed my progress.

'I should finish this afternoon,' I said, 'as long as we don't linger too long over our lunch.'

'Then I promise not to keep you.' Lightly, he touched the back of my hand with his finger. 'Perhaps we'll allow ourselves more time another day?'

I nodded, my cheeks growing warm under his gaze.

'Flavia called by,' he said. 'She called at the Palazzo degli Angeli and left you an invitation to her lunch party on Thursday.'

'How kind of her!'

'I wouldn't let her come and disturb you while you were working.' Dante laughed. 'She'll show you off to her friends, quite shamelessly, as her latest discovery.'

The waiter brought the spaghetti and I suddenly realised how hungry I was.

Later that afternoon, I finished taking the photographs and returned the annexe keys to reception. Disappointed there was no sign of Dante, I returned to the palazzo.

I hadn't been attracted to any man since Lorenzo. But now I'd discovered the chains around my heart were unshackled, I freely admitted to myself that Dante aroused feelings in me I hadn't experienced for a very long time.

On Thursday morning, Enzo and Marco finished the darkroom. I was excited at the prospect of arranging my new equipment and planned to visit Signor Tonello to see if the items I'd ordered had arrived. That would have to wait, however, until the following day because I was going to Flavia's lunch party.

She lived close enough to the Palazzo degli Angeli for me to reach her apartment on foot. I crossed the bridge over the Rio de la Fornace and turned right onto a footpath that ran beside the canal. The building I sought had once been a fine palazzo but was now divided into apartments. Flavia's was on the second floor and reached by a decorative iron staircase. A maid opened the door and showed me into the drawing room.

Flavia came forward to kiss me on each cheek and introduce me to the other guests. 'You already know my sister-in-law Paola,' she said, 'and this is my school friend Amalia.'

Both of them greeted me with a friendly smile.

'And Ines here is my husband Salvatore's cousin.'

Petite, dark and intense, Ines patted a place on the sofa beside her. 'Come and tell me how you came to Venice,' she said. 'Flavia tells me you're a photographer?'

Ines drew me into conversation and I soon felt at ease with my new acquaintances.

The doorbell rang again and a moment later I tensed when I saw that the latest guest was my sister. She looked at me and her smile faded.

'I hope you've fully recovered from the influenza, Eveline?' I said.

'Perfectly. I didn't know you were coming today.' She turned away, obviously no happier than I that we were to be guests at the same table.

Paola went to kiss Eveline, drew her over to sit down beside her and soon they were chatting together.

Ines gave me a questioning look. 'Is there some difficulty between you and your sister?' she murmured.

I hesitated. 'Eveline and I hadn't seen each other for many years before I returned to Venice recently.' Ines studied my face until I felt myself redden. 'It's complicated,' I said.

She gave me an understanding smile. 'Families usually are. What happened?'

There was no avid curiosity in her question, only compassion, and I found myself explaining that Eveline had expected to inherit the palazzo. 'It was a great shock to both of us when we discovered our Aunt Lavinia had left it to me instead.'

'But why did your sister believe it was fair for her alone to inherit the palazzo?'

'My aunt and I quarrelled many years ago,' I said, 'and she disinherited me.'

Ines frowned as she considered the problem. 'Wouldn't the fairest thing now be for you to share the inheritance?'

'I agree with you but I haven't said as much to Eveline yet. She's so angry with me, it's impossible for us to discuss anything calmly.

She's too proud to accept what she sees as charity, and her anger makes it hard for me to feel generously disposed towards her.'

'Do you have a good lawyer to advise you? Perhaps he might find a way to smooth the way?'

'My aunt's lawyer, Signor Benedetti, is dealing with the inheritance papers.'

'Benedetti? Ah, yes.' Ines smiled. 'Venice is a small city and everyone knows each other's business. Cosimo Benedetti took over the practice when his father retired, didn't he? The Benedetti family is old and was once noble, though I understand Cosimo's grandfather was forced to sell the ancestral family home to clear his debts.'

'How humiliating for him.'

'Especially as he was left with only enough to purchase an apartment and a warehouse with a boathouse. It's in the Rio del Duca, on the opposite side of the Grand Canal from your palazzo. He continued to trade in spices for a while but, eventually, the business failed.'

'Poor man,' I said.

Then Flavia announced lunch was ready and led us all into the dining room.

There was plenty of laughter as she and her friends gossiped their way through lunch, but I found it awkward when I couldn't join in with the talk about their children's antics and achievements. Surreptitiously, I watched Eveline smiling at something Paola and Amalia had said and was struck by how attractive my sister was when she lost the sullen expression she habitually wore while dealing with me.

When it was time to leave, it was heart-warming to hear Flavia and her friends insist that Eveline and I must join them for the next lunch, which would be at Amalia's house.

I said goodbye to my sister, who merely nodded and turned

away. Irritated by the snub, I set off for home. Home! I realised it was the first time in many years I'd thought of the palazzo as my home. Perhaps that was because I now had more friends in Venice than in London.

Approaching the palazzo along the alley that ran behind the garden, I saw the dark silhouette of a priest walking briskly away from me. My heart began to thud but then I chided myself for imagining that, of all the priests in Venice, this must be Lorenzo.

When I opened the front door of the palazzo, there was a note on the hall mat. Opening the envelope, I saw Lorenzo's signature. So it *had* been him I'd seen hurrying away!

Dear Phoebe,

Mindful of the manner in which you discovered Sofia's existence, I studied my mother's household account books and discovered something interesting. For the last seven years, she made substantial twice-yearly payments to the Convent of the Sacred Heart in Bologna. This may have been a purely charitable gesture but the timing suggests that it was probably intended to pay for Sofia's upkeep after she left the Vianello family.

After my mother's funeral, I must return to Molina and confess to my superiors that I have fathered a child. Until I have received their instructions and permission, I am not in a position to visit the convent to make enquiries regarding Sofia. I imagine you will not wish to wait and suggest you visit the convent yourself.

I hope this information will assist in reuniting you with our daughter and bring you the peace of mind you so desperately need.

Lorenzo

I sank down onto the hall chair, my legs suddenly incapable of supporting me.

Chapter 23

I found the Convent of the Sacred Heart in an unassuming side street. I tipped back my head to study the faded paint of the stucco wall towering above me. A row of small barred windows had been set high up under the eaves. Larger windows with decorative iron grilles flanked a nail-studded entrance door twice my height. I shuddered at the thought of Sofia shut away behind such a forbidding façade and pressed the brass bell-push set into the wall.

Several minutes later, my finger was poised to press it again. I hadn't travelled all the way to Bologna to leave with my questions unanswered. Then I heard the scrape of a series of metal bolts being dragged back. The door opened a crack.

'Hello?' I said. A pulse fluttered in my throat as I wondered if this was the day I would meet my daughter at last.

The door creaked inwards and an elderly nun regarded me with rheumy eyes. 'Yes?'

'May I come in?' I asked. 'I wish to enquire about a girl who may reside here.'

'This is an orphanage so there are many girls here.'

'Her name is Sofia Vianello.'

The nun muttered under her breath and turned away.

Uncertain as to whether I was to remain on the doorstep or to follow her, I hung back until the gatekeeper had disappeared into the gloomy passage, leaving the door ajar. Slipping inside, I pulled it shut behind me.

The nun's sandalled feet scuffed along the tiled floor and came to a halt at the end of the passage. 'I will speak to Mother Superior,' she said, and pointed to a wooden bench.

I inferred I was expected to sit and wait. Five tense minutes later, my knee was jiggling up and down with impatience when the nun opened an interior door and beckoned me inside.

The Convent's Mother Superior sat behind a large desk, her hands folded upon it. She gestured to me to sit down. 'You may wait outside, Sister Maria Elena.' The door closed and her superior gave me a wintry smile. 'I understand you wish to enquire about Sofia Vianello?'

'Yes. I have reason to believe she has resided here for the past seven years.'

'What is the nature of your business with her?'

'Sofia is my daughter.' I met the nun's gaze, determined not to show shame for having given birth to a love child. 'She was taken from me as an infant but, a few weeks ago, I discovered she'd been fostered by the Vianello family. They told me a lady had taken Sofia away to be educated in a convent. I believe Signora Albani was that lady.'

'And how did you arrive at that conclusion?'

'Signora Albani passed away last week. Her son revealed to me that she has made substantial payments to this convent twice a year for seven years, ever since Sofia was ten years old.' I held my breath.

The Mother Superior tapped a finger on the desk. 'Since Signora Albani has departed this life, I do not believe it will break any confidences to confirm that the child did come to the Convent of the Sacred Heart.'

I exhaled sharply. 'Thank Heavens!' A delicious warmth flooded through my whole body and I couldn't contain my smiles. 'May I see her?'

'That will not be possible.'

The smile faded. 'Please,' I pleaded, 'I've waited so long ...'

'It will not be possible because she is no longer here.'

'But ... where is she?'

'I have no idea.' The Mother Superior pressed her lips together. 'Sofia has caused us a great deal of trouble. We have thirty girls in our care at any one time, orphans as well as babies abandoned by mothers who have fallen from grace.' She fixed me with a meaningful glance as she said this. 'Sofia has been a thorn in our side since the moment she arrived. She absconded from the convent no less than three times and had to be brought back at considerable inconvenience to others.'

'I daresay she was made unhappy by being torn away from her loving foster family by an unknown woman.'

'Signora Albani was concerned about the child and desired the sisters here to give her moral instruction, to prevent her from falling into the ways of sin.' She leaned forward and hissed: 'Like her mother did.'

Heat raced up my throat and flooded my cheeks. 'You know nothing about me or what happened.'

'Nor do I wish to know. The children in our care are raised in humility to fit them for a life of service to the community, either as a Bride of Christ or in some useful occupation. Sofia was unsuited to a humble religious life but had some capacity for learning and demonstrated an interest in the younger children. Last week, a position was found for her as governess to a family. The ungrateful girl ran away after only one night in the post.'

'Ran away?' To have come so close to finding her and then to discover I'd missed her was a bitter pill to swallow.

'To compound her wrongdoing,' continued the nun, 'she stole money from her employer's purse. Naturally, the police have been informed.'

'She must have been badly treated,' I said. 'I must meet the family who employed her.'

'Absolutely not.' The Mother Superior rang a little brass hand-bell on her desk. 'Sofia has chosen her own path to damnation, despite our best efforts, and I wash my hands of her. This interview is at an end.' The door opened and the elderly nun re-entered the room. 'Sister Maria Elena, please accompany our guest out of the building.'

'But I need to know more about my daughter,' I protested. 'At least tell me what Sofia looks like!'

'She is entirely unremarkable.' The Mother Superior rose from her chair. 'Now you must leave.' She swept out of the room.

'Come,' said Sister Maria Elena.

Trembling with rage at her superior's abrupt dismissal of me, I had no choice but to follow.

When Sister Maria Elena opened the entrance door, I caught hold of her sleeve. 'Will you at least tell me the name of the family Sofia Vianello went to work for?'

The nun blinked rapidly. 'I do not know it.'

'Then what did Sofia look like? Was her hair dark or blonde like mine?'

'She was a girl like any other. Now you must leave.' She pulled her sleeve from my grip and waited impassively by the open door.

Later, still furious, I boarded the train to Venice. I found myself an empty compartment and slammed the carriage door behind me. A middle-aged man followed me in and I gave him such a scowl that he backed out again with an apology. The whistle blew and the train puffed out of the station.

I stared out of the window, simmering with rage at the Mother Superior's implacable attitude. Why could she not have found the compassion to describe what Sofia looked like? Gradually, my anger gave way to despair. The search for my daughter had come to a dead end, yet again. There was a tightness in my chest as I fought back the fear that now I would never find her.

Refusing to allow myself to cry, I pondered on what I would have done in Sofia's position. Since she'd absconded several times from the forbidding confines of the convent, surely she would have welcomed the opportunity of finding genteel employment elsewhere? Why then would she run away with no financial support other than a few coins from her employer's purse? And where might she have gone in her friendless state?

I was jolted out of my brooding thoughts when the train drew into Ferrara station. Doors slammed, a whistle blew and an old lady entered the compartment. Thankfully, she showed no inclination to talk but began to work on a complicated piece of crochet.

I returned to the question of where Sofia might have gone. It was some while later that I suddenly sat bolt upright. Of course! She had been snatched away from her foster parents' home, a place where she'd been happy. Why else would she repeatedly attempt to escape from the convent, except to return to the safety and love of the only family she'd ever known?

A thrill of triumph made me laugh aloud and the crocheting passenger eyed me uneasily. I smiled reassuringly at her and went back to my ruminations. It was highly likely Sofia had returned to Benaco and the Vianello family. And Rovigo station from which I could reach the village was only a few miles away from Ferrara on my return journey to Venice.

Half an hour later, the rhythm of the train began to slow its rattling progress. Springing to my feet, I lifted my overnight case from the luggage rack. The brakes squealed and the train pulled into Rovigo station.

I arrived at Ristorante Angelina as Signor Vianello was locking the door after the departure of the last lunchtime customer.

'Signora Wyndham! Come in, come in!' He ushered me inside and called out, 'Angelina, come quickly!'

His wife appeared from the kitchens, wiping her hands on a tea towel. She halted when she saw me. 'How did you know?' she said. 'I only posted my letter to you this morning.'

I glanced around the restaurant, my stomach churning. 'Sofia? She's here?'

Angelina shook her head and blotted her eyes with the tea towel.

Suddenly dizzy, I sat down on a chair. 'I was so sure she would be.'

Signor Vianello collected three glasses and a bottle from the counter. He poured me a brandy and pushed the glass towards me.

'She was here yesterday,' said Angelina. There were dark shadows beneath her eyes as if she hadn't slept. 'I couldn't believe my eyes when I saw her. My baby girl has grown into a beautiful woman. The first thing she did after escaping from that terrible place was to come home.'

'But she left again?'

Angelina's face crumpled. 'She was so angry with us, she said she'll never come back.'

'I don't understand,' I said. 'You showed her nothing but kindness.'

'Drink your brandy, Signora,' urged Signor Vianello. 'You've had a shock.'

I took a sip and felt its bracing warmth spreading inside me. 'Please, tell me what happened.'

'I recognised her at once,' said Angelina, 'even though she's no longer a child.' She smiled through her tears.

'What does she look like?' I asked.

'Tall and slender, like you. Her hair is dark but her complexion is fair.' Angelina hid her face in the tea towel.

Signor Vianello patted her shoulder. 'Sofia asked why we'd allowed someone we didn't know to take her to the convent. She said that woman barely spoke to her while they travelled, except to tell her she'd been born in sin and must atone for her mother's wickedness.'

Anger burned in me again at Signora Albani's inhumanity. 'What a cruel thing to say to a child!'

'Sofia protested that her mamma and papà weren't wicked,' said Angelina, 'and that monster slapped her face!'

I couldn't speak for distress. I'd known Signora Albani was cold-hearted but I hadn't imagined she'd strike her own grandchild.

'That heartless woman told Sofia that Luigi and I weren't her parents,' wept Angelina. 'She said her birth mother hadn't wanted her and that we'd been paid to care for her. Sofia hoped it was a lie but over the years, because we never came to take her home, she came to wonder if it was true.'

Tears scalded my eyes. 'She must have been bereft.'

'She tried several times to escape from the convent but, each time, they found her. Then she was sent to work for a family and, at the first opportunity, came here and demanded we tell her the truth,' said Angelina. 'I tried to explain we'd always loved her as much as if she were our own and that all we wanted was her happiness, but she was too angry with us to listen.'

'I can only imagine how desolate she felt,' I said, 'torn away from everyone she loved and given into the care of nuns who showed her little compassion.' I squeezed my eyes shut at memories of my own despair after the discovery of my pregnancy and subsequent banishment.

'She was distraught,' said Signor Vianello. 'For the seven years she suffered at the convent, she hoped that woman had lied to her. She came here expecting us to confirm that she was our daughter.' A muscle clenched in his jaw and he looked away.

'But we couldn't,' whispered Angelina. 'We told her how Carmela brought her to us and that her mother was too young to keep her, but she screamed at us: "I would never give up *my* child!"'

'I didn't give her up,' I said, my voice breaking, 'she was stolen from me.'

'I told her about you and that you were looking for her,' said Signor Vianello, 'but she was too upset to listen and ran out into the street. We followed but she was too quick for us.'

'I'm frightened for her,' I said. I drained the last of the brandy for courage. 'Where can she go? She's an unworldly young woman without friends to support her or family to guide her. What will become of our Sofia?'

Chapter 24

Defeated, I returned to Palazzo degli Angeli and wrote to Lorenzo to explain what had happened. I received a brief but compassionate note in response. His mother's funeral had taken place and he was on the point of returning to Molina. He thought it best we didn't meet before he left but asked me to inform him straightaway if I found our daughter.

I was tormented by thoughts of Sofia, alone and friendless. I imagined her in one dangerous situation after another. How could an innocent girl, inexperienced in the ways of the world, and men in particular, remain safe? It was painful there was no one I could confide in, except for Eveline, who was too caught up in her entrenched resentment of me to listen to my woes.

Valentina, conscious I was unhappy about something, kept up a non-stop flow of gratingly cheerful conversation, cooked all my favourite dishes and chivvied Jacopo to keep the fires burning brightly. She mentioned Dante had called several times and that Cosimo had left a message asking me to visit his offices to sign some papers.

After a few days of wallowing in my misery and wracking my

brains as to where Sofia might be, I gave myself a mental shake. I placed advertisements in the newspapers offering a reward for information leading me to Sofia. There was no other immediate action I could think of to find her.

In the new darkroom, I opened the window to dispel the lingering smell of damp, and asked Jacopo to light a brazier to warm the room. I ventured out to visit Signor Tonello and collected the supplies I'd ordered, taking Jacopo with me to carry the boxes back to the palazzo. I called into a haberdasher's shop and bought a sturdy pinafore to wear in the darkroom.

Once back at the palazzo, I fetched the photographic plates in their light-proof bag from the bottom drawer of the wardrobe and took them into the darkroom, which now felt warm and dry. I closed the window shutter. Opening the boxes, I positioned the developing tanks on the new workbench adjacent to the sink and arranged the bottles of chemicals on the shelves near to hand.

Jacopo fetched the steps and fitted a filtered lamp to the newly installed electrical point above the workbench.

Once he'd closed the door behind him, I poured out some developing solution into a deep tray and arranged the stop bath next to it. Now I was ready to set to work.

Two hours later, in the dim red glow of the darkroom, I lifted the last glass plate out of the water bath. Taking care to hold it only by the edges with my fingertips, I rested it on the wooden draining rack beside the other negatives. I poured the fluids from the developing tanks down the sink drain and tidied away the bottles of chemicals. Switching off the red lamp, I left the darkroom, locking the door behind me.

'Phoebe!' Dante was standing behind the water gate to the canal. I hadn't wanted to speak to anyone since returning from the convent but now I smiled involuntarily. 'Hello, Dante. I've been developing the negatives for the photographs of your annexe.'

'Valentina told me when I called to see you earlier.' He didn't respond to my smile. 'How do they look?'

'One was overexposed but I'd taken an alternative and that one is good. They're on the drying racks at present. If the day is bright and clear enough tomorrow, I'll make the prints in the late morning. You can come and watch if you have the time.' Over Dante's shoulder, a movement caught my attention. A nun was standing on the walkway on the opposite side of the canal, her black habit billowing in the breeze.

'I'd like that.' He glanced at me uncertainly. 'I wondered if . . .'

'If what?'

'If you've been avoiding me. Have I upset you?' The expression in his green eyes was troubled.

'Of course not.' After hesitating, I said, 'I had to go away on business and I've had some things on my mind, that's all.'

He regarded me steadily for a moment and then smiled. 'Until tomorrow then.'

I noticed the nun was still there on the opposite side of the canal, watching us. Curious, I stared back at her. Then my view was obscured by a barge laden with furniture, the oars creaking as it glided by. Water slapped against the landing stage, stirring up a faint smell of decay. I glanced over the canal again but the nun was hurrying away along the path.

Nonplussed, I wondered why she'd been so interested in us. Was it a coincidence or might she have come from the Convent of the Sacred Heart? Perhaps one of the nuns there had taken pity on me and had news of Sofia? The hurrying figure was some way off now. There was no continuous walkway on the palazzo side of the canal so I couldn't chase after her. Infuriated that I was powerless to speak to her, I had no choice but to return indoors.

When I went in, Valentina reminded me Cosimo had asked me to call on him. I changed out of my pinafore and put on my hat and coat.

I walked through the garden towards the back gate. A builder's cheerful whistle and the sound of hammering drifted over the wall from the Hotel Falcone's new annexe.

A short while later, I arrived at Cosimo's office in Campo Santa Margherita.

'How delightful to see you, Phoebe!' he said, ushering me to a chair.

'Valentina told me you'd called.'

'It's good news. Probate on your aunt's estate has been agreed.'

'So now the palazzo is mine?'

'Absolutely.'

I had mixed feelings about owning it. Now I could no longer postpone making a firm decision about whether or not to share the inheritance with Eveline. It would be so much easier if only she'd welcomed me back into her life.

'The deeds are here in my safe,' said Cosimo, 'and the funds, less my fees, have been transferred to your new bank account. I also have the documents ready for you to sign regarding the trust you wish to set up for your sister's children.' He opened a door and went into his file store, returning a moment later with some papers. 'Will you see if this meets with your approval?'

I took the document and read it, asking him to explain some of the legal terms.

'And you're quite sure you wish to do this?' he asked. 'Your relations with your sister are ... difficult.'

'I'm not doing this for Eveline,' I said. 'May I borrow a pen to sign the papers?'

Cosimo sighed heavily. 'I'll call my secretary to witness your signature.'

After it was done, he gave me two copies of the document. 'One for you, one for Eveline to keep on behalf of her children. The third will remain on file here.'

'Thank you.'

He drummed his fingers on the desk. 'Have you considered any further whether you are ready to sell the palazzo? As your aunt discovered, it's a very large property for one person and expensive to maintain.'

I'd been so intent upon my search for Sofia recently that I hadn't thought about it again. 'I haven't decided yet,' I said. I couldn't leave Venice when I hadn't yet found my lost daughter. 'There are so many opportunities here to further my photographic career,' I said. 'I've made myself a darkroom in one of the store rooms. I intend to take photographs in the coming spring and summer to contrast with the winter scenes.'

'I see,' said Cosimo, leaning towards me over the desk. 'Then I strongly suggest you undertake a survey of the palazzo. It would be as well to have that done in good time in case you do decide to sell. Or, if you decide to stay, to undertake any repairs before they become any more pressing.'

'I really don't believe there's any problem—'

'I hope you're right.' He sighed. 'Please, let me arrange it for you. The Conte discussed his concerns with me before he died. Your aunt meant to deal with them but I suspect she was frightened of what might be found.' He shrugged, palms to the ceiling. 'I've admired Palazzo degli Angeli for years and can't bear to think of the foundations suffering from that level of neglect. Left too long, it may become impossible to remedy.'

'I suppose that's sensible advice,' I said. After all, I could always seek a second opinion if anything worrying was found.

Cosimo positively beamed. 'Then I shall speak to Signor Nardone and ask him to call upon you at his earliest convenience.'

I stood up, drawing the meeting to a close.

Outside, in the Campo, I decided to visit Eveline and tell her about the trust fund for Carlo and Rosetta. Perhaps that would go some way towards easing our prickly relationship.

I used the map Dante had given me and navigated my way through the narrow streets to the Grand Canal, where I boarded a vaporetto.

Pale sunshine reflected from the windows of the ancient buildings lining the canal and scattered spangles of light over the surface of the water. I was growing to love Venice all over again.

Disembarking at San Stae, I set off for Eveline's apartment and soon arrived at the little square with the plane tree in the centre. A group of women carrying kitchen knives and scissors gossiped together while waiting for a knife-grinder to sharpen their blades. He had only one hand but he wore a medal on his shabby military uniform.

Washing still hung limply from the balconies of the salmon-pink apartment building. When I opened the entrance door, a mangy cat slunk past me into the square.

At the top of the dismal staircase, I heard voices as I knocked on my sister's door. They ceased abruptly. 'Eveline? It's Phoebe.' Silence. Perhaps the voices had come from another apartment? I tapped on the door and called out again. I strained my ears but all was silent.

After a moment, I gave up and returned to the square. I gave the knife-grinder a fistful of lire as he was packing up to leave. He smiled and saluted me.

I glanced up at Eveline's window. Did I imagine it or was that a face moving away from behind the casement? Exasperated, I wondered if my sister would ever cease to be so obstinate. Her behaviour made it a wearisome business for me to be as generous towards her as I wished to be. Sighing, I set off for the palazzo.

At eleven o'clock the following morning, Dante tapped on the darkroom door. 'Am I too early?'

'Not at all,' I said. 'Once I've prepared the printing frames, I'll lay them out on the table in the courtyard. At this time of year, we need good light close to midday to expose the negatives to the print paper.'

I pulled on a pair of white cotton gloves. 'I don't want to spoil the prints with fingerprints on the glass,' I explained, in answer to Dante's enquiring look. Next, I sandwiched photographic paper and a plate negative in a glass-and-timber printing frame.

Dante watched closely while I closed the cover and tightened the thumb screws. 'Do you see?' I said. 'The glass presses the paper into perfect contact with the negative.'

'I suppose you have to be careful not to overtighten it, in case it cracks?'

'Exactly.' I carried the frame outside, placed it on the table and then opened the cover to expose the glass slide to daylight. I glanced up at the sky. 'It's bright for early February,' I said, 'but it will still take a while. In the summer it might only be a few minutes.' I shivered. 'Why don't we have some coffee, while we're waiting?'

We went to the drawing room to warm our hands by the fire and dip *cantucci* into our coffee.

The sun came out and I adjusted the window shutter so the light didn't dazzle me. I frowned. 'Dante,' I said, 'is there a convent nearby?'

'There are many of them in Venice but I'm not aware of any in the immediate vicinity. Why do you ask?'

'There's a nun standing on the other side of the canal. She was there yesterday, too, watching us.'

'You see nuns and priests every day in Venice,' he said.

'I suppose so. Will you excuse me for a moment?' I hurried out of the room, ran downstairs and through the courtyard to the water gate. I dragged it open and went out onto the landing stage. There I waved my arms at the black-clad figure and called out, 'Hey!'

She took a step back.

I scrambled into the *sandalo* moored to the landing stage. It had been years since I'd rowed the old boat ... but then I realised the single oar was missing. Jacopo must have taken it indoors for safe-keeping. Looking across the canal, I saw the nun had gone. Infuriated, I already knew I'd be too late to find the oar and row after her. I returned to the palazzo feeling annoyed with myself for not being better prepared.

Valentina sidled out of the drawing room as I went in.

Dante stood up when I entered the room. 'What happened? Are you unwell, Phoebe?'

'Not at all.' I rubbed a smear of mud from my hand. 'I thought I saw a friend outside and ran downstairs to catch her but she'd already gone.' I smiled brightly to conceal my agitation.

'Valentina is worried about you. She said you were very unhappy when you returned after your business trip. Look, I don't want to interfere but if it helps to talk or if I can do anything ...'

Forcing another smile, I said, 'Thank you, but there's no need.' There was a tight knot in my chest. I longed to unburden myself but how could I tell the man I'd begun to have feelings for that I'd been searching for my illegitimate daughter? Not yet anyway. I didn't want to lose him as well as Sofia.

Sensing I wasn't prepared to discuss the matter, Dante made light conversation until it was time to go back to the courtyard and see what progress had been made with the first contact print.

'A few more minutes,' I said, glancing at my watch. 'Meanwhile, the light is still good so I'll set up some of the other printing frames to bring out here.'

Soon, I had several more laid out on the table. Once the first frame had been sufficiently exposed, I carried it back to the darkroom.

All the time I was developing the photographic paper, I was very aware of Dante standing close beside me in the dim red light. 'Do you see the image gradually appearing?' I said.

He peered over my shoulder as I gently rocked the developing bath from side to side. I scrutinised the contact print. 'That's perfect, so I'll put it in the fixing solution for a few seconds.' I lifted it out of the tray with tongs and placed it in a small tank of water set in the sink. 'Now I'll turn on the tap and let it gradually replace the water I tip out as the print is washed.'

'For how long?' asked Dante.

'About two minutes.' It was hard for me to concentrate while he was so close but at last the print was washed. I fished it out of the water and pegged it on the line I'd stretched over the draining board. 'Now it has to dry.'

He leaned in close beside me as I studied the print. 'I can hardly believe the detail,' he said. 'It's like magic!'

The warmth of his breath tickled my ear. My pulse pounded and I was powerless to move.

'And you, Phoebe, are a sorceress,' he whispered. Turning to face me, he touched his palm to my cheek.

Something in my eyes gave him the permission he sought. He took me in his arms and kissed me.

Chapter 25

A few days later, I looked out of the drawing-room window and saw the nun was on the opposite side of the canal again. Stealthily, I opened the casement then ran upstairs and collected my camera, tripod and the long-focus lens and set it all up in front of the window as quickly as I could. I focused the lens and calculated the exposure.

Then wind gusted across the canal, billowing the nun's habit like a sail. She turned and clutched at her veil. I took the photograph a second before she walked away.

Later that afternoon, I developed the plate and was surprised to see the image was better than I'd expected for a photograph taken in such a rush. The nun's face was in profile. She had a straight nose and a pointed chin. There was some blurring to the veil and habit from the wind but that only endowed the image with life and movement.

There wasn't a single response to my newspaper advertisement but I arranged for it to be reprinted fortnightly over the following three months. During this time, I kept my eyes open, hoping I might see the nun again and find a way to talk to her. If she hadn't been watching the palazzo so intently, I'd have dismissed her from my mind. Had she come from the Convent of the Sacred Heart or, a thrilling thought, was it possible this was Sofia herself? If she'd planned to run away, she could have stolen a habit from the convent before she left, to give her some protection in the outside world. Luigi Vianello said he'd told her about me, even though Sofia hadn't wanted to hear. Had she been curious enough to come and find me? If this was my daughter, I prayed she'd return and let me speak to her.

Meanwhile, I kept busy to distract myself from my melancholy. I continued to work on the prints of Dante's annexe and, when they were finished, developed some of my photographs of Venetian scenes. I was quietly confident that *The Glory of Venice* would be another success.

My spirits also lifted because Dante and I were growing closer. He became a regular visitor to the palazzo, spending evenings with me in the drawing room or taking me out to dinner or a concert.

One morning, the surveyor, Signor Nardone, arrived. He spent several hours examining the palazzo, prodding and tapping the walls, inside and out, and inspecting the attic. He finished a short while before I had to leave to meet Flavia and her friends for lunch.

I returned home later in a cheerful mood. It did me good to have new friends and I decided I'd offer to host the next lunch.

Spring arrived. Inspired by Dante's enthusiastic encouragement, I roamed the city photographing unusual views as well as the popular landmarks. I wanted to capture the essence of Venice and convey its unique qualities to others. The distinctive personalities of the people of the City of Water were a part of the city's character and I took a series of photographs to demonstrate this:

fishermen unloading their catch at dawn; elegant elderly ladies drinking coffee and gossiping in Caffè Florian; gondoliers dressed in their finery as they ferried the dead to San Michele.

I returned to the palazzo after one of my expeditions and found Valentina looking out for me in the hall.

'Signor Benedetti is waiting to see you,' she said. 'Since it's nearly dark, I thought you wouldn't be long so I made him coffee.'

I left my camera, tripod and photographic bag in the hall and went to see Cosimo.

'I'm afraid I bring unwelcome news,' he said. 'I have a copy of Signor Nardone's report.'

'He sent it to you?'

Cosimo dropped his gaze when he saw how annoyed I was.

'There are many technical terms you won't understand and I wanted to save you the bother by explaining them to you.'

'I was married to an architect for many years so allow me to be the judge of that,' I said, holding out my hand.

The report was very clear. The piles that supported the palazzo, driven into the mud of the Lagoon, were rotting. The mortar in the brickwork was crumbling and there was a woodworm infestation in the roof. If extensive work wasn't undertaken very soon, there was a risk the building would sink into the water. I felt sick.

'I did warn you,' said Cosimo when I looked up from the report.

'I'd no idea the situation was so bad.'

'I advise you to sell the palazzo as soon as possible. The proceeds of the sale ought to be enough to buy you an elegant apartment more suited to the needs of a single lady.'

I lifted my chin. 'Or I could manage the restoration work myself.'

Cosimo chuckled. 'I doubt you'd care to live in a building site for the best part of a year while walls, roof and foundations are being replaced. The funds required will soon absorb what is left of your aunt's inheritance.'

'How much would it cost?'

'It's the nature of an extensive renovation that no one knows until the job is finished. The foundations are centuries old and it's impossible to fully determine their condition until the floors are lifted and the excavations begin.'

I felt as if there was a heavy stone pressing on my chest. I'd fallen in love with the palazzo again and it was immensely painful to discover its existence was under threat.

'What a shame you tied up such a large sum in the trust fund for your sister's children,' said Cosimo. Looking thoughtful, he said, 'Did you tell her about it? Perhaps it's not too late to dissolve the trust?'

'I won't do that!'

He shrugged. 'As you wish. The buyer I mentioned when you first arrived in Venice is still interested. He's aware the palazzo needs work and his offer is priced to reflect that.'

'Signor Falcone offered me a larger sum,' I said.

'Of course he did. He has a greater interest because the palazzo is attached to his hotel, but he didn't know then that Palazzo degli Angeli is rotten to the foundations. He won't want it now.'

'I need some time to think about the best course of action.' Certainly I needed a second opinion. I decided I'd speak to Dante about it and take the risk that he would change his mind about buying the palazzo.

Cosimo stood up. 'Don't wait too long, Phoebe. The longer you leave it, the worse the situation will become. And don't let Falcone lead you into false expectations.' He narrowed his eyes. 'Either personally or professionally.'

Later, I was in the darkroom when there was a thunderous banging on the door. 'Who is it?'

'Jacopo. Please come at once, Signora Wyndham!'

'I'm working. Can't it wait?'

'Valentina's had an accident.' He rattled the door handle.

I covered the glass plates with a black velvet cloth before slipping through the door and closing it behind me.

'Please hurry, Signora Wyndham!' Jacopo's face was creased with worry.

'What happened?' I asked as we sprinted across the courtyard.

'She fell in the bathroom and hit her head. I can't wake her!'

I raced up the outside stairs to discover water dripping through the hall ceiling and pooling on the parquet. I ran up the next flight, where the landing carpet was sodden, and went into the bathroom.

Valentina lay crumpled on the white marble floor in a lake of blood. The dolphin-headed bath tap lay on the floor and water spurted in a fountain from the pipe. Gasping in horror, it took me a moment to realise that the blood running from the cut on Valentina's forehead had coloured the water on the floor, making it look infinitely worse than it was.

Moaning, she lifted her head. I snatched up a towel and pressed it to her wound.

Jacopo, panting, arrived in the doorway and dissolved into tears when he saw she was conscious again.

'Jacopo, can you find the stopcock to turn off the water?' I said.

He opened an access panel beneath the bath and, with some difficulty, turned the stopcock. The fountain slowed to a dribble.

I lifted the towel from Valentina's head and inspected the wound. 'It's almost stopped bleeding. Shall we sit you up?'

Jacopo kissed his wife's cheeks and encouraged her to be brave but Valentina shrieked in pain when she tried to stand. 'My ankle!'

It took some while for Jacopo and me to perch her on the side of the bath, remove her sodden and blood-stained clothing and wrap her in a dressing gown. Her ankle was rapidly swelling and she cried out when I gently pressed it. 'We'll put you to bed, Valentina.'

Jacopo, suddenly heroic, hefted his wife into his arms, staggered to their bedroom on the top floor and dumped her on the bed. Scarlet-faced with exertion, he sank down beside her.

I found her a clean nightgown and went to the kitchen to brew her a glass of herbal tea.

When I returned, Valentina was still pale and trembling so I sent Jacopo to fetch Dottor Bucchi. 'What happened?' I asked her.

'I was cleaning the bath and the tap came off when I turned it.' She gesticulated wildly to add drama to the account. 'There was so much water I thought it would never stop! I put a towel over it but the force of the torrent threw it off. I ran to call for Jacopo to help but the marble was so slippery, my feet flew away from under me and I fell onto the corner of the bath.' Her mouth trembled. 'It wasn't my fault the tap broke, Signora.'

'I'm quite sure it wasn't. Drink your tisane,' I said, patting her hand. 'There's honey in it to help the shock.'

Dottor Bucchi arrived a little while later and inspected Valentina's head and ankle. He pronounced the ankle badly sprained but not broken and advised Jacopo to remain nearby for the next twenty-four hours in case she had concussion. After disinfecting the head wound and applying an adhesive dressing, he bound up the empurpled ankle and advised the patient to keep her leg elevated.

Valentina clutched at her ears. 'But I cannot!' She made an effort to rise, crying out as her swollen foot touched the floor. 'Who will cook Signora Wyndham's meals and do the cleaning?'

I put a firm hand on her shoulder. 'You must rest here until you're better. Jacopo will sit beside you in case you need anything.'

Later, after I'd said goodbye to Dottor Bucchi, I set to work in the bathroom with a mop, wondering where I could find a plumber.

I was carrying the mop and bucket downstairs when there was a deafening crash in the hall below and a thick cloud of dust surged up the stairs. Holding my pinafore over my mouth and nose, I ran down to see what had happened. Waving the dust away, I caught my breath in dismay. A large chunk of plaster had fallen from the frescoed ceiling and the painted angels on their rose-pink clouds now surrounded a dark hole where the chandelier used to hang. Shattered fragments of crystal drops were scattered over the floor and a pall of plaster dust and debris was settling on every surface. Aghast, I clung to the newel post.

Jacopo appeared at the top of the stairs and his eyes widened at the scene of destruction.

'Don't come down,' I said. 'You'll spread the dust with your feet and Valentina needs you, in case she has concussion.'

He disappeared again.

I picked my way over the rubble and broken crystal, assessing how I might remove it. Then I brushed down my skirt and went to find Dante.

He was in his office, working on a pile of paperwork, when his secretary knocked on his door and admitted me.

'I'm sorry to disturb you,' I said, 'but there's been an accident next door and I was wondering if Enzo or one of his men might be able to help.' I explained what had happened and Dante arranged for a tray of coffee to be brought to me while he went to speak to the workmen.

Before long, Enzo and his apprentice were busy shovelling the damaged plaster into buckets and carrying it away down the palazzo stairs. Enzo said he'd arrange for a plumber, an electrician to make the chandelier cable safe and a plasterer to mend the ceiling.

Marco, his dark curls bouncing, set vigorously to work with his broom, raising a choking cloud of dust.

Enzo let out a muffled oath and clipped the boy's ear. 'Marco, you idiot! Use some common sense!' He shook his head and gave a wry smile. 'Nothing but trouble that boy, but I promised his mother I'd give him a second chance.'

Finally the workmen left.

Wearily, I picked up the mop and bucket. 'I'd better start cleaning up.'

Dante took the mop from me. 'Come back to the hotel for dinner. I'll send some of my cleaning staff to deal with this.'

'Oh, I couldn't ask . . .'

'You didn't.' He smiled and wiped a streak of dust off my cheek. 'Your clothes are sodden. Go and change and I'll fetch some help.'

By the time I came downstairs again, three uniformed maids were busy dusting, sweeping and mopping. They looked up from their labours when I asked them where Signor Falcone was.

'In the drawing room, Signora,' said the youngest of the women.

Dante was reading the newspaper in a chair by the fire. 'Thank you, Dante,' I said. 'I'd have been up all night setting this to rights if I'd had to do it by myself.'

'I'm happy to help.'

'Valentina told me my aunt lost most of the servants during the war. I agree with her that this place is too large for only a couple to manage properly. Standards have slipped. My photographic work is time-consuming. I'm trying to capture each season and don't want to miss opportunities because I'm busy scrubbing floors. Do you know of a good domestic staff agency I could speak to?'

'I'll give you an address,' he said. 'Valentina is going to have to rest for a while and it will take time for you to interview suitable applicants. Why don't you borrow one of my maids as a temporary housekeeper until she's recovered? You could have Caterina.

I employed her recently to train as a chambermaid for the new annexe, when it's open. She's young but willing and has been helping out in the kitchens when we're extra busy.'

I felt as if a weight had been lifted from my shoulders. 'Are you sure you can manage without her for a while? I'd pay her wages, of course.'

'I don't need her until the annexe opens and that won't be for a while yet. There's another reason I'd be happy to have her out of the hotel for a while. I've found Enzo's apprentice hanging around her at every opportunity. She's a pretty girl and a bit of an innocent so I don't want Marco attempting to take advantage of her.'

'Certainly not!'

'I've warned him about it but removing her from out of his way for a while is a sensible idea. Shall I call her and you can speak to her?'

Dante brought Caterina to meet me. 'I've explained the situation and she's agreed to work for you for a few weeks, if you find her suitable.' He discreetly returned to the hall, leaving me to speak to the girl.

Caterina, a slim, neat figure in her uniform, stood before me with her hands clasped and her eyes lowered.

'Signor Falcone tells me you're a willing worker?'

'Yes, Signora.'

'I understand you've been helping out in the hotel kitchens?'

She nodded.

'Are you capable of plain cooking? I live alone, apart from Valentina my housekeeper and her husband Jacopo. Simple meals will be perfectly adequate.'

'My mother taught me to cook from a young age,' she said, 'and sometimes I've helped out in the hotel.'

'That's excellent,' I said, relieved. 'I daresay Valentina will be more than happy to advise you on the household routine. Jacopo sees to the fires and any heavy work but you would be required to clean and tidy the rooms that are in use.'

'Yes, Signora.'

'Then welcome to Palazzo degli Angeli, Caterina. There's a room for you on the top floor, near the housekeeper's room. Could you please finish up in the hallway and then prepare a light supper for yourself, Valentina and Jacopo? He can take it up to their room if you tell him it's ready.'

'Thank you, Signora Wyndham.'

'Then I'll tell Signor Falcone we've come to an agreement.' Caterina looked up at me with a flash of her hazel eyes. She was a pretty girl and seemed biddable.

We returned to the hall and Caterina resumed her duties with the dustpan and brush.

Dante offered me his arm and led me back to the hotel for dinner.

Chapter 26

At first, Valentina was ruffled by Caterina's presence and, until I set her mind at rest, suspicious I might be trying to replace her. I was amused to see the young maid carefully deferring to Valentina and meekly accepting her orders. She obediently carried neatly laid trays of dainty dishes up to the invalid's bedroom and before long Valentina was in no hurry to return to her duties. I didn't chivvy her out of her sickbed because Caterina went through the palazzo like a silent tornado, polishing, dusting and tidying until everything gleamed. Dante had found a jewel of a maid for his hotel and I would be sorry to lose her.

Meanwhile, I boxed up the damaged chandelier and took it to Murano to be repaired by a glass manufacturer Dante had recommended. Enzo found a craftsman to repaint the freshly plastered area of the ceiling, to blend in with the original fresco, and the bathroom tap was replaced. I visited a domestic staff agency, who promised to notify me when they had a suitable applicant.

I spent time in my darkroom developing and selecting images to send to my publisher for *The Glory of Venice*. I packaged up the contact prints between sheets of cardboard to protect them and took them to the post office.

Several times a week, a letter arrived for me from one of the convents I'd written to, all telling me what I already knew – that Sofia had never stayed with them. Each letter rubbed salt into a wound that would never heal. There was still no response to my newspaper advertisements.

Now that spring had arrived, I frequently rose before dawn and went out with my camera and folding tripod, before the street beggars had stretched themselves awake in their makeshift beds in doorways. The light was luminous in the early morning when Venice was waking up and the air filled with the aroma of sausages and eels roasting on gridirons, coffee and newly baked bread. I would often warm my hands on a steaming cup of coffee amongst a crowd breakfasting at one of the food stalls. Many people were curious about my camera and happy to pose for me. I photographed a greengrocer building pyramids of cabbages and carrots studded with garlic and onions, fishermen with weather-beaten faces setting up their stalls and gondoliers washing their boats and shaking out the cushions to ready themselves for business.

Whenever I saw a nun, my heart thudded, as I wondered if it might be the one who had watched me from the opposite side of the canal. I knew it was unlikely but, in any case, I made a collection of wonderfully graphic images of nuns in the city.

One afternoon, I laid out my best photographs on the vast table in the dining room to show them to Dante.

'These are truly excellent, Phoebe,' he said. 'Now you've made enlargements, I can see details I might not have noticed before.'

'My enlarger is in London but Signor Tonello has been very helpful and allowed me to use the one in his darkroom.'

'What will you do next?'

'I've sent my publisher some of the small contact prints and I'm pleased to say he approves of the content for *The Glory of Venice*. In fact, I've taken so many photographs that I'll soon have enough for two books. He's agreed to a second entitled *The Faces of Venice*. Photographing the people here going about their daily work fascinates me.'

'How could your publisher *not* like these wonderful photographs?'

'It never does to be complacent,' I said. 'I'll suggest that if there is a dual text in both English and Italian, the book can be sold in both countries.'

Dante picked up an image of a blind ex-soldier in a tattered uniform, holding out a begging cup with his scarred face turned up to the sun. 'Heart-breaking, isn't it?' he said, his tone bleak.

There was pain in his eyes. 'There are many similarly disabled soldiers in London, too,' I said.

'Perhaps people who buy your book will be moved to help others like him?'

'I hope so. There must be charities in Venice for the welfare of ex-soldiers? I'd be happy to make a donation from my royalties.'

Dante lifted my fingers to his lips and kissed them. 'And I could sell the books in my hotel shop.'

'I imagine they'll be popular with tourists as a memento of their stay here.'

'Ask Flavia about suitable charities,' said Dante, smiling 'My sister-in-law has a finger in most pies in this city. You might start your enquiries by showing her your photographs.'

'I could invite her here for lunch, together with her friends. Or perhaps host a party and put the photographs on display?' I laughed, suddenly full of enthusiasm. 'Aunt Lavinia and the Conte used to give wonderful parties here.'

'Legendary!' said Dante.

My smile faded. 'It may be the first and last party I host here.'

'But why? You aren't leaving Venice, are you?' He caught hold of my wrist.

I shook my head and his fingers loosened their grip. 'I want to stay.' And I realised then that, even if Sofia hadn't been in the country, I would want to stay to be near to Dante.

'Good,' he said, letting out his breath.

I wanted to think about what this might mean but now wasn't the right time. 'I meant to tell you about the survey,' I said. 'It went out of my mind with everything that happened: the incident with the bathroom tap and then I was busy with the photographs. The survey showed the foundations of the Palazzo degli Angeli are decaying. I must either sell it to a buyer prepared to spend a great deal of money on it or undertake extensive restoration work myself.'

'But ...' He shook his head. 'How can you be so sure?'

'Cosimo Benedetti commissioned a surveyor to write a report.'

Dante frowned. 'I see. Is his surveyor reliable?'

'Signor Nardone was thorough and the report looked professional.'

'Would you think it rude of me to ask if I might see it?'

'Cosimo has it at the moment but I'll ask him to return it to me. He knows someone who wants to buy the palazzo. It's a low offer but I'd have enough to buy an apartment.'

'Phoebe, the palazzo is a treasure. Don't be persuaded into selling it for a handful of pasta!' Dante ran his fingers through his hair. 'And if you do want to sell, I'd still like an opportunity to buy it.'

'But the place is a liability. I don't want to shift the burden onto your shoulders.'

He flashed a smile. 'Others in this situation wouldn't be as honest as you. In any case, I'd employ another surveyor first, to see if he confirms Signor Nardone's view. I'd have to know what I was taking on.'

'Truthfully, I don't know what to do,' I said. 'I set up a trust fund for my niece and nephew before I knew about the condition of this place so I no longer have the disposable income I did before. And I don't know how much the restoration will cost.' I folded my arms. 'My head knows the palazzo is too large for me but I've grown so fond of it . . .'

'Don't look so worried!' Dante caressed my cheek. 'Put all this aside for a while and plan your party. Will you invite me, too?'

'Of course, if you'd like that. I'd imagined a simple lunch for Flavia, Paola and their friends.'

'Why not be more ambitious? If this might be your first and last party at the palazzo, make it truly memorable!' His face shone with enthusiasm.

I hadn't been able to find Sofia and give her a better life but perhaps I could make a small difference to some of the soldiers who'd returned damaged by the war. 'I don't know many people to invite to a party,' I said, 'but an exhibition of my work would be an excellent way to promote it, while raising money for disabled soldiers, too. The ballroom would be a perfect gallery.'

'I have many business contacts and know people with money to spend,' said Dante. 'And the hotel kitchen could prepare the lunch.'

'That would be marvellous! I used to arrange parties regularly for my husband's business associates and exhibitions for a photographer called Solly Goldman, but my New York address book for florists, vintners and musicians is useless to me here.'

'Again, Flavia will guide you. Why don't you talk to her?' He grinned. 'She'd absolutely love to see inside this place.'

'Thank you, I'll do that.'

'Meanwhile I'll arrange for my surveyor to inspect the palazzo.'

'Thank you, Dante. You've been such a good friend to me since I arrived here.' I slipped my arms around his waist and he kissed me. I knew now that I wanted more than friendship from him but there was time to allow love to grow at its own pace.

I took the finished photographs to the framers and chose a narrow black surround with an ivory mount. Then I enlisted Flavia's help. She was enthusiastic about the idea and took me to Caffè Florian to meet her acquaintance Signora Argento, who was already fund-raising for ex-servicemen.

'My son returned from the war missing an arm and with his lungs weakened by mustard gas,' she said. 'Alfio is a brave boy and has made every effort to find work but no one will take him on.'

'So what is most needed is not merely financial support but some way for these wounded men to earn their own living?' I said.

'Precisely,' said Signora Argento. 'Paid work gives a sense of worth.'

'Then the first step must be to raise awareness of the problem. I'll take more photographs of war veterans to include in *The Faces of Venice* and display them at the reception. Would your son allow me to use him as a subject? And perhaps he knows others in a similar position who might volunteer?'

'I'll ask him.'

Flavia sipped her hot chocolate. 'We should speak to business owners and persuade them to provide work for wounded men, even if it's only part-time.'

'Send me the names of your contacts and I'll invite them to my reception,' I said. 'I'm framing some of my photographs for sale and display and anyone interested in purchasing the books, once they've been published, can leave their name on a list.'

A few days later, I met Alfio Argento and photographed him looking out soulfully from behind the water gate of the Palazzo degli Angeli, to symbolise the unrecognised constraints placed upon him by his wartime experiences. He was an engaging young man who talked freely about his frustration at being unable to find work.

'Despite my limitations,' he said, 'I could perfectly well do clerical work. The problem is that now so many men have returned from the war, most of them more physically able than myself, there isn't enough work to go round.'

'It's very hard for you,' I said.

'I have a dream for the future.' He leaned forward, passion for his cause burning in his dark eyes. 'I want to found an employment bureau where disabled soldiers may register for employment to suit their abilities.'

'That's a very worthwhile ambition. If you come to the reception, you could speak to the gathering and describe your situation. Say that, having made such a sacrifice while fighting for your country, you now need an opportunity to become independent.'

'I'd be happy to do that,' he said.

I had invitations printed for the buffet lunch, exhibition and sale of my work. I asked the printers to include my photograph and a brief biographical note on the back, and stated my intention of making a donation from each sale to the Work for Ex-Soldiers fund.

I was in my study writing addresses on the invitation envelopes when Valentina announced Cosimo's arrival.

'I haven't heard from you,' he said, 'so I've called to see if you've made a decision yet.'

'Decision?'

A flicker of annoyance passed over his face. 'About selling the palazzo.'

'I've been so occupied with my photographic work and planning a reception,' I said, 'that I've pushed thoughts of anything else to the back of my mind.'

'Phoebe, this isn't something you can simply ignore,' he said.

'I know! I'm waiting for another surveyor to inspect the foundations.'

'But you've had a report already!'

He looked so outraged that I raised my eyebrows. 'Dante Falcone is still interested in the palazzo and he prefers to use his own surveyor.'

'That's monstrous! It's tantamount to accusing me of presenting you with false information.'

'No, it's not!'

'Why do you want to sell the palazzo to him? I've found you a buyer already.'

'You said you *thought* you'd found a buyer. And that offer is considerably lower than Dante's. If your buyer's still interested, perhaps he can let me know his highest bid.' I assumed Cosimo was so pressing because he expected to earn a decent introduction fee out of the buyer, if the sale progressed.

His jaw clenched. 'Very well. I'll ask him to write to you.'

'Look, Cosimo, I haven't made any decision yet and I'm currently very busy.' I leafed through a pile of addressed envelopes on the desk and extracted two. 'Here are invitations for you, your sister and her husband, to attend my reception.'

'What kind of reception?'

'I'll be displaying photographs taken for *The Glory of Venice* and another book in the series to be entitled *The Faces of Venice*. I hope to collect pre-publication orders and I'll give a donation from the sale of each book, or photograph, to a charity set up by Signora Argento to raise funds to assist war-wounded and unemployed ex-soldiers.'

'Is that the wife of Orazio Argento, the violinist, by any chance?'

'I expect so. She mentioned her husband performs at La Fenice. He's attending the reception to support his wife and son.'

'My sister thinks highly of Signor Argento.'

'And the chef from Hotel Falcone is going to prepare a buffet with a wonderful centrepiece of shellfish.'

Cosimo gave a bark of laughter. 'Falcone is certainly attempting to ingratiate himself with you, Phoebe.'

'Not at all! I'm pleased to have his help,' I said, remembering the several romantic evenings we'd spent together, planning the event. 'He's given me the names of some influential businessmen to invite, in the hope they'll support the cause. Perhaps you might find it a useful opportunity to make new business contacts?'

'I have perfectly good contacts already.'

'It never hurts to increase your connections,' I said.

Cosimo tucked the invitations into his pocket. 'You're quite right, of course, Phoebe. I'm only annoyed because I don't care to see anyone take advantage of you. I'll see myself out since you're busy but, when this is all over, let me take you out for lunch.' He turned back. 'Oh, by the way, the handle on your garden gate is broken. Another small sign of the lack of regular maintenance here.'

After he'd gone, I picked up my pen. I'd written invitations to everyone now except for Eveline. I wrote her name on one of the cards. She wouldn't thank me for it but at least I couldn't be accused of excluding her.

Chapter 27

On the day of the reception, the ballroom was flooded with sunlight and fresh spring air wafted in through the open windows. I took a moment to enjoy the sense of calm the palazzo instilled in me. Dante had sent his surveyor and I expected his report in a week or so. I knew any renovations he might make to incorporate the palazzo into his hotel would be carried out in good taste. And, if I did sell it to him, I decided that I'd retain my own apartment within it. I wanted to keep my independence while remaining close enough to Dante to give love a chance to flower at its own pace.

The ballroom made an excellent gallery. The Conte's art collection had been temporarily removed from the walls and replaced with my photographs. I walked around the perimeter of the room, checking that each framed image was perfectly straight. I'd grouped the new studies of war-wounded men on one wall and believed they couldn't fail to move the onlooker. The portrait of Alfio looking steadily back at me from behind the wrought-iron water gate, his empty sleeve folded and pinned neatly to his shoulder, struck exactly the right note of vulnerability and bravery.

I moved on to look at the landscapes of Venice through the seasons: pearly mist wreathing the canals, frost tipping the bare twigs of a plane tree in a sunny square and dawn light glinting on the Byzantine domes of the Basilica di San Marco. I anticipated with pleasure adding images of a Venetian summer to the collection.

I straightened the frame of a view of the Giants' Staircase, the imposing flight of stone steps in the Doge's Palace that led up to the landing where doges were crowned. A pile of copies of *Behind the Lines on the Western Front* was displayed on a side table, sent by my publisher and available for sale.

Caterina stepped into the room carrying a pile of freshly ironed napkins. She hesitated when she saw me.

'Come in, Caterina!'

The girl bobbed her head and placed the napkins at one end of the buffet table before retreating as quietly as she'd arrived.

The table was spread with a snowy linen cloth and decorated with vases of irises, tulips and trailing wisteria. Smaller tables, decorated with bowls of sugared almonds and nougat, awaited the guests. Dante's catering staff had brought and arranged the china and glassware earlier.

I walked across the hall, perfumed with more flower arrangements, and glanced up at the newly refurbished crystal chandelier, the sunshine catching it and casting rainbows onto the walls. In the drawing room, the parquet floor gleamed and the centre carpets complemented the pale green panelling and rose-coloured upholstery. I smiled in satisfaction. Everything except the buffet lunch was ready. It was time for me to change.

Later, dressed in a sea-green silk dress and pearls, I went downstairs to the ballroom to wait for the guests. Caterina was leaning forward to study the details of a photograph of a dark and narrow alley lit by a shaft of bright sunlight reflected from the canal at the end. So absorbed was she that she didn't hear my soft tread.

'What do you think of it?' I asked.

She jumped and turned to face me. 'I'm sorry,' she stammered, 'Valentina sent me to check the sofa cushions are plumped up.'

'Do you find the photographs interesting?'

She frowned while she considered her answer. 'I was wondering how you, an Englishwoman, have caught the spirit of Venice so well.' Her cheeks flushed and she dropped her gaze. 'I'm sorry, it's not for me to comment . . .' She turned and walked towards the door.

I called after her. 'Caterina!'

She turned around, her posture rigid.

'Of course you're entitled to have an opinion about the photographs! And, in answer to your question, although I'm English, no doubt Valentina told you I spent seven years of my girlhood here in the palazzo before I married and went away. Returning after so long, I've fallen in love with the city all over again. It's impossibly beautiful, that mixture of grandeur and decay, isn't it?'

Caterine opened her mouth as if to speak then simply nodded and walked away.

The doorbell rang and Valentina hurried through the hall to admit Dante and the catering staff, bringing the food in hampers. He sent them to the ballroom to lay out the buffet, open the red wine and chill the white.

'Let's hope it will loosen our prospective benefactors' purse strings,' said Dante. 'I'd better check on the buffet.' He patted my arm and hurried away.

A moment later Valentina announced Flavia, Signor Argento and his wife and son. Flavia kissed me on both cheeks.

'We're a little early,' said Signora Argento, 'but I wondered if you might need any assistance?'

'Thank you but everything is in hand.'

'When the guests are assembled, if I may, I'll say a few words about the cause? And I understand you've invited Alfio to speak, too.'

'Are you nervous, Alfio?' I asked.

'A little but it's important to me. Besides,' he shrugged, 'once you've been under fire on a battlefield, nothing else can ever be so frightening again.'

Before long Valentina, who still limped when she remembered, was fully occupied with answering the door. Caterina took the guests' coats. Soon after that the hall and ballroom were crowded with chattering guests. Waiters worked their way through the throng with trays, ensuring that everyone had a glass of wine.

I was pleased to welcome Paola, Ines, Amalia and their husbands, who were full of praise for my photographs.

'I'd no idea you were so talented, Phoebe,' said Ines. 'My husband has said he'll buy the view of Piazza San Marco at dawn.'

'That's one of my favourites, too. I'll put a red sticker on it and reserve it for you.'

Cosimo arrived with his sister Livia and her husband Francesco.

'My dear Signora Wyndham,' said Livia, her gaze sweeping around and missing nothing, 'how interesting to see inside the Palazzo degli Angeli. My father used to tell me about it after one of his visits to the Conte di Sebastiano. As a girl I developed quite a fascination with the place.'

'Really?' I said. Over Livia's shoulder, I saw that Eveline had arrived and was talking to Paola. Perhaps I'd be able to have a few quiet words with my sister, to tell her about the trust for her children.

'I used to spend hours imagining what it might be like to live here . . .'

'Livia, don't dwell on old times,' said Cosimo briskly. 'We're here to see the photographs and hear about charitable works.' He smiled at me. 'It's good to see a party at the palazzo again.'

Livia ignored her brother. 'How many staff do you employ? It's so difficult to find good servants these days, isn't it?'

I was relieved when Signora Argento and her husband moved over to join us. 'Signor and Signora Rinaldi,' I said, 'allow me to introduce you to Signor and Signora Argento.'

I slipped away, leaving them discussing music.

Dante returned and greeted me with a kiss on the cheek, murmuring that the buffet was now ready. 'It looks splendid,' he said.

'Bless you, Dante!' I laid a hand on his arm. 'It's reassuring to know that you've thought of everything.'

He grimaced. 'Actually there was a last-minute problem when the fishmonger failed to deliver due to illness. Luckily, his cousin appeared with everything we needed.' He glanced behind me. 'I see Benedetti is looking daggers at me.'

'I mentioned you'd proposed sending in your surveyor to look at the palazzo. He took umbrage at the implied suggestion you didn't trust his man.'

'We'll have to wait and see what the new report finds.'

'Most people have arrived now,' I said, 'and I must introduce Signora Argento and her son.'

'Ready?' asked Dante. I nodded and he clapped his hands and called for attention. The guests turned towards us.

'Welcome to the Palazzo degli Angeli,' I said. 'It's been a great pleasure for me to return to Venice and to capture images of the City of Water in all her moods. I hope you will enjoy looking at the photographs and please come and talk to me if you wish to purchase a framed print or a copy of *Behind the Lines on the Western Front*. Now I'd like to introduce you to Signora Argento, who will tell us about Work for Ex-Soldiers.'

She thanked me for hosting the reception and explained there would be a donation from every sale to support the welfare of wounded men. 'Work for Ex-Soldiers is a cause that's very dear to my heart,' she said, 'since my son Alfio is one of these men. He is far better placed than I to tell you what this cause means to him.'

Alfio stepped forward and smiled at the guests. 'Please will you look at me? Really look at me. So many people can't bear to. What do *you* see?' Briefly he touched his empty sleeve. 'An invalid with a missing arm? Or an ordinary young man who has served his country and now yearns to return to normal life? Or at least as normal as possible. Society has relegated me to the scrapheap but although I've lost my arm, I can still write. And it's a surprise to some, I know, but I can still think for myself too.'

He scanned the room, fixing his gaze upon one person after another. 'I don't want charity,' he said, 'despite my admirable mother's fund-raising efforts. The proceeds must be used for men who are far worse off than I. What I want is to work. I'm not useless and I'm not proud. I'll take any job that I can do – and please let *me* be the judge of my capabilities. I want, need, to earn my keep.'

A ripple of applause followed this declaration.

'I assure you,' continued Alfio, 'that all businesses open-minded enough to offer work to those of us who are disabled by war, will find their new employees loyal and hard-working.'

Someone cheered.

Alfio bowed in acknowledgement.

Dante clapped and the room resounded with ringing applause.

I stepped forward. 'Thank you, Alfio Argento. Now I invite you all to enjoy the buffet lunch and the photographs.'

The crowd chattered amongst themselves as Signora Argento, her eyes shining, came to join Dante and me. 'I'm so proud of my boy.'

'And so you should be,' I said.

Dante nodded. 'An excellent young man and most eloquent. Excuse me while I go and have a word with him.'

Eveline was standing on the other side of the room and I gave her a little wave. She nodded then quickly looked away. I tried not to mind and distracted my thoughts by exchanging pleasantries with various guests.

I was putting red labels on several of the photographs when Cosimo arrived at my side. 'You've sold quite a few, I see.'

'Yes, I'm delighted.'

'Falcone seems very at home here. I noticed he took on the duties of a host without deferring to you.'

'He's been extremely helpful with the arrangements.' I hoped I didn't sound too defensive.

'You shouldn't rely on him too heavily. In my experience, and from some comments that your aunt made, he isn't trustworthy.'

I frowned. 'You've implied that before but without offering any justification.'

He pursed his lips. 'This is neither the time nor the place.'

'If there is something I should know, we will speak of it soon,' I said.

'Indeed. Shall we join the others for lunch?'

Valentina and Caterina were assisting the guests with the buffet. The table was spread with tempting dishes of all kinds but the vast tiered platter of crab claws, prawns, mussels, clams, scallops and smoked eel, bedded onto crushed ice, formed a magnificent centrepiece.

Livia Rinaldi had already heaped her plate with an assortment of delicacies. 'The seafood looks divine,' she said. A piece of smoked eel slipped from her fork but Caterina managed to catch it in a napkin before it fell to the floor.

'Don't be too greedy, Livia,' cautioned Cosimo. 'You know your digestion is delicate.'

'Nonsense! You'd better help yourself before it's all gone.'

'I don't care for shellfish,' he said.

'Signora Wyndham,' said Livia, 'I was wondering why you've taken so many photographs of nuns? Do they hold some special significance for you?'

Nonplussed, I said, 'There are nuns everywhere in Venice. I like to take views that are bustling with people. It adds vivacity to a scene, don't you think?'

'Perhaps.'

I noticed Eveline sitting alone at one of the side tables 'If you'll excuse me, I must speak to my sister.' I made my escape.

I collected two plates of appetising tit-bits from the buffet and threaded my way through the guests towards my sister.

'I'm pleased you came,' I said, placing one of the plates in front of her.

'You seem very thick with Cosimo,' said Eveline, 'as well as Dante Falcone.' She speared a large prawn with her fork. 'Are you trying to make them jealous of each other?'

There was an accusatory tone to her voice that got under my skin like a burr. 'I don't know what you mean!'

'You know Cosimo's only after your money, don't you?'

'I'm not interested in him. Look, Eveline, I've been wanting to speak to you about something but you weren't at home when I called.'

'You surely don't imagine I sit at home all day awaiting your convenience?'

I pressed my fingers over my eyes in exasperation. 'Can we stop bickering for just one moment? This is important.'

Eveline sighed. 'I can't imagine what—'

'Then listen to me and I'll tell you!' I took a deep breath. 'I instructed Cosimo to draw up a trust fund to benefit Carlo and Rosetta. I'd like Carlo to have the opportunity of attending university, if he wishes, and there's an equal sum of money for Rosetta when she attains her majority. I don't want her to be in a position where she might feel obliged to marry for security. She can use the fund to have a degree of financial independence, or she might wish to go to university or set up a business. I want her to be able to make choices about her life.'

Eveline's cheeks flushed a dull red.

'I so nearly found Sofia ...' My mouth trembled. 'It's probably too late for me to help her now but it's not too late to give your children some assistance in finding their way in the world.'

Eveline's hands were clasped so tightly her knuckles were white. 'It's so easy for you, living here in this palazzo and playing Lady Bountiful. I've not had your good fortune and it's painful to see you in a position to give my children what they need, while I—'

Dante arrived, two glasses of wine in his hands. 'Hello, Eveline. May I join you both?'

'I was just about to leave,' she said, standing up.

She didn't look back when I called after her.

'Trouble?' Dante handed me a glass of wine.

'No more than usual.' Why couldn't my sister be gracious, just for once? I picked at my lunch, barely noticing what I was eating.

He stole a little pastry confection from my plate. 'I've invited Alfio to come to the hotel tomorrow, to discuss the possibility of work for him in the hotel office.'

'That's excellent!'

'And more excellent news is that the guests are admiring your photographs and adding their names to the waiting list for your books,' he said.

I put down my fork. 'I should go and talk to them.'

Dante linked his arm through mine and we went to chat with the guests.

247

It was late afternoon and my head ached and I felt queasy by the time the last guest departed. The hotel staff collected the chinaware and glasses lent for the occasion, while Valentina and Caterine restored order.

Dante and I retired to the drawing room with a glass of wine.

'Well,' he said, 'that was a success, wasn't it?'

'Several of the guests bought framed photographs or pre-ordered the Venice books,' I said, 'and Alfio tells me he was involved in some ongoing discussions about employment for disabled soldiers in local businesses.' I sipped my wine and then put the glass down because it suddenly felt uncomfortably acidic in my stomach. 'Today reminded me of the wonderful parties my aunt and uncle used to give. The palazzo came to life again when it was full of guests, exactly as I remember it.'

'It did, didn't it?'

'Aunt Lavinia would have loved it.'

'That's one of the reasons she decided to sell it to me,' said Dante. 'She didn't want to see the Palazzo degli Angeli become a mausoleum. And I can't help thinking what a marvellous hotel it would make,' he said. 'The Hotel Falcone reception area is spacious but just imagine your elegant drawing room as a place for guests to sit quietly without the hustle and bustle of a busy lobby. The ballroom would be perfect for wedding receptions and the dining room would allow us to offer private dining facilities, with a canal view, for family celebrations. And then there's the garden ...'

I listened for several minutes to his enthusiastic plans. With growing dismay, I realised I felt horribly nauseous. 'Dante, please stop!'

His flow of excited chatter ceased abruptly.

'Cosimo says he only wants the best for me,' I said, 'but he keeps pressuring me to sell the palazzo to him before it slips below the surface of the Lagoon. Eveline expected to have it for herself and now she hates me because Aunt Lavinia disinherited her. Now *you* appear to be carrying out plans to continue extending your empire into my palazzo even before I've decided if I want to sell.'

'Phoebe—'

'Let me finish! I may not have the choice of staying here if it's so rotten it can't be restored, but I love it and now I hate the thought of having to leave.' Furthermore, the prospect of returning to my lonely life in London filled me with misery. 'Everyone thinks they know better than I what I want, but I won't allow anyone, not even you, Dante, to steamroller me into selling my home.'

He blinked rapidly and his animation drained away. 'I'm so sorry,' he said. 'My intention was not to hound you to sell. I merely wished to show my earnest desire to support you in your wish to save the palazzo. Like the Contessa, I believe it should be enjoyed by many.' He placed his half-drunk glass of wine on the table. 'Please excuse me. I'm sure you have things to do.'

'Dante—'

'I apologise if I overstepped the mark. I shan't trouble you again.' Stiff-backed, he strode from the room.

I heard the front door close firmly behind him, leaving an echoing silence. My head hurt and my stomach churned unpleasantly. I hadn't meant to upset him after he'd been so kind but it was insensitive of him to rattle on about his plans for my home. Upset and out of sorts, I wandered into the ballroom to collect the list of advance orders for my books.

It was then I discovered that one of the framed photographs had disappeared from the dining-room wall: the image of an unknown nun, studying the palazzo from the far side of the canal.

Chapter 28

Wretched after my contretemps with Dante, I felt too sick to eat any dinner. I went to bed and lay awake, wondering if I'd over-reacted. It also upset and angered me that one of my guests must have stolen the missing photograph. Neither Valentina nor Caterina had seen anything but how on earth had a guest concealed a picture frame about their person without being noticed? I finally fell asleep wondering if one of Dante's staff might have taken it away in a china crate.

In the depths of the night, I awoke with sharp stomach cramps. Shivering, I turned on the bedside light. Nausea made my forehead clammy. Sickness roiled inside me and I made a frantic dash for the bathroom. After a most unpleasant interlude, I crept back to bed and wrapped myself in the blankets. Still nauseous, I revisited the bathroom several times and didn't sleep again until dawn.

It was early afternoon when, heavy-eyed, I went downstairs. Valentina was nowhere to be seen but Caterina was in the kitchen.

'Shall I fetch you something?' she asked.

I shook my head with a grimace. 'A cup of peppermint tea will do.'

The girl looked at me with appraising hazel eyes. 'You are unwell, Signora Wyndham?'

'I was ill during the night.'

'So was Valentina. She remains in bed.' Caterina put the kettle on the range. 'I'll bring the tea to you.'

I picked up the post from the hall and took it into the drawing room. Listlessly, I glanced at the letters. There were a few brief notes thanking me for my hospitality and complimenting me on my photography. Signora Argento thanked me from the bottom of her heart for hosting the reception. She wrote that Alfio had been so excited at the prospect of his forthcoming interview with Signor Falcone that he'd succumbed to a weakness of the stomach.

Frowning, I put the letter down. Was there some gastric infection at large?

I drank the peppermint tea and then went upstairs to tap on Valentina's bedroom door. There was a muffled response and I peeped through the doorway. 'Are you still unwell, Valentina?'

Her complexion was milk-white and there were shadows under her eyes. 'I thought I would die!' She clutched a hand to her tangled hair.

'Tell me, did you eat any of the seafood at the party yesterday?' I asked.

She shifted her position but didn't look at me. 'There was so much left over,' she muttered. 'I don't like waste so I may have nibbled a few morsels.'

'What about Jacopo?'

Valentina shrugged. 'He felt ill for a while but he ate very little.'

'I was ill, too, and so was one of the guests,' I said. 'I suspect it may have been the shellfish. I'd better tell Signor Falcone so he can complain to the fishmonger.' I didn't relish having to speak to Dante so soon after our upsetting exchange the previous afternoon but he ought to know.

A short while later, I walked into the hotel lobby to hear raised voices. Cosimo was banging his fist on the reception desk and shouting at Signor Fortini, the General Manager, who was doing his best to appease him.

Guests were watching, whispering in small groups or peering out from behind their newspapers.

'Get Falcone immediately!' bellowed Cosimo.

'But Signore—'

'Now!'

The office door opened and Dante hurried out. 'What seems to be the matter?' He saw Cosimo and came to a halt.

'My sister is at death's door!' raged Cosimo. 'The buffet you supplied to the Palazzo degli Angeli yesterday was contaminated and it's poisoned her. God only knows what state of filth there must be in your hotel kitchens to make her so ill!'

'Come into my office, Signor Benedetti,' said Dante. 'We can talk it over calmly with some coffee.'

'You don't imagine I'd let anything that comes out of *your* kitchens pass my lips, do you?' he spat. 'Not unless I care to risk my life.' His lips curled in contempt.

I pushed through the small crowd that was gathering to watch the altercation. 'Cosimo?' I said. 'Is Livia going to be all right?'

He covered his eyes with his palms and gave a loud sob. 'It is in the hands of God. All I know is how terribly she suffers. She fell violently ill soon after she ate the food Falcone provided. I fetched a doctor and stayed at her side all night.'

'I assure you,' said Dante, 'our kitchens are spotless. You're welcome to look—'

'I suspect it was a problem with the shellfish, Dante,' I said. 'Valentina, Jacopo, Alfio and I were all ill, too.'

'Four more of you were struck down?' Cosimo turned to address

252

the gathering crowd. 'Do you hear that? Victims are falling like flies! God knows how many more there will be or even if they will survive. I plead with you all: stay away from Hotel Falcone if you value your health!'

White-faced, Dante stepped towards him. 'That's enough!' he said. 'Please come into my office where we can discuss this in a civilised manner.'

'My silence cannot be bought,' said Cosmo grandly. 'I will not rest until all Venice knows about the risks your guests take when they eat in your hotel.'

'Then you will hear from my lawyers if you persist in spreading vile and unfounded rumours.'

'And you'll hear from me again but for now I must return to my sister's sickbed.' Cosimo grasped my hand. 'Come, my darling. You must rest and recover your health.'

Dante stared at our clasped hands and a muscle flexed in his jaw. 'Don't let me keep you.'

'Dante—' I said.

'Don't let me keep *either* of you.'

I was distressed by the flinty expression in his eyes and angered by Cosimo's blatant attempt to imply close familiarity with me. Flustered, I failed to snatch my hand from his grip before Dante turned on his heel. He disappeared into his office and the door closed with a sharp click.

Dismayed, I wondered whether to follow him.

The hotel manager shepherded the guests back to their armchairs with offers of free drinks and Cosimo caught my hand again and led me away.

I shook myself free from his grip. 'Let me go! Was it absolutely necessary to make such a scene in front of Dante's guests?' I asked. 'Comments like that could do a great deal of harm to the hotel's reputation.'

Cosimo pinched the bridge of his nose. 'I've been awake all night, frightened my sister was going to die. Perhaps I over-reacted a little but the hotel guests must be made aware of the danger.'

'I daresay the shellfish, which didn't come from the hotel's usual supplier, caused the sickness rather than any lack of hygiene.'

'We can't know that and hotel kitchens are notoriously dirty.' His tone softened. 'Are you quite recovered, Phoebe?'

'Thankfully, I didn't eat much of the buffet.' I recalled Livia's loaded plate and remembered Cosimo's comment about her deli-cate stomach. Perhaps it wasn't surprising she'd been so ill, after she'd overindulged like that.

We went downstairs to the landing stage.

'I apologise if I've annoyed you.' He cleared his throat. 'It's so hard to say nothing when I know how much harm that man has caused.'

'It may have been the fishmonger's fault—'

'That isn't what I was referring to. Phoebe, I care for your safety and happiness and it's hard to stand back and watch you fall under Falcone's spell when I know him to be calculating and devious.'

'That's not true! And I'm perfectly able to look after myself.'

'You think you are.' He sighed heavily. 'I have a gondola waiting for me. I promised Livia I'd return soon.'

'Please send her my best wishes.'

'Thank you. May I call on you tomorrow? If you're quite recov-ered, we might take a boat to the Lido and have lunch at the Hôtel des Bains?'

'Let's wait and see how Livia is,' I said. I was too distressed by the deepening rift between myself and Dante to anticipate such an outing with any pleasure.

Cosimo kissed my hand, his dark gaze fixed upon my face.

'Until tomorrow.' He boarded the gondola and waved as the boat glided into the canal.

It was as I turned to walk back to the palazzo water gates that I saw something beneath the landing stage. I crouched down to peer at it and, as the canal undulated with the wash from a passing boat, the item bobbed up and down. Unable to believe what I was seeing, I kneeled on the timber decking and pulled it from the water. There was no doubt now: it was my missing photograph, the hastily taken shot of the nun I'd seen across the canal, her habit and veil blowing in the wind. The frame was damaged and the water-soaked print curled away from the warped mount. Seething with indignation at such an act of vandalism, I took it into my darkroom and placed it on the workbench.

I went into the palazzo and was crossing the hall when I heard a noise in my study.

Caterina was standing on the desk chair in front of the bookcase. She held a ledger in her arms but another had fallen to the floor, scattering pages far and wide.

'What are you doing, Caterina?'

The girl flushed scarlet. 'I was ... I was dusting.'

'Then where's your duster? Have you been prying through my files?'

She scrambled down from the chair but lost her balance and fell, sprawling on the rug.

I hurried to help her. 'Are you hurt?'

She shook her head.

'Valentina must have told you that I prefer to clean my study myself?'

She turned away and reached up to straighten her maid's cap.

I stared at her. Her nose was straight and her chin pointed. I gasped when I realised the significance of what I was seeing. It was the same profile I'd seen only minutes before in the shot of the nun who'd watched me from across the canal.

I froze, my heart beating so rapidly it felt as if it would burst out of my chest. I looked into Caterina's defiant hazel eyes – a duplicate of Lorenzo's. 'Sofia?' I whispered. 'Is it you?'

Her mouth trembled.

I let out a sob of joy. 'My darling girl, I've been searching everywhere for you! But in the end, you came to find me.'

'Angelina told me where you lived, here in your fine palazzo.'

I reached out to her, desperate to hold her in my arms.

'Get away from me!' she hissed.

Her words were like a bucket of cold water thrown over me when all I longed for was to give her my unconditional love. 'But—'

'Don't touch me!'

'Don't you understand?' I said. 'I'm your mother, Sofia.'

'No, you're not! You discarded me at birth as if I were no more than a piece of rubbish. And all to save your reputation. Angelina Vianello was my mother but ...' Her eyes filled with tears. 'I discovered even she didn't love me in the end.'

'She did! Of course she did. Your foster parents have *never* stopped loving you.'

'They only took me for the money and they *lied* to me all my life. And then they let that hateful woman take me away.' Sofia's voice rose to a wail. 'Why didn't they stop her? If they loved me, how could they have allowed me to be imprisoned in that place, where I starved and shivered and was humiliated every day?'

There was an ache in the back of my throat. My child had been so desolate and I hadn't been there to help her. 'Angelina and Luigi didn't want to let you go but they had no legal rights. The woman who took you away was your grandmother.'

Sofia's indrawn breath shuddered in her breast. 'My own flesh and blood? But she despised me. She said I must suffer to atone for my mother's sins. And I did suffer,' she sobbed. 'I was humiliated and so miserable, every single day, all because you abandoned me.'

'Oh, my dearest!' I swallowed back my tears. My own misery had been nothing compared to my daughter's agonies.

'I found work at the hotel so I could be near you.'

My heart was bursting. 'Sweetheart, I promise I'll do everything I can to make it up to you. Why didn't you tell me sooner who you are? All I want is for you to be happy again.'

'Happy?' she said. 'I'll *never* be happy again. I don't want to be with you but I knew I'd never rest unless I saw you. I needed to understand what kind of unnatural woman could abandon her own helpless baby. Why did you do it?'

'I didn't! You were taken from me. And more than anything in the world, I want you by my side.'

'I watched you playing the part of the grand lady here in your palazzo. You showed no sign of guilt about your immoral past or regret for the baby you abandoned. I watched you acting the gracious hostess and offering charity to wounded soldiers.' She laughed harshly. 'But I *know* you for what you really are.' She pointed a finger at me. 'You're a wicked, selfish woman without a shred of compassion, not even for your own child.'

'You're wrong! So very wrong.'

Sofia put her hands over her ears. 'No more lies!' she screamed. 'I can't stand it any more. I wish I were dead!'

'Listen to me . . .'

Her face was twisted with hatred as she rushed at me with outstretched hands and thumped me in the chest.

I staggered backwards and tripped over the fallen desk chair.

Sofia darted out of the door into the hall.

Scrambling to my feet, I rushed after her, running down the stairs two at a time and following her out into the garden. The back gate slammed in my face as I reached it. I wrenched at the handle and it came loose in my hand. I gave the gate several hefty kicks but it wouldn't budge.

My daughter's running footsteps faded away down the alleyway.

Chapter 29

I sprinted inside and shouted for Valentina.

Still in her dressing gown, she came to see what I wanted.

'Caterina and I had a misunderstanding,' I said. 'She was very upset and ran away so I'm going to search for her.'

'A misunderstanding?'

Hesitating, I said, 'I found her in my study looking through my files. I was angry.'

Valentina shrugged. 'I've noticed she's very inquisitive about you and the palazzo. She asks questions all the time.'

'If she returns, will you try to persuade her to stay?' I took a panicky breath. What if I never saw Sofia again? Then there would never be the chance to explain that I'd been as much a victim as she had. 'Are you well enough to go to the hotel and speak to Signor Falcone, in case she returns there?'

Valentina nodded.

'And tell Jacopo to mend the garden gate. I asked him to fix the handle ages ago.'

I hurtled out of the palazzo and ran through the city streets and alleys. There was a knot of dread in my stomach as hard as a brick. I remembered my own heightened emotions at Sofia's age. The note of hysteria in her voice had made me fear she might harm herself.

Halting on the crest of each bridge I came to, I rapidly scanned the canals and walkways for Sofia, before racing down another street. My feet were sore and the breath harsh in my throat as I darted into the railway station to ask at the ticket office if they'd sold anything to a young maid.

Later, I stopped pedestrians in Piazza di San Marco to ask if they'd seen her – surely everyone turned up there at some point? They backed away from me, as if my anguish might be catching. I glanced into churches and shops and hurried through street markets but there was no sign of my daughter.

When darkness fell, I sank down onto the steps at the foot of the Rialto Bridge. Exhausted and heartbroken, I buried my head in my hands and sobbed. All I wanted was to ask Sofia for her forgiveness and heal the rift between us.

At last, I pushed myself up again and hobbled homewards on blistered feet.

When I arrived at the palazzo, Valentina must have been looking out for me because she opened the front door and led me into the drawing room, all the while pouring out a flow of exclamations and expressions of concern. She sat me down and bustled off to warm chicken soup.

I eased off my shoes and closed my eyes but I couldn't shut out the memory of the hatred in Sofia's eyes. Rubbing my cheeks, itchy with dried tears, I heard the door open. Expecting Valentina, I started when I opened my eyes and saw Dante.

'Caterina is safe,' he said.

Relief and exhaustion made me burst into tears. 'Thank God! I've been searching all over the city for her. Sit down, won't you, and tell me how she is?'

'I'll remain standing,' said Dante. He glanced at my blistered feet and torn stockings but his face might have been carved from granite. 'Enzo was working at the back of the new annexe when he saw her hurtling along the rear alleyway. He guessed something was very wrong and ran after her, which was just as well because she threw herself in the canal.'

Shock coursed through my body and I reared to my feet, momentarily unable to speak. My fears had been realised.

'Enzo pulled her out and carried her back to the hotel,' continued Dante. 'Fortunately, she's as well as can be expected after swallowing a bucket of canal water. She was utterly overwrought. The housekeeper put her to bed and I called a doctor. She's expected to make a physical recovery but he's concerned about her mental state. I've instructed that one of the chambermaids is to stay with her at all times.'

Light-headed, I sank down onto the chair again. 'May I sit with her?'

'I hardly think that's advisable in the circumstances, do you?'

His voice was so cold that I shivered.

'What happened to cause her such anguish?' he asked.

I folded my arms defensively over my chest. 'I found her in my study, looking through my private files.' How could I possibly tell him the whole truth? At least, not while he was looking at me with such contempt. 'I was angry,' I said, 'and she ran away.'

'Angry? Is that all?' His gaze bored into me.

I hesitated, wondering if I should tell him everything, but then I nodded.

'Caterina is a hard-working and conscientious girl. You must have been exceedingly harsh to drive her to attempt to drown herself. She fought Enzo like a wild cat when he pulled her out of the water.'

'I believe she was already upset about something else,' I said. 'Perhaps my anger exacerbated her distress.'

'I'm sure you'll understand when I tell you her emotional state is too fragile for her to return to your employ.' He gave me a pointed look. 'And I will protect her from visitors, any visitors, unless she chooses to see them.'

My face burned, knowing he blamed me. 'I had no intention of causing her any harm,' I protested. 'Quite the reverse.'

'Unfortunately, whether you intended it or not, the result is the same. It's shocked me to discover how volatile your temperament can be. I had thought better of you but now I understand how it was you became estranged from your family.' He walked towards the door.

'Dante!'

Frowning, he turned back.

'I apologise if I gave you the impression I'd definitely sell the palazzo,' I said, 'and realise you spent money on the survey. I was feeling horribly nauseous when I snapped at you but I still haven't made a final decision. And about Cosimo Benedetti, I'm so sorry—'

He turned away, as if he couldn't bear to look at me. 'Don't embarrass either of us. What you do with your palazzo, as you've made perfectly clear to me, is absolutely no concern of mine. And neither are your close friendships.'

'Cosimo shouldn't have made such a disturbance in your hotel.'

'It's far too late for you to apologise on his behalf. The damage to my hotel's reputation is done.' He strode through the doorway, narrowly missing Valentina as she carried in some soup on a tray.

Unsurprisingly, I barely slept. My heart ached, knowing Sofia was lying in bed next door, anguished and despairing. It was unbearable that my precious daughter had attempted to drown herself rather than live with the torment of what she imagined was my desertion of her, followed by the betrayal of her foster parents and grandmother.

The long hours of darkness trapped me in my miserable thoughts. I remembered now that Lorenzo had been wiser than I when he warned me Sofia might not welcome us into her life.

I went downstairs in the small hours to brew a tisane but the range had gone out. Wrapping myself in a blanket, I curled up on the window seat in the drawing room, waiting for the sun to rise. If there was to be any further chance of becoming close to Sofia, I'd have to take it slowly. The truth was, we shared the same blood but none of the memories of a life together that were the foundation of the loving bond between a mother and daughter.

Eventually, the sky began to lighten and I watched the sun rise. The beauty of the dawn dulled the edge of my pain. When boats began going about their business on the canal, I unfolded myself from the window seat. It was time for me to face the world.

Later, somewhat restored by a cup of strong coffee, I remembered Cosimo was hoping to take me out to lunch, though all I wanted was to see if Sofia would talk to me.

I waited impatiently until mid-morning, to give her a chance to rest and have breakfast, and then I went to Hotel Falcone.

Dante was by the reception desk talking to the hotel manager when I arrived. He glanced up and took a step back when he saw me.

I gripped my hands together. 'I came to find out if Caterina is feeling any better?'

'She passed a troubled night. The housekeeper gave her some of the sleeping draught the doctor prescribed.' His eyes didn't meet mine.

'May I talk to her when she wakes? I want to apologise for upsetting her.'

'I can't answer that. She's likely to sleep for most of the day. I'll send a message if she's prepared to speak to you. Now, if you'll excuse me?' He walked into his office and closed the door.

I left, my face burning with humiliation, and returned to the palazzo.

I attempted to write to Sofia but threw four different versions into the wastebin. I'd thought it would be easier to explain in a letter what had happened when she was born, but it wasn't. I needed to speak to her in person and attempt to gain her trust.

I wrote to Lorenzo to tell him Sofia had been found but that she'd been so angry and hurt she'd tried to drown herself. I promised to write again if I had better news.

I was sealing the envelope when Cosimo, looking very dapper, arrived with a large bunch of freesias and roses for me.

I buried my nose in their heady perfume. 'How lovely. Is Livia better today?'

'Improving but very weak. Falcone has a lot to answer for.'

'I'm not sure he should be blamed,' I said.

'That's a matter of opinion.' He smoothed his hair, as black as a raven's wing. 'You're still very pale. How about a little outing to Hôtel des Bains for lunch?'

'I don't think I—'

'The weather is clement and the boat trip across the Lagoon will make you feel better,' he said. 'Perhaps we might venture along the seafront after lunch?'

'It's kind of you but I really don't feel up to it.'

His face fell. 'How disappointing! Another time perhaps?'

I nodded. 'I'll spend the day wrapping the prints I sold at the reception, ready for Jacopo to deliver.'

'Did I tell you how impressed I was by your photographs?' He gave me an appraising look. 'Somehow I hadn't expected such a decorative lady to be a talented photographer, too. Work like yours demands a high level of technical competence, doesn't it?'

'I've practised hard to improve my skills,' I said, trying not to be irritated by his condescension.

'I'd be fascinated to see your darkroom. Perhaps you might show me?'

'If you're interested,' I said. It would pass the time since I wouldn't know until later if Sofia would speak to me.

I led Cosimo to the *portego*, unlocked the darkroom door and stood back to let him enter.

He turned to face me, one hand held to his nose. 'What a strong chemical odour! Isn't it bad for you to work in such an atmosphere?'

I turned on the light switch and then stopped abruptly in the doorway. My carefully arranged bottles of developing solutions lay smashed on the floor and the new sink and tap had been wrenched off the wall, leaving water gushing from the pipework. The table and workbench had been turned over and ashes from the brazier scattered over the whole mess. Stunned, I read the words scrawled in chalk on the black-painted wall.

LEAVE VENICE NOW!

Cosimo took it all in, his face expressionless. 'Dear God! I take it that it wasn't you who had a fit of temper in here?'

I shook my head, too shocked to speak.

'This is monstrous!'

I stepped over the stream running across the floor from the damaged pipe and picked my way through the broken developing tanks, pools of chemicals, sodden paper and splintered wood.

'Everything's ruined!' I pressed a fist to my mouth. What distressed me most was the vindictive nature of the attack. This wasn't random mischief-making by young hooligans. The writing on the wall was a deliberate attempt to frighten me away.

Cosimo righted the overturned brazier and grimaced as he wiped his fingers on his handkerchief.

The shutter hung from one hinge and I pulled it aside to study the window set high up in the wall. 'Even a child couldn't have squeezed through here and there's only one key to the door, which I keep with me. Who on earth could have done such a wicked thing?'

I went cold at the thought that Sofia might hate me enough to take this revenge on me. Then I remembered I'd brought the photograph I'd pulled out of the canal into the darkroom only minutes before I'd discovered her in the study. Everything had been in order then. And later, after Sofia had tried to drown herself, she'd been in no fit state to cause such destruction.

Cosimo called to me from the corner of the darkroom. 'Phoebe, have you seen this? There's a door.'

'I'd forgotten about that,' I said. 'It leads into the Hotel Falcone's furniture store. Dante wasn't aware it was there but said he might have a key for it in his office.'

'Then I'm very much afraid that's your answer.'

'What is?'

He pointed at the chalked words scrawled on the wall. 'It's obvious. Falcone has the key to the door and he wants to frighten you away so he can buy the palazzo.'

'But ...' I shook my head. 'He wouldn't! We're friends.' But *were* we still friends?

'He didn't look very friendly towards you yesterday,' said Cosimo, echoing my thoughts. 'Oh! Don't look so woebegone. Come here!'

I found myself firmly enfolded in his arms.

He patted my back. 'It's hard for a woman alone in the world to realise it when a man is flattering her purely for his own gain. I know you don't want to hear this but Falcone wormed his way into the Contessa's affections, too. And now he's attempting the same trick with you.'

'I'm sure Aunt Lavinia wouldn't have fallen for that.'

Cosimo sighed. 'I've tried to warn you about him. Did you know he persuaded, or perhaps frightened, the old lady who lived in the house behind his hotel to sell to him? Everyone knew she didn't want to leave but now he's converting it into an annexe. He'll stop at nothing, not even murder, to fulfil his ambitions.'

'*Murder*?' I pushed myself away from him.

'Your aunt became very anxious. It was not so surprising – a single lady rattling around in a huge old palazzo all alone.'

Involuntarily, I shivered.

'You might well tremble, my dear. She was an independent lady, like you, but a few days after she changed her will, she sent me a note, imploring me to come immediately because she thought there was an intruder. Valentina and Jacopo were away so she wrote that she'd wait for me in the alley behind the palazzo.'

'Why didn't she run to the hotel for help?'

'It's significant that she didn't, don't you think?'

'Surely she wasn't afraid of Dante?'

Cosimo shrugged. 'Anyway, I ran straight there and accompanied her inside but I didn't find any intruder.'

'She imagined it?'

'I didn't say that. I believe someone was attempting to frighten her into leaving.'

'I can't believe Dante—'

Cosimo kicked aside a piece of shattered glass. 'Evidence of the lengths he'll go to is here, right under your feet.'

Uncertainly, I glanced around at the mess. 'Murder is an entirely different matter.'

'Indeed it is. I promised to call on the Contessa the following day to be sure she'd recovered from her fright. Since I had to visit my warehouse, I came to the palazzo in the *sandolo* I keep there. The Contessa had said she'd unlock the water gate and meet me at eleven o'clock.'

'And did she?'

'As I approached the palazzo, I saw her on the landing stage. Suddenly, she jerked forward and fell into the water. Falcone was behind her on the landing stage.'

I caught my breath in disbelief. 'You can't think he pushed her?'

'I didn't see that but I shouted to him to help the Contessa and rowed towards her as fast as I could. She was floundering in the water and there was blood on her forehead. I didn't wait to moor the boat or remove my jacket but dived straight in. I grabbed hold of her but she was so terrified she tried to fight me off. And then Falcone jumped in beside us.'

'He said he saved her.'

'That's a lie! He punched me in the face and I was so shocked, I let go of the Contessa. Falcone pushed me underwater. When I surfaced again, coughing and choking, I'd drifted away but was close enough to see he was holding the Contessa's head under the water. By the time I'd caught my breath and swam back to them, he'd dragged her onto the jetty.' Cosimo's face was expressionless. 'She was dead.'

My gorge rose and I covered my mouth. 'But he wouldn't ...
You say you *saw* him drown her?'

'He called the police.' Cosimo's lips thinned. 'A clever move
because it drew suspicion away from himself. He denied the
murder and tried to blame me. I had a black eye from his punch
and there were no witnesses to corroborate my side of the story. I
don't know if he bribed the police but, in the end, they decided it
was an accident. I considered whether to take the matter further
but, without witnesses, it would be impossible to prove anything.'
He ran a finger around the inside of his collar, as if it felt too tight.
'You understand now why I was anxious about your friendship
with Falcone and why I tried to warn you against him?'

'But what would Dante gain by drowning Aunt Lavinia? She'd
decided to sell him the palazzo.'

'She'd told me she'd changed her mind.'

'But why?' I asked.

'She was frightened. And who was the intruder in the palazzo?' He shrugged. 'Well, you've discovered that for yourself
now. Falcone has a key and could come and go as he pleased
through this store room. And now he's destroyed your darkroom
to frighten you away. As I said, he'll stop at nothing to get his
hands on this place, decaying or not.'

I couldn't grasp the idea that Dante had murdered Aunt
Lavinia. Everything I'd thought was true was a lie. Suddenly
dizzy, I began to shiver uncontrollably and black spots floated
before my eyes.

Cosimo caught me as my knees buckled. He supported me
into the garden and sat me on the bench. Chafing my icy hands,
he said, 'You've had a shock. I'll call your housekeeper to tend to
you and then arrange for a plumber to cap off the water. Jacopo
can fix some stout timber over the door to the hotel and you'll be
quite safe, but keep all the gates locked.'

'Thank you,' I murmured.

'Will you be all right for a few minutes while I fetch Valentina?'

I nodded and he'd hurried away before I realised he'd dropped a kiss on my forehead.

Chapter 30

Valentina made me a tisane and insisted that I lie on the sofa until I'd stopped shaking. My thoughts went round and round like a rat trapped in a barrel. Dante had lied to me all along, his honey-coated words working their charm on me just as they had on Aunt Lavinia. Once he'd realised I might not sell him the palazzo, he'd dropped all pretence of affection for me. I'd sworn I would never allow myself to fall in love again but I'd been foolish enough to forget that.

Dante had been exposed as a murderer and now Sofia was in his care. If he was prepared to destroy my darkroom, what might he do to her if he discovered she was my daughter? I sat up and smoothed down my skirt. I would have to confront him about Cosimo's allegations but, first, I must persuade him to let me speak to Sofia and bring her back to the palazzo and safety.

I went straight to Hotel Falcone. At the reception desk, I approached Signor Fortini. 'May I speak to Signor Falcone?'

He didn't greet me in his usual friendly way but said abruptly, 'He is not here.'

'Please send someone to find him for me.'

'He's out of the hotel for the afternoon but he left a note for you, Signora Wyndham.' He handed me an envelope.

Signora Wyndham,
    I have spoken to Caterina and she does not wish to talk to you under any circumstances. Please <u>do not</u> attempt to contact her, either in person or by letter, as she is still in a state of distress. My staff have clear instructions that you are not to be allowed to enter this hotel again without my express permission.

Dante Falcone

I crumpled up the note, burning with anger and hurt. To think I'd imagined myself in love with him! Head held high, I stalked out.

I returned to the palazzo and called for Jacopo.

He appeared from the kitchen, his mouth full.

'Where will I find the police station, Jacopo?'

He swallowed. 'Piazza San Marco. Is something wrong, Signora?'

I shook my head and ran upstairs to fetch my coat.

I took a vaporetto. When I arrived at Piazza di San Marco, I asked a passer-by to direct me to the police station where I explained that I wanted to speak to the officers who had been called to the scene after Aunt Lavinia drowned. After waiting for what seemed like an interminable time, I was called into a cubby-hole of an office with a name plate on the door inscribed *Commissario Mazza*.

Mazza, a thin man with weary eyes, glanced up from a pile of paperwork. 'Signora Wyndham? I understand the Contessa di Sebastiano was your aunt and you wish to make an enquiry about her death?'

'Yes,' I said. 'She drowned last October, before I arrived in

Venice. Please can you tell me what happened when you questioned Signor Falcone and Signor Benedetti afterwards?'

Mazza opened a file and scanned the contents. 'I remember now. Falcone, a hotelier, called us to the scene. He accused Benedetti of drowning the Contessa but it was clear straight away that there was long-standing animosity between the two men.'

'That's still the case,' I said.

'Falcone admitted he'd punched Benedetti in the eye. He said it was because Benedetti failed to pull the Contessa from the water quickly enough. Falcone then dragged the lady onto the jetty but by that time she was dead.'

'And there were no witnesses, Commissario?'

He shook his head. 'Other boats arrived at the scene shortly afterwards but no one had seen anything suspicious. The two men had to be held apart when each accused the other of murdering the Contessa.'

'I was told she'd slipped.'

'We found marks on the jetty indicating that. There was also a trace of blood, corresponding to her head wound. We concluded that after suffering an accidental blow, the Contessa was knocked unconscious and then drowned. Falcone and Benedetti, a hitherto respectable lawyer, used the accident as an excuse to cause trouble for each other.'

'I see,' I said. 'And you're sure Signor Falcone didn't drown the Contessa?'

Commissario Mazza shrugged. 'I have told you our findings, Signora.'

I left, still turning everything over in my mind. I kept remembering the righteous anger in Cosimo's voice when he recounted how Dante had drowned Aunt Lavinia. Furthermore, he was a respected lawyer and, even if the police disbelieved him, would hardly lie about something as serious as murder.

Still, I had no real reason, despite Dante's unpleasant note to me, to believe Sofia was in imminent danger from him. The thought that I might make her even more distressed if I attempted to comfort her was painful to me. All I could do was to wait and hope she would allow me to speak to her when she felt better.

I arrived back at the palazzo and saw the light in my darkroom was on and the door ajar. Inside, the floor had been swept clear of the shards of glass and damaged equipment, the water pipe capped off and entry to the hotel basement barred by oak planks screwed securely to the door frame. The splintered workbench had gone and the table was upright again. Several of the glass plate holders had remained unscathed and were stacked on the table, along with a single undamaged developing tray.

The door creaked behind me and Jacopo stood in the doorway. 'I tidied up as much as I could,' he said.

'I'm grateful to you for saving me from an upsetting task,' I said.

He shook his head. 'So much destruction. Valentina scrubbed those words off the wall.'

I shuddered at the memory. 'At least my camera and glass slides are safe,' I said. 'It's too damp to keep them in here so they're in my wardrobe. Everything else but those can be replaced and I can make new prints.'

'God is merciful,' said Jacopo.

I went inside and Valentina came to greet me.

'Several letters arrived for you while you were out.' She handed me a clutch of envelopes.

I went into the study and read the notes with dismay. All were from guests at the reception who had been struck down with food poisoning. I wrote a reply to each of them, apologising and mentioning that an unknown fishmonger had supplied the shell-fish. Despite all that had happened, it wasn't fair for Dante to be blamed for this.

Then I attended to the painful task of writing to Angelina and Luigi Vianello, to tell them I'd found Sofia but that she'd been too angry and distressed to allow me to explain that I hadn't abandoned her. I promised to let them know if anything changed. After sealing the envelopes, I took them to Jacopo and asked him to post them.

I felt restless and went to sit in the garden. The last thing I'd wanted had been to come to Venice but in the past few months here I'd discovered I had a living but lost child. I'd met Lorenzo again and laid the ghost of our long-ago romance. I'd made friends, fallen in love with Dante and decided to make the palazzo my home. Now, everything had changed once again.

I'd found Sofia, but she despised me. The man I'd grown to love was probably a murderer. If I remained in the palazzo, my life might be endangered. Lastly and unsurprisingly, my impoverished sister hated me for inheriting the palazzo. I felt utterly alone and miserable at being at odds with those I cared for. I couldn't bear it. Something had to change.

Then, all at once, it was perfectly clear to me what I must do. I couldn't solve all the problems I faced but, in the end, *nothing* was more important than family.

I was sensible enough to sleep on my decision but, in the morning, hadn't changed my mind. After breakfast, I set off for Campo Santa Margherita. As I approached Cosimo's office building, the front door opened and a young man hurried out. He paused on the step to tuck a fat envelope into his pocket before hurrying away.

Puzzled, I watched him go. It was Marco, Enzo's curly-haired apprentice.

Cosimo's secretary ushered me inside and minutes later his employer welcomed me into his office.

'My dear Phoebe!' He kissed my cheeks. 'This is an unexpected pleasure. I had planned to come and call on you later today, to see if you'd recovered from your shock.'

'It was upsetting,' I said, 'but at least my camera and the glass negatives weren't damaged. The darkroom is too damp for me to store them there.'

'That was an unexpected stroke of luck for you,' he said. 'So there's nothing to stop you completing *The Glory of Venice*? I'd wondered if you might have lost heart after so much was destroyed . . . if maybe you'd return to London?'

'I'm not sure yet. Meanwhile, I've come to ask for your assistance in writing my will.'

'You're still young,' said Cosimo, 'but it's an excellent idea to have your affairs in order. You never know what is around the corner.'

I pictured Aunt Lavinia drowning right outside her home and a chill of fear ran down my spine. 'There's something I have to tell you before you prepare the document.' I hesitated, buying time as I ran my finger over a bronze statuette of Mercury displayed on Cosimo's desk. 'It's an extremely delicate situation,' I said. 'Can you assure me that I may speak to you in the strictest confidence?'

'But of course!'

I swallowed. 'I wish my estate to be shared equally between Eveline and . . .'

'Your sister? Phoebe, are you *quite* sure about that?'

'Yes, I am.'

He puffed out his cheeks. 'It's your decision, of course.' He drew a sheet of paper towards him and wrote down Eveline's name. 'And your other heir?'

'Sofia Vianello.'

'And she is?'

I was unable to meet his eyes. 'Sofia is my daughter.'

He dropped his pen with a clatter. 'Your *daughter*? But you said you and your husband were childless.'

'We were.' Despite my embarrassment, I forced myself to look at him. 'Sofia is seventeen years old and the result of a youthful liaison. It wasn't until I returned to Venice after my aunt died that I discovered that my baby, who I'd been told was stillborn, had in fact survived. As you can imagine, it was a great shock to me but the discovery also filled me with joy. I'd thought I would never have a child.'

Cosimo pressed his palms to his cheeks, seemingly struck dumb. Then he drew a deep breath. 'Where is she now?'

'At the Hotel Falcone.'

'But why?'

'It's a long story. Sofia was sent to live in a convent but recently she came to find me.' I outlined for him what had happened.

'She doesn't want to know you,' said Cosimo, frowning, 'but you still want to make her your beneficiary?'

'Through no fault of her own, my daughter's life has been unhappy. It's the least I can do for her. If she'd allowed me, I'd have taken her in and loved her and made sure she came to no more harm ...' My voice broke and I fumbled for a handkerchief. 'I would do anything, anything at all, to have my daughter restored to me.'

'My dear Phoebe!' Cosimo hurried around the desk, proffered his handkerchief and patted my back. 'What a dreadfully painful situation this must be for you and you've had to bear it all alone.' He pursed his lips. 'Does Eveline know about her?'

His compassion and lack of censure made the tears flow faster. It took a minute or two for me to regain my composure. 'Eveline knew I'd had a baby but not that she'd survived. I only told her that very recently.'

'It must have been a shock for her, too.'

'It was. And there's something else, Cosimo. I've come to the sad decision that I must sell the palazzo.'

He drew in his breath sharply. 'You won't sell it to Falcone, will you?'

'Not after what you told me about him. Eveline and Sofia will be my beneficiaries but, as soon as the palazzo is sold, I want them to share the proceeds. They are both in great need of financial security. You said you had a buyer in mind?'

Cosimo drummed his fingers on the arm of his chair. 'Yes. I'll have to . . .' He seemed distracted. 'Funds will need to be arranged and another property sold. I don't know how quickly . . .'

'What is it, Cosimo?'

'You've forced my hand.' Running his fingers through his hair, he said, 'I'd planned to ask you later, in quite different circumstances, but now . . .' He kneeled down beside me and took my hand in his. 'You must know how much I admire you, Phoebe? You're so unlike any other woman I've ever met. Headstrong perhaps, but so clever and beautiful. I confess, you've completely swept me off my feet. I don't delude myself that you might love me as I love you, but perhaps, in time, I might persuade you to care for me a little?'

I caught my breath in a mixture of astonishment and confusion.

'Phoebe, dearest Phoebe, will you marry me?'

'I . . . Cosimo,' I stammered, 'this is so unexpected. I never imagined . . . especially since only minutes ago I told you I have a child born out of wedlock.'

'A youthful mistake.' He kissed her hand. 'Once Sofia is over her shock and comes to know you, she'll be sure to love you. And if you become my wife, I'd gladly welcome her into our home. Who knows? Perhaps we might even have children of our own.' His expression was wistful. 'How I would love a son.'

My pulse raced. I'd had no idea he had such feelings for me. I'd been so caught up in my attraction to Dante that I'd never looked at Cosimo in that way.

'Phoebe?' His gaze was fixed on my face.

'But, Cosimo,' I said, 'if it becomes known that Sofia is my love child, it will bring shame down upon us all.'

He pulled his chair to my side and we sat with our knees touching. 'It need not,' he said, 'though a little subterfuge might be necessary. Perhaps we might say Sofia is your ward, the child of a friend killed in the war? She might stop blaming you for everything that has happened if we give her a secure and loving home.'

'I'm not sure—'

He squeezed my hands. 'I know you don't want to leave the Palazzo degli Angeli and I have a suggestion for a way in which you may remain there and still release the funds. Suppose I buy it from you at the price I previously mentioned? I'd be responsible for the repairs, leaving you to share the sale proceeds between Eveline and Sofia. And we will live in married bliss together in the palazzo.' He laughed. 'Don't you see? That solves all the difficulties.'

There was a fluttering sensation in my stomach. 'This is completely unexpected,' I said. 'I'm aware of the honour you do me but I must have time to consider your proposal.'

Cosimo's smile wavered as he bent to kiss my hands.

I stared down at his dark head of lustrous hair and tried to imagine waking up every morning to see it on the pillow next to mine.

He looked up at me. 'I understand my proposal appears to come out of the blue but I was waiting for the right moment. I knew Falcone had wormed his way into your affections but I guessed that, eventually, you'd discover he isn't the man you thought he was.'

'That's certainly true.' The realisation was painful.

'I fell more in love with you every time we met,' said Cosimo. 'I'd have preferred the opportunity of wooing you over a longer period but, please, Phoebe, I beg you to consider my proposal. Our marriage would make me the most fortunate of men and I'd do everything possible to make you and your daughter happy.'

His velvet brown eyes looked so earnest that it was hard not to be moved. 'I need time to think,' I said.

He sighed. 'I'll draw up your draft will and perhaps you'll come and see me again this time next week with your answer?'

I stood up. 'I will,' I agreed.

He put his arms around me. 'Please don't keep me waiting too long,' he murmured into my hair.

Chapter 31

'Signor Benedetti has sent you flowers again,' said Valentina. 'Lilies this time. The drawing room will smell as if there's going to be another funeral.' She gave me a sideways look.

'Put them in water, will you?' I refused to enter into a discussion about it and pretended to read my book until she left.

Cosimo's proposal had come as a bolt from the blue and I vacillated between shock and relief that he'd offered me an opportunity to continue living in the home I loved, while also providing Sofia and Eveline with financial security. Perhaps, in time, Sofia might come and live with us. I didn't love Cosimo, of course, but love makes you vulnerable and I wasn't prepared to expose myself to the risk of being hurt again. Gradually, I was warming to his proposal.

On the morning before I was due to give him his answer, Alfio Argento came to visit me, bringing a box of chocolates and a letter of thanks from his mother.

'I'm delighted to tell you I now hold the position of Signor Falcone's private secretary,' my visitor told me. A beaming smile spread across the young man's face.

'Congratulations!' I shook his hand. 'I couldn't be happier for you.'

'And,' he said, 'I have an assistant. She'll train beside me and take over my role next year. You see, Signor Falcone has promised to teach me how to manage a business and then will make me a loan. I'll be able to realise my dream of setting up an employment bureau for disabled soldiers. I'm determined to make a success of it.'

'I don't doubt that you will,' I said.

It disconcerted me to hear that, for all his duplicity, Dante could also be generous and philanthropic. 'I wonder,' I said, 'if while you've been at the hotel, did you by any chance come across a young maid called Caterina?'

'Caterina? Why, yes. She's my assistant. A very personable and diligent young woman, although a little nervous. Apparently, she's been ill and Signor Falcone asked me to look after her.'

'He must trust you,' I said. I was relieved to hear Sofia had recovered sufficiently to work. 'Signor Falcone allowed her to work for me here while my housekeeper was incapacitated. Would you tell her . . .' What message could I send to a daughter who hated me? 'Just tell her she's always welcome here.'

After Alfio left, I went out. I'd procrastinated long enough, wondering how I was going to explain to Eveline why I hadn't given her a share of the palazzo before now. It didn't show me in a very good light.

It was raining and there was a squally wind that blew my umbrella inside out. I took the vaporetto and hurried through the drizzle to her apartment.

In the hallway, the drains still smelled, making me even more ashamed I hadn't already taken steps to improve Eveline's lot.

Outside her door, I leaned my dripping umbrella against the wall. I stiffened my resolve and knocked.

The door opened. 'Oh, it's you,' said my sister.

'May I come in?'

'It's not very convenient.' She wouldn't look at me and blocked the entrance.

'Please,' I said. 'I really haven't come to cause difficulties.'

Sighing, Eveline turned and I followed her inside.

There was an ancient sewing machine on the table, and the floor and the armchairs were heaped with white, ruffled shirts and black breeches in various stages of manufacture.

'What are these?' I asked.

'Some of us have to scratch a living wherever we can,' she said. 'I do piecework, making costumes for the opera house.'

There was a lump in my throat that she'd been reduced to this. I should have insisted on helping her as soon as I heard of my aunt's bequest.

Eveline snatched up an armful of shirts and dumped them on the table. 'Sit down. I can't offer you coffee. I haven't been paid yet.'

'I didn't come for coffee,' I said. 'I came to see you.'

'Why?'

'To tell you I've found Sofia. At least, she found me.'

Eveline became very still. 'Thank God,' she murmured, pressing a hand to her breast. 'I've prayed and prayed that you'd be reunited. Is she well?'

'She ...' My breath caught on a sob. 'She tried to drown herself.'

Eveline gasped. 'But why? Now you've found her, surely you'll take care of her?'

'It's awful. She hates me and won't let me anywhere near her. All I want is to have her by my side and to let her know she's loved.' The whole story came tumbling out. At the end of it, I drew a shuddering breath and wiped my eyes.

'It must be unimaginably painful,' said Eveline, 'to have found her and now ...' She rose from her chair and came to hug me.

I was too distressed to feel surprise. 'She wouldn't even let me explain,' I sobbed, clinging to my sister.

'The important thing for now is that she's safe. Give her time. When she's calmer, you can try again.' Eveline perched on the arm of my chair. 'You can't know how thankful I am that you've found her. I've been in an agony of guilt knowing that, because of what I did, she was stolen from you.'

'I thought you didn't care?'

'You asked me how I would feel if Rosetta had been taken from me, and I realised then how poisonous my jealousy was. I was too proud and ashamed to admit it but guilt has eaten away at me like a canker ever since. Whenever you showed me or my children another kindness, it was like acid in my stomach.'

I let out a long sigh. Perhaps everything could be peaceable between us again. 'I came here to beg *you* for forgiveness.'

'But why?'

'For all those times I blithely took pleasure in the good things that came my way without noticing your unhappiness. I should have been more sensitive to your feelings.'

Eveline bowed her head. 'I'm aware my surly manner made ... still makes it hard for you to like me. I have never matched up to you. I remember the Conte used laughingly to call you the Golden Child.'

'But you were, are, pretty. You'd have been prettier still if you'd smiled more often and hadn't nursed your grievances.' I reached for her hand. 'Can't we draw a line under all that and be friends again? I really want you back in my life; the loving sister who mothered me when we were at boarding school. I know now that *nothing* is more important than family. And we have no other family, have we, except for each other and our children?'

'It's exhausting trying to hate you all the time but is it possible to forgive and forget the past?'

'We can try.'

Eveline's smile was shaky and tears glistened in her eyes.

'And, for a start, this is what I want to do,' I said. 'I never expected to inherit the palazzo, not after Aunt Lavinia's disappointment and anger with me. When I received her telegram, I only came to Venice out of a sense of obligation and a half-hearted hope I might mend the rift between us. Discovering that she'd died and made me her sole heir, I was utterly shocked. I would have shared the inheritance with you but ...'

'I behaved so atrociously you changed your mind?'

'It was childish and spiteful of me,' I said, 'particularly after I saw how you and the children were living.'

'You did try to help me but I was too angry and proud to accept.'

'That's in the past and I want to put it right. If you agree, I've decided to sell the palazzo. We won't get as much for it as I imagined because there are severe problems with the foundations but, whatever money it realises, I'll share between you and Sofia. As you pointed out, my husband made sufficient provision for me.'

Eveline's complexion turned as waxen as a church candle. 'Oh, Phoebe ...'

'If I hadn't discovered the palazzo is sinking into the Lagoon, I might have suggested again that you and the children come to live with me—'

'I don't want to live in a draughty old palazzo.' Eveline looked into the distance, her eyes misty. 'I've always dreamed of a nice modern house or a newly renovated apartment. Not too big to keep clean but somewhere the children could each have their own bedroom.' She blinked. 'But what about you, Phoebe? Must you return to London? I wish you'd stay in Venice.'

'There's little to make me want to return to London.' I smiled at my sister. 'Especially now I've found you again.'

She gripped my hand, her mouth working while she tried to

keep control of her emotions. 'So will you buy an apartment here? Carlo and Rosetta keep nagging me about when they can see their aunt Phoebe again.'

'I'd love to see them, too,' I said. 'I might buy an apartment, but I do have another choice. I could remain in the palazzo.'

Eveline stared at me. 'I don't understand.'

'Don't worry! I'm not going back on my promise; you'll still have your share of the proceeds. But I've grown to love the palazzo again and don't want to leave. The thing is, I've received a proposal.'

Eveline jumped up and clapped her hands. 'You're going to marry Dante and he's going to buy the palazzo to add to his hotel? I'm so happy for you! He's perfect for you.'

Something in my heart turned over. 'No,' I said. 'It's not Dante. It's Cosimo.'

There was a moment of silence. 'But, Phoebe, you can't!' My sister's eyes were wide with alarm.

'Why not? He's charming and good-looking. He loves me and has enough money to buy the palazzo and pay for the repairs. If I marry him, I'll be able to continue living there and will share the value of it between you and Sofia.'

'I'll tell you why you can't marry Cosimo.' Eveline drew a deep breath. 'He proposed to me, too.'

'What?' I stared at her. 'When was this?'

'Last year. I don't deny I was flattered when he started to pay court to me. My marriage had been ...' She closed her eyes for a moment. 'It was not a success and I felt only relief when Matteo died.'

'Eveline, I saw the burn marks on your thighs,' I said. 'Did Matteo do that to you?'

'He derived pleasure from other people's pain. When the war began, he was exhilarated at the prospect of shooting the enemy.

286

It turned out that we were wrong for each other. As I said, the marriage wasn't a success.'

'Except that he gave you your children.'

Her features softened and she nodded. 'Anyway, during the war I went to live with Aunt Lavinia. Cosimo visited her often about business matters. After Matteo died, he invited me to the opera and the theatre and took me to expensive restaurants. Orchids, chocolates and flowers arrived for me every day. He even invited me to bring the children on a pleasure outing to the Lido.'

There was a sinking feeling in my stomach.

'Aunt Lavinia didn't like it,' my sister continued. 'I thought she was jealous because Cosimo had paid her a great deal of attention since he took over managing her business affairs. But she told me he wasn't worthy of me and tried to make me promise not to encourage him. I ignored her. Of course I did. Cosimo made me feel I was beautiful and funny and clever ... when he proposed, I was ecstatic. But after I told Aunt Lavinia, she forbade the match and we had a fierce argument. I said I was no longer a child and nothing would stop me marrying the man I loved.'

'Did she say why she didn't approve?' I asked.

'She called him an upstart with delusions of grandeur and said she thought he'd embezzled some of her investments. I accused her of lying.' Eveline fell silent for a moment. 'I flew into a rage and stormed out of the palazzo with the children. And you know how that ended.' She grimaced as she looked around the apartment. 'Soon afterwards, Cosimo came to see me. He told me I wasn't a suitable wife for a man in his position and that my children would be a burden to him.'

'Oh, Eveline! What a swine!'

'It was a lucky escape and it was Aunt Lavinia who saved me from making another dreadful mistake. Though she never mentioned your baby, she'd made several cryptic comments about the "harm" she'd done to you and how she must make amends.'

'She never said that to me.'

'When you came here and I discovered she'd disinherited me, I realised that she must have suspected Cosimo would show his true colours and ditch me once he knew she'd changed her will. He drew up the new one, so he knew I no longer had financial expectations to bring to a marriage with him.' She looked at me, her grey eyes steady. 'But *you* did.'

Horror washed over me in an icy wave. 'What a snake he is! I've been such a fool.'

Eveline shrugged her shoulders. 'Join the club.'

'At least I'm not in love with him, but this means I've lost the opportunity of remaining in the palazzo while releasing the funds from it. I'm damned if I'll let him buy it now!'

'Staying there wouldn't make up for being trapped in an unhappy marriage, Phoebe.'

'It certainly wouldn't.'

'And he'd probably renege on his promise to make a home for Sofia,' said Eveline.

I thought for a moment. 'When Aunt Lavinia sent me that telegram asking me to visit her, it said, "do not fail me". And Dante told me she'd said to him, "Whatever happened in the past, I know Phoebe won't fail either me or Eveline." If you're right, and she disinherited you so that Cosimo wouldn't marry you, perhaps what she meant was that she knew I'd share the inheritance with you?'

'Maybe. But what will you do now, Phoebe – sell the palazzo to Dante? I know Aunt Lavinia discussed it with him.'

'I can't.'

'I thought he wanted to buy it?'

'He does but he wanted the palazzo badly enough to do

something heinous.' I squeezed my eyes shut. 'He drowned Aunt Lavinia.'

'Dante? I don't believe it!'

'Cosimo was there. He *saw* Dante push her in the canal and hold her underwater.'

'And you believe Cosimo, even after the way he's deceived you?'

'I didn't want to believe him so I went to speak to Commissario Mazza, who investigated Aunt Lavinia's death. He said it was an accident, but Cosimo was so clear that he actually saw Dante holding Aunt Lavinia's face underwater that I had to believe him. And it's not only that,' I said. I related how Dante and I had fallen out and how, later, my darkroom had been vandalised. 'He must have had the key to the door between the buildings.'

'But there's no proof he actually carried out the act, is there?' said Eveline.

'I don't know what to believe any more,' I said. 'If you'd seen how Dante changed in his manner to me.' I shook my head. 'All I know is that tomorrow morning, at ten o'clock, I'm to go to Cosimo's office to sign my will. Afterwards, I'll tell him I won't marry him. Knowing what I know now, I daresay he'll be very annoyed.'

'Shall I come with you?'

Her offer was heart-warming. 'Bless you but it's better he doesn't know you've told me how he tried to dupe you, too.'

Eveline nodded. 'May I wait for you at the palazzo? I'd be happier ... ' She shrugged. 'Men can become angry when they're thwarted.'

'I've never seen any signs of violence in Cosimo.' Standing up, I hugged my sister. 'I feel as if a lead weight has been lifted from my shoulders,' I said. 'I regret more than I can say all the years we've been estranged.'

'We'll look to the future now.'

I glanced around the mean little apartment with its damp-stained walls. 'I don't know where I'll find a buyer for the palazzo, or how long it will take, but until then, why don't you and the children move in with me?'

Eveline lifted her chin. 'I've done the best for my family that I could.'

'I know that but—'

She smiled and suddenly looked pretty again. 'I want us to be friends but maybe living together might put a little too much of a strain on our new friendship?'

'I hope not,' I said, returning her smile. 'There's plenty of room for us all at the palazzo. We could each have our own space. Think about it, will you? Meanwhile, I'm going home to throw away every single one of Cosimo's bouquets.'

Chapter 32

The following morning, I was putting on my hat to visit Cosimo when Eveline arrived.

'You're dripping wet!' I exclaimed.

'The rain is almost horizontal and there's a high wind.' She kissed my cheek and unbuttoned her coat.

A smile spread across my face. Her kiss gave me hope that, in time, we'd strengthen our sisterly bond.

'Come into the drawing room. Jacopo lit the fire for you and Valentina will bring you coffee.'

'There was a full moon last night,' said Eveline, 'so I wouldn't be surprised if there's an *acqua alta* today.'

'I shan't be visiting Piazza San Marco anyway.'

'That's not the only place in Venice to experience floods in a high tide.'

I glanced out of the window at the canal lapping over the walkway on the opposite side; the walkway where Sofia had lingered to watch me. 'If I hadn't agreed to visit Cosimo,' I said, 'I wouldn't go out in this weather, but I want to sign my will. And then I'll tell him I'm turning him down.'

Eveline squeezed my arm. 'I'll be here, waiting for you.'

I let myself out of the palazzo and strode through the streets, head down into the teeming rain, rehearsing the words I'd say to refuse Cosimo's proposal.

He opened the door himself and greeted me with a wide smile, kissing my cheeks.

Judas kisses, I thought. He smelled as if he'd bathed in Acqua di Parma.

'I hope you'll excuse the informality,' he said. 'I gave my secretary a day's holiday to visit his mother so we might be undisturbed. Give me your hat and coat, they're soaked!'

I followed him into his office, hoping he hadn't sent his secretary away with the intention of sealing our engagement by seducing me.

'Sit down, my dear.' He pulled out a chair for me at his desk. 'I'll fetch your file.' He unlocked a door at the back of the office, switched on the electric light and disappeared into his file store.

I noticed a bottle of champagne in an ice bucket and two glasses on the side table and smiled grimly to myself. Cosimo had presumed too much.

He returned and moved aside the bronze statuette to make space for the documents.

'That looks like an excessive amount of paperwork for my will,' I said.

'You're quite correct,' he said. 'I've taken the liberty of preparing several documents.'

I looked at him with a puzzled frown.

'Depending upon your answer to my proposal, we may have a different set of circumstances,' he said. 'I've drawn up a deed of sale for the palazzo and also revised my own will, to take effect upon our marriage, naming you as my beneficiary. Naturally, we'd mirror your will in the same way.'

'I see.' So I wouldn't be able to sign my will before refusing his proposal.

'Phoebe, waiting for your decision this week has been agony.' He spoke quickly, as if it were a speech he'd prepared earlier. 'Tell me, dearest, will you give me your answer now?'

My mouth was dry. 'It's been a difficult week for me, too,' I said. 'I've given your proposal a great deal of thought.'

'And?'

'I'm conscious of the honour you do me,' I said, noting a tic at the corner of his eye, 'but I'm sorry to tell you that my answer is no.'

There was a momentary silence, while his countenance flushed an alarming shade of beetroot. 'No! You can't refuse me. How *could* you do this to me, Phoebe? Have I not behaved towards you with every consideration? I sent you flowers and took you to the opera. I even promised to overlook your immoral past and take in your illegitimate daughter.' He spread his hands wide. 'How many men would do that?'

I bit back an angry retort and forced myself to speak in calm tones. 'A marriage based on a wife's sense of obligation to her husband, knowing he condemns her for her past, will never be happy, for either spouse. Since I don't need a husband to provide for me, I am free to choose whether to marry or not.'

Cosimo sprang to his feet and paced across the room. After a moment he sighed. 'Have it your own way but you'll end up as a lonely and embittered old woman, like your aunt.'

'I doubt it,' I said. 'I'm perfectly happy in my own company.'

He made a visible attempt to compose himself. 'Well, I'm sorry you refused me. I'd hoped we might have a child together to continue the Benedetti line.'

I noted he made no further mention of his great love for me. 'No doubt you'll find a younger woman who will be happy to oblige in that respect.'

'That is a consideration,' he said, nodding his head. 'It's a nuisance not to have the use of your husband's money but you'll still sell me the palazzo?'

If I'd had any lingering doubts that comment decided me. 'No,' I said.

His head jerked around and he stared at me. 'But you must – you promised!'

'Actually, I didn't.'

'But you wanted to sell it, to give the proceeds to your sister and your illegitimate daughter?'

'True but I don't wish to sell the palazzo to you. Eveline and I have become reconciled and she told me how you proposed to her and then cast her aside after the Contessa disinherited her.'

Cosimo regarded me with brooding eyes. 'You had better sell the palazzo to me, Phoebe. Who will accept you in Venetian society when it becomes common knowledge that you had an illegitimate child?'

'There's no point in blackmailing me,' I said, attempting to sound indifferent to his threat. 'I'm not a part of Venetian society anyway.'

'So where do you envisage you'll find a buyer for your crumbling palazzo?' His mouth twisted in a sneer.

I picked an imaginary piece of lint from my skirt, perturbed by how quickly his manner had changed. 'Since both you and Dante Falcone are so keen to buy it, there's bound to be someone else who'll be interested. I have wealthy friends in New York.' I smiled up at him and spoke in an American drawl. 'They'd just love to have their very own darling little palazzo in Venice. It's sooo romantic!'

'You can't!'

'Of course I can. Or I might change my mind and let Dante have it after all.'

He thumped his fist on the desk. 'You will not! All this irrelevant chitter-chatter has taken an inordinate amount of time. I want you to sign the deed of sale right now and bring this matter to a close.'

I stood up. 'It isn't about what you want, Cosimo. I won't sell my palazzo to you and that's an end to it.'

He rushed towards me and caught hold of my arm. 'You don't understand, Phoebe! I must have it—'

'Venice is full of elegantly decaying palazzi.' I tried to pull free but his grip tightened.

'Listen to me! It *has* to be the Palazzo degli Angeli! It belonged to the Benedetti family for generations – from the fourteenth century. My ancestors were important spice traders, merchants and explorers.'

There was a fanatical light in his eyes that made me uneasy. I spoke in soothing tones. 'That's a marvellous family history to remember.'

Scowling, he said, 'Until my wastrel of a grandfather made bad business decisions and sold the palazzo to the Conte di Sebastiano for a pittance.'

'My uncle?'

He clicked his tongue with impatience. 'Of course not! *His* grandfather. So you see, I must have the Palazzo degli Angeli back, to restore the Benedetti name and fortunes.'

'Then it must be worth a very great deal more to you than the price you offered me,' I said.

'Don't you *dare* renege on the deal!'

'We didn't make one!' I said.

Cosimo shook my arm and pushed his face close to mine. 'You will sign the paperwork,' he hissed, his spittle landing on my cheek, 'and make the palazzo over to me.'

'I will not!'

'If you refuse, it will be the worse for you, just as it was for your aunt.'

'What do you mean?'

'The arrogance of that woman ... How dared she think a Benedetti, from a long line of nobility, wasn't good enough for her niece? I warned her what would happen if she didn't sell the palazzo to me but still she refused.' He spread his hands, palms up. 'So she drowned and I knew I'd have another chance to regain the palazzo when you came to Venice.'

The hairs on the back of my neck stood up. 'You murdered Aunt Lavinia!'

'Shall we say that it's definitely in your best interests to sign the palazzo over to me?'

'Never!' I shouted.

He let out a bellow of rage and twisted my arm up behind my back.

I screamed in shock at the jolt of agony in my shoulder.

He dragged me into the file store and thumped his fist onto my back so hard it sent me flying. The ground hurtled towards me and smacked my face.

The door slammed, the key turned in the lock, the light snapped off.

Stunned, I breathed shallowly, my cheek pressed against the dusty floorboards.

'You're not coming out until you see sense!' yelled Cosimo. 'And, by God, I'll make sure that you do!' He kicked the door three times.

And then I was all alone in the pitch dark.

Sometime later, I wasn't sure how long, I pushed myself into a sitting position. Gently, I touched my cheek and my fingers came away sticky with blood. I rotated my shoulder, wincing with the pain. Nothing was broken but my heartbeat was unsteady and I couldn't stop trembling. There was a faint line of light beneath the door but otherwise inky blackness pressed down on me like a suffocating blanket.

'Stupid!' I said aloud, my voice quavering. But it was too late now to berate myself for imagining Cosimo would do me no harm. The fanatical glint in his eye when he'd spoken of his family history demonstrated hitherto unsuspected depths of instability.

Standing up, I rattled the handle, already knowing the door was locked. Fumbling in the darkness, I made a fingertip search of my prison. I found nothing other than dusty files on the shelves; certainly nothing I could use to help me escape.

I sat on the floor again, my eyes fixed on the thread of light beneath the door. None entered by the keyhole. And then I had an idea. My fingers groped blindly about until I found a box file on the nearest shelf. I tore out a handful of papers and pushed them under the door so that only a sliver of paper remained on my side. Running my palm over the door, I found the keyhole and then thumped the wood above it with my fist.

The key remained firmly in the lock on the other side. I ripped another sheet of paper from the file, rolled it into a tight spill and inserted it into the lock. After a few minutes, I laughed aloud when I dislodged the key and it fell onto the paper behind the door. Slowly, I pulled the paper towards me, only to howl in frustration when I discovered the key was too large to slide through the gap.

I leaned back against the wall, thinking. Cosimo had as good as admitted he'd drowned Aunt Lavinia – and that changed everything. Driven by his passion to possess the Palazzo degli Angeli, he'd slandered Dante, his competitor, from the moment I'd arrived in Venice.

It was Cosimo who'd driven a wedge between Dante and me by giving him the false impression we were close. After all Dante's kindnesses to me, he must have been deeply hurt. And then Cosimo set out to destroy Dante's business reputation, while I stood by and said nothing. Hardly surprising he rebuffed me when he thought I'd driven Sofia to attempt to take her own life.

I wondered now if Cosimo had bribed Signor Nardone to write a false report about the condition of the palazzo to persuade me to sell it to him at a low price. If so, it was no wonder he was angry when Dante arranged his own survey.

How could I have been so gullible as to allow Cosimo to persuade me that Dante had murdered Aunt Lavinia, when all along he had been the villain? My heart ached to think that my own foolishness had caused me to lose Dante.

Chapter 33

I was huddled on the floor, throat raw from shouting for help and my fists bruised from pounding on the door, when I heard the key turn in the lock. Before I could struggle to my feet, Cosimo had grabbed me by my collar. He dragged me out of the closet and pushed me onto a chair.

'Read this!' he said, thrusting a folded sheet of paper into my hands. He leaned over me, drops of rain falling from his hair.

I unfolded the note and read it.

Please, please do exactly as this man says. If you do not agree to give him the palazzo, I will drown. The water is rising fast and there is little time. I beg you, do not forsake me again or my death will be on your conscience forever.

Sofia

Horror-struck, I glanced up at Cosimo. 'You can't—'

'Oh, but I can,' he said.

'Where is she?'

He snorted with laughter. 'You don't imagine I'll tell you that, do you? What I *can* tell you is that she's tied up with only her head and shoulders above water. She doesn't have long before the *acqua alta* rises and drowns her. And before you ask, yes, it is still raining.'

'You might be trying to trick me. I don't know if that's Sofia's writing.'

'Are you prepared to take the risk?'

I wasn't. 'Please, don't do this, Cosimo!' My heart thudded and I felt sick.

'The matter is in your hands.' His smile was smug. 'All you need do is to sign the contract and make the palazzo over to me.'

I didn't hesitate. 'Give it to me!'

'Certainly.' He reached across the desk and placed the paperwork in front of me, together with a pen. 'Here.' He pointed at the space left for my signature.

I stared at the pen, my mind working furiously. There was no one present to witness my signature but I supposed he was crooked enough to arrange that later.

'Sign it!' He prodded me between the shoulder blades.

'I wish to read it first,' I said, mustering as much of my shredded dignity as I could. If he was prepared to risk drowning Aunt Lavinia and Sofia, what else might he do? And if I signed the palazzo over to him and then went to the police to say he'd coerced me ... I grew icy cold right to my core at the sudden realisation that, of course, he wasn't going to allow me to do that. Once I'd signed, he'd do away with me, along with Sofia and probably Eveline and the children. He wouldn't risk any witnesses or heirs surviving. How would he do it? An accident with a boat perhaps? I could imagine his shocked expression as he cried crocodile tears. *What a tragedy that the whole family drowned! Those poor children!*

'You're wasting time!' Cosimo forced my fingers around the pen. 'Sign it now!'

I turned my head to look at him. 'Let go of my hand,' I said coldly, 'or my signature will look as if you've forged it.'

He released me, making an exclamation of disgust.

Now! Without hesitating, I spun around on the chair and jabbed the nib of the fountain pen into his eye.

Screaming, he reeled backwards, one hand clapped over his eye.

Snatching up the bronze statuette with both hands, I swung it in an arc and whacked him on the side of his head.

He sank to his knees with a groan. Blood blossomed from a gaping cut on his forehead and he toppled forward onto the floor.

Not waiting to see if he was unconscious, I snatched up Sofia's note, ran along the passage and out into Campo Santa Margherita.

The rain was torrential as I bolted across the open expanse of the square and into a narrow passage between two shops. I pelted along the backstreets, crying out in frustration when I could see the other side of the canal but a dead-end prevented me from reaching the bridge. I retraced my steps and found another route. Splashing through puddles and slipping over cobbles, all I could think about was where Cosimo might have taken Sofia.

Soaked through and heaving for breath, I arrived at the palazzo. I raced up the outside stairs and burst through the door, shouting for Eveline.

Valentina hurried into the hall. 'Sainted Mother! Look at you, dripping all over my clean floor! Where is your hat and coat? And what has happened to your poor cheek? There's blood—'

'Is my sister here?'

'She was worried you hadn't returned but couldn't wait any longer and went to collect the children from school.'

'I must see if Sofia ... I mean Caterina ... is at the hotel.'

'I saw her this morning.'

'When? Where?'

Valentina gave me a puzzled look. 'I was cleaning the windows in the drawing room and saw her down on the hotel's landing stage, climbing into a boat with that youth. I called out of the window, asking what she was doing going out in such weather. She looked up but didn't answer.' She shook her head. 'Young people today have no manners.'

I felt as if there was a lead weight inside me. I already knew Sofia wouldn't be at the hotel. 'What youth?' I asked.

'You know. The boy with the curly hair. He came here with Enzo to make your darkroom.'

It was all falling into place now. I'd seen Marco leaving Cosimo's office so they obviously knew each other. Had Cosimo paid him to apprehend Sofia and lure her out of the hotel on some pretext? But where would he take her? Something teased my memory. Cosimo had told me he needed a new tenant for his warehouse and had mentioned he kept a boat there.

It was then that I remembered Flavia's lunch party and Ines telling me Cosimo's warehouse was above a boathouse. It would be an ideal location for him to keep his captive hidden.

'That must be it!' I exclaimed. I pressed my knuckles against my mouth, desperately trying to recall where Ines had said it was. 'Not far from here,' I murmured. 'Valentina, what's the name of the canal on the opposite side of the Grand Canal from our canal?'

'The Rio del Duca,' she said, 'but why—'

'Tell Jacopo to make the *sandolo* ready. I need him to take me to Rio del Duca. Quickly!'

'You can't go out in this rain again,' she protested.

'You don't understand! Caterina has been kidnapped.' I pulled the damp and water-stained note from my skirt pocket. 'Listen carefully. Keep this safe to show to the police. I'm going to the hotel to make sure it wasn't a hoax, but if Caterina isn't there, I'll ask Signor Falcone to send the police to Rio del Duca.'

Valentina clapped her palms to her cheeks.

'And tell Jacopo to bring a sharp knife and a crowbar or something to force open a locked door.' Ignoring her shocked exclamations, I ran outside again and entered the hotel.

Signor Fortini's eyes widened when he saw my sodden and dishevelled state.

'Signora Wyndham, you shouldn't be here. Signor Falcone gave express instructions—'

'Is Caterina here? It's very important!' He must have heard the desperation in my voice.

'Let me see.' He went into the office and returned a moment later with Alfio.

'Signora Wyndham!' said the young man. 'Did you fall?

I shook my head. 'Is Caterina with you?'

'She had to run an errand.' He glanced at his watch. 'But she should have been back long ago.'

'So it is true!' I whispered. 'Is Signor Falcone here?'

Alfio shook his head. 'He had a meeting out of the hotel. That's why Sofia went out. He sent her a message to bring his diary.'

I drummed my fingers on the reception desk. 'I'm not sure what to do. There's so little time! Caterina has been kidnapped by Signor Benedetti.'

'What?'

'I believe she's tied up in a boathouse somewhere in the Rio del Duca. The water is rising and I fear she'll drown. I can't delay any longer. Will you send for the police?

Signor Fortini drew in his breath sharply. 'But of course.'

'Ask for Commissario Mazza. Tell him Signor Benedetti confessed to drowning the Contessa di Sebastiano and my housekeeper has the ransom note for Caterina that he sent me. And send the police with a doctor to Signor Benedetti's office, too.' I bit my lip. 'I stabbed him in the eye and then knocked him out.'

Alfio's mouth fell open.

I told him Cosimo's address. 'And will you tell Signor Falcone I said I was sorry? I was completely wrong. I know that now.'

Alfio nodded and I ran out of the hotel and into the driving rain again.

Jacopo was outside, waiting for me in the *sandolo* moored at the landing stage. 'Valentina says you must put this cape on or you'll catch your death.'

I clambered into the boat. 'Did you bring a knife and a crowbar?'

He pointed to the leather bag of tools by his feet.

'Let's go, then. Hurry!' I snatched the oiled rain cape from him and shrugged it on, grateful for Valentina's care.

Jacopo, a man of few words, stood in the stern and rowed silently and swiftly away from the palazzo. Rain drummed down on my head and shoulders and water dripped from Jacopo's nose and drooping moustache as he worked the single oar.

A few moments later our small boat was being buffeted by the wind as we crossed the Grand Canal. Shivering in my sodden clothing, I gripped the sides of the *sandolo* as Jacopo navigated the wide stretch of choppy water. Brown and murky, the surging canal reeked of decay. I averted my gaze as the bloated corpse of a cat floated past.

Mist shrouded the air and Jacopo cursed as the boat rocked dangerously when we encountered the heavy wash created by a vaporetto.

The buildings on the other side loomed out of the mist and Jacopo skilfully manoeuvred the boat into the narrow opening of Rio del Duca. Tall buildings to either side reached up to a grey ribbon of waterlogged sky.

'Where now?' he asked.

I looked helplessly at the blank façades with their shuttered windows. 'I don't know,' I admitted. What if I was wrong and the boathouse wasn't here?

Jacopo shook a drop of rainwater off his nose. 'We'll go to the end and see what we can find.'

He'd rowed more than halfway along the canal when I craned my neck. 'See that sign, Jacopo? *Building to Let*. And look! Could that be a boathouse?'

Taciturn as ever, he said nothing but rowed closer until it became clear that the canal flowed under a pair of flaking timber doors set into a stone archway. A padlocked chain was looped through the iron handles.

'Can you open it?' I asked.

He rattled the door and shrugged. 'I might be able to saw through the chain but let's try this first.' He took a long, thin screwdriver from his tool bag and inserted it into the padlock. He twisted it carefully a few times, muttering under his breath. And then the shackle sprung free. He grinned at me, pulled the chain away and pushed open the doors.

I peered into the shadowy interior. A timber landing stage ran around three sides of the boathouse in a U shape with mooring posts around the edges and an enclosed staircase in one corner. The stone steps to the landing stage were already underwater. There was no sign of Sofia.

'Hello?' I called softly.

Silence.

Had we broken into the wrong place and might a furious property owner appear and accuse me of trespassing? 'The stairs must lead to the warehouse,' I whispered. 'I'm going to take a look.'

'You wanted this,' said Jacopo. He rummaged in the toolbox again and handed me a sturdy knife in a leather sheath.

I took it gingerly. It was too large for my pocket so I tucked it in the waistband of my skirt.

Jacopo rowed into the boathouse and I stepped onto the landing stage, which was covered by half an inch of water. 'Wait outside,' I murmured. 'If you see either the police or Signor Benedetti approaching, shout a warning and then come back for me.'

He nodded and pushed the boat away from the steps using the oar.

I picked my way towards the stairs through coils of rope, broken tea chests and an abandoned boathook. Icy water lapped at my shoes. Glancing over my shoulder, I saw Jacopo and the boat had already disappeared.

The door to the enclosed staircase wouldn't open. I tugged it and all at once it moved. It hadn't been locked, only swollen with damp. Tiptoeing up the stairs with my heartbeat pounding in my ears, I reached a large open space, empty except for the supporting columns, an old tarpaulin and festoons of cobwebs. The stale air was suffused with the musty smell of spices and my footsteps echoed.

I hadn't realised I'd been holding my breath until I was sure the warehouse was deserted. I hurried to the grimy window and rubbed away the bloom of dust with my fingertip. Outside, Jacopo sat hunched over in the rain in the *sandolo*. There were no other boats in view. It was likely I'd found Cosimo's vacant warehouse but it was devastating that Sofia wasn't there. Where could she be?

Shivering, I hugged my arms across my chest. Had Cosimo forced her to write that note purely to frighten me? Had he lied to me, as he had about everything else? Or was Sofia imprisoned somewhere else? There was so little time! My breath came in panicky gasps. There were hundreds of boathouses in Venice and my precious daughter would drown before I could find her. I let out a mew of fear and raked my fingers down my cheeks.

A small noise came from below, no louder than a mouse scratching in the wainscot.

I tipped my head, listening. There it was again.

I let out a hoarse cry and ran downstairs.

Chapter 34

At the foot of the stairs, I gasped when cold water covered my ankles. If Sofia was imprisoned with only her head above water, the level was rising so fast now it might already be too late. I stood still, looking and listening. The khaki-coloured water in the dock undulated in the silence. Taking slow breaths, I focused my eyes on the water under the landing stage in case Sofia had been held there and had already drowned. Nothing. There was nowhere else to look.

Or was there? The outer side of the stairs was boarded over but there was a door to an understairs cupboard set into it, fitted with a bolt. A mallet and a pile of splintered timber decking was heaped close by. I dragged back the bolt, feeling fearful and hopeful at the same time.

The interior of the cupboard was dark and I leaned to one side because I was blocking out the light. There was no sign of Sofia, only shelves on the back wall, littered with rusty tools and old paint pots. Most of the floor had been removed, making an opening a yard long and the width of the stairs.

Ink-dark water rippled below the damaged flooring and something pale stirred in the gloom.

I leaned forward to see better and my head jerked back in shock.

Sofia, entirely submerged in the water, lifted her face above the surface to gasp for breath. She stared at me with terrified eyes before sinking again.

I cried out, fell to my knees and lifted her chin. I fumbled to loosen the gag that had been so cruelly tied over her mouth. The knot in the cloth was tight and I had to be careful not to let water wash over her face. But would I be able to get her out before she drowned? At last, I pulled the gag away.

'He's tied my hands behind my back and then to a ring on a post under the water.' Her voice was thin and high with terror as she struggled to keep her mouth and nose clear.

'I'm going to get help.' I forced myself to sound calm and in control but failed. It would be too late.

'Don't leave me!' Sofia shrieked. She swallowed water and choked, thrashing her head from side to side in terror.

I put my hand under her chin again. 'Sofia, keep still!' I stroked her hair until she stopped panicking. I didn't dare leave her in order to yell for Jacopo but, even if I could reach her bonds under the water and cut her free, how would I find the strength to lift her through the opening in the floor? Then I remembered the coil of rope on the landing stage.

'Keep very still and breathe through your nose,' I said. 'I'm going to fetch a rope.'

Splashing back along the boards, I grabbed the rope and the worm-eaten boathook and carried them back to the cupboard. I looped the rope a couple of times around the nearest mooring post and trailed the ends into the water beside Sofia. Then I slid the boathook across the opening in the floor.

Filled with fear, I said, 'Sofia, I'm going to cut you free now but you must stay very still.' Only her nose and eyes were still visible above the water and I was filled with dread that there wasn't enough time.

She gave a slight nod.

I kicked off my shoes and dropped the waterproof cape on the floor, drew the knife from my waistband and held it between my teeth. I sat down and, in one swift movement, swung myself down through the hole. Gasping at the cold shock of the water, I kept a tight grip on the splintered edge of the boards. I pointed my toes down through several inches of mud until they found more-or-less solid ground beneath.

Taking a deep breath, I closed my eyes and ducked under the surface. Salt water seeped into my mouth and nose. My questing fingers felt the rope tied around Sofia's wrists, crossed behind her back. I slid my hand along the rope to the point where it was tied to ring on a mossy post supporting the landing stage above. Inserting the knife into the knotted rope, I sawed at it.

I must have nicked Sofia's skin because she flinched, knocking the knife from my hands. I reared out of the water, gasping for air. Time was running out. There was no choice; I *had* to find the knife. I dived down again, hampered by my skirts that tangled themselves around my legs. Stretching out my hands, I combed frantically through the mud with my fingers. Something wriggled unpleasantly against my palm and then my breath ran out.

On my third dive, I touched something hard and, as I gripped it, the blade of the knife sliced my thumb. I burst up to the surface, took another breath and went down to find Sofia's bonds again. This time, it took only a moment to sever the rope and free her.

She jerked her head out of the water, flailing her limbs and taking fast, panicky breaths.

I caught her in my arms. 'You're all right now, my darling girl,' I said. I stood on tiptoe and supported her head on my shoulder, thankful I was taller than she was. 'Breathe slowly now!'

Sofia's hair had come loose from its pins and wrapped itself like seaweed around my face. It was the first time I'd ever held my daughter and I pressed my lips to her forehead. But there was no time to waste.

'We need to get out of here,' I said. 'Can you hang onto this?' I lifted her hands and clasped them over the boathook resting over the opening in the floor.

Weeping with relief, she clung on.

I could see she hadn't the strength to hold on for long and hastily tied the loose ends of the rope under her arms. It took me several attempts to get myself out of the water. My shoulder hurt like the devil and I was shuddering with cold but eventually I managed it.

Sofia looked up at me, her eyes dark with fear. 'Help me!' she mouthed.

I hauled on the rope tied under her arms, my muscles trembling with the effort.

Whimpering, she scrabbled at the splintered timber with desperate fingers.

Grasping her clothing, I heaved her up and eventually dragged her from the water and deposited her in a dripping and ungainly heap on the landing stage.

Then there was silence, apart from our laboured breaths and the sound of the rain sheeting down outside.

'We can't sit here in two inches of water,' I said. 'Can you stand?'

She shivered uncontrollably and mumbled something, her lips mauve with cold and shock.

I pulled her to her feet and supported her to the staircase. 'Sit here on the stairs,' I said, chafing her hands. I wrapped the rain cape around her. 'I saw a tarpaulin upstairs. We need to get you warm before I fetch Jacopo with the boat.'

Sofia closed her eyes and rested her head against the wall.

Every step I took felt as if I were wearing lead boots. My teeth chattered as I crossed the warehouse and found the tarpaulin. It was heavy and dusty and smelled of fish. As I dragged it towards the top of the stairs, Sofia cried out. Then came the rumbling tones of a man's voice. Dropping the tarpaulin, I hurried to the top of the stairs and looked down.

Sofia wasn't there.

I guessed it was Jacopo I'd heard and hurried downstairs.

A boat was tied up to one of the mooring posts and my heart nearly stopped when I saw Cosimo, his back turned towards me. He had gripped Sofia by her wrists and was shaking her like a rag doll.

'Where is Phoebe?' he shouted. 'Tell me now or you'll go back in the canal!'

Cowering, Sofia shrieked as he gave a vicious twist to her arms and dragged her towards the side of the jetty.

Rage seethed in my breast. I snatched up the boathook. Holding it like a lance, I rushed towards him with a scream of fury.

He turned, mouth open in astonishment.

I didn't hesitate but thumped the boathook against his breastbone with every ounce of force I could muster.

Breath left his body on a loud groan. He released Sofia's wrists and fell backwards into the water.

I ran to my daughter and hugged her.

'I thought he was going to drown me,' she sobbed.

I stroked her hair and crooned comforting words. Then I gasped, feeling a sudden vice-like grip on my ankle. I caught a fleeting glimpse of Cosimo as he yanked my foot from under me. Toppling sideways, I landed in the water with a great splash.

'Got you, you bitch!' His hands were around my throat. Blood oozed from the wound on his forehead. One eye was swollen shut but the other burned with hatred.

Frantically, I tried to loosen his fingers but he pushed my head under the water and held it there. I thrashed my legs in a panic-stricken attempt to reach the surface. If I died, he'd kill Sofia and then we'd never be reconciled. I fought back, twisting and turning in Cosimo's grip, but the last of my breath was inexorably seeping away. My ears boomed and echoed as I struggled, knowing it was hopeless because my body would force me to inhale and then I would drown. Just like Aunt Lavinia . . .

All at once, the pressure on my throat was released.

Scissor-kicking my legs, I burst above the surface, gasping and choking, waiting for him to grab me again. I turned my head to scan the dock.

Sofia was sobbing hysterically and repeatedly jabbing the boathook into the water. Each time Cosimo's face surfaced, she attacked him again, pushing him under.

'Sofia!' I shouted. 'Stop it! You'll drown him!' I floundered towards the steps and hauled myself out of the water.

A shout came from behind me and a gondola slid through the gap between the boathouse doors. Dante jumped out seconds before the boat bumped against the mooring. He ran towards me, touched his palm to my cheek for a heartbeat, then wrested the boathook from Sofia's grip.

I caught her in my arms and drew her away from the water.

Dante snagged Cosimo's collar with the boathook and dragged him to the side of the dock.

Cosimo lay on the steps, heaving for breath. When he tried to push himself into a sitting position, Dante forced him down onto his front. 'The police are on their way,' he said. 'You can be grateful for that because otherwise we'd have reported an accidental drowning.'

'I *wanted* to kill him,' whispered Sofia.

'Me, too,' I murmured, 'but neither of us need have that on our conscience. And you saved my life.'

'As you saved mine.'

A police boat arrived shortly after with Commissario Mazza, two police officers and a doctor.

The doctor fixed pads of gauze over Cosimo's eye and forehead and then the police officers handcuffed him and bundled him into the boat.

The doctor examined Sofia and me and told Commissario Mazza we were unfit for questioning until we were warm and had recovered from our shock.

Sofia refused to go in the police boat with Cosimo and in the end we left together in Dante's gondola, accompanied by another officer.

Sofia, still trembling, drooped against my side. She didn't flinch when I gathered her in my arms and rested her head on my shoulder.

As Dante rowed us away, he smiled at me. 'Look,' he said, 'it's stopped raining.'

Chapter 35

Sofia and I were taken to the Palazzo degli Angeli where my sister and the children waited for us.

'I've been out of my mind with worry,' Eveline sobbed as she hugged me. 'I was sure Cosimo would drown you both.'

If I'd had any doubts about our reconciliation, they left me right then.

The police officer cautioned us that we were not to communicate with each other until we'd been interviewed, and remained stationed in the hall to make sure of it.

Valentina, unusually quiet, bathed us and put us to bed. She whispered to me that Cosimo had rammed the old *sandolo* and knocked Jacopo out with an oar.

The following morning, after Sofia and I had breakfasted in our rooms and the doctor had seen us, I was called into the dining room to be questioned.

It was painful to describe in minute detail the harrowing events that had almost destroyed my entire family. Once I'd given my statement, I went next door to find Dante.

He hurried out of his office, his hands held out to me. 'How are you? They wouldn't let me see you but I spoke to Jacopo and Valentina this morning after we'd all been questioned.'

'I haven't been able to speak to ...' I hesitated ' ... Caterina. But it's all over now,' I said. 'Though there will be a court case, of course.'

'And probably a hanging. Come into my office. I shan't make you talk any more about what happened. Not unless you wish to.'

I followed him in and sat down. 'I want to thank you, and Alfio, too, for what you did. Also to apologise.'

'Alfio gave me your message but I'm not quite sure what you meant.'

I rubbed a palm over my face. 'Cosimo tried – with some success, I'm sorry to say – to poison me against you. He told terrible lies and, for a while, I was stupid enough to believe him. In my heart of hearts it felt wrong, but he was very convincing.'

'What did he tell you?'

'That you didn't want me for myself but only because of the palazzo. And that you murdered Aunt Lavinia.'

A muscle flickered in Dante's jaw. 'I wondered if it was something like that.'

'But yesterday, I realised that he was the one who killed her.'

Dante picked up his pen and idly twirled it between his fingers. 'I tried to convince the police of that at the time but he can be very plausible.'

'I can't believe I let him take me in.'

'I made it my business to investigate Cosimo and discovered he arranged for one of his hirelings to sabotage my fishmonger's delivery for your reception. The shellfish that was finally delivered was contaminated.'

'I never thought it was caused by a dirty kitchen,' I said, 'not in your hotel anyway. Then Cosimo manipulated the situation to make it look as if he and I were especially close. And another thing: he refused the shellfish, saying he never ate it, but I remember now that he once ordered spider crab when we had dinner together.'

'My chef told me Enzo's apprentice, Marco, offered to find an alternative fishmonger when the order failed to materialise. Subsequently, I found no trace of the new supplier.'

'And I saw Marco leaving Cosimo's office recently. He was tucking a thick envelope into his pocket. I wonder if . . .'

'You'd be right to wonder. There have been several petty thefts in the hotel in recent weeks. When a guest had his wallet stolen, my manager saw Marco where he shouldn't have been so I accosted him and insisted he turn out his pockets.'

'Did you find anything?' I asked.

Dante gave a thin smile. 'The wallet was there. Enzo sacked the boy on the spot. He was also in possession of a rusty key with a faded label attached to it; the same kind of label as on the ancient keys that came with this building when I bought it. I returned the key to the tin in my office and I'd have thought no more about it, if Jacopo hadn't come to tell me later about your darkroom being destroyed.'

'While working on the new annexe, I suppose Marco had the opportunity to creep into your furniture store and let himself through the communicating door to my darkroom.' I covered my mouth. 'How could I have believed Cosimo, for even one second, when he told me that it was you who caused that damage?'

'Your aunt was an intelligent woman,' said Dante, 'but even she was taken in by Benedetti's wiles. It wasn't until she suspected him of embezzling her savings that she finally lost trust in him. Then she changed her will and we know what happened afterwards.'

'Cosimo told me he saw you drown her. He was so convincing, telling me one lie after another until I didn't know what to believe.'

'And I thought I saw Benedetti holding the Contessa underwater. Accusing someone of murder is a serious thing and I wasn't *absolutely* sure or I would certainly have warned you about him.'

'Dante ...' I glanced away from him. 'I was upset about you making plans for my palazzo, as if it was already a done deal. We parted on bad terms, and when you thought I'd been cruel to Caterina, the chasm between us grew even wider. Oh, Dante, I wish I'd overcome my pride then and spoken freely to you.'

'I did think you must have been very harsh with her.' He shrugged. 'And I was hurt you'd mistaken my intentions about the palazzo. I had my pride too. Benedetti did everything he could to come between us. And yesterday, when I received the report from my surveyor, I knew for certain that he had tried to cheat you. Phoebe, there's nothing very much wrong with your palazzo.'

I closed my eyes momentarily. 'What a complete and utter swine he is.'

Dante reached out to touch my cheek. 'If I promise never to speak again about you selling the place to me, can we put all this behind us now?'

'There's still so much to tell you,' I said, resting my face against his palm. He leaned forward to kiss me but I drew back. 'Dante, no!' I said.

He let me go, his expression stricken. 'I'm sorry. I hoped you loved me as much as I love you and now that we've cleared the air ...' His green eyes were full of hurt.

I wrung my hands. 'Oh, but I do love you!' It was unbearably poignant that he had declared his love for me at the very moment I was going to make him despise me. 'Dante, I've not been completely honest with you. Once you know the truth, you may no longer feel the same about me.'

318

His face was impassive. 'Tell me.'

'I didn't lie,' I said, 'but it was a sin of omission. You see, Caterina's name is really Sofia.' I cast him a darting glance. 'And Sofia is my daughter.'

There was a moment that seemed never-ending.

A pulse fluttered in my throat and I held my breath.

'Go on,' said Dante.

'I was young, no older than Sofia is now, when she was stolen from me at her birth,' I said. Unable to look at him, I related the whole story. When I was done, I stood up. 'I'm sorry, Dante. It's probably for the best if I leave Venice, so if you're still interested in the palazzo, I'd be happy for you to buy it. I want Eveline and Sofia to share the proceeds.'

'Wait!' Dante caught hold of my elbow as I reached the door. 'You're not the only one keeping secrets. Phoebe, I knew you'd had a child, even before you came to Venice.'

'*What?*'

'The Contessa enjoyed a glass of whisky.' His mouth curved in a smile. 'Or two. And she was lonely and sometimes she confided in me more than she meant to. It troubled her very much that you lost your daughter but she'd genuinely believed that having Sofia fostered was in the best interests of you both.'

Tears sprang from my eyes and I pressed my knuckles against my mouth. 'But it wasn't! We've both been miserable for years and now Sofia despises me.'

'Oh, Phoebe! I can't bear to see you so unhappy.' Dante hugged me and kissed my hair. 'Sofia doesn't really hate you but she's very hurt and troubled. When she discovered the Vianellis weren't her real parents, and then that her birth mother had also apparently abandoned her, it was a devastating blow. The very foundations of her world had collapsed.

'I can only imagine how alone she must have felt.'

'I sat with her when she was recovering and she told me everything,' he said. 'Throwing herself in the canal wasn't from any real desire to take her own life, it was a plea for understanding. What she needs is to be loved, unconditionally.'

'But I already *do*,' I sobbed. 'I want so much to repair the damage I have done and make the rest of her life happy.'

'We all need to be loved,' murmured Dante into my hair. 'Without love and family, we have nothing.' He dropped small kisses over my forehead and cheeks and then sought my lips. He kissed me, gently at first but then with rising passion.

It was impossible not to respond to his fervour and I slid my arms around his neck.

He tipped up my chin and gazed steadily into my eyes. 'I love you, Phoebe, and it's nothing to do with your palazzo. What happened in the past doesn't matter to me. I want us to be together. Always. Please, will you marry me?'

Happiness blossomed in my heart and all my vows never to marry again disappeared like mist in the sun. Dante was a good man and it was impossible for me not to love him. I laid my head on his shoulder and smiled. 'I will,' I said, and he kissed me again.

A little while later, he said, 'Shall we celebrate tonight? I'll put some champagne on ice. We can talk quietly about our plans over dinner. Once we announce our engagement, my family will descend on us, full of clamour and questions.'

Bursting with happiness, I nodded. 'But I must go home now and see if the police have finished speaking to Sofia.'

Floating on a cloud of euphoria, I returned to the palazzo. In the hall, a sweet smell of vanilla and sugar drifted from the kitchen.

Eveline and the children were in the drawing room. Rosetta and Carlo jumped up and ran to hug me.

'Why don't you go and see Valentina?' I said. 'I think she's cooking something delicious.'

Carlo sighed. 'What you really mean is, will we go away while you talk in private with Mamma?'

'Absolutely right, young man,' I said, winking at him.

'You look very pleased with yourself,' said Eveline once the children had closed the door. She raised her eyebrows. 'It's Dante, isn't it?'

'Is it so obvious?'

'You're glowing like a lantern,' she said. 'But I'm absolutely delighted for you.' She laughed. 'Truly!'

'Thank you. That means a great deal to me.'

'Neither of us has had much luck with husbands to date,' she said, 'and perhaps we'll talk about that sometime – or perhaps not – but you'll be happy with Dante.'

I sat down beside her. 'I hope, one day, that you'll find the right man to make you happy, too. What a shame both Dante's brothers are already married.'

'I shan't hold my breath, sister dear. I've wasted so much of my life waiting for a man to come along and love me. Perhaps we make our own happiness? I've seen how fulfilled your photography makes you and I'm going to look for some work that does the same for me. Perhaps I'll learn to type. I might find work as a bilingual secretary or as a translator. And my children are healthy, and now that you and I are friends again, what more could I want?'

The door opened and Sofia stood hesitantly on the threshold.

Eveline beckoned her in. 'Have the police finished with you?'

Sofia nodded and closed her eyes for a moment. 'All night I kept waking up, thinking the water was closing over my face.' Shuddering, she rubbed at the rope burns on her wrists. 'It made me realise how silly I'd been to throw myself in the canal, when life is so precious.'

'We all learned yesterday how much we wanted to live,' I said.

Diffidently, Sofia perched on the sofa next to me. 'I wouldn't

321

be here today if you hadn't saved me. I don't know what to call you,' she said, her cheeks flushing. 'Signora Wyndham sounds wrong now—'

'Simply "Phoebe" will do. Although I'm your birth mother, Angelina is the woman you'll always think of as Mamma, isn't she?'

Sofia nodded. 'But Aunt Eveline explained everything to me this morning, how it nearly killed you when I was taken away—'

I let out a sob. 'It was the cruellest thing. I've thought of you every single day since you were born. When I discovered you hadn't been stillborn after all, I searched frantically for you. Then you turned up here out of the blue but you despised me ...'

Sofia's eyes, Lorenzo's eyes, swam with tears.

'I missed the delight of watching you grow up,' I said, 'but I've always loved you.'

'How lucky I am,' she said, 'to have *two* mothers to love me.'

'And perhaps you'd like to meet your father, too?'

'I know he's a priest now but, if he's allowed to see me, I would like that.' She shook her head in wonder. 'Suddenly, I'm no longer a lonely orphan. I have a whole new family. Two families.'

'Perhaps it's time,' said Eveline, 'that we all made a new beginning?'

Tentatively, I opened my arms, hoping Sofia wouldn't refuse me.

But she smiled through her tears and came unhesitatingly into my embrace.

Breathing in the scent of her freshly washed hair, I felt my daughter's heart beating against my own, in perfect harmony.

'A new beginning,' I echoed.

Acknowledgements

Mothers and daughters. I thought about the connection between mothers and daughters a great deal while I was writing *The Lost Daughter of Venice*. I come from a long line of mothers and daughters who, despite the usual ups and downs, enjoyed strong and loving relationships. As a child, I was lucky enough to think this was normal. As an adult, I know that sadly, this isn't always the case; mothers die young, become ill or mired in conflict with their children. So thank you, Polly – it would have been so much harder to write this novel without our unbreakable mother-daughter bond.

My grateful thanks also go to my wonderful agent, Heather Holden-Brown and my lovely editor, Eleanor Russell and all the team at Piatkus who made it possible for this book to be published. Thank you to Lynn Curtis for copyediting the manuscript so sensitively.

Huge thanks to my supportive writing group, Wordwatchers and to fellow author Liz Harris, who all read and commented on the manuscript and told me where I was going wrong!

Thank you to my husband and family for understanding

that, a large part of the time, my thoughts are somewhere in another century.

Finally, a special thank you to those of you who have read and reviewed my books – it makes all the hard work worthwhile to know you have enjoyed them